Corey shrugged. "She's  met her, and my wife scarcely knew her. But that death still bothers her. My wife, I mean. And I started looking into it because I was going daffy doing what I was doing, and she wanted to move here, and the more I looked, the more it stunk. Even to an amateur like me, there are just too many loose ends to the story of how that property changed hands. There's no question in my mind, even at this point, that Jim Mandeville was murdered, and it seems pretty clear why. All I'm looking to find out is maybe who did it. And what prompted him to do it."

" 'Who' I don't know," Oldham said. " 'Why' I do know. What got him killed was a sweet little deal. He'd packaged a deal for himself so sweet that somebody had him killed for it."

Also by George V. Higgins:

THE MANDEVILLE TALENT

1

The man signed the registration card at the Brass Lantern Motel in Easthampton, Massachusetts, shortly after 6:30 P.M. on December 21, 1967. The handwriting was illegible except for the initial consonants of the first and last name—J and M— but since the clerk was principally occupied with his reading of Malraux's *Man's Fate* for a term paper due after the Christmas break at Amherst College (it bored him and he therefore found it baffling), he made no effort to read the handwriting. "Will that be cash or credit card?" he said. "We accept only BankAmericard and MasterCard, I'm afraid."

"Cash," the man said, reaching for his wallet. He was a white male about forty years old, approximately five feet, nine inches tall, weighing somewhere around 150 pounds. He had receding black hair. He wore a tan London Fog raincoat with a red melton zip-in liner, open on a grey Harris tweed jacket and grey flannel trousers. He had removed his necktie and unbuttoned his white shirt at the collar. The clerk, behind the counter, could not see his footgear: black leather chukka boots, whitened and cracked along the welting from repeated and unprotected wear in wet weather. "I have to get an early start." His pronunciation and inflection were clear enough, though non-New England, and the clerk did not take any notice of them. He seemed to be tired.

"We have someone on duty starting at six every morning, sir," the clerk said.

The man shook his head. "I'll be long gone by then, I'm

1

afraid," he said. "Got a long drive ahead of me." He produced two ten-dollar bills and placed them on the counter.

The clerk frowned and inspected the registration card for the first time. "Ah, sir," he said, "I'm afraid you forgot to put down the license plate of your car. We have to have that for our records, you know?"

The man smiled. It was an old-blue-blazer kind of smile: practiced, not quite shiny, loose-fitting, comfortable, and suitable for all occasions. "Well," he said, "I can go out in the yard and look at it if you want, and come back in and write it down, but it's cold out there and I don't see much point in it. I don't even know what state it's registered in. It's one of Mister Avis's buggies there. I borrowed it from him down in Hartford, and when I finish this trip, if I ever do, I plan to give it back to him." He paused. "You want that number so bad, *you* just take a hike for yourself out into that cold and look for the green car with the out-of-state plates. It's the only damned car in the lot anyway."

The clerk opened the cash register and put the two tens in the second currency slot from the right. He thought for a moment and then removed one five-dollar bill and three ones from the third and fourth slots. He gave them to the man. He said: "If you make any long-distance calls—"

"I never do," the man said. "Not from the room. My employer pays for no calls made after five P.M. Says they're bound to be personal and you pay for them yourself. So I use pay phones for them, and not often. When I call him, which I may very well do, I call him collect. If he calls me, as he often does, he will pay for the call. Now let me tell you something: if you go to the switchboard and block that room from making or taking calls, I will put my clothes back on and come back down here and kick your teeth in. The key."

The clerk started to say something. "The key," the man said. The clerk turned and scanned the open cupboard divided into numbered small boxes. "An even-numbered room," the man said, "the first number being a 'one.'"

2

The clerk, his right hand extended toward a box, stopped his motion. "Sir?" he said.

"The odd-numbered rooms are on this highway side," the man said. "I saw a lot of trailer trucks coming in. My guess is they'll be rolling all night. They're just as anxious to get where they're going before Christmas, and do what they have to do when they get there, as I am. Fine by me, but I don't want to listen to them any more'n absolutely necessary. So, an even-numbered room, on the other side, and one with a 'one' for the first digit because I don't feel like climbing icy stairs."

The clerk handed him a key tagged 14. The man grinned. "Uh-huh," he said, "comes right after twelve, I bet. Well, I wish you the best of luck too, and a Merry Christmas, too. Gimme a receipt. All I want to know is where the ice machine is. And the pay phone."

"It's in the hallway between the two wings," the clerk said.

"Which?" the man said.

"Both of 'em," the clerk said. "The pay phone's next to the ice machine."

"Thank you," the man said. He turned quickly and headed for the door, hunching his shoulders in preparation for the cold.

"Good old Saint Nick," the clerk said to himself, and went back to reading *Man's Fate*.

The man went to the room and put the valise on the luggage rack. He took the brown plastic ice bucket off the top of the bureau and left the room. He went to the passageway between the wings of the motel and put the ice bucket on top of the machine. He fished in his pocket for coins and took the handset of the pay phone. He deposited one dime and dialed 0. He told the operator the number that he wanted in New York. She asked him whether he knew the area code, and he said: "Sorry: two-one-two." She asked him to deposit seventy-five cents for the first three minutes. The dime came back. He dropped three

3

quarters through the slot. The phone on the other end was picked up on the first ring. The woman who answered said: "Yes?"

"I'm in Easthampton, Massachusetts," the man said. "It's about an hour away. I went through the town again yesterday and today. It hasn't changed. Shropshire hasn't changed. The bank's still where it was. He saw me, and he hasn't changed. Things stay the same in Shropshire."

"Will that be a problem?" the woman said. "That he should be concerned about, I mean?"

"No," the man said. "The guy's basically kind of a bunny. A great, big, happy bunny. Rich bunnies are usually happy, I think. I went up to his office for a drink. The closet was half open. The Browning's in it. I won't need my piece, except for persuasion. I stopped at a store and got some shells. He even invited me to his party. I don't think I'm gonna go. I don't think anybody's gonna go." He paused. "Except him, of course. He is definitely going. But he is going before the party."

"So, then . . . ?" she said.

"So," he said, "unless something's changed and I don't know about it, or I decide to clip the desk clerk here instead of the guy I came to clip, we're right where we were before. Three-thirty tomorrow morning I get on my pony and ride. The boss makes his call at quarter of five. That sends the bunny to the bank. When I get near there I call him and then I call the other guy and find out if everything's still on track. If it is, I wait fifteen minutes. Then I go to the bank, and he's there, and I do it. Then I get out. Looks good to me."

He hung up the phone and opened the bin of the ice machine. He was glad there was no wind across the flats in the foothills of the Adirondacks. It was cold, but when there was a wind, he recalled, it could penetrate any garment known to man. He used the brown plastic bucket to scoop up a full measure of cubes. He went back to the room and removed the

4

raincoat, hanging it in the closet. He took off the sports jacket and laid it on the bed. He took a water glass from the tray on the bureau and filled it with ice. He opened the valise and took out a brown paper bag. There was a fresh fifth of Smirnoff red-label vodka in it. He opened it and filled the glass halfway. He went into the bathroom and topped off the vodka with water from the tap. He returned to the room and switched on the television set. He watched Chet Huntley deliver the last item of the *Huntley-Brinkley Report*, in monochrome. Shortly before 10:00 P.M. he went to bed.

The clock was a Westclox Traveling Alarm. It always worked. He set the alarm for 3:15. When it rang, he awoke and showered. He got dressed and made another vodka and water, this time without ice, and stronger. He poured the remaining vodka down the toilet, flushing it. He put the empty bottle in the valise and stuffed his dirty linen on top of it. He took out a box of 12-gauge Remington shotgun shells and put three in the left pocket of his raincoat. He took a .45 Colt automatic out of the valise, worked the slide, chambered a round. He put the .45 in the right pocket of his raincoat. He inspected the room and correctly concluded he had left nothing behind.

There was a wind now, in the early-morning darkness. It whined down through the gaps in the hills of western Massachusetts like a meat saw, nothing personal but well-adapted to separating joints and ribs. He went south in the Plymouth on Route 5 to the Massachusetts Turnpike at West Springfield and headed west toward the New York Thruway. He got off at the Stockbridge exit and went south until he hit Route 7. There was a gas station, closed at that hour, with a phone booth on Route 7. He stopped and used it to make two calls. It was 4:40 A.M. The first call required three quarters. The second required one dime. He returned to the Plymouth, started the engine, and cursed the engineers who had built it for failure to anticipate the car might be occupied in cold weather. He shut off the engine and went to the trunk, removing the partial box of shotgun shells from his valise. He emptied it into a small brook beside the gas station, crumpled the box and put it into a rubbish can.

At 5:35 A.M. he approached the Foothills National Bank in Shropshire, Massachusetts, from the north. There was snow falling. There were lights illuminating the second floor of the brick building housing the bank. He turned left into the parking lot, down the incline, and parked his car. There was a Cadillac Coupe de Ville, dark-colored, in the lot. The wind was lighter in the Berkshires than it had been in Easthampton, and the snow was light. He put on unlined black leather gloves. He shut off the headlights and closed the car door carefully. He did his best to follow the tracks to the bank made by the driver of the Cadillac. The back door opened to his grasp. He went inside and climbed the stairs to the second floor, proceeding with the confidence of a person revisiting familiar places. He went directly to the president's office at the front of the building and found James Mandeville, Jr., pacing in front of the windows fronting on Washington Street. He rapped his knuckles once on the open door.

Mandeville turned. *"You?"* he said. "I just saw you. You didn't say anything. He said he was sending somebody who had to see me right off. I thought he must need some help."

"He did," the man said. "I'm him. The one who needs help."

"Well," Mandeville said, taking things in the way a vestryman takes up a church collection, "not that that changes anything. I know what I owe, and I know when it's due, and I'm going to pay it. In full. To him. Not *you*. You get nothing from me."

"I don't think so," the man said. "He doesn't think so, either."

"Doesn't matter what you think," Mandeville said. "Doesn't matter what he thinks, either. What matters is the agreement. The loan agreement. Three years from now I have to pay. I'm going to. The gamble paid off. Claretian Shores is worth at least—hell, much more—than I paid for it. When he called me this morning and said he wanted me to meet somebody at this ungodly hour, naturally I obliged—I'm doing business with the guy. But I assumed this was some other business. Not involving you."

The man backed toward the closet and opened it fully. He took out a Browning automatic 12-gauge shotgun.

"Hey," Mandeville said.

"Very nice gun, Jim," the man said. "Beautiful gun." The grip was checkered and the receiver was engraved with a picture of a hunter leading a rising pheasant while a retriever stood frozen at point. The man took one of the shotgun shells from his pocket and chambered it.

Mandeville started toward him. "Gimme that thing," he said.

The man shifted the shotgun into his left hand and drew the .45 with his right. "Into the bathroom, Jim," he said. "Wouldn't want to make a mess on this lovely carpet."

"What the hell are you doing?" Mandeville said.

"I've got a new line of work," the man said. "I'm better at this one. Into the bathroom, Jim. Or here. Doesn't matter to me." He approached Mandeville and rammed the .45 into his side. "*Move*," he said.

"You can't do this," Mandeville said, moving. "You'll be caught. . . . "

"Into the bathroom, Jim," the man said. "Back to the sink, 'atsa boy. Okay now." He put the automatic back into the pocket of the raincoat and used both hands to ram the muzzle of the shotgun under Mandeville's lower jaw. He noticed abstractedly that Mandeville had gotten a bit jowly in his later years.

"You can't do this," Mandeville said. He put his hands on his face and shook his head. "I knew you. We were friends. I

7

know you didn't like it when I did it, but you knew I had to do it."

"This has nothing to do with that," the man said. "I didn't hold that against you then, and I'm not doing that now. I'm just doing what I do now. I do what the boss says. He says to do this."

"But we've known each other—"

The man pulled the trigger. The pellets in a load of number 6 birdshot cover a thirty-inch circle when they are fired at a paper target from a shotgun bored or choked to full, at fifty feet. The pellets in the shell the man fired from the Browning with its muzzle against the flesh of James Mandeville's lower jaw emerged at nearly 900 feet per second in a group approximately three quarters of an inch wide and dispersed only slightly before they collided with the maxillary, zygomatic, nasal, temporal, parietal, and frontal bones of his head, so that the force that carried them sufficed to blow out the back of his head against the wall and the mirror over the sink—it cracked on the impacts of bone fragments and emerging pellets.

Mandeville left his feet at the instant of impact, but then gravity took over and he began to descend rather gracefully toward the tile floor, his back arching over the washstand, his blood and shredded particles of his brain draining down the wall and broken mirror, some coming from his mouth, a small amount spurting from his nose and ears onto his hands before they dropped, the external carotid artery having been severed along with the internal. The crash of the shot in the acoustically hard room dissipated almost instantly.

The man used his right hand to wrap Mandeville's right hand around the fore end of the stock of the Browning. Tenderly he took Mandeville's left arm above the wrist and placed it on the pistol grip so that the thumb rested on the trigger guard. Then he tore toilet paper off the spool next to the commode and used it to wick blood coming out of the hole in

8

Mandeville's cranium, and dripped it over the shotgun and the front of Mandeville's clothing. He flushed the toilet paper away.

At Bradley Field in Windsor Locks, Connecticut, at 7:25 A.M., the man repacked the .45 in his valise, discarded his black gloves in a rubbish receptacle, along with the vodka bottle and the two shotgun shells he had not needed. He turned in the Avis car.

"Leave this on your MasterCard, sir?" the young woman said.

"No," he said, taking out his wallet, "I'd rather settle it in cash."

"Very well, sir," she said, tearing up the credit card voucher, "that will be fifty-eight thirty-eight, please." He took his wallet out and gave her six ten-dollar bills. "Did you have any problems with the car that we should know about, sir?" she said, ringing up the payment.

"Well," he said, "at one point I thought I was going to spend the rest of my life in a parking lot, because it'd been snowing, and the drive was up a grade, and whatever you've got on that junker for snow tires doesn't do the job. But other than that, no, no problems."

She handed him a receipt. She smiled brightly, having practiced. "Thank you very much, sir," she said. "We appreciate your business, and we hope to see you again. We try harder, you know."

He stopped at a bank of pay phones outside the airport coffee shop and dialed the operator, this time remembering to give the area code before telling her the number. The woman at the other end accepted the charges. "The job is done," he said.

"He'll be very pleased," she said. "When he wants you for something else . . . ?"

"He knows where to find me," he said. "I'm going back where it's warm. I'm freezing my ass off up here. I'd forgotten how cold this place is."

2

The slick-paper photocopied reports of the investigation of the death of James Mandeville, Jr., that Joe Corey read at the small desk in the room he shared with his wife at the Unicorn Inn at Goshen, Massachusetts, had been stored in the accordion-bellow file for about twenty years when Corey accepted them in Shropshire that morning from Amelia Feldt. They curled from the top and bottom when he removed them, and the type had become faint. He used a volume of the *Reader's Digest Condensed Books* from the inn library as a paperweight, and Jill said as he struggled with them: "Are you really sure you want to do this?"

"Yes," he said.

"Why?" she said.

He put down the report he was studying and turned in the chair to look at her. "Because," he said, "in the going-on six years we've been together, you've talked in your sleep at least twenty times about how your grandfather was murdered, and the cops did nothing about it, and then you apologize to your mother for not caring more about it. And also because it's much more interesting than what I've been doing since law school, as would be almost anything this side of a tire fire." He turned back to the reports.

"I hope so," she said.

Between 4:20 and 4:30 A.M. on the morning of December 22, 1967, Patrolman Robert Gates finished trying each of

11

the three doors and checking the windows of the two-story brick building that housed the only office of the Foothills National Bank on the hill overlooking Washington Street in Shropshire, Massachusetts, southwest of Pittsfield. He shone his flashlight into each of the four six-paned windows flanking the main entrance doors and stooped to shine it as well into each of the basement windows. He then proceeded around the building, beginning at the northeasterly corner and continuing around to the rear, placing his gloved left hand on the sills of each of the three first-floor windows in order to rise on tiptoe to shine his light into the lobby of the bank and the three tellers' cages that served it. The two lights illuminating the front of the Mosler vault were burning, and he saw no signs of tampering, or any other indication that any person was inside the bank.

Three inches of fresh dry snow had fallen since just before midnight; the storm would end around 5:00 A.M. It carried very light winds, and therefore the footprints he left during his 4:30 inspection of the entire exterior of the bank—the lighter impressions he made walking, as well as the deeper ones at each of the three basement windows on the side and rear of the building and the ones he made on tiptoe at the windows on the sides and at the rear—remained clearly visible four hours later alongside the marks he had left during his identical inspection two hours before. There were no footprints other than those he had made at the sides of the building when observations were made and photographs taken at 8:45 A.M.

On each occasion he had paid particular attention to construction of the one-story wing, not yet connected to the interior of the existing structure, that would expand the bank's office space on the southerly side overlooking the parking lot, making sure that no one was hiding in the enclosed shell of the new addition. By maneuvering his cruiser around the perimeter of the parking lot and the temporary access road behind the addition, he had employed both the headlights and spot-

12

light to ascertain that no one was lurking in the area. The cruiser was equipped with traction chains on the rear wheels, which, along with the front wheels, were equipped with new Goodyear Town & Country studded winter tires, size 8.50 × 16 inches.

At approximately 4:55 A.M. Patrolman Gates completed his regular inspection of places of business on both sides of Washington Street south of the bank and entered the rear door of the lighted kitchen of the Shropshire Inn. Owner Jack Davis was preparing breakfast for himself before preparing to serve guests. He advised it had been a quiet night as far as he knew. They exchanged small talk. Davis offered, and Gates accepted, four containers of coffee and six pieces of Danish pastry.

Jack and I'd become old friends by then," Attorney Gates had told Corey that morning. "He and Winifred were still newcomers, mind you, only'd owned the place four or five years at that point, but Jack and I were the only people up and about at that ungodly hour every day of every week— well, he was up the seven days; I did get one day off, when I didn't see him. But it wasn't because I was home in bed, sleeping away—when you've been on the early shift for a while, your body stays on it, even on days off. The farmers out in the country, of course, they'd all been up for hours, but even the people had the early shift up at the G.E. engine plant in Pittsfield, they weren't up at that hour. Of course, old Bill Slinger, back at the station, he was *supposed* to be up, same shift as I was, but I don't think there were five mornings, in all those years I spent as a member of the force, when the first thing I had to do when I came back with the coffee wasn't: wake Bill up. And those were mornings when he'd had something for lunch that disagreed with him, so his stomach was acting up and keeping him awake. He was much better company when he was asleep.

"For Jack and I, that morning was pretty much the same

13

as any other morning. We talked about the storm, just about perfect for the season, we both thought. Nice for the tourists— Jack said half his rooms were full, and the other half were all reserved and'd start filling up that day. Real New England Christmas, just like Norman Rockwell'd trained them to expect. And we just had the usual chitchat. It's funny how some conversation you'd forget eight hours later on an ordinary day just sticks in your mind on a day like that. Gets glued there. But, just the usual chitchat. Neither one of us could understand why the selectmen thought it was cheaper, leave the Christmas lights on all night, six weeks every year, than it'd be to put in just once a separate circuit for 'em so you could shut 'em off at midnight but still leave the streetlamps on and leave them off during the day. But they didn't.

" 'Now,' I recall Jack saying this, 'now after being here awhile I'm beginning to understand how a town with *one* school,'—see, the older kids've been taking the bus up to Regional, soon's they finish elementary, ever since 'fifty-six. Did the last two years there, myself. 'How a town with just one school,' this's what Jack was saying, 'eight cops, and a volunteer fire company can have such damned high taxes. Now I think I know. They're throwing money away. Must have Light Company stock.'

"Well anyway," Gates said, "I suppose we stood around and shot the bull there for fifteen, twenty minutes, while the Danish finished baking. They were usually coming out, time I got there mornings, but that morning Jack said he'd overslept. Forgot to set his alarm. And he'd just barely put 'em in before I got there. Which is when the phone rang, like I said in my report, out at the desk.

"Now, that was unusual. Who the hell'd be up to call at that hour? So Jack went out and answered it, and I heard him say: 'Shropshire Inn.' And then: 'Nope. Must have the wrong number, my friend. No one by that name registered here. Nobody up in the whole town, in fact, 'cept for me and one

14

hungry cop.' Then he came back out and said to me, like I said in my report: 'Wrong number.'

"So the Danish got ready, and he took 'em out, and then as soon as they got cool enough for him to touch 'em, frost 'em, Jack popped the usual half a dozen in a bag for me, and I helped myself to the coffee—by that time of the morning, the stuff back in the station pot'd turned to motor oil—two cups for me, two for Bill, as usual, and then I told him I hoped he had a good day, also as usual, and he said what he usually said, something to the effect that he hoped all of his men guests'd had good nights with their ladies 'cause it made his days more cheerful, and I went on back to the station."

At approximately 5:20 A.M., the files stated, Patrolman Gates was proceeding in the cruiser north on Washington Street toward the intersection of Berkshire Street. The snow had stopped.

"Jim Mandeville was coming up the hill on Berkshire," Gates recalled, "so I stopped—the light was flashing yellow—and let him through. He had his blinker on to go left, or put it on as soon's he spotted me, but of course I didn't know where else he'd be going at that hour, unless it'd be to the bank, but then when I thought about it later on, I didn't really understand why anyone as rich as Jim was, driving his big Cadillac and owning his own bank, only local bank in town, why he'd even have to go there, that time of the morning. Jim was a man, did his work, but he wasn't all that strong on it, to go in at that hour of the day. But that was where he was going all right, and he waved to me and I waved back, of course—man as rich as Jim was, town as small as Shropshire, man like that wields a lot of power. Even if you are a cop. Like to stay on his good side, if he behaves himself enough so's you don't have to make him mad. Man with that much money can have quite a lot to say, when it comes to Town Meeting and the police budget comes up.

"But I have to say this about Jim: he never gave us, any of

us that I know of, the slightest bit of trouble, that regard or any other. Never tried to throw his weight around. Didn't ask for special treatment. Just lived in his big white house out on Berkshire there, he and Mimi raised their kids, always had a wave for you, 'How's it goin',' knew your name. Lived a little *better*'n most people did, of course, but nothing showy, never went around acting like he thought he was better'n they were. He just had a lot more money. And he kept it to himself."

The report said that Miss Katherine McCormack, head teller, at approximately 7:50 A.M., her customary time, was the first to arrive at the bank, in order to perform her duties of opening the doors and admitting personnel arriving at 8:00.

"I've always liked that first hour of the day," she told Corey. "Mister Mandeville Senior, I recall it was in 'forty-nine, August of 'forty-nine, when Josie Shanahan announced she was finally going to retire and move to Florida with her sister. My God, she must've been seventy-five if she was a day, but nobody ever thought she'd retire. She'd been there when Mister Mandeville's father was still alive, he'd put her in the job, and there were some who thought she'd been there even before that, when *his* father started the bank. Back in the eighteen nineties. Anyway, Mister Mandeville Senior called me into the office and said to me: 'Well, Kate, would you be willing to take on Josie's job, now that she's leaving?' And I was, well, not *shocked*, exactly, because I've always flattered myself I knew what I was doing, once I learned the job and all, but there were two other ladies there who'd been there longer'n I certainly had, one of them *much* longer, if you want the truth, and I just said, well, I don't know what I said, but he could see I was surprised.

"And he said, this was Mister Mandeville Senior, very imposing man, too, he said: 'Well, Kate, I look at it this way. Mildred'll be leaving in a few years herself, and she's not been

16

feeling well. This bank's done pretty well now, good many years, I'd say, and I think a good part of the reason has been continuity. Continuity in office. Experience, and staying power. So I'd like whoever succeeds Josie to look like she'll stay awhile. And then, of course, Christine is married, so even though the two of you are about the same age and all, and she has been here a bit longer, I imagine pretty soon she and her good husband there'll want to start a family, so of course she'll have to leave, and we'll have to get someone new. Who the head teller'll have to train. So I think that should be you. And the job does pay a bit more money—five dollars every week.' So that settled it, of course.

"But the reason I tried to get there every morning, not just that one that turned out to be the start of such a terrible, awful day, was because I'd liked to have the place all to myself a little bit. Before all the others got there. So that day was no different. Except of course it was.

"The first thing that I noticed was Mister Mandeville's car in the lot. It was the only one there. And that was unusual because Mister Mandeville—Mister Mandeville Junior, I mean—wasn't like his father. Mister Mandeville Senior always got to the bank by nine, usually about eight forty-five or so. But Mister Mandeville *Junior*, well, he seldom strolled in until around nine-thirty or ten. He had a different attitude about business than his father did.

"I remember he said once, he came in one morning to sign some papers that had to be signed and go out, first thing. Then he was going home to shave and get dressed and come back. And he was still in his fishing clothes. Well, not his boots, or any of his equipment, but a flannel shirt and old pants and this terrible-looking old hat, and he hadn't shaved or combed his hair or anything—and he was just in the best mood you ever saw. Said he'd been up since two and he'd gone fishing somewhere down in East Lee there, 'at the very crack of dawn,' this was in the spring, and he'd caught his limit of

17

trout. And I remember clearly him saying this: 'Before anybody else was even out of bed. Fishing luck's no different than business luck—first guy on the stream gets the fish.' And another time, well a good many more times than once—this was something that happened every year; he made a habit of it, once his father'd died—when the season opened on birds, you simply just couldn't find him in the afternoons. He was out shooting pheasants, or quail, I forget what he said. Once or twice, when he had a lunchtime conference in the office, he even brought his dogs in with him, had two beautiful English setters, handsome dogs, very well behaved, and they were in the meetings with him, just like they'd been bankers themselves.

"And his guns, too, of course. His shotguns. He had several of them. When it wasn't bird season, he was always going out of an afternoon to shoot clay pigeons. He said: 'skeet.' It was the longest time when I thought a 'skeet' was some kind of real bird, and I remember I thought it was just awful the first time he said he'd 'broken a hundred yesterday,' and I said: 'Mister Mandeville, really. You can't possibly eat that many. Even give them away.' And didn't he just laugh and laugh at me? I can't say how embarrassed I was. But he always kept some of his guns in the office. In the closet behind the door, where he hung his coat. He was very proud of them, always taking them out and showing them off to his friends. I think they cost quite a lot when he bought them. I don't know much about guns. Guns scare me, and they always have. I've always been afraid, since I've been a teller, that someone will walk in with one and point it at me. But they were very beautiful guns. Anyone could see that.

"But as I say, he did come in late, and he did leave early. I'd never known Mister Mandeville Junior to be at that bank that early in the morning. I recognized his car, of course. But the lights were still on, but the sun was up by then, and the door on his side was open. So my first thought was that there

18

must have been a robbery, or maybe a fire or something, or the alarm went off and the police called him and he'd come to shut it off. So that would explain why he was in too much of a hurry to shut the door on his side.

"But the sun was *up*. And the car lights were *on*, and Mister Mandeville Junior would never have left his car lights on when the sun was out, because that would run the battery down. And that was when I noticed that the motor was still running, because it was cold and I could see the exhaust smoke. So I knew he must have come in a terrible hurry, and I parked my car and got out and ran to the back door of the bank, which was the one he always used, and it was open. Which was another thing he never did, leave the back door of the bank open. And not just because of all the heat getting out, either—because of maybe someone coming in to do something that he shouldn't. And I went in, and I climbed the stairs, and I was saying his name—'Mister Mandeville, Mister Mandeville, are you here?' Although of course I knew he was, that he must be. But he didn't answer from the first floor, and the vault was still closed like it always was when I got there in the morning, and so I ran upstairs to see if he was there. And I got upstairs and he wasn't in the board of directors' room, the first door when you come to the top of the stairs in the back, because I looked in there, and he wasn't in the bank conference room, where we have our conference meetings, our bank conference meetings, and so I knew he must be in his own office at the end of the hall at the front of the building, and the door to it was open.

"So I ran down the hall to his office, saying 'Mister Mandeville, Mister Mandeville, where are you?' And I was—I think I was crying by then. I knew something was terribly wrong, because why didn't he answer me? And I went into his office, and he wasn't in there, either. I couldn't see him. I started thinking: 'Can he be in the cellar? Could there be something wrong with the boiler, so that he went down there to fix that?'

"That was when I noticed that his closet was open, and, I don't know what made me do it, I know I didn't mean to, but I just looked up toward that door of his lavatory, and I saw the wooden part of the gun there on the floor, and then I saw his foot and the bottom part of his leg, and I ran in there and . . . I found him."

3

Katherine McCormack paused and wept quietly for less than a minute into her handkerchief. She raised her eyes and chewed once on her lower lip. "I could see right off that he must be dead. There was blood everywhere, on the walls, the mirror—the mirror was broken—and the sink and the toilet. Everything. So I guess I must have screamed, and I was trying to think what to do. At first I thought I could ring the alarm, but then I thought: 'No, I'll just call the police.'

"And so that's what I did. I called the police. And they came. They came right off. Sergeant Barry was there in jig time, and two other men after him. I think one of them was State Police, but he came a little later. Sergeant Barry was very bossy. I was surprised. He'd been banking with us for years, although of course almost everyone in Shropshire did. Wasn't much choice in those days—us or the Savings Bank, and they didn't offer checking, couldn't in those days. Not like now, with all the branches of the banks in the big cities, and all those automatic teller machines so you almost never meet a human being when you do your banking now. Sergeant Barry'd always been very nice, when he came in with his paycheck—of course, since he was a policeman, it wasn't a very big check, and he always needed to get some in cash. But we were good about that. It was a town check, after all. The town's credit was good.

"But that day, he was still very polite and all, but I guess he must've had eight or ten dollars in his pocket or something, because when he said you had to do something, well, that was what you had to do. He said I had to leave my car right where it was until after the State Policeman questioned me, and then he, Sergeant Barry, I mean, he had Patrolman Gates give me a ride home, after they were through with me. No one could use the parking lot, and the bank had to be closed until they finished what they were doing. I didn't get my car back until late that afternoon."

Mandeville's Cadillac Coupe de Ville was equipped with metal-studded Goodrich mud-and-snow-cleated tires, 8.50 × 15, on the rear wheels, and Goodrich Super Cushion 8.50 × 15 tires on the front wheels. Investigation showed one set of tracks indicating that the vehicle had been driven into the parking lot after Gate's 4:15 A.M. inspection—the tracks were superimposed—and stopped at the place where it was found by officers. One set of footprints, apparently made by a man walking fast, was found leading from the Cadillac vehicle to the concrete step at the rear door of the bank, where several other persons had also stepped, obliterating all footprints. The car remained untouched until forensic specialist Owen Moore arrived from SP Northampton to examine scene, having been secured by Patrolman William Slinger, on orders of Chief Albert Feldt, pending Moore's inspection. Moore ordered it impounded. Upon subsequent examination, no latent prints other than those identifiable as family members, friends, or Mandeville himself were found.

No evidence of forced entry was found at the rear door. All other possible means of entry, including all first-story windows and doors, and basement windows and door, were inspected and found to present no marks of forced entry. No footprints other than those of Patrolman Gates were observed at any other potential points of entry.

Katherine McCormack stated it had been decedent's invariable practice to lock his office when he left it. Further stated

22

that he had the only key, and that she had found the door open upon her arrival. No sign of forced entry was found on the office door.

Katherine McCormack's vehicle, a Ford Galaxy sedan, was inspected and found to be equipped with metal-studded Goodrich mud-and-snow cleats, 7.50 × 15, rear, and Goodrich Super Cushion 7.50 × 15 front.

I always relied on Mister Mandeville Senior for advice on all my business dealings," Katherine McCormack told Corey. "He knew much more about such things than I did, and he was often able to get a much better price for me than I would have been able to get for myself. And he was always very kind and helpful whenever I asked him for advice, and then after he died, so was Mister Mandeville Junior, and I relied on him in exactly the same way. And that's why my tires are the same brand as the ones on his car. Because he was convinced that they were the best tire for the money, and that was good enough for me."

A third set of tire marks was found leading into the parking lot to the space adjoining that occupied by the Cadillac, indicating by the similarity of their depth and the relative freshness of the tread marks that they had been made at about the same time as those made by the Cadillac. Two sets of footprints, not made by a man wearing low boots or rubbers—he had tried as best he could to use the same footprints Mandeville had made going in, and had succeeded well enough to prevent identification of his shoes by brand or type—led to and from the rear door of the bank.

Observation showed that the vehicle causing the incoming tread marks had subsequently backed out over the last fifty feet of them. The Unknown Motor Vehicle not found at the scene had faced the street and thereupon returned to it. Acting at the direction of Mr. Moore, photographs were taken of all tracks.

Patrolman Gates stated the pattern of the rear treads of the

UMV appeared to him to resemble the Goodyear Suburbanite winter tires he had installed on his personal vehicle two years previously, but expressed the opinion they were newer because the tracks appeared to be deeper. He noted also that the tread did not appear to carry metal studs.

I was driving back and forth to Westfield three days a week in those days," Gates told Corey, "getting my college degree. And I'll tell you it was hell. I was young in those days and could almost believe I could do it, all right. Today that kind of duty, working all night here, and then driving down there and back—today that routine'd kill me. I think it probably would've then, if I hadn't wanted it so much.

"But no one in my family'd ever had much of anything. I was the first one in it who ever went to college, and I had the fire in my belly. Gil Rogers'd lighted it up. Knew me from my father's house-painting business—I worked for Dad in the summers in high school, and one summer we worked on Gil's house. Gil told me if I could make it through law school, he'd give me a job in his office, and to me what Gil made was big money. His house wasn't as big as Mandeville's, of course, all that land, private mountain—nothing else in this town ever was. But Gil's was plenty big by my standards, you bet, and the minute he said that, well, my ears went up—I was *sold*. He had the biggest practice here, and small-town pay's good if you're all of it, when it comes to practicing law. So I was a cop nights, and a student days, and therefore I didn't get drafted. But still, that commute was a genuine killer. Taught me something, though, that punishment for those eight years, and it wasn't just law cases, either. I learned how to figure things out. The minute I saw those tread marks, and no car there to go with them, I told Sergeant Barry right off.

"I said: 'Sergeant, whoever drove in here and parked next to Mandeville's car, he's not from this neck of the woods. You've got to stud those Suburbanites out here, unless you want to get stuck. Now this new snow isn't what you'd call deep, and it's nice and dry, and there's no ice under it—fine. But if it had been, or there *had* been some ice, or maybe a good ten-inch blow, nice and wet and heavy, he'd've still been here when we pulled up. Or at least his car would've been. I know, believe me, I know. I saved thirty bucks, not getting my last set of those studded. And after the first year, well, I left 'em on, and burned them right down the next summer. Bought myself new ones, next winter. Because I found out the hard way, you know, if you want to travel in this part of the world, in the winter, and you want to get home when you do, you've got to have those spikes under you. Otherwise you'll sleep in a ditch.'

"So I don't know if Paul believed me, or if it ever did anybody any good, but if you're trying to figure out now what went on there, whoever can tell you came from someplace else. Down in the flats he came from."

Officers at the scene were unable to make a positive identification of decedent pending autopsy, due to extreme degree of trauma to facial and cranial region. Powder burns and associated trauma to upper neck and frontal lower-jaw area together with related damage to clothing of upper body—collar of grey flannel sweater, white dress shirt—warranted a working hypothesis that the muzzle of a shotgun had been placed in contact with and against the skin at the junction of the lower jaw and throat while the decedent was standing erect, and that the weapon was then discharged by person unknown. A Browning Automatic shotgun, caliber 12-gauge, was found between the decedent's legs. The decedent's right hand was clasped around the fore end of the stock, and the decedent's left hand was on the breech of the weapon. The breech was open, and a single expended shell, 12-gauge, number 6 shot, was found on the carpet of the office approximately forty-one centimeters from the decedent's sinistral pelvic bone. Dr.

Thomas Lowden, M.D., medical examiner, determined the probable cause of death, pending autopsy, to have been a single round fired from a shotgun at extreme close range.

Preliminary examination of decedent showed a well-developed, well-nourished white male, between sixty and sixty-five years old, height approximately 5'10", heavy build, weight approximately 210 pounds, clad in grey flannel sweater, white shirt, dark brown wool trousers, wool stockings, leather-topped boots with rubber bottoms. A red woolen parka, size 46, a felt hat, size 7⅜, and a blue woolen scarf were found on a chair near the desk and identified by Katherine McCormack as the property of James C. Mandeville, Jr., age sixty-two, president, Foothills National Bank, Shropshire.

Following observation by Dr. Lowden of the body undisturbed, it was placed upon a gurney and examined for evidence of identification and personal property. A gold wedding ring was removed from the third finger of the left hand and found to have been engraved on the inside surface. The engraving appeared to have worn away. A gold Rolex wristwatch, engraved on the back J.C.M., A.D.M., with gold bracelet was removed from the left wrist. A brown wallet was found in the left rear pocket, containing $68 in currency; an American Express card in the name of James C. Mandeville; a MasterCard issued by Foothills National Bank in the name of James C. Mandeville, Jr.; and a valid Massachusetts driver's license issued to James C. Mandeville, Jr., date of birth January 17, 1905, height 5'11", weight 195 pounds, hair grey-brown, eyes brown, no restrictive codes, address Overlook Hills Farm, Shropshire, Massachusetts. Also contained in the wallet were eight business cards in the name of James C. Mandeville, Jr., President, Foothills National Bank, Shropshire, Massachusetts.

Chief Feldt stated that on information and belief, and based upon lifelong acquaintance and familiarity with the appearance of James C. Mandeville, that the decedent was that individual. Chief Feldt stated that in his opinion and belief, there was no reason to subject Mirion Mandeville, known to him to be the wife of the decedent, to what he termed "the ordeal of viewing him like this."

Det. Lt. Insp. Warren Oldham, Massachusetts State Police, having taken charge of the homicide investigation, authorized entry of the name of James C. Mandeville, Jr., as tentative identification of the decedent, and authorized Dr. Thomas Lowden to order the body removed. Tentative identification was so recorded, to be withheld pending actual notification of next of kin, and the body was removed to the morgue at Berkshire General Hospital for autopsy and postmortem.

The interior and exterior of scene remained secured, per order of Lt. Oldham, and Specialist Owen Moore conducted a complete inspection of the premises, concluding at 3:51 P.M. December 22, 1967.

It wasn't much of a Christmas that year," Katherine McCormack said. "When Officer Gates was driving me home that morning—I lived then on the southern edge of town in the house that I was born in, did, until just three years ago, when it got too much for me to handle by myself—it just seemed so *strange*. To've come from that terrible sight, the man I worked for just lying dead like that there—he was so proud of that rug. Everything in the whole bank, really. His grandfather'd bought that rug from a real Persian he'd met in New York City, he was down there on business with the Morgan people and they introduced him to this man—they bought all their rugs from him—and Mister Mandeville's grandfather'd bought it on the spot and had it shipped back home, and said that his wife couldn't have it for that lovely home; it was going in the bank. And all the furniture had history, too, the furniture in his office. That wonderful old chiming clock on the mantelpiece; the matched leather chairs and so forth: what Mister Mandeville's grandfather hadn't bought and put in there, Mister

27

Mandeville Senior had brought. And now it was all ruined, and him lying dead so horribly in the midst of it all, and I just couldn't get the sight out of my mind.

"So here was the village, then, all dressed up for Christmas. All the Christmas decorations over Washington Street, all silver, and red and green, all the lights burning of course, the old inn looking so nice and inviting again. It really is what Mister Mandeville Junior always said it was: 'the natural centerpiece of town, and as long as it's rundown, the town'll be in the same shape.' And he had a lot to do with getting it going again, finding a new owner to spruce it up and so forth, loaning him the money to do it, and then, when that didn't work out, the first one—he drank—well, didn't Mister Mandeville Junior just say: 'All right, I'll get another one'? You bet he did. There was no stopping Mister Mandeville Junior when he made up his mind to do something.

"His father always said that," she said, "and he wasn't always happy when he said it, not by any means. I remember when Mister Mandeville Junior was in college—all the Mandevilles, well, the boys, anyway, all of them'd always gone to Brown, all the way back to Mister Mandeville Senior's grandfather—and one day Mister Mandeville Junior, well, he just came home in a brand new car. A Ford convertible. Red. And his father said, Josie Shanahan told me this, he was just about beside himself.

" 'Now that's his mother's handiwork you see there, that blasted brand new car. Doesn't that kid know there's a Depression on? How people out of work in this town're going to feel when the banker can't give them a loan because they can't pay it back, and then they go out the door and the first thing they see's the banker's son, kitin' around in that confounded thing like the Prince of Wales or something? She's spoiling the blamed kid rotten, and there's not a thing I can do about it. Not one single thing in the world.'

"Well, I suppose he *was* spoiled. But still, he was goodhearted, and he was determined that the inn was going to get

28

started again, and he was the one who did it, and he stuck with it, and there it was that terrible morning, in the fresh new snowfall for Christmas, looking just as proud as it could be. And Mister Mandeville Junior lying dead up there in his office.

"It was all just so sad. Mister Mandeville's daughters, he'd told me this, one of them was your wife's grandmother, on their way with their families to spend Christmas, two of the grandchildren he'd never seen; he was so looking forward to that. Everything else in the whole blessed world, all ready for Jesus' birth. The happiest time of the year. It just made no sense to me at all. It was all just so terribly strange."

4

The birds had been up and chattering in the sunshine about four hours, and therefore Corey had been up four hours when he parked his rented maroon Ford Escort for the second time in the shaded driveway of Amelia Feldt's white Cape Cod house among the pines along Jefferson Street in Shropshire. The tail end of the *Today* show was playing on the television on the counter in her kitchen when she opened the door. She was no more than 5'1"; and Corey at 6'0", married to a woman slightly taller than he when she put on her low-heeled pumps, was thankful for Amelia's brisk notion of the rules of decorum that ought to be observed between a man of twenty-nine and a woman of seventy-six.

"Because if you didn't make it pretty plain she might haul off and belt you one if you patronized her one small bit, I really would be tempted to pat her on the head like a miniature schnauzer. That's exactly what she reminds me of: a little grey miniature schnauzer. She doesn't have the whiskers, and she gets around on her back legs only, but she's got that same bright bounciness as those little dogs."

Jill said: "So what am I? Your giant schnauzer? I told you when we started thinking about doing this that you could have your puppy if we moved up here. I knew that'd get you. All that liberated male stuff—'My wife has a career, too'—it's just a load of buncombe, and so's all your endless whining about logging all those hours and wanting to get out so you can do

30

something that's real. The only reason you went for the whole idea of getting out was that you knew if you did it, I'd get you a puppy, of your very own."

"You can be pretty hostile, when you put your mind to it," he said.

Now, Amelia scrutinized him. "Well," she said, "come in, come in. I'll get you a cup of coffee. You look like the wrath of God." She went to the counter and shut off the TV.

He closed the door behind him and nodded. "That's about the way I feel, too," he said. "It's the darned birds up here that do it. They won't let me sleep. I'm on a winter, city schedule. I can sleep through traffic noise, and metal garbage cans, and people blowing horns at four A.M. they're not supposed to blow at noon. I can sleep through gunfire, and through sirens and loud cursing, just as long's the room stays dark. But put me down out in the country where it's quiet after dark, and lodge me in an old inn where the shades don't quite fit the windows, and then start the birdies singing around five A.M. or so, and I can't sleep at all. So I got out of bed around six, I guess it was, drove into Lenox and had myself breakfast, then read all the papers and drove down."

Amelia brought the coffee to the small round table at the two shaded windows that gave out on the pine grove and a meadow to the south. They sat down. "Does it bother your wife, too?"

"Not as much, I think," he said. "She's more a morning person anyway. It makes for good teamwork. One of us is most alert just when the other one is stupid, at both ends of the day."

"Katherine seemed to think you were alert enough, both times that she saw you," she said. "You charmed the pants off of her."

"Well," he said, "because I'm generally crafty enough not to go calling on people before ten or so in the morning. As for the charm stuff? I doubt that. I like the lady. Here I am, a

31

total stranger, rooting around in bad things that happened over twenty years ago, things that really hurt and are none of my business. . . ."

"Well," Amelia said, "they certainly are, young man. At least I assume it's still the case that if a thing concerns a wife, then it concerns the husband. And surely your wife has some stake in this, being Jim's granddaughter."

He shrugged. "She has what I guess you'd call an intellectual interest," he said. "She was only four when Gampy died. She'd only seen him twice. It's hard for a kid that age to form any real, lasting impressions of someone that they saw so little, so young, when their minds were on Christmas and Santa more'n anything else."

"Well, *Christmas*," Amelia said, "Christmas alone should've done it, if she was visiting Jim. Jim was Old Saint Nick himself, when it came to putting on Christmas. One of the saddest parts of the whole awful business, one of the details that sticks in my mind, was when Al came by here on his way to tell Mimi—Al'd just come from the bank, and when I saw the look on his face, I thought he was dying himself, or that he'd had terrible news that he didn't dare tell me by phone. And then when he told me, well, of course he had. And after he told me, so'd I. He said I had to come with him to tell Mimi. He couldn't face her alone. And I said of course, I'd insist on going, but first we were having a big drink. Al didn't approve of Dutch courage at all. The most that he'd take was one highball, and his friends knew he wanted it weak. But that day the ginger ale was very dark, and Al didn't complain, not a bit.

"Then we drove out Berkshire Street, with our terrible secret and not wanting to tell it at all, and as we came 'round that long curve where you first see that big beautiful white house—you've been out there to see it yourself?"

"Oh yeah," he said. "Jill didn't want to come with me. She said: 'It's great and it's gorgeous, and gone. Why go see it and get all worked up again, as Grandmother said when she sold

32

it. I think Grandmother was right.' It's beautiful all right. Up on that knoll there? Out in the country? Jill was a child the last time she stayed there, but it impressed her even then. 'The thing I remember most,' she said, 'was all the *rooms*. Amy and Josh, and Aaron and I, could play hide-and-go-seek the whole day long, and not use the same hidey-hole twice."

"Yes," Amelia said, "well, you should've seen it at Christmas. Jim'd found his grandfather's collection of brass candlesticks, which of course people used to use to set their curtains afire before electric lights, and he had them all wired for Christmas-tree bulbs, and there was one in every window. He'd have one of his men cut a tree that they picked out, the whole family out in the woods, and I don't recall one that didn't fill up, it seemed like, that whole big front hall. He had laurel rope around the banisters of that big double staircase, and more laurel and holly all over the dining room and the sitting room and the library, and those great big fireplaces burning whole logs, and oh, my heavens, the *smells*. Mimi was a wonderful cook. Insisted on doing her own. They had money enough, God knows, to hire people, but a hired cook she wouldn't permit. She'd let Joe hire maids, and farmhands and so forth, people to take care of the place, but while she never said it, I know Mimi thought she was the best cook in the county. Maybe the whole Commonwealth. Turkeys and hams, the great roasts of beef, and Joe's own special punch, in case eggnogs or mixed drinks weren't to your liking, and each Christmas a mammoth plum pudding.

"They'd throw the house open, did it every year, the Sunday before Christmas came. If there was somebody in Shropshire he didn't invite, I don't know who that might have been. Al used to dread that annual Sunday—oh, how he dreaded it. He was in a foul temper for days. It wasn't because he didn't like Jim—Al just thought the world of Jim Mandeville, called him 'Duke of Overlook Hills.' And it wasn't because Al disliked big parties, or seeing his friends have good times. It was because Jim asked all the cops, just like he asked all the firemen, all the people from the post office, from the school, the churches, naturally from the bank—why, there wasn't a store open on those Sunday afternoons along Washington Street, not even Bruce Tappett's drugstore. The whole town was at Overlook Hills.

"And naturally all of Al's men, all of them all wanted to go, too. Well, Al couldn't very well just throw up his hands and say: 'All right, Jim Mandeville's having his Christmas party. We'll close up the shop and raise hell.' Because what if there was a car accident, or somebody's house caught on fire, the fire chief up at Overlook Hills, and all of his volunteers up there with him? So two of Al's men had to miss the big party, and I'll tell you, they didn't like it. 'Well, what can I do?' Al said that every year.

" 'They tell me to rotate the duty that day, so everyone goes for a while. Well, I'll rotate it by years, but not by hours, because I know what'll happen if four men go up there in two shifts: the two that go first to the party will get drunk, do it fast, because they know they'll have to leave. And the ones they replace will do likewise when they get there, making up for all the lost time. So what does leave me with? Police protection? Not if you know what the word means. It leaves me with four drunken cops on the second rotation, and that's not protection to me.'

"So every third year, two men missed the party, and Al took his turn with the rest, and every year both men, including Al when his turn came, were madder'n hornets to be at the station. That was what kind of party it was.

"So," she said, "the year that Jim died, Friday before Christmas, two days before his big party, there we were in the car, rounding that bend, with what we had to tell Mimi. And when we saw that house—the sun was barely up, it was only about nine, but it was still quite dark, this being December and all—with all the house lights blazing, and Mimi inside with her cooking and baking, not knowing the terrible news, well, it hit us. We hadn't planned on that. We were both

34

crying before we even turned in the driveway, and when we got to the back door and one of the maids answered it, well, she took one look at us and stepped back, put her hand over her mouth: she knew. Without us saying a word. And Mimi came 'round from where she was working, wiping her hands on her apron, and saw us and *she* knew, just like the maid did. Without saying a word. Not the shooting, of course, she didn't know that, but right off, she knew Jim was dead."

She sighed. "Al said many times, and I never once doubted him, that the worst part of his job, the very worst part, was going to the house to tell someone that their boy or girl'd been killed in a car accident, or their brother'd been shot in some fool hunting thing, or someone'd drowned—things like that. But the very worst thing, of all the worst things that he ever had to do, was drive out to Overlook that Friday before Christmas, to tell Mimi what'd happened to Jim."

She shook her head. "Al always insisted on making those visits himself. He said he was the chief, and it was the chief's responsibility to make an example for the rest of the men, that when something that nobody wants to do came along and had to be done, the chief was the one who would do it. 'For one thing,' he used to say, because Al did have a sense of humor, 'any one of those monkeys starts getting it into his head that he might do a little dirty politicking, get me kicked out and take my job, the second I get wind of it, all I'll have to do is take him aside and remind him: "You sure you want to do this, Sam? You want to be the one that has to go out and tell the families?" And that'll settle him right down.' But that day, I think if someone'd said to him that he'd drive out and tell Mimi, if he could have Al's job, Al would've told him: 'Take it. I don't want it anymore.' "

"It must've been tough," Corey said.

"Tough?" Amelia said. "Tough, you think it was? If Al knew what religion the family was, what church they went to, when he had to make one of those calls, first he'd call up the minister, or the priest, or the rabbi from the Pittsfield congregation if the dead person was a Jew, and arrange either that he'd pick him up in his cruiser or meet him somewhere near the house. So at least he'd have some backup, in case the family collapsed. Once or twice, when he knew the new widow was pregnant, about to deliver, or when the boy or girl's parents—one of the parents of one of those junior prom fatals—had a heart condition or something, he'd take the doctor along.

"But when Jim died, he couldn't do that. They weren't churchgoers, Jim and Mimi weren't—they were from different religions, him Episcopal, much as anything else, and she was a Catholic. But not much of one. I guess when they got married there was some kind of row, the families really opposed it. And that soured them on churches, I guess, so no clergyman could've done much. I don't know; Al told me several times, when something got him to thinking about it—and to the day he died, as many things as Al always had on his mind, I doubt there was a day went by he didn't think about it. That's how I happened to have had that copy of the files I gave you— Jim's death absolutely *haunted* Al.

"If he started thinking about it in the middle of the night, he wouldn't be able to sleep, and he'd get up and get dressed and go up to the station and sit there at his desk there, going over that file again. I told him he had to stop. It was costing him his health, and I didn't want *him* dying on *me*. He told me: 'I can't help it. I keep thinking that there must be something in that file, something that I've overlooked, that everybody's overlooked, some tiny insignificant detail that'll explain this whole thing. Just unravel it. I can't get it out of my mind.'

"And that was when I said: 'Well then, you just take that file and put it through the Xerox machine, and don't tell me it's against regulations, because you're the chief and you're the man who makes the regulations. Make a new one: "When the chief can't get the rest he needs because he's up all night at the station thinking about a serious case, the chief can make a copy of the file and bring it home." And you put that copy together and you *bring* it home. And then when you get to tossing and turning over that case in the middle of the night so you can't sleep, get up and put your robe on, and get your copy out of the desk, and read it right here in the study. And then come back to bed, and at least try to get some sleep. You have to take care of your health. *I* won't peek at it, I promise you. I declare, I don't know how you can even stand to go over it and over it again so many times. I'm doing my best to forget it.' And he said: 'It isn't that I want to, or that I can stand it either. It's that I can't stand *not* to go over it again.'

"Anyway, Al said several times he guessed I must've been his clergyman that day, there to comfort Mimi after he told her. Maybe he was right. But I didn't do a very good job. Trying to comfort Mimi was like trying to comfort a statue. It was almost as though she refused to show grief. Felt it, but wouldn't show it. At least not to me. Old friend that I may have been. I wasn't worthy of that. Maybe grief was only for family. I don't know. And as far as Al was concerned, well, I didn't do much for him, either."

"Jill said her mother told her Mrs. Mandeville took it like Joe Louis," Corey said. "She said they were on their way here from Chicago to spend Christmas that year, and naturally they were in the air somewhere when Jill's grandmother got the news. So they didn't, it must've been eight, nine hours before they finally arrived here from Albany or Hartford, wherever they landed, and discovered what'd happened. And Jill, like I say, was still pretty young—she doesn't remember that much, except that something very sad'd happened, and Gampy was going to miss Christmas."

Amelia shook her head. "This is a small town," she said. "It's a lot bigger now than it was then, although the building'd already begun then. But it's still a small town, and it's not very often, almost never then, that when somebody dies who's lived here all his life, most of the people don't know him. Or her. And know all the family, too. And they *watch* you when someone close to you dies, just to see how you'll behave. When Al died, back in 'seventy-eight, two years shy of retirement,

37

people came around to the house here, bringing food and sympathy to me and Julie and the grandkids, or making like that was what they were doing, and I could see them watching us. Studying us. 'How're they taking it?' Al's the one who tipped me off to that, naturally enough, him being a policeman and all. 'Surveillance,' that was what he called it. 'They put you under surveillance. And you can't get away from it, nohow.' At the funeral home. At the church. The watching, watching eyes.

"So when Mimi chose not to have visiting hours—not that she could've had an open casket anyway, as Al said, after what'd happened—and made the burial private except for family and close friends, all the gossips felt like they'd been cheated. Of a circus or something, some big treat like that. So they said that she was glad, glad that Jim had died. Because Mimi spared her family, spared herself, when they were grieving.

"Mimi didn't collapse. She didn't fall in a heap on the floor, and she didn't beat her fists. Mimi stood there with her hands in her apron and her face all red and sweaty for Christmas, and just stared at us as though she had never seen us before in her life. And she hadn't, not like that.

"It seemed like a long time went by. Like Mimi was off someplace else for a while. Then she seemed to come back. I don't know where the maid'd gone. She disappeared. Mimi told us to come and sit in the big room. We went in there. Al and I sat on the big sofa in front of the fireplace—it was all laid for a fire that night, but it hadn't been lighted—and Mimi said: 'Something's happened to Jim.' And Al told her Jim'd been found dead at his office at the bank. Just like that. I don't know how many times after that he told me he'd made a mess of it, just saying it like that, and as many times as I told him it didn't make a bit of difference, because she already knew, for the rest of his life Al thought he made a mess of it.

" 'Do they know what caused it?' Mimi said. Al's been dead over twelve years now. I know what the certificate says caused

38

his death, and I also know that doesn't matter in the slightest, what it says. What matters is: he's dead. What Al never understood, and you, Joe, probably don't either, is that every woman with a man knows that someday someone that she doesn't know is going to clear his throat and tell her that she's had all the time she's ever going to with that man. Because he's dead. That's all those certificates say, no matter what else they say: 'He's dead.' Men die before women do. They do things that blow up in their faces and kill them, because they have to make a living and it's the only way they know. They do things that blow up in their faces and kill them because other men do those things, like driving fast, or hunting, or drinking with the boys, or being soldiers. And some of them don't know what they're doing, and some of them just plain aren't lucky. So they die. We all know that. You men don't. You never seem to learn. In Al's case it was worry. In Jim's case it was a gun. If your wife's mother tells you Mimi was very brave, well that's what explains it: she'd always expected it. Only question was when it came.

" 'He was shot,' Al said. That sort of stopped her. She didn't say anything for what seemed like a couple minutes. Her face wasn't red anymore. 'Shot?' she said. She put her hands up to her face. I got up and went over to where she was sitting and made a place for myself to sit down, and put my arm around her shoulder, which I probably should've done when we went in there, but I didn't. She was shaking. I was . . . the tears were just running down my face. Finally she said: 'Who would want to shoot Jim?' "

"What did he say?" Corey said.

Amelia shook her head. "Just what he said till the day that he died himself. 'I don't know.' Of course Jim had people that he knew who didn't like him. Jealousy, most of them. Or he'd had to say no to a loan. But, shoot him? No one would want to shoot Jim."

She shook her head again and got up from the table, grabbing her coffee mug and going around behind the counter and the overhanging cabinets where Corey could not see her face. She did not say anything for what seemed like a long time. She remained there when she spoke again. "I made one or two mistakes that day," she said. "I know that. With Mimi, mostly, though, but I wasn't married to her. I wasn't as good a friend to her as I should've been. So they were bad mistakes, but not important ones. But the ones I made with Al, started making with Al, on that awful Friday, *those* were bad mistakes. Al was my own *husband*. I should have helped him more. I should have found a way."

She made a fist of her small right hand and slammed it on the counter. Corey could see her body bend, and hear her breathe in deeply. Then she straightened up, inhaling deeply again. "*Ohhh,*" she said, "and still, after all these years've gone by." Corey did not say anything. After a while she raised her left hand out of his sight. Then she brought it down to the countertop again, took another audible breath, picked up the mug with her right hand and refilled it from the pot.

She emerged slowly around the counter and sat down at the table. "I thought I was doing the right thing," she said. "You *always* think you're doing the right thing, when you're in an awful situation and you have to do something right off, and so you do. Nobody ever does the wrong thing, on purpose. I thought I was doing the right thing, when I went with Al that day. I thought I was doing the right thing when I tried to comfort Mimi. And maybe I was right, those times, maybe I was right. But then, afterward, after Jim was buried, after that awful Christmas . . . they took the lights down the next day, the Christmas lights across Washington Street, the Saturday before Christmas. They flew the flags at the town hall and the fire station and of course the police station, but even the postmaster did it—they flew the flags at half-mast. Tappett took the decorations out of his windows, and as soon as he did that they came down in the hardware store and the Western Auto and every other store. Two days before Christmas came. If you'd driven through it on Sunday, the day Jim was having the party, you wouldn't've seen a single soul out on the sidewalk. It was like the whole town had gone into mourning. It had."

She paused. "Except for the inn. Jack and Winifred Davis said they had to keep their decorations up because people'd driven all the way up from New York and New Jersey to have a cosy little, quaint, Hallmark-card Christmas, here in good old New England. Sleigh bells ringing, roast goose in the old cellar tavern—all that kind of stuff. 'A real country Christmas this year.' So they owed it to their guests. They said. Well, maybe they did. Maybe if you're running an inn, the feelings of the people who come and stay in it and give you money should be more important than the feelings of the people who live in the same town. But there was a lot of bad feeling around town about that decision of theirs. It may've been the right one, as Al said, but it sure wasn't the popular one. Those guests didn't live here. Jim did. And so did dear Jack and dear Winifred. And Jack'd always before that gone out of his way to cultivate Jim, too. From the day that he arrived. Always telling people what a great guy Jim Mandeville was, and how much he admired him. Jim went for it, too. He may've been a banker, but he was a banker in a town where he'd lived all his life. He wasn't suspicious of people, like I guess most bankers are.

"Al couldn't understand it, the way that Jack behaved. 'Here they've gone to so much trouble to get themselves accepted in the town, not just passing through like their guests do, the minute something happens that just knocks the whole town flat on the floor, they act like they're just passing through.' "

"Where'd they come from?" Corey said.

"Oh, I don't know," she said. "I suppose, like you, from New York. Dawson Nichols owned the inn before them. He ran it into the ground. Al said Dawson liked to spend too much time in his own saloon. After a while Jim just couldn't let him have any more money to fix it up because Dawson always spent it on something else, seemed like. And the inn still needed paint, and the rooms were so ratty not even the most desperate Tanglewood people would ever stay there more than once. And Dawson kept missing payments. So Jim foreclosed on it, much as he hated to, and Jack Davis came up and bought it.

"He told people he and his wife were sick of the rat race, which is what the New Yorkers always say, so I don't know if they ever said where it was they came here to get away from. If they did, it wasn't to me. What mattered to Jim and the bank at the time, and the town, too, far as that goes, was that they could fix it up, run it right, get the trade coming back so they could pay the taxes.

"That inn is important to Shropshire. The tourist money, I mean. Back then the inn was the biggest single taxpayer we had, when it was running right. Not today, I guess, with those big time-sharing condos all filled up the way they are. But back then it was. And Jack did make his payments on time. He got the inn *all* spruced up. That was a nice change from Dawson, and I guess Jim was grateful, one worry off his back. He even set it up so that Jack went on his board, the directors at the bank. Took him fishing, I guess, too, in the summertime.

"And then when Jim died, Jack acted like that. 'Ho hum, no kidding, Jim's really dead? Well, I'm alive. Business as usual.' "

She reflected. "I suppose it didn't hurt them much in the long run," she said. "Ignoring Jim's death, I mean. Most of their trade comes from tourists. But for quite a long time no locals went there, for dinner or just for a drink. Taxes or no taxes, they'd drive down to Stockbridge, or over to Lenox, put themselves out to avoid it. So maybe it doesn't matter to them, and never cost them much money, but people remember things in small towns. And a lot remember that one, to this very day. I think Jack made a big mistake.

"But I did, too," she said. "When I saw how Jim's death was eating, just *eating* at Al, I tried to get his mind off it by telling him he had to forget it the same way I did, just put it out of his mind. Which I hadn't done either, of course, but it didn't bother me the way it bothered Al. Al said: 'Of course it doesn't. You're not the police chief. Not supposed to bother you until it's all cleared up. If it ever is. I'm the police chief. Something like that happens, it's supposed to bother me.' "

5

Except for the small conference room off the reception area of Investigations, Inc., Warren Oldham seemed to have the only private office in the small sixteenth-floor quarters in the Valley Bank Tower in Springfield, Massachusetts. His office had floor-to-ceiling glass walls on the three sides of its protrusion into the open space, where sixteen men and women worked at desktop computer stations. The two windows behind him looked out on the Connecticut River and Memorial Bridge, and the morning light that came through them dazzled Joseph Corey's eyes so that he had to angle his head and inch his chair to the right to see more than Oldham's silhouette.

That night at the Unicorn, Corey said to Jill: "Until you get that light out of your eyes, you think that you're Marlene Dietrich, *Witness for the Prosecution*, and any minute now Charles Laughton, with his back to the light, pops in the bloody monocle and blinds you with it good. And then, when you move your chair so you can see his face, you wonder if you should've, if that was a good idea. He looks like an old eagle, but with full use of his wings, and never had a bit of trouble with the talons. You thank the Good Lord Jesus you are not a nice fat fish, swimming upstream by his tree."

Oldham sat with his hands clasped at his waist. He had grey hair that swept back in a widow's peak from the center of his brow, and his facial skin was leathery, stretched taut over his cheek- and jawbones. His nose was prominent. He nodded when Corey said that he appreciated Oldham's time.

"You're the first one, then," he said. "I spent eight years in the Army, twenty-four in MSP, and that comes to thirty-two, and that's the first time I've heard that."

"Yeah," Corey said, "but you got paid for that time, plus vacation, health insurance, and the pension you're collecting while you get your salary here. I'm not paying you a dime. So I have to say thanks."

"Uh-*huh*," Oldham said. He leaned forward and rested his elbows on his desk. "Just what is it you want?"

"I want to find out who killed Jim Mandeville back in nineteen sixty-seven," Corey said. "And why."

"Is that a fact," Oldham said. "Well, I know the feeling. Had it myself, matter of fact, over twenty years ago. Your chances are not good. You've got the thing bassackward."

"I don't follow," Corey said.

"I know you don't," Oldham said. "That's what I just said. Amelia told me you're a lawyer. A fine young New York lawyer. Just what is it that you do, when you're lawyering down there?"

"Amelia Feldt?" Corey said.

"No," Oldham said, "Amelia Earhardt. She calls me every week. Collect from the Pacific. Asks me when she can come home. Is the damned war over yet. Regular pest, that woman is, worse'n old Judge Crater. He calls me, too. Wants to know: Should he come home? His calls I don't take."

"Amelia told me she wasn't sure whether you were still alive," Corey said.

"Son," Oldham said, "when you get to our age, we're not even sure ourselves. Every day's a brand new gift. One gratis, free, and for nothing. We've been to lots of funerals. After a while it's not just dirt that sinks in over graves. The understanding sinks in, too. 'You may be next, my friend.' "

"She told me to call the barracks in North Adams, and they'd know where you were."

"And you did that," Oldham said, "and they told you that they weren't sure if anybody there knew. Ancient history's what I am. And they said to call them back, and they would check around. And while you were doing that, Amelia called me here. And I said: 'Sure. Case's pissed me off for years.' Well, I didn't say that. Amelia wouldn't let Al swear, for God's sake, not when she could hear him. She believed that was vulgar. So I didn't use coarse language. But that was what I meant. 'This volunteer wants to come in, little late, maybe? I'll tell him what I know, which won't take very long, and then I'll tell him what I don't know. That could take a week.'

"You're new at this, son," Oldham said. "Amelia made you go look for me so she'd have time to warn me you were looking for me. And let me make my own decision, whether I should talk to you. And if I'd decided no, you know what would've happened? North Adams would've told you they had no idea where I went. Because I would've told them no. Now, I've got a question pending. What kind of law you do?"

"Mergers and acquisitions," Corey said. "Hostile takeovers mostly."

Both of Oldham's eyebrows ascended into the wrinkles that formed on his forehead. "Really," he said. "Are we talking junk bonds here?"

"*Defensive* mergers and acquisitions," Corey said. That night in the small room at the Unicorn, he said: "Thought he was going to pounce."

"I work for Birnam, Barkley, Morris. We represent old-line corporations, mostly. Some have new owners, of course. But old-line. Outfits that reluctantly decided to diversify, hedge against the markets, ten, fifteen years ago. And got themselves into a lot of stuff they didn't understand. Their core businesses are stable, making regular profits. But their subsidiary operations bounce around like basketballs, and eat up the dividends. That puts the price-to-earnings ratios completely out of whack, and then some sharking arbitrageur circles for the kill. What we do is fight off raiders. Nothing more than that."

"In other words," Oldham said, "you protect the indigenous crooks against the new swindlers, and get paid handsomely for doing it."

"We get paid handsomely, yeah," Corey said, "but we work too damned many hours every week of our lives earning those gaudy checks, and I think you've been out here with the happy squirrels in the peaceful woods too long. I don't know how much you know about markets, not in stocks but selling goods, but the way you talk, I'd say not much. You have to predict things, way ahead, and that isn't easy. And if you're right, then you get rich. And if you're not you go bankrupt."

Oldham snickered. "Right," he said. "And that explains why Coca-Cola took the old brand off the market and put the new brand on."

"Stupid decision," Corey said. "In retrospect, I fully agree. They should have talked to us."

Oldham did not say anything. "And I didn't say anything, either," Corey said to Jill. "We just sat there like a couple of cigar-store Indians, and it seemed like an hour went by. I think the sun passed through two meridians, or whatever the hell those lines on the globes are, and the people outside the glass cubicle came and went, talking of Michelangelo, and I looked at him, and he looked at me, and then he cleared his throat and backed his chair up, like he was backing up a tank, and got out of it and turned around, and grabbed the rods that shut the Levolors, and closed the blinds, and turned around, and said: 'It's time for lunch. No one but a fool in Springfield ever goes to lunch except at Mario's.'"

After his salad, Warren Oldham finished a platter of roast pork with brown gravy and hash-browned potatoes before Joe Corey had proceeded a third of the way through his plate of schnitzel. Oldham began on his second glass of the house red; Corey's first remained half full. Oldham belched quietly. "There are things you don't understand," Oldham said.

47

"Many," Corey said.

Oldham belched silently. "Well," he said, "a man has to eat." He put his right hand to his breastbone and straightened up. "Ahh," he said.

"Yeah," Corey said, "but he doesn't have to eat like the Great White Shark does. The stuff on the plate isn't going to get away. It's already dead, for God's sake. It's been cooked."

"Ahh," Oldham said, "but not *hot*. Cold dead stuff's no fun at all. I've seen lots of cold dead stuff. I know. And you don't."

"You've got me there," Corey said. "I've seen no cold dead stuff at all."

Oldham nodded. He picked up his glass. He held it in both of his hands. He stared at Corey over it. "When four men—this is your ideal gang—go in to rob a damned bank, three go in the bank. One stays in the car. They rob it and they run away with the money.

"In such an operation you start with one element: you know the motive right off. Four men wanted money. The bank had the money. Three of the four men went in and took it. The other one drove them away." He drank.

"Your job, to catch them, is find out who those four men are. Sometimes you cannot do this. They don't call you up before they hit the bank and say: 'Watch the Hampden Trust Branch in Indian Orchard today. We've been feeling a little bit short.' But you know what they wanted; you know what they got; and you know what they're liable to do with it. So you put out your feelers, and set your small traps, and sooner or later, most times, you catch them. Not always, but usually. Because people that you know must've had motive will sooner or later betray it. All you don't know is who they might be.

"The only times that you don't catch bankrobbers is when they're too smart for you. And that doesn't happen too often. Bankrobbers tend to be get-around guys. Play the horses. Wear good suits. Chase the girls in big cars. Hardware clerks do not rob banks. Not more'n once, and you catch them. It's ridiculously easy. Real bankrobbers, the ones that you don't ever catch, unless you get very lucky, need lots of cash for that action. But they get it and then wait to spend it. They always live the same way. They plan ahead. They rob the next bank before they run out of the money they got from the last one. They never give it away.

"The amateurs give it away. First they blow the cash, and therefore how they got it. There's very few bankrobbers, numerically speaking, that have the good sense to lie low. Lie low and let it cool off. You don't buckle a swash in your everyday life, and you make a big score, you will buckle a swash when you shouldn't. It takes a certain kind of a man to become a successful career bankrobber. Most bankrobbers are not of that kind. In most cases, if you're the kind of man that's willing to go in a bank and take the money out, your temperament is not the kind that lets you sit on it. Put it under your mattress, and wait till two thousand and one. You didn't rob the bank so you could start a Christmas Club. You robbed the bank 'cause you were broke, and you don't like being broke. We're prisoners, all of us, of our characters. No better, no worse, than we can be.

"Jim Mandeville's bank was not robbed. The dog did not bark, you remember your Holmes, 'Silver Blaze,' but the man was killed at the bank."

"Then you think it was murder," Corey said.

"Well," Oldham said, "I think Christopher Columbus discovered Santo Domingo, and thought it was something else, and I think that Ted Williams was a good hitter, and Jesse James may've robbed banks. But yes, I'll agree, I do think that someone rubbed out Jim Mandeville. I doubt very much that a man like Jim Mandeville did the following things:

"One: for no reason at all, that anyone knows, he leaped out of bed in the dark, threw his clothes on and rushed to the bank. Okay, a phone call is possible. A phone call is more than possible. It's the only explanation why a man who would get out of bed at that hour to go and torment a trout would get out of bed at that hour when even the trout were sleeping, and if they weren't, they were out of season. And they weren't jumping at Jim Mandeville's bank. This means he did have a reason, and it wasn't trout. When you have eliminated every possibility except one, then that possibility is the explanation for the event.

"The problem in this case is that you don't know who made that phone call. I didn't find out, when I worked the case, and you're not likely to either.

"The person who made the phone call knew the reason. If the person who made the call is alive, he is an accessory before the fact of murder, liable to be charged as a principal. That's life, as Frank Sinatra says. If he's not alive, he's not liable to say much, to you or anyone else. Therefore it's unlikely that any person is about to swagger up and say to you, or anybody else: 'I called Jim Mandeville down to the bank to set him up, the morning he got shot.'

"Two. Go back to the bankrobbers. Robbers rob banks to get money. If Jim Mandeville had bad habits, and he did—he killed small animals and birds, and he was more than a bit of a blowhard, and when it came to banking, well . . . I'll get to that—they were the same kind of bad habits I've got, and you've got, or will have, when you get a little bit older."

"He asked me how old I am," Corey said to Jill at the Unicorn that night. "I said: 'Twenty-nine.' He scowled at me. 'I was twenty-nine once, too. Recall it. Not too clearly, but I know I must've been. Nothing memorable about it. That's why I don't recall it.' "

"He sounds like a perfectly awful man," Jill said.

"Oh, he is," Joe said. "I've met snakes kinder'n he is. He was a combat soldier when he was a kid, and I don't think anyone ever convinced him the combat was over and we're at peace. He isn't. He never will be."

"Jim Mandeville's bad habits did not get him killed," Oldham said. "What got him killed was his money. Well, not his money, exactly. What he owned that somebody wanted. And he wouldn't give it to them, so they killed him. That was what got Jim Mandeville killed.

"What he owned was that land. His own land, with that house, and the other land. The land that he bought from the priests. The man who killed him didn't want that land; he wanted the money for making the hit. He made it, and he got the money. The man who called him did not kill him, either. He was in it for straight salary. But the man who killed him, and the man who called him, were hired by the man who wanted that land, who was nowhere near that bank that day. He was snug in his bed miles away. And he was one damned smart robber, I'll tell you. That's why nobody's caught him."

"Obvious question," Corey said. "Who was he? The man who wanted the land."

"I never found out, equally obvious. If I had I would've grabbed him. But I retired in 'seventy-six, and between the morning when Mandeville died and I picked up my first pension check, I had some other things on my mind. If I hadn't've, maybe I would've. The closest I ever got was Gilbert Rogers, the lawyer who worked for the bank. And everyone else who needed a lawyer and had a house somewhere in Shropshire. I think he made the call."

"You do," Corey said. "What makes you say that?"

The waitress came by and Oldham ordered coffee. Corey said: "I'd like some coffee myself."

Oldham sighed. "Same rule," he said. "The elimination of other possibilities. All the ones I know about, at least. Whoever called Mandeville, and got him up, and caused him to go to the bank, was someone he knew, and he trusted. Trusted to know his bank's business, and his. If you'd've called him, he wouldn't've gone. He wouldn't've gone if I'd called him. Therefore the person who got him out of bed was almost certainly Gil Rogers. He was Jim Mandeville's personal lawyer, along with being the bank's. He knew what Jim owned, by inheritance, and he knew what Jim Mandeville'd bought, and where he borrowed the money to buy it. He did the titles on

51

the Claretian property, which was given to them years ago. By some Gay Nineties looter, or his descendant, who'd used up the family cash, so his heirs couldn't pay estate taxes. And then the good fathers ran out of recruits, and they coudn't keep it up, either. It wasn't worth much in the late fifties, and Jim Mandeville snapped it up fast. A hundred and ten acres of prime real estate, abutting Overlook Hills Farm. He borrowed half of the money—five hundred thousand American dollars, no small sum, to be sure, but a mill for the land was a bargain.

"But I interviewed Rogers, and he said he didn't make the call. He said he was shocked that I asked. He said he was home fast asleep, and when he heard he was all broken up. Of course he would say that, if he made the call, and knew what would be the result, but that didn't change the fact that he said it, and I couldn't prove he was lying. Rogers lived in Shropshire, too. No toll records on local calls.

"The fact that he brokered and titled the transfer of Mandeville's land later on—none of that meant the slightest damned thing, when it came to disproving what he said. Of course Mimi Mandeville hired him to do it. He was the family lawyer. She wanted no more to do with the house, and as for the land, the same thing."

"The file says Chief Feldt interviewed Mrs. Mandeville six times," Corey said. "She certainly didn't seem to have any interest in keeping the place after he died."

"Yeah," Oldham said. The waitress served the coffee. When she went away, he said: "Don't misunderstand me, now. I'm not knocking the dead. Al Feldt and his wife were damned good to me. They welcomed me into their home." He sat back in the booth. "Because I liked both of them so damned much, and because I like company, I probably made a mistake in that case. I let Al take complete charge of Mimi."

Corey did not say anything. "They were old friends," Oldham said, almost apologetically, "and she had to be all broken up. The first rule in murder is: grill the spouse good, but she obviously didn't pull the trigger. So I guess I used that as an excuse to break the rules.

"See, there was a possibility there, that at the very least she had information that she didn't know she had, and Al didn't know how to get, and at the very most that she connived in the murder. Likely or unlikely doesn't matter. I failed to eliminate any of those possibilities, and therefore I didn't do my job right.

"See, the first point is that maybe she might've known who did it, without knowing she knew. That happens a lot. People don't pay attention. Important details slip right by them. And Al, a real nice guy, wouldn't get at them. He was limited, know what I mean? He wouldn't've known what question to ask, the one that would lead you to the ultimate answer of who put the damned contract out. The perfect police chief for a small town. A natural leader of men. Set an example, call your own number, when the going gets heavy and so forth.

"This's great when the problem you have is a car crash. Wonderful when there's a flood. Spectacular when someone's dog runs away, or the neighbors have too many loud parties." He exhaled. "They don't have too many contract killings in small towns like Shropshire, you know."

He leaned forward and stabbed the wooden table with his right index finger. The skin on his forehead creased. "But as a result, when someone gets killed on a contract basis, that kind of man's not much good." He poured cream into his coffee and pulled the saucer toward him. He leaned back in the bench and stirred it. He shook his head. "He just didn't know what questions to ask. He didn't know when to press. And if he'd known, he wouldn't've pressed. She was an old friend of his. So he and Amelia thought, anyway."

"You don't think they were friends, the Feldts and the Mandevilles? Is that what you're telling me now?" Corey said.

Oldham shrugged. He stirred his coffee again. "The Feldts thought they were friends, so maybe they were. I'm not sure the Mandevilles did." He stopped stirring and stared at Corey.

"Jim Mandeville was not a stupid man, and his wife was smarter than he was. They were very astute in their cultivations, their cultivations of townsfolk. They spread the manure on crops that they wanted. They didn't spread it on the weeds. Even Al Feldt, that good, simple man, called him 'the Duke.' So even Al Feldt had an inkling of things, a glimmer of what Mandeville really was doing. Jim Mandeville patronized people in Shropshire. He did it because it helped business, and what helped town business enriched him. The reason he liked Jack Davis so much was that Jack met his note on the inn. The reason that Jim put old Jack on his board was because he thought he controlled him. His reasoning was that Jack owed him money, and therefore would do what he said. If Jack gave him trouble, making a loan, or thwarted him in any way, well, Jack knew that Jim could call his demand notes, and pitch him right out in the street."

He shook his head. "No," he said, "don't kid yourself. At least don't kid yourself the way Al and Amelia kidded *them*-selves. Jim Mandeville was a very calculating individual. The people in the town, their high regard for him: those were factors that were important to him. But *not* determinative. If an opportunity came along that would be enhanced by their approval, he wanted to be sure he would get it. As was exactly the case when the Claretian Fathers decided to unload their property on the lake, and he bought it and then had the zoning changed. If he'd lived, his plan was to develop that land, just about as it's developed now. It was a very good plan. So good that someone who knew about it decided to get rid of him and take it over.

"That was how Jim's annual Christmas parties really paid off—zoning changes and that stuff. I don't know how much twenty or thirty years of whiskey and turkeys and hams, four salads, plum pudding, and eggnog cost Jim Mandeville out of pocket, but whatever it was, when that Claretian land was rezoned for development, by damned-near standing ovation, he made it all back, and then some.

"Now," he said, "I'm being candid with you here, as I would not've twenty years ago, when I still worked for a living. I did not do a good job on that case. I had a lot of territory to cover, and when I ran into some local cop who wanted to do some of my work for me, well, I was glad to let him do it. But I still should've interviewed Mimi myself. That woman was awful cold. I explained her behavior back then to myself by saying: 'She's an aristocrat. The only reason she played Lady Bountiful was because it was good for Jim's business. And once he was dead, well, that ended that, no more reason to grease up the peasants. And she kept her grief to herself.'

"But what if she didn't have any grief? What if that sterling self-control she showed was the grim satisfaction of success? What if Jim Mandeville bored the ass off her? What if she didn't like her life? Which it certainly appears that she didn't, by the way—soon's he went in that ground, she was off it. The pair of them had a whole set of friends that never set foot into Shropshire. They met them at tracks, on winter vacations, and some of those people could do things. They had access to professional talent. So, who were those people? Did Mimi hire one? Or maybe, did Mimi hire three? To set up her country-squire husband and send him off to meet Jesus? And did she then recline and wait until I got off the case, so all she would have to worry about was Al and his deep trust of her, before she sold off the whole parcel? Could've been, my son, could well've been. Can't prove the contrary by me.

"But still, probably not," Oldham said. "Al sure didn't think so, that Mimi knocked off her husband. The thought never entered his mind. But it did enter mine, and I should've explored it, and not let him monopolize her the way I did." He sighed. "It was easier—that's why I did it." He paused. "I realize," he said, "I'm being a trifle, well, hard on your grandmother-in-law."

Corey shrugged. "She's dead," he said. "I never met her, and my wife scarcely knew her. But that death still bothers her. My wife, I mean. And I started looking into it because I was going daffy doing what I was doing, and she wanted to move here, and the more I looked, the more it stunk. Even to an amateur like me, there are just too many loose ends to the story of how that property changed hands. There's no question in my mind, even at this point, that Jim Mandeville was murdered, and it seems pretty clear why. All I'm looking to find out is maybe who did it. And what prompted him to do it."

" 'Who' I don't know," Oldham said. " 'Why' I do know. What got him killed was a sweet little deal. He'd packaged a deal for himself so sweet that somebody had him killed for it."

6

In what he described as "a previous life, with a previous wife," the proprietor of the Unicorn at Goshen had been an accountant. The "spacious and comfortable library" he boasted about in his three-color leaflet was the parlor in which he had stocked the shelves with *Reader's Digest Condensed Books* and the textbooks dating back over forty years to his student days in business school; his copies of the *Internal Revenue Code and Regulations*; and his collection of books interpreting and explaining those provisions. "But it could've been worse," Jill Corey had said after browsing through it: "Just suppose what he'd offer if he'd been a mortician."

"Well," Joe Corey said, "as a matter of fact, I'd prefer that. Couple good treatises on embalming, rigor mortis, lividity, stuff like that, they'd be a hell of a lot more useful to me right now'n *Opinions of the Commissioner* and *The Hundred Best Decisions by the Court of Claims*, or whatever the other stuff is. 'Hey, kids, it's a cold, rainy day out. Let's curl up by the fire with some tax court opinions, a nice cup of weak tea, some stale cookies.' "

"No self-pity, please," Jill said. "No morbid brooding here now. I didn't tell you to dig into Gampy's death."

"Not much," he said.

"Look," she said, "if you want to drop this whole business and go back to being an adult, it's okay with me; I'm quite satisfied, having a husband who agrees we should have a life, too, and is willing to follow me to it."

"Does that mean you're going to be in the mood after dinner?" he said.

"Probably," she said. "But what's wrong with late-afternooners? You all tired out from your drive?"

"I don't see how the first one rules out the second," he said. "Or why it should, anyway."

So he was hostile," she said to the mirror in front of the vanity table, while she repaired her makeup afterward.

He sprawled on the bed built for people much shorter, who'd come to the inn when it was new in the mid-nineteenth century. "He wasn't quite as accessible as you are, if that's what you mean," he said.

"Did he seem like he resented your interest?" she said.

"Yeah, he did," he said. "Lieutenant Oldham's of the old school. He can't shake the habits he made. When he was called to a homicide scene, he was the person in charge. When he took command, his word was the law, and everyone stayed out of his way. He didn't relinquish command of those cases when he retired from police work. He had it then? He's still got it now. Everyone's a trespasser, see? And he wants no damned volunteers butting into things, messing up prints and his day. As far as Warren Oldham's concerned, the cordon he put up around that bank that day twenty-three years ago, that's still in place, and you'd better not cross it without his permission. Which you will have some trouble getting. I wouldn't go so far as to say Warren Oldham doesn't trust anyone, but he sure doesn't make new friends fast. The first thing he does is size you up good, and there's no hurrying that. I think that if maybe I show staying power, stamina, fortitude, grit, in six months or a year he might accept me. But right now I'm just an out-of-town shyster, bored with his job, and a meddler."

"Maybe," she said, brushing her hair, "maybe he thinks he missed something. Something that you might find out, and embarrass him twenty years later."

"Oh, there's no question about that," he said. "But he's ambivalent on that matter. He knows he missed something. No doubt in his mind. He's convinced your grandfather was murdered. And that, as he says, he knows that 'some bastard blew smoke and I bought it, just like a fool. Because I couldn't prove he was blowing smoke, and he knew I couldn't. He beat me.' He thinks that bastard was Rogers." He sighed. "Maybe I should've been an accountant myself. I would've done better with him than I did, as a younger version of Rogers."

He sat up on the bed. "I want a cigarette," he said.

She pushed her chair back from the vanity table and surveyed herself in the mirror. "Well, you can't have one, and you know that. You've gone eight months now, unless you've been cheating, and you haven't coughed once, or snored. You smell better, sleep better, don't burn holes in your clothes, and fidgeting won't hurt your health."

"I still want one," he said. "It's not the same when you can't have a cigarette afterward."

She stood sideways to the mirror. "Do you think I should have breast augmentation?" she said. "I'm pretty tall for the size of these things. They're not in the proper proportion. The rest of me's all right, except for the thighs." She pinched the flesh of her left thigh. "I should do my leg bends more often."

"No, I do not think you should spend four grand we don't have to buy fiberglass boobs for yourself," he said. "The deal agreed to was we buy a house, a genuine house of our own, and we need that cash for down payment. Plus something left over for my dog, and it's possible we may need two cars. Nor do I think you should have liposuction, or start to live only on celery. We're both in the same fix, and we both know it. We spend most of our days on our butts. That's what we do to make money. Either we do that, so we can eat, or else we do not, and we don't. Which I suppose will in due course slim your thighs, if we can't buy any food, but then if that happens your tits will go first, and how will you feel about that, huh?

59

You want to exercise your legs, put your ankles behind your ears more. It'll take your mind off your troubles."

She turned from the mirror and gazed at him. "The level of this conversation is well beneath my standards," she said. "I'm going to take a shower."

He swung his feet off the bed and stood up. "I'll join you," he said. "I could use a quick rinse myself."

He told me he'd call the District Attorney here, give him my name and so forth," Corey said over onion soup at the Turning Brook Inn. "I can't say he warmed up, but he did start to thaw, after we'd eaten our lunch. 'But he won't know much,' this is what Oldham said, 'he's another young fellow like you are. He grew up around here,' this was Springfield he meant, 'before he went off to law school. And then later he was a federal prosecutor, not a bad one from what I've been told. Actually put guys in jail without weeping salt tears when he did it. Man after my own hardened heart.

" 'The thing of it is, he does not know the case, even if he did get the papers. His office, the Berkshire one, didn't exist when Jim Mandeville got himself killed. That jurisdiction was part of this one. The Hampden D.A. had 'em both. That dated back to the days when John Adams tried cases. Not so many people around then. Man on a horse could cover the territory, visit it three times a year. Talk to the sheriffs and the constables, pretty much handle what went on. Now there're more people, and the roads are better. So now it's a separate district. But that split was made well after it should've been, and long after Mandeville's murder.'

"I put it right to him," he said. "I said: 'So was the case tanked?'

"He played dumb with me. I said: 'Nonchalanted. Did it get swept under the rug? And if that was what happened, why did it happen? Why didn't anyone care?'

" 'Look,' he said finally, 'understand this. It wasn't a real

60

easy case. The medical guy was a damned fool, of course, and a real lazy bastard to boot. But even a bright one would've been stumped. He wouldn't've said it was suicide—he would've left it at "gunshot." But to prove it was murder he would've needed some evidence, and that stuff was in short supply.

" 'That Browning was covered with blood,' he told me. 'All I could think of was Shakespeare. Who would've thought the old man to have had so much blood in him? Now, for the life of me, I can't imagine how a man who blew the back of his own head off could somehow manage to've bled all over his hands and forearms, and bled on his weapon as well. I couldn't that day, and I still can't today. Someone else dipped him in it that morning.

" 'The reason that someone performed that small service was to cover his own fingerprints. If he left any—the guy who did that job was careful. But knowing that didn't help me. Blood's slippery stuff, and when it congeals on a surface, as this did, it's pretty hard to remove without also dissolving fingerprints under it. If the killer forgot his cheap gloves.

" 'Result is I sit here, all these years later, and tell you I know what happened. Someone Mandeville trusted, or at least respected, called him that morning at home. The reason I know there was trust or respect there is that whoever called him knew that office. He knew that Mandeville had a gun there. So he'd been in there, and seen it.

" 'Very few people got into that office. Only the ones that he trusted. Business he did in the conference rooms, or at one of the desks on the floor. Jim Mandeville was not an approachable man. He pretended he was, but he wasn't. To get into his office, you had to know him, and had to've for a long time. And since every so often he took his guns home, to clean them or rack them, whatever, the man who called him'd been in there within a few days before the killing happened. He knew that shotgun was still there.

" 'He also knew what gauge it was. I say that because Jim

Mandeville was a very careful gun owner. Al Feldt would've given him a license, no questions asked, for machine guns or anything else, because Al Feldt was Jim Mandeville's slave. But in fact his friend was responsible. No guns stored loaded by him. When he had it in mind to go shooting clay pigeons, or brought his dogs in with him at lunchtime because woodcock had come into season, he had his shells in his car or his jacket. That Browning was not to repel boarders. Therefore the man who used it on him had his own shells on him when he came, and he knew it was not sixteen-gauge that he needed, or twenty-, or four-ten, either.

" 'I'm not saying the man who pulled that trigger was the man who called him at home. I'm not saying that because I don't think it was. I think the man who made the call knew what was going to happen as a result of it, and I think he was in cahoots with another man who wanted the hit made, but I don't think the guy with the telephone ever had coffee, before or after, with the guy who pulled the trigger. I think your learned brother Gates got it exactly right. I think the triggerman was out-of-town talent, experienced, careful, and quick. Most likely he never met the man who paid him his fee. He got a call, two or three days before, and he met a man in a bar. The man in the bar gave him an envelope. That envelope was full of cash. He put it in his pocket and got his directions, and finished his drink and went out. He went where he was told, and did what he agreed to, and then he went back where he came from.

" 'Now I'm guessing, but I had a lot of cases in my time, and my guesses were usually damned good. The out-of-town man got a second phone call from our friend Mandeville trusted. Our friend told the man all systems were go, and the target'd left for the bank. The out-of-town talent put on his clothes and tucked a gun into his pants. He went to the bank and saw Mandeville's car there. He got out of his car and went to the back door. He opened it. He went inside. He went up the stairs—he'd been tutored on this, or he'd been there—and directly to Mandeville's office. By the time he was halfway down the hall to it, he had his gun out in his hand.

" 'He went into the office and caught Mandeville flat-footed. This was not the person who'd called him to get up and come to the bank pronto. This man was someone else, and he had a gun, and what the hell could be going on now? It's a wonder he didn't have a heart attack and save everybody the trouble.

" 'The talent kept his gun on Mandeville and grabbed the Browning out of the closet. He loaded it with one shell, number-six shot, which no one who owns those things does. They fill up the magazine: five. He pointed the Browning at Mandeville and told him to go into the bathroom. They got into the bathroom and that's when he did it. He stuck the muzzle under Mandeville's chin. Mandeville put his hands up around his chest, probably pleading for his life—which is not much defense against a shotgun and an out-of-town hitman at the other end of it. The talent pulled the trigger, and that was curtains for Jimmy. After Mandeville's brains hit the walls behind him, and the rest of him landed down on the tile, the talent took his forearms and dipped them in the spouting blood. Then he put the shotgun between the hands and smeared them all over it, and that was how we found Mandeville.

" 'The talent went out the same way he came in. No real trouble. Nobody lives near the bank. No one'd heard him or seen him. He got into his car and backed up in the lot, and went out to the street, headed north.'

" 'Why north?' I said to Oldham.

" 'You've got two choices when you come out that bank lot,' he said. 'If you go south, you go through town, to no place in particular, and you run the risk of being seen. If you're seen at that time of the day, at that time of year, in a town of that size, you're remembered. If you go north, well, you still might be seen, but the chances are not as good. And if you go north you'll hit the Turnpike, and then you can go anywhere. To

Albany, west, or Springfield or Hartford, get some sleep, turn the car in, and fly.

" 'There was never a way to locate the killer until we found out who hired him. To do that we needed to know what the motive was. But he was smart and lay low. He thought if he waited, the widow would hide it, and he was right. She did that. Once her husband'd been cremated and scattered on the cold, cold ground, the only thing Mimi Mandeville could think about was getting her tail out of Shropshire. Which meant after she'd been away for a while, and found out her suspicions'd been right, that life without Jim was easier elsewhere and she didn't miss Shropshire a bit, she said to her lawyer, our friend Gilbert Rogers: "Sell everything, Gil." And he did.'

" 'What she didn't know, and we didn't catch, was that some of it'd already been sold. And that was why, I'm sorry to say, we didn't catch it, either.'

"Your grandfather was rich," Corey said to Jill, as the waitress removed the remains of their steak Diane, "but he was rich by small-town standards. He had more money than anybody else around did, but he didn't have as much money as he wanted. When the Claretian Fathers reached the conclusion that they had to get rid of that hundred-and-ten-acre plot of prime lakefront land, and the house and all that went with it, he knew what that place would be worth in ten years, or twenty—it didn't matter to him. He was in good shape, he was fifty-five then, and he planned to be ninety when he died, at least. He had time to accumulate more.

"What he didn't have was money enough to finance the thing by himself. So he set up a trust, a partnership trust, and Gil Rogers drew up the papers. He and Gil Rogers were the trustees. Jim and Mimi were the beneficiaries. If both of them died before the land sold, well, their wills would take care of your mother and your aunt. In the meantime he wouldn't have somebody moving in next door, opening up a new piggery. So that meant that Overlook Hills became more valuable. It would stay safe and serene.

"Your grandfather was also a smart man," Corey said. "He knew that the Claretian property was well worth the investment, but if he floated it all by himself he'd be strapped, so that meant he needed a loan. He was utterly honest. He would not take chances on putting his own bank in trouble. So he hedged his bet by borrowing privately, signing a ten-year-term, fifty-percent mortgage on it. Until those ten years elapsed, all he had to do was pay taxes. After ten years, that paper became a demand note, and he had to pay it all at once. How he did that would be his own business.

"If he couldn't or wouldn't refinance—in other words, if he didn't think that land by then was worth fifty percent of what he'd paid for in nineteen sixty, he'd lose it, plus his fifty percent of the price. That was the gamble he took.

"The gamble the investors took was that the value of the land wouldn't appreciate enough by nineteen seventy to make it good business for him to hold onto it. Or that he wouldn't have some other business reverses that would prevent him from doing that—pretty unlikely in his case, but a possibility still. Or that he'd die early, and there wouldn't be enough liquidity in his estate to make his heirs decide to pay off the loan. Kind of a cold-blooded gamble on both sides, but that's how big money is made.

"Well, with Johnson inflating the currency like a giant beach ball to run the Vietnam War and all his other programs without raising taxes to pay for them; and the edge of the World War Two baby boom just getting into the markets; and with the regional economy improving faster than it ever had before; sometime in 'sixty-seven those investors—whoever they were; nobody ever found that out—didn't need a palm reader to guess who'd get rich when that mortgage became due. It was going to be Jim Mandeville. Still hale, still hearty, and richer by far than he'd been when he'd borrowed the money. They would've gotten straight interest on their cash, but he'd make big bucks for himself. What'd looked liked a straightforward business deal, less than eight years before that, had be-

65

gun to look to those big-city boys as though the local rube'd snookered them good. They weren't going to sit around and let that happen. They'd guessed wrong but intended to win.

"You look back on it now and see that he signed his own death warrant when he gave that mortgage in 'sixty."

"And no one ever went to the trouble of finding out who they were?" Jill said, sipping her coffee. "That's simply incredible."

"There Oldham was no help at all," he said, "and if I ever wondered what the word 'chagrin' means, a look at Oldham's face when he admitted it would have spared me a trip to the dictionary.

" 'We traced it as far as a Delaware corporation,' he said, 'the consortium that bought the mortgage. We got documentation from Wilmington on it, and it told us nothing, of course. Just an investment pool, all of them bankers, scattered all over the place. Which meant that behind them was somebody else who funneled his money through them. Keep in mind now: when that property changed hands, over two years'd gone by since Jim Mandeville went to the bathroom and got his brains blown all over it. By then it was the front part of 'seventy, and more things've happened, and I was working on them first. Al Feldt and Paul Barry, down there in Shropshire, never gave up on that case, but Al was a nice man, and that's about all, and Paul was chained to that town. He wasn't your globe-trotting cop. When I got the Delaware papers, I bumped them along to Al Feldt. But I didn't have time to run them down myself, and those two did not have the range. Or the imagination.

" 'So the bottom line is, as we say today, that one person ordered that hit. But who it was, I still don't know. Why don't you figure it out?' "

"What're you going to do?" she said.

He drew a deep breath. "Well," he said, "I'm going to the Berkshire D.A.'s office tomorrow, I made an appointment, using Oldham's phone and his name, and I'm going to ask him if it's okay if I tackle this thing on my own. Oldham says he's a good guy and won't mind a bit if I roam around in his jurisdiction, provided I make sure he gets all the credit when I corner the bad guy and nail him."

"And you believe that, of course," she said.

He grinned. "I believe what Warren Oldham says: 'That D.A.'s not stupid. It's in his best interest to give you your head, and it's in your best interest, too. He's short of staff with the state budget problems. A volunteer's just what he needs. You round up the suspect and bring him in, he will put you on his staff. You won't get much money—compared to New York, you'll get nothin'—but you'll get headlines, and those don't hurt young lawyers at all.' "

7

Burton Magoun was forty-one, burly, with receding sandy red hair and a big nose. He had six assistants, four fewer than he would have had but for budget problems.

When Joe Corey entered his office in Pittsfield, Magoun remained seated behind his desk and said: "Skip the preliminaries. We're not old friends about to meet for the first time. I agreed to let you in because Oldham called me up and told me you might make us both look good. I've got five overworked assistants—out of six; one isn't worth a damn—with too much on their minds. I have to run for reelection two years from now. If Attila the Hun came in to volunteer to do me some good, I'd talk to him. That's the only reason. So, what've you got and why do I want it?"

Corey told him what he had learned. "Yeah," Magoun said, "well, that's not enough. Oldham thinks every case he didn't solve's the Lindbergh kidnapping. He's wrong. People forget in due course. The Mandeville thing was a long time ago. I went over the file after Oldham called me, and I agree with him, and, I gather, you: Murder One. But it was a *good* Murder One. Whoever did it knew what he was doing. What they were doing. When there's a lot of money involved, people with problems to solve seek professional help, and if they get good help, they solve them. Permanently."

" 'Permanently' may not be the right word," Corey said. "I think that may be why there's no limitations on murder. It will, as the saying goes, out. Oldham told me that he thinks the motive was to get the Claretian land. Katherine McCormack tossed me an aside about all the condo and time-share units that've gone up since Mandeville got it.

"I checked the records in the tax assessor's office. Old Katherine in fact is dead right. Nearly fifty percent of the town's annual revenue comes out of those new developments. Most of the people who own them—not all, by any means, but most— or own shares in them, don't live in them all the year 'round. They're out-of-towners, skiiers, music lovers, leaf peepers, and general riffraff. Those are their second homes. People with second homes in Shropshire don't go to town meetings and bitch. They get their tax bills at their primary homes, bitch a lot to their roommates, and pay up. I believe the term for their species is 'sitting ducks.' And the shorefront stuff at Claretian Estates accounts for half of that revenue. The people who live in the rest home that used to be Overlook Hills can't even get the hang of pudding anymore.

"I'm not the only one who knows this. Those lakefront properties are cash cows for the town. The town's counsel, succeeding the late Gilbert Rogers, is Robert Gates. Our learned brother Gates also represents the trusts that own and developed the land.

"The person behind those Delaware corporations that invested in the trusts is the person who hired the shooter. It's possible that person is dead, which means he or she can't be indicted and brought to justice, which in turn means it will do you no good at all to put on a big show if you ever do manage to solve the case. So you can't take the outside chance of solving it, because you haven't got enough money or manpower to put on a full-court press, and that's what this thing will take.

"At first for family reasons, later for personal reasons, this thing engaged my interest. I've spent the last five years and more as a drone in the hive, and I'm sick of it. Fed up to my eyeballs. I went to law school to be a real lawyer, not a businessman with a degree that didn't come from business school."

"The money'll trap you pretty soon," Magoun said.

"Exactly," Corey said. "My wife'll be trapped at this end of the world, doing something she loves."

"Your wife," Magoun said. "Just what does she do she's so eager to do it up here?"

"She's a college teacher, American history," Corey said. "For the past five years at NYU, and she's very good at it, too. Ph.D. from Columbia, bachelor's from Brown before that. Her father's a lawyer in Chicago. She liked the idea of teaching real well, but she'd thought about being a lawyer. So the summer between her second and third years in grad school she decided to make sure, had Daddy yank on a rope, and got herself a paralegal job at Birnam. I was between my second and third years at Yale, clerking at Birnam that summer. Well, she didn't like law, but she liked me."

"You're a New Yorker, then," Magoun said. "What makes you want to want to leave now?"

"I'm a New Yorker to the same extent that any kid who grows up in Saint Paul and comes east to Princeton for college, and then goes to Yale with being a lawyer in mind, thinks that he wants to be one. After six years in those two places, taking the train into New York on weekends, your priorities get all out of whack. You go into your seventh year thinking it'd be nice to live there. And it can be, no question about it. My wife was teaching there, doing real well. We both were young and on autopilot.

"Then around the end of June," Corey said, "one of Jill's professors at Brown called her up and told her this history teacher at Mount Holyoke'd had a cerebral accident and dropped dead, age about thirty-eight, I guess. And it was late in the year to be filling those jobs, so they were on sort of a scramble. He asked her if she might be interested. Well, how many twenty-nine-year-old assistant professors wouldn't be interested in becoming tenured associates at one of the Seven Sisters? She was happy where she was. But chances like that don't come along every day, and New England's always been

70

a kind of green mecca to her. Her mother and her aunt grew up here, out there on Overlook Hills, and they loved it. But they went away to school, and both of them'd married men whose best careers were elsewhere. So neither one of them ever got back, and Jill's mother at least regretted that till the day that she died.

"She called me at the office and said to me: 'Just once, okay? Just this one time? Let me pull rank on a client, and you meet me for dinner tonight.'

" 'Hey, I said, 'this must be serious.'

" 'It is,' she said. 'I am not telling you on the phone. A real dinner at eight, at Monte's, all right? You won't stand me up, will you?'

"I thought she was pregnant," Corey said. "I really thought she was pregnant. And that sort of flustered me, you know?"

"You don't want to have kids?" Magoun said. "Can't say as I blame you, some days at least, but when you've got five it's a little too late to start having feelings like that."

"No," Corey said, "as a matter of fact, we did. And it was something that was at the back of our minds all the time. Except that even though the years were going by, there always seemed to be some reason to put it off another year: her career, mine, and the money. And when we did it we'd have to move, up to Connecticut, most likely. Which meant hiring a nanny and giving up what little freedom we had—once in a blue moon to have dinner, a weeknight—so we'd put it off one more year. Well, before I met Jill for dinner that night, thinking what I told you I'd thought, I'd gotten to thinking: 'Hey, which ought to count more in this world?' And that brought me back to the work I'd been doing. Pay's great; job isn't. So I was already telling her in my own mind I thought it was great, our first baby, because I want to change something myself, and not just the diapers, either.

"Well, she wasn't," Corey said. "But when she told me what her happy news actually was, I couldn't see how it changed anything in the train of thought I'd been having. So

I said: 'Great, we'll move up there. This is your big chance, so grab it. If they offer the job, you take it. We'll buy a big house and a dog.' She said: 'What will you do, if we do that? You'll go nuts as a house husband.' I said: 'I'll practice some law—that's what I'll do. If I can't get admitted to the Mass. Bar on reciprocity, I'll take the Mass. Bar exam. But this is as good news for me as it is good news for you. It's gotten me off of the dime.' And that's our story till now."

"Yeah," Magoun said. He frowned. He shook his head. "I don't know," he said. "This is the kind of situation that makes me uneasy. I can spot the ambushes long before I walk into them. But the ideas that look like a day at the beach, with hot dogs and beer and the ball game, those make me suspicious. When I can't find something wrong in the plan, I think there's something gone wrong with me."

"What's your downside risk?" Corey said. "I'm not asking for anything official from you. Not at this point, at least. Jill's grandfather was murdered. She's bothered by it, to this day. Everyone who knows anything about the case agrees with her. I'd like to see if I can find out what went on, because that might settle her mind. I'll never reach the point of asking you for anything unless I do come up with something. For now you can say, and I can say, too, this was a courtesy call. I've got a legitimate family interest in the thing—you wouldn't deny a man that. And I'm not asking, nor have you given to me, anything out of this office."

Magoun snorted. "Chiefly because you've already got all I've got," he said. "Hell, you've probably got more."

"But you can still say that because it's true, and then say: 'How could I stop him, if I wanted to? His family's got rights. If they want, they can certainly hire a lawyer or a private investigator to dig into old records, and go around talking to people. Happens they don't need to hire one—they've got one in the family. But what difference that makes, I don't see.' "

"Yeah," Magoun said. He nodded. "Okay," he said, "I'll go for it. You understand, though: I'm agreeing to do nothing whatsoever to help you. We've got all we can do in this circus trying to stay five steps behind the eight ball as it is. I'm going out in public all the time and screaming about scarce resources. I'm not going to put myself in a position where some wise guy stands up says: 'Oh yeah? Well, if you haven't got the manpower to handle what's happening now to the poor and the downtrodden, how come you reopen a case that's over twenty years old, then? Is it because the victim was rich? Or because you're in somebody's pocket?' So, you're free to do what you like, but I can't help you at all."

"I understand," Corey said. He stood up.

"Wait," Magoun said. He took a memo pad and wrote on it: *Baldo Ianucci.* He handed it to Corey.

Corey read it and looked back at Magoun. "Understanding I'm not helping you," Magoun said, "but on my review of that file, if I were doing what you're doing, that would make me want to take a little walking tour of that Claretian land. Nice summer day, pleasant walk in the Berkshires—at least you'll get some fresh air, after all that New York grit and grime. And you'll also get a feel for the place—what it looks like, why it's worth so much, too."

Corey looked puzzled. "Okay," he said.

"Jim Mandeville bought that property for five hundred thousand dollars of his own and five hundred thousand that he borrowed, back in nineteen sixty," Magoun said. "I'm not sure, but I think gas was about forty cents a gallon then, and when I got my first mortgage, one year after that—I was down in Boston then, starting my lifetime career as a white-shoe-firm trial lawyer—the interest rate was five and three-quarters. What's it today? Ten and a half? The house was a four-bedroom in peaceful suburban Wellesley; it cost us thirty-nine grand and some change. When we sold that house twelve years later, we got a hundred forty-one.

"Now, property out here hasn't shot up quite as much as it did back there, but you'd be pretty hard-pressed, even with the economy sucking brown wind like it is now, even to find

73

a buildable acre today fronting on that lake, and get it for eight or nine thousand. Ten'd be more like it, at least. So that makes me wonder what that Claretian property's worth today. Not as much as it was when this state was still boomtown, but still, I would guess, quite a lot. Well, Baldo knows everything. Baldo can tell you. And if you're nice to him, Baldo will do that for you."

Corey's eyebrows went up. "I don't know," he said.

"Well," Magoun said, "neither do I. But maybe if you went down there, oh, say, tomorrow, around eleven or so in the morning, and parked your car in a visitor's space—for God's sake, don't take one of the residents' numbered spaces; probably get away with it this time of year, but in the high summer there's been near-gunplay over those spaces—and just started walking around, you might run into someone like Baldo, semi-retired person, year-'rounder, old-timer, who might help you a little, you know? Purely on the off chance. The shoreside units, southerly end."

"Ahh," Corey said. " 'Baldo'?"

"Only name I've ever known him by," Magoun said. "Nice fella, though. Lived around here a long time, knows lots of things. You run into him, give him my best."

Jill had the library at the Unicorn at Goshen all to herself when he returned late in the afternoon. She sat at the game table at the westerly window with dozens of index cards stacked in seventeen piles around her lap-top computer, her posture perfect, her dark blond hair and her profile back-lighted, and he stood in the doorway for a moment before he cleared his throat and said: "Hey lady, you own this place or something? 'Cause you're sure acting like you do."

She looked up, momentarily startled, grinned at him, got out of the chair, stretching her back, and met him on the mid-dle of the oriental rug. When he started to release her from the clinch, she held on. "Uh-uh, stranger," she said, "give the

74

old lumbar region a good working over with your famous knuckle rub, all right? Those perchy little side chairs sure do look real pretty, but they're sheer hell on your bottom and back."

When they separated, he said: "So how did your day go?"

She returned to the table and began gathering the index cards, wrapping an elastic band around each bundle and putting it into her briefcase. "Oh, according to plan, I guess," she said. "One of the people I have to see won't be back until Thursday or Friday. They asked me if I could wait, and I said sure. I wonder what they expected. 'Like hell I'll wait, for this crumby job. Get the guy back here. My time is valuable. Who the hell does he think he is'? So I told them I'd only wait a reasonable time, such as till hell freezes over. How was yours?"

He pulled one of the wing chairs up to the table and sat down, giving her a full report as she finished with the cards and began to fold up the computer. When he finished, she said: "That sounds almost too good. Is this guy on the level with you?"

"I don't know," he said. "Is anyone but you?"

8

The next morning the parking lot at Claretian Estates was about two thirds full and the doors of the vast stone main building were open, but there was no other person in sight when Joe Corey at last located the visitors' spaces and put the Escort into one of them. He heard only birds nattering in the surrounding tall maples and pines flanking the building, and in the far distance the mutter of an outboard motor somewhere out on the lake.

He climbed the four steps under the maroon canopy and went into the lobby. It was furnished with heavy green bamboo furniture deeply cushioned with bright, flowered pillows. There was a large spray of yellow, orange, and red flowers on a table opposite the reception desk—no one was there. A small brass sign in script advised visitors to ring the small brass bell next to it. He continued on through the lobby toward the French doors that opened to the west on the veranda and then on the bright lake and dark hills beyond.

The veranda extended about two hundred feet on each side of the French doors. It was shaded by a green awning and was abundantly supplied with white wicker rocking chairs and white settees, cushioned with pink and blue pillows. No one sat in them. To his right there was a large putting green, unused, and beyond that there was a launching ramp; an empty trailer attached to a red Ford Mustang was parked unattended up the slope. Farther up the shore at an inlet, a dozen or so small boats rigged with outboards were tethered to a wooden pier.

He descended the three steps to the white gravel walk and turned left toward the south. He heard a rapid clicking sound that he recognized but could not place; a workman wearing a blue baseball cap and pushing a hand-powered mower appeared at the end of the veranda, his head down, intent on his task. "I was actually relieved," he told Jill that afternoon back in Goshen. "That place was downright eerie. Plenty of physical evidence of human habitation, but not a soul in sight. I thought: 'God, I should've bought a paper this morning. Have we been hit by nuclear fallout? I'm the only survivor?'"

The workman turned the mower and vanished behind the end of the main building again. Corey increased his pace and came to the end of the veranda just as the man completed that row and turned back toward the lake. He still had his head down as he approached the white gravel—the cap was embroidered in white script: NY. He appeared startled when Corey said "Excuse me," and seemed to have some momentary difficulty locating the origin of the sound. He was about sixty and had spent many years out of doors. "Sorry to interrupt you," Corey said, "but there doesn't seem to be anybody else here."

The man stared at him. "Usually isn't on Thursdays," he said. He relaxed his forearm muscles but not his grip on the mower. "What can I do for you?"

Corey smiled. The workman remained impassive. "Well," Corey said, "I've heard a lot about this place, and my wife and I, well, we've been thinking of getting a place up around here, and so I thought if it was all right, maybe I could look around? I mean she's not with me or anything. What I mean is: I'm by myself. But would that be all right, you think?"

The workman turned his head slightly to his left and spat a small bit of saliva. He looked at Corey again. "Fine by me," he said. "Anything else?"

"Ah, no," Corey said, "nothing else. Thank you."

The workman nodded. He tensed his forearms again and completed his pass to the walk. He stepped onto the gravel and turned the mower to begin his next row. He looked at Corey. "You all right?" he said.

"Well, yeah, I'm all right," Corey said. "I was just waiting here until you turned around. Didn't want to get in your way."

"Not in my way," the workman said. He bent his head again and started back toward the front of the main building.

Corey continued along the walk through a small but dense grove of young oaks, emerging from it into a clearing that curved around the shore of the lake for six hundred yards or more. To his left began a series of clusters of two-story, grey-clapboard condominiums, each boasting two or three front doors. The roofs were sharply peaked, and the second-story windows in the centers of the units were Palladian arches, each with matching white shutters. Each of the units on the shoreline had a picture window facing the lake. Some of the small front lawns had white metal tables under blue umbrellas with white iron chairs grouped around them.

"They seemed to go on forever," he told Jill. "The only way I could've counted them was from the air. But at least I could hear sounds of normal human existence. I don't mean anything noisy, or anything like that. In the city at night that amount of noise would make me think: 'must be a blackout.' But someone had a radio or a CD player on, and I heard someone calling someone else, and I began to feel much better. I straightened my shoulders and stepped forth boldly, like any confident yuppie scoping out the *actual* desirability of a vacation home in the Berkshires—'no fooling me with your fancy brochures, your smooth-talking salesmen and unction; I'm going to see for myself.' Of course that still left me with the question of how the hell I was supposed to locate this guy who's supposed to know so much, in this place the same size as Switzerland, but I thought: 'trust to luck. You've done all right so far. Besides, luck's all you've got anyway.'

"I was about, oh, maybe a hundred and fifty yards into this what, settlement? There were people around, although very few kids, going out to errands, coming back. But as far as I could tell, nobody paid the slightest bit of attention to me. They're used to strangers wandering through. Normal occurrence, that's all. Makes sense, I suppose. The people who own those things have them in time-share—you're used to seeing new neighbors today. Different ones'll come next year, most likely.

"So there I was in the midst of my charade, 'getting the feel of the place,' and in front of me I see this guy sitting at his table under his umbrella on his lawn, having a nice cup of coffee. There's another cup opposite him, but nobody using it, I could see. I figured this had to be Baldo."

"Oh, my brave, handsome man," Jill said. "You were born to be a detective."

"He's about five-ten," Corey said, "standing up or on his side. This mane of white hair—he did not get his name on his looks, unless he was wearing a wig, and he didn't seem like the type. He looked to be in his early fifties. But those mesomorphs can be deceiving. Most guys born with that build run to fat pretty early, though not as much fat as they used to. But some guys're all muscle. And he was all muscle. They have to send their new polo shirts out, in order to have them stretched, hard. They keep themselves in shape, and after they get to be fifty or so, they stay at that same age forever. When they finally do decide to die, undertakers have to send out for piano crates to hold them."

The man at the table wished Corey a good morning. "And the same to you, sir," Corey said. "A very fine morning indeed for a stroll."

The man at the table displayed many white teeth. "Still," he said, "no need to hurry. Care to join me for coffee?"

"Why, thank you, I will," Corey said. He crossed the small lawn and offered his right hand. The man at the table stood up. "Very nice of you, sir. I'm Joe Corey."

79

"I imagine," Corey told Jill that afternoon, "that the Jaws of Life take a stronger grip on a wrecked car when they're cutting the poor victims out than Baldo took of my hand. But I don't know, and I wouldn't put money on it."

"Baldo Ianucci," the man said. Corey sat down and Ianucci filled his cup. The coffee poured out with cream in it. Ianucci put the thermos down, and when he sat back in his chair there was an expressionless look of appraisal on his face. "What do you think of this place?" He gestured vaguely behind him.

"It's enormous," Corey said. The heat of the coffee did not bother him; it was the strength of it under the cream.

"Six hundred and fifteen units," Ianucci said, "in two hundred fifty-one structures."

"Two or three to a structure?" Corey said.

"Yah," Ianucci, "threes, most of them. Couple of fours. Mine here and two others: one unit only. Same size building but just your own dinner."

"I don't follow," Corey said.

"No matter how sound your basic construction is, party walls make you close with the neighbors. When they have fried fish, then you have fried fish, regardless of whether you want it. When they have the grandkids up for the weekend, the grandkids visit you, too. I've got nothing against fried fish, keep a boat down at the pier and catch dinner myself now and then, but I want to decide when I want to have fish for dinner. Same with grandchildren, small kids or teenagers. Completely approve of nice kids. Bad kids I don't approve of. Approve of the parents still less, letting them become bad kids. So my three-unit's just one."

"You're by yourself here?" Corey said.

"Nope," Ianucci said. "Live here year 'round with my wife. Gets pretty quiet after the leaves fall, doesn't pick up till late spring, but that suits us fine. Makes a nice change, have the place all to ourselves half a year, some company the other half."

"I came in through the main building," Corey said. "Didn't seem to be much company. All I saw was a gardener. Surly guy in a Yankees ballcap. All he said was because it's Thursday."

Ianucci laughed. "That'd be Deacon," he said. "Old Deac wastes no words. I think it's because he doesn't have many. Afraid to spread them around.

"The Thursday thing is actually simple. Open rehearsals at Tanglewood. Management here offers free bus transportation; parking's tough and expensive there in season. Time-share owners rent out their units, mostly to middle-aged people, lot of them closer to my age, and most of them come for the music. Not many musicians, classical, at least, have money, and a lot of the people who like what they do don't have a great deal of it, either. The rehearsal music comes at a lower price than the actual performances do. Lots of the people who rent here're on fixed incomes. That makes prices important. They can afford a regular concert, one concert, no more, per weekend. Thursdays are bonuses. So Thursdays are popular here. They fix a picnic lunch, take a bottle of wine, get on the bus and ride over. No parking fees. No big meal expenses. It's a very odd thing these days: a genuine bargain. Looks like an evacuation's been ordered around here, those buses pull up Thursday mornings. They have a nice day, they don't spend much dough, they come back at night tired but happy.

"And then they go back where they came from, of course, and rave to all their friends what a great time they had here, and the next year their friends rent units here too. And that means the real owners have no trouble renting. These units are full up most weekends. Which in today's condo market's a real inducement to buy here 'stead of someplace else. That's why the management offers the service, and why almost everyone uses it. It's a loss-leader that works. There's a lot of developments around here like this, and a good many of 'em're starving. Right on the brink of Chapter Eleven, and their balance doesn't look good. But Claretian's in profit. I think it'll survive—and do better, the more of them fail." He paused as though interrupting himself, thought for a moment, then poured more coffee into his own cup.

"You were going to say something," Corey said.

"The people who own this place are smart," Ianucci said. "When the condo thing got started, fifteen years or so ago, everybody but these people went the plush-resort route. Not only were they offering you a vacation-home deal that you might be able to swing, one twenty-sixth of the purchase price, upkeep, in exchange for one twenty-sixth of the year—which two weeks were probably all you had or wanted to spend in the Berkshires every summer—but those other guys were also gonna give you swimming pools and golf courses, tennis courts and horseback riding, top-notch food, a great clubhouse, canoeing and fishing, and, some of them, band concerts Saturday nights.

"There was only one way they really could do all that. Either they'd have to price the units to reflect their actual costs, overhead, and investment return, in which case their competition would underbid them so far that they'd never sell a unit, or else they'd have to do cheap construction, stall on building the facilities, run the operation without enough skilled help, let the whole plant go to hell and try to unload 'fore it did. And that's what most of them're trying to do now, while the buildings fall apart around them and the weeds come up through the one tennis court that got built in place of the six planned, and the brambles take over the golf links, and their kitchens give people ptomaine. This will not be easy for them to pull off.

"The Claretian people were smarter. The main building was here when they got the place. The New York broker-type that first came up in eighteen ninety and grabbed all this land dirt-cheap had that house built like a fort. It's been here now ninety years, and it looks as good today as I bet it looked back then. You couldn't duplicate that place today for ten million dollars; probably not for any price: those kind of builders aren't around this world much now.

"Now you look at the acreage. Nothing that God's been taking care of for years, doing a fairly good job, has been changed except where it had to be. God didn't put a golf course in. God didn't play much tennis. Probably because God's smart too, and didn't want the upkeep. But anyway, no golf course here, all overgrown and shaggy, and no place for tennis you can't play on 'cause the fence's fallen down and there isn't any net. If God felt like a swim, He swam in the lake, so the lake's still here, but there's no Olympic-sized pool, cracked and leaking, breeding bugs and stinking up the place. Hell, about the only lawn you see here's what's around the main house."

"They even save on that expense," Corey said. "One man with a hand mower. Didn't know they still made them."

Ianucci laughed. "Well," he said, "that one, no, that's not for cheap. The hand mower is for quiet. I don't know if you've ever gone on vacation and tried to sleep late, which on vacation you should be able to, you want, but there's nothing like the sound of four guys riding gang mowers all around the property to get you out of bed at daybreak in a really lousy mood. Michelle and I decided, couple years ago, we'd splurge: a month in Florida, all of February. Cost a lot of money, too, height of the season like that. Real nice cottage on a golf course, nice and warm—it looked just great.

"Yeah. The first night we were there they watered that damned course all night, right under our windows—sounded like we had a hundred elephants pissing outside. Finally managed to get to sleep, and six A.M., no later, bang, the power mowers start. It's invasion time. Couldn't sleep there. Can here."

A brunette woman in her early forties came out of the house. She was wearing jeans and a loose-fitting blue pullover, and her feet were bare. She carried a coffee cup. "She was," Corey told Jill back in Goshen, "a *very* attractive woman."

83

Ianucci introduced them. She sat down at the table and filled her cup.

"That's why Deacon pushes the mower," Ianucci said. "Because of the noise otherwise. These little patches in front of the places—when you see one, it belongs to the owner, and the owner takes care of it. Ninety good fathers lived in the main house, when there were ninety to live there. Now there are rooms for seventy guests, who pay good money to use them, and that plus the winterized units in this place means it's a year-'round operation.

"So, when the music stops and the leaves fall down, there's still business at this place. Very few weekends unbooked for conferences; quite a few weeks're booked, too. The ski crowd's not really much of a factor—cross-country's okay, but most of the market wants downhill, and we're too close to Vermont to get them. Vermont has real mountains; this doesn't. But those business meetings keep cash coming in all year 'round, and very few outfits like this get that."

"I see what you mean about 'smart,' " Corey said.

"Yeah," Ianucci said, "but I'm not as smart as I think I am. You came in through the main house. You did not see a bar. You did not see a dining room, or a breakfast room. You saw a lobby, and two big rooms off it, and you saw just about all that there is. You'd've come tomorrow, you would've had to fight your way through a big music tour coming in for the weekend. That's why it's so quiet today.

"Three more places where they didn't spend money, putting the place together, I mean. When they get a conference, they cater the thing, some big outfit up in Pittsfield. The kitchen is big enough so they can cook banquets. They set up portable bars. Breakfast is served in the room by the lake. The meetings are in the next room. Then back to the lake room for lunch, and back to the other one after lunch, drinks in the lobby, upstairs to change, dinner looking out on the lake. Kind of boring, maybe, but the companies love it: nobody sneaks out for drinks in the bar in the middle of the afternoon—where can they sneak to? There's no bar. They'd have to drive into town and be missing. That'd cost them their jobs. So it's great for the bosses: they get their people locked up nice and tight, meter their liquor intake—they make them live cleaner'n the good fathers did. It's a comptroller's dream, I tell you."

"Yeah, but at night," Corey said. "What stops them from going out then?"

"Well," Ianucci said, "unless they feel like driving all the way to Pittsfield, really—and keep in mind that their bosses have breakfast served early; you're there by seven or skip it— there's really just one place that they can go: the inn in the center of town. And a lot of them do, a lot do that, just to escape for a while."

He paused. "Now do you see what I mean?" he said. "About how I'm not always smart?"

Corey shook his head. "Not really," he said. "So far what you've told me is that this is a very tightly run operation that's cut overhead to the bone, targeted exactly the mark it wants, and hit it, right on the bull's-eye."

Ianucci leaned forward in his chair. "You're no smarter'n I am," he said. "And I dunno what I'm bragging about either. Took me several years to piece this together, knowing much more'n you do. But just think about this: if you were planning this whole operation, spending only on what's essential, making very efficient use of a building that'll last forever, doing solid, durable, top-quality construction on the structures you were adding, so they won't fall apart either, eliminating full-time kitchen staff, even leaving out a lobby drugstore and a newsstand because they'd cost more than they'd bring in— in other words, if you were putting all your eggs strictly in the basket that your fattest, warmest hen was going to sit down on and hatch, would you leave out a *bar*? Bars with captive markets make money hand over fist. Anyone who's smart enough to plan this setup like they did, putting nothing in that would cost more than it would bring them, going absolutely first-class on anything profitable, has to've known that. 'If we don't have a lounge in there, a nice, big, comfy tavern, all those people that come in here will go up the street. Large groups of thirsty people, too. To Jack Davis's.' "

He paused. "It's almost as though," he said, "someone involved in this liked Jack Davis so much he wanted to make him rich. Of course it could have been that that someone wasn't really generous, but wanted to avoid a lot of problems with the town, building permits, stuff like that. And Jack did have some power by then—on the bank board and all. He could've made some trouble if he got some competition that he didn't want to have. Better just give him his little windfall and shut up. Could've been, I s'pose."

He slapped the top of the table with the flat of his hand. "But I don't believe it for a minute. Not one minute. The someone who was running this was running Jack as well, and Jack was his employee. What people spend at Shropshire Inn they're really spending at Claretian. This whole deal got under way years before the murder. Jack was the advance man. He was sent here to set this up."

9

Corey did not say anything for a while. At last he frowned and said: "Did Jack Davis make the call that got Mandeville out of bed?"

Ianucci slumped back in his chair. "I doubt it," he said. "Davis could've, but I doubt it. He was on the board of directors, sure, and Jim Mandeville liked him—mostly because the bank'd had a mortgage on that inn since the Year One, but when Dawson Nichols was running the place, that loan'd been a real problem. At least that's what Amelia told me."

"Amelia Feldt, this would be," Corey said.

Ianucci looked mildly surprised. "Yeah. What other Amelia?"

"You didn't say her last name," Corey said. "That means you knew I'd talked to her, and I didn't tell that to Magoun. So either he knew it, and mentioned it to you, or else you and Amelia've talked since I saw him."

"I called her last night," Ianucci said, looking innocent. "Is there something wrong with that or something?"

"Not at all," Corey said. "It's just that among all the other things that entertain and interest me about this project is the way the person I go to see next always knows where I've been before."

Michelle shook her head once and looked down at her hands.

Ianucci scowled ("It was not a pretty sight," Corey told Jill that afternoon. "It was a fairly scary one"). "Now look, fella," he said, his voice dropping into a rasping growl, "I'm an old man now, I know that. But I know a lot of other things, and one of those things is that I don't need any smart-ass stuff from any fresh kids, you got that? I'm willing, I'm eager, to work with you on this. If you'll allow it, that is.

"Until last night I'd never exchanged a word with Amelia in my life. I still haven't met the nice lady. One of Burt's assistants lives down this way, and Burt sent the file down with him. I went through that file, as I've done with files for years, when somebody's handed me one that I know nothing about. I saw her name there as someone who might know things, so when I got through, I called her.

"That's what you do when you know what you're doing: you talk to the people who might know a little more about the facts than you do. And, in case you want to do a little more Sherlocking here, kid, she's in the phone book, all right? That's how I got her number: I picked up my phone book and looked under 'Feldt,' and there the name was, plain as day. Wasn't that clever of me? You've read that file, so I assumed you'd seen her. And when I called her, she told me you had. Okay, boy gumshoe, that clear?"

"Okay," Corey said. "Sorry. I mean that."

"I," Michelle said, starting to get up, "I'm going into the house and fix some lunch for us, all right?"

Ianucci put out his right hand and touched her left arm. He did not shift his gaze from Corey's face, but his voice was quite gentle as he spoke to her. "Please sit down, honey," he said, "I'll do that." She sat down again. He stood up. "I've got to take a leak anyways. I'll bring the food out when I come." He pushed the chair back, glared at Corey once, and started up to the house. In the distance the outboard murmured.

"Well," Corey said, "that was pretty stupid of me, I must say."

She looked up at him. "I know," she said, "he can be an old bear at times."

Corey nodded. "Yeah," he said, "I figured that just from looking at him. Which makes what I did even stupider."

She gave him a small smile. "Yes," she said, "it was. I did it once or twice myself, riled him up like that without meaning to, when I first knew him, and he made it just as clear to me that what I'd done was stupid. You got off easy, if you want the truth. All he did to you was insult you two or three times, and he didn't even swear once, which he usually does when he gets angry with another man. I guess he must've slowed down a little, over the last twenty years." She enlarged the smile. "Woman married to a normal man would expect that to happen, but somehow, when you're married to Baldo, that thought never crosses your mind. That he could mellow, I mean."

Corey told Jill in the late afternoon that when Michelle started talking, "I decided I'd already said enough as it was, and maybe if I just sat still, looked ashamed, and kept my damned mouth shut, maybe she'd give me a check for absolution I could cash with him."

"I met him down in Hartford in the spring of 'sixty-nine. We were building engines, of course, that was what the plant was for, for the Navy and the Air Force in Vietnam. F-4 and A-4 Phantoms at that time, I think, but I can't say I'm really sure—we made engines for so many kinds. Civilian, military, all kinds."

Corey frowned. "The G.E. plant in Hartford," she said. "That's what we built there, jet engines. And there'd been some problems with them. And no matter what they did to try to correct them, the same things kept going wrong. I think it had something to do with impeller blades, whatever they are—you have to understand: I was in personnel, not production, so all I really spent my time on was making sure security clearances were in, getting tax forms prepared, strictly clerical stuff. All I really knew about what we actually did, and what we did, or what we did it with, was from scuttlebutt around the cafeteria and so forth. They called me a secretary, which is nice when you're twenty-two, and it paid more, but what I really was was a clerk.

"Baldo was still with DID—DOD—then, and apparently when the problems kept coming up again and again, and pilots who survived crashes or ditchings began to write home about them, some senator or congressman got furious about it and demanded an investigation into whether sabotage was involved. Or deliberate failure to make sure parts met specs— everybody was all spooked then about the longhairs infiltrating arms plants and screwing up on purpose. Or anyway, just what was causing them.

"So the Defense Department, the Intelligence Division, sent Baldo up to investigate, and the first place he had to come to was personnel, to present his credentials, have his plant badge issued, and get shown around to where the files were he might want. He had one of the high mucky-mucks with him, of course, a very *nervous* high mucky-muck—but then that isn't really fair; it's pretty tough not to be intimidated by Baldo even now, but when he came rolling in in those days with the power to shut down your plant, cost you your job, and maybe get you prosecuted and put in jail, he was *really* intimidating.

"That plant was no convent," she said. "The girls—we called ourselves 'girls' then, the young single women; the others were married ladies and the old biddies—had plenty of chances for a romance, and it was a good place to start one. At least it seemed like it was in those days. Those single guys all had good steady union jobs, and that plant was booming back then. Most of the married guys out on the line were married to women they'd met there. The town itself was no New York City, but there were enough bars and stuff. Pay was good, two or three shifts were running, everything looked pretty nice. So all the girls joked with all of the guys when they saw them at work, or, you know, around.

"What I'm saying is that Baldo didn't exactly walk into the Island of Lost Women there. There were lots of young, good-looking guys around, in good shape, making good money. And good God, he was forty-nine then—I had his records, you see. But the day he came in, all the girls zeroed in on him: 'Who the heck is this guy?' 'Is he married?' I'm not saying it was an Elvis thing, you know, it didn't get quite that bad, but Baldo, well, he was certainly different than anyone else that we'd seen. And I don't want to give you the wrong idea here: I was sort of going with a guy out on the line, had been for almost a year, and he was a really nice guy, and pretty good-looking, I do say so, but I was just as bad as the rest of the girls. Baldo was just fascinating. And none of us really knew why.

"He must've noticed it," she said, "all the giggling and blushing when he came into the office, how all the other girls all of a sudden found excuses to get something up at the counter while I was waiting on him, holding their breath all the way up, wiggling their fannies like little bunnies, going back to their desks. And you know what he did? He ignored it. Which of course made it worse until the day he exploded at me— after that they all ignored *him*."

"What set him off?" Corey said.

"The usual thing," Michelle said, "a screw-up by someone else, somewhere else—he wasn't getting his check. It wasn't really my fault that he wasn't, of course; he wasn't on G.E.'s payroll. It was some jerk down at Langley. Baldo'd been in Newport News, down in Virginia, oh, I don't know, five or six months, something about parts durability on ships, and Defense was supposed to change his address to up there, and somebody didn't. That's all. It wasn't my error at all.

"But he said it was. 'I told you to'—not 'I asked'; 'I *told*'— 'you to double-check for me on that. You've got to ride those clowns to exhaustion, you incompetent smile in a skirt, if you ever want anything done, and I haven't got enough time to do that, so I told you to do it. And you didn't. I'm beginning to understand why the hell everything in this sorry lash-up's disorganized. It's a party all day, whee, let's all have fun, and never mind if things get done, let alone whether they get done right. This sideshow in here's symptomatic. Looks to me like it shows the whole atmosphere here, all the way onto the line. Now you listen to me and you listen up good, and feel free to pass it along: this slipshod attitude doesn't fight wars, and it doesn't build aircraft to win them. You may all think this is Mardi Gras time here, every day of the year, but we've got young men over Vietnam in the planes that those engines push, and their lives're important to me. Even if they're not to you.

" 'Now there's nothing I can do if those planes take ground-fire and go down, but there's one hell of a damned lot I can do if they're going down because the engines that're built here stop pushing when they need them at forty thousand feet. And I *will* do it to you, every sorry meatball in this sorry operation, and do it *gladly*, got that? Now get off your butt and get on that horn and get those checks routed up here.' Then he turned and stomped out of the office."

"Wow," Corey said.

"You bet," Michelle said. "And you can also bet I moved my tail back to my desk and phone, and I got on that phone to payroll at DOD, and I think I shocked the other girls—I *know* I shocked the ladies; I'm surprised the biddies didn't all faint dead away—with the tantrum that I threw. Here was sweet little Michelle, always ready with a smile, snarling, 'Give me the supervisor, *now*, you jerk, if you can't handle this.' And when I got the supervisor, I said: 'Listen to me now: I've got about two hundred pounds of damned-mad Baldo Ianucci breathing fire and smoke into my face here, and it's all because someone down there screwed up and didn't shunt his pay-checks. Now you get on the stick and find those checks wherever they are, and you get'em up here *pronto*, lady, no delays, no excuses, and no bullshit. Because the next time that dragon comes in here for me, I've got your number written down and I will dial it in a hurry, and let him talk to *you*.'

"When I put the phone down, well, *slammed* it down, you could've heard a cotton ball if someone dropped one in that office. I looked around and said: 'What's the matter with you guys?' Kinda pleased with myself, you know? Figured I'd shown 'em a side of me they hadn't seen before. Of course they hadn't—I hadn't seen it myself.

"But they weren't looking at me," Michelle said. "They were looking at the doorway. Baldo was standing in it. I don't know how long he'd been there. I don't know how much he'd heard. But it must've been enough, I guess." She sighed and looked down at her hands, twisting her diamond ring with her right thumb and forefinger. She looked up. She grinned. "I never saw that particular approach to catching a man in *Cosmopolitan*," she said, "but I know one time when it worked."

He laughed.

She leaned forward. "Now let me give you some pointers here, all right?"

"Sure," he said. "I can use all the help I can get."

"Baldo's making chicken Senegalese salad. He *loves* Senegalese salad. If I weren't around, I think he'd make drums of the stuff, and eat it at least once every day all summer. I don't mind it at all, kind of like it actually, but I'd like something else now and then. Since I do feel that way, he only makes it in small batches, one lunch at a time, boiling the chicken, draining the chicken, chilling the chicken—he does all that the night before. What he's doing now is chopping the celery— very important not to chop the celery until you're actually ready to serve; won't be as crisp if you do—and making the mayo, from scratch. Most people like their mayo cold. Baldo does not. Well, he does, but to chill it you have to make it the night before, which means it won't be as fresh when you eat it. He likes fresh better'n cold. Then he'll blend in the curry powder. He used to like enough of it to power downtown Calcutta, and I guess he probably still does, but his belly's gotten older, and it doesn't.

"So," she said, tapping him on his left wrist with her right forefinger, "*you* love Senegalese salad, Mister Corey—got that?"

He nodded. "Got it," he said.

"Even if you don't," she said. "*Especially* if you don't. Got that?"

93

"Well," he said, "I like the soup okay. I don't think I've ever had the salad."

She settled back. "Well," she said, "I can assure you, if you like the soup okay, you will love the salad. So there should be no problem there.

"Now," she said, "the nice thing about having Baldo chew your ankle is that when he's finished biting you, he's finished. It hurts like hell while he's doing it, but it doesn't last too long, and it does end. Unless you ignite him again, when he comes back out here, he'll be sweet as a lamb—wait and see."

"That's good to hear," Corey said.

"He was really excited after Burt called him yesterday," she said. " 'Burt's sending a kid down to talk to me,' he said. 'Looking into the Mandeville case.' Burt didn't let on I called him back in June and begged him, please, to find something Baldo could do. No pay. Just activity. Genuine work. Something to occupy him. Of course I did tell Burt I'd kill him if he told Baldo I'd called, but still, he could've and he didn't.

"You see, you can't take a man who's worked all his life, and then just suddenly put him out to graze like an old bull. Not if the man is Baldo. He doesn't know how to do it. He doesn't know how because he never did it, and the reason he never did it was because he never wanted to. A man like Baldo's used to doing what he wants to do. When you tell him he can't do what he wants to anymore, you're not telling him he's retired—you're telling him he's dead. Baldo says he's not dead. He says he's alive. That means you're lying to him—he does not like liars.

"Baldo enlisted in the Army right out of school in nineteen forty. When the Second War ended, he stayed in. Along the line his branch was split off into Air Force. He retired from that in nineteen sixty and joined DID, and when some crackbrained rule made them retire him in 'eighty-two—they didn't want to—he was beside himself.

"Burt Magoun's a good guy," Michelle said. Ianucci emerged from the house. She stopped talking at once. He used both hands to carry a large tray. He brought it to the table and rested its forward edge on it. She removed a large glass bowl draped with a pink linen napkin and put it in front of his chair. She lifted off a bottle of red wine, its label concealed by a grey marble chiller, and put it in front of her place. While she removed first three wineglasses and then salt and pepper grinders and put them on the table, he lifted off three white plates rimmed with blue, and a glass bowl of Boston lettuce. She distributed tableware wrapped in pink napkins. He sat down.

"Sorry it took me so long," Ianucci said. It was evident to Corey that he was not sorry at all. He used the tongs to distribute lettuce on the plates, then spooned the salad onto the lettuce and served it. Michelle poured a slightly sweating Juliénas from the bottle in the granite cylinder. "Takes time to do this stuff properly, like everything else in this world." He looked at Corey. "You like Senegalese salad, I hope?"

"Never tried it," Corey said. That afternoon in Goshen he told Jill: "The last thing I was going to do at that point was start lying."

"Huh," Ianucci said. He ate with Oldham's avidity, but with a deliberate delicacy that made it difficult to understand how his first helping had disappeared so quickly; Ianucci was taking a second when Corey was no more than two thirds through his first. Ianucci stood up again suddenly. "I'll be right back," he said, peaking his napkin over his plate. "Coffee's ready by now. Got to get it in the jug before it cooks down to molasses."

"He and Burt worked with each other when Burt was in the U.S. Attorney's office in Boston," Michelle said softly and rapidly. "Burt was out here when DOD let him go, heard about it, called him up, and asked him to come up here as his chief investigator. It was a godsend. And the only reason, *only* reason, that Burt let him go last year was because those fools down in Boston said he had to hire a woman lawyer. Right off. Didn't give him any money to do it with, of course, just told him to get with it and do it. Feminists were raising hell because all the other D.A.s had at least one female assistant. Well, the only way Burt could hire a woman lawyer was by letting Baldo go. There wasn't enough money in Burt's budget to give another first-year lawyer, either sex, the same salary he was paying to the first-year men lawyers he hired, and of course if Burt paid a woman less, he'd get in even more trouble for doing that. So, Baldo had to go."

She shook her head. "It really was too bad," she said. "Burt hated to do it, absolutely hated it. Baldo understood, but that didn't change the fact. He was retired again, for the third time, every single time not because he couldn't do the job anymore but because of some silly rule, and now it looked like he was *really* retired. He was very, very low." They heard the door open. "So," she said, in a hushed voice, barely audible above the outboard far out on the lake, "you're a godsend, Corey. Treat him real good, okay?"

"Promise," Corey whispered.

10

So," he said to Jill in their room at the Unicorn, "given the fact that I did my level best to screw it up, I'd have to say that all in all, my day went pretty well. Baldo's working plan is that we start by cataloguing every piece of paper in the town hall, and the Registry of Deeds, that pertains to Claretian Shores, and copying every single name that we find on them."

"Then we'll do a chron from that," Ianucci said at the table in front of his house. "It'll tell us who came in and who went out, and when the changes happened. There's nothing like a time line to clarify your thinking when you're going back and sorting out what it is that happened. Otherwise all you've got when you get finished is an indigestible mass of data that tell you *what* happened—most of which you already knew, because you've read the reports, walked around the territory, seen the buildings and so forth—but not *when* it happened, and the when is often the why.

"It's the why that interests you, because that's where you get your peeks at who had the motive. You already knew what the motive was, of course, but the trouble with one in this particular case is that greed's a pretty common failing. If everyone who ever envied Jim Mandeville the ownership of this land was a suspect, then we might as well write up a one-page memo to Burt and tell him to saddle up a grand jury to indict every last soul who ever knew Jim'd bought the land. Not too practical. We've got to narrow it down some. We've got to find the particular greedy people whose envy was strong enough, and whose methods were coarse enough, to allow them to murder to get it. So the when in this case that gives you the why also gives you the who, that not only had the same greedy motive any sensible person would've had, but also the willingness and the means—the out-of-town talent—to commit one or more apparently innocuous acts that in due course led to Mandeville's murder. Just as the greedy killers had in mind when they started committing the acts."

He grinned. "Only if you're damned lucky, of course. But I always begin these impossible projects with the assumption that *naturally* when I need a hod full of luck to get me over an obstacle, a kindly God will provide it. That's the kind of harebrained attitude a kid gets, growing up the only child of a bible-belting Christian gone so completely nuts on religion he'd name his son 'Baldad.'"

"You've got me there," Corey said. "I don't claim ever to have been a member in good standing of the Third Order of Saint Francis—hell, I never even joined the Newman Club at Princeton. But I thought I knew most of the players, and I never heard of Baldad."

"Baldad the Suhite. Job Two: eleven. 'Now when Job's three friends heard all the evil that had befallen him'—this being right after God'd starting kicking the slats out of poor old Job, showing off to Satan, like a headstrong little kid, just to prove that He could do it; cripes, how my poor old father could've admired that whimsical old Rascal the way he did, I'll never know—'they came each one from his own place, Eliphaz the Themanite, and Baldad the Suhite, and Sophar the Naamathite. For they had made an appointment to come together and visit him, and comfort him.'"

Ianucci grinned again. "After all, what're friends for, anyway? And what good're friends, if they don't come around and lift up their eyes afar off when they get a close-up look at you and see you've taken such a pounding they can scarcely even recognize you, huh? Well, I tell you, Baldad and those guys were *all right*. They were the kind of friends to have. They cried out, and they wept, *and* they rent their garments and they got their hands all dirty, and then they sat down on the ground with good old Job, their pal, for seven days and seven nights. You can look it up. Job Two: twelve; thirteen. And Job, well, he really appreciated it. He let it all come right out. He said he wished he was *dead*."

Ianucci shook his head. "I look at it this way," he said, "it could've been worse. Daddy could've named me Eliphaz or Sophar, and God only knows what people meeting a little kid with one of those names would've decided to call him. I understand why he did it, of course—Daddy had a hard life, and he didn't think he deserved it. He wasn't quiet about it, either—even my mother got sick of listening to him gripe, after a while. He thought it was unjust that the son of a cobbler who'd worked his fingers to the bone in Calabria so his son could go to university and be something better than a cobbler in Calabria couldn't find a better job in America than working as cobbler in the North End of Boston. Land of Opportunity? *Basta*. He did not think it was fair, and he wanted everyone to know it. It's a good thing for him at least that his daddy'd taught him the cobbling business well, helping him out in the shop, before he went off to school. Because if my daddy hadn't been a *damned* good cobbler, the kind of shoemaker Caruso was a tenor, nobody in the North End after a few years would've put up with the griping they had had to listen to when they took their shoes in for repair. It's a wonder Daddy didn't hook up with Sacco and Vanzetti, but I suppose the Jesus stuff was too strong for anarchy.

"Job was Daddy's favorite book in the bible—he was reading the Book, as he called it, all the time; he'd finish, go back to the first page and start again. But Job was his favorite book. He thought he was Job. A godly man, churchgoing man, family man, hardworking man, who for some reason or another just never caught a break. A graduate of the University of Bologna with a degree in Italian history, but absolutely nothing else, such as speaking English, for example, who brought his pregnant wife to America in nineteen twenty, with no job waiting for him, so his child would be born here, and could not understand why no college here would hire him. It just wasn't fair. And that enraged him. Permanently. Daddy had a stronger sense of justice than he did reality. To him justice was all; God stood for justice; he loved God a lot, and he could get none. There was only one answer: God had it in for him.

"Well, after a while, no one would listen to him. So I came along and he named me Baldad. Because he wanted someone on this earth, one person, at least, who would *want* to listen to him, and I was going to be that person. I would have to be, because I was his son. Care to speculate about the reason why I joined the service the day after I got out of MIT, year before we were at war? Give you a hint: it was not so I'd have seniority when the inevitable happened. And that's why *I've* carried a burden all my life—the burden of my name. It's automatic with me now, the habit of a lifetime: when I have to show my papers and the person's eyebrows go up, before he can even ask, I say: 'It's a family monicker. Most people call me Baldo.'

"Anyway," he said, "obviously there's nothing to all that heredity theory. I'm my father's son, but I've always believed in luck, and I've always run into a patch of it, just when I needed it most. I hope for your sake I haven't used it all up yet, and you've got some of your own. We're going to need all we can get."

I envy you," Jill said, preparing gin and tonics with the makings they had purchased in New York. "We should've brought limes, too. And a knife."

"I bet they have limes and knives in Massachusetts," he said. "They have indoor plumbing and electric lights, central heat too, I've heard. I've even seen air conditioners sticking out of windows here and there. Your day was not so good, I take it?"

She handed him his drink and took the other wing chair at the southwesterly corner of the room. "Oh," she said, "it wasn't really bad. Inconclusive, that's all. Carlson wasn't back when I left the campus today—I went over there after you left this morning and worked in the library. It's just as quiet there this time of year as it is in the Museum of Archaic Accounting Practices downstairs here, but the chairs in the library there were chosen by someone who apparently had an idea someone might want to use them to sit in for long periods of time, thinking and reading and so forth.

"I figured I'd check in with his office after lunch, and if I didn't have any luck then, once more before I came back here. That way if he did come back, I'd be right there to see him, and we could get it over with. It's just a formality, anyway. He's read all my papers, seen my C.V., read all my recommendations—two of the other people on the search committee've told me that. And they've also told me, confidentially of course, that they know he's very favorably impressed. So I *know* it's just a formality, his interviewing me. But he can't sign off on my candidacy until he does that. And like all formalities in academia, it's therefore critically important that he see me, because making things that aren't important *critically* important is what we do in order to account for all the time we spend not working. Lodge rules, my friend, and I want to join this lodge, so I'd better obey those rules."

She sighed. "But he didn't come back," she said, "and the secretary in the department office said he didn't call in either. So I couldn't get it done today. Does this mean I'll be able to tomorrow? Well, I don't know. If his failure to call means that he's on the road, then the chances are that I will. If it means he's detained at whatever gathering or convocation he went to, then I won't, and I'll have to make a choice between staying over the weekend on the assumption he'll be back Monday, and going back to New York. Because you've got to get back to the office, and I don't want to stay around here all by myself. But if I do that, I know very well that sure as shootin' he'll show up bright and bushy-tailed Monday morning, just as eager as you please to see Professor Corey." She snickered. "Then he'll probably call me 'Irwin,' and be disappointed when he finds out that I don't do doubletalk."

"Well," he said, "I wouldn't get too down, if that's all that's bothering you. There's no new glitch in your candidacy. He has to come back sooner or later. Other people've told you he's prepared to like you, and I've known one or two in my time who liked you even though they weren't prepared at all. The job's still something that you want a lot, prime cut and all that, and as for going back for the weekend, well, if this place were a little closer to Tanglewood, or it was Columbus Day, and the entire region was a glorious blaze of breathtaking colors from Nature's choicest palette, well, Uriah Heep downstairs'd probably have the place reserved up to the rafters. He'd have to throw us out. But it's neither of those things, and although I do have to get back sometime at the front of next week and start cleaning up the stuff I'm working on, nobody's going to give me too much grief if that's not until early Tuesday afternoon or so, even Wednesday morning if it suits me.

"They're aware I'm thinking of leaving. I've been candid with them. I haven't been *entirely* candid with them, I'll admit, but that was only because I didn't want to march into Ed Birnam's office and as much as tell him that now that I've tried it out, I'm satisfied that the life that goes with working at the firm his grandfather founded isn't fit for a rational man. No point in offending people needlessly. I'll just call in Monday morning and tell them I'm going to need another day or so to talk to some more people. I won't be losing anything I wasn't going to give up anyway, as soon as I get back."

She gazed at him. "You've really done it, haven't you," she said.

"What?" he said.

"You've really made up your mind to take a sure partnership at a Wall Street law firm that you've mostly already earned, with a lot of damned hard work, one that'll almost certainly make you a million a year in ten years, and just chuck it and move to the country."

"I told you when we first talked about your job at Mount Holyoke that I seriously wanted to do it," he said. "You've known me long enough to know I'm a spoiled brat, and that when I get it into my head that I want to do something, I'll scream and stamp and hold my breath if that's what it takes. Why shouldn't I want to, anyway? Half the shining appeal of jobs in those noble houses is their inaccessibility to all except us few, we happy few, my little band of brothers, who have written evidence covering every year of our lives after our seventh birthdays, showing impeccable and spotless progress in all matters great and small, academic, athletic, intellectic—is there such a word? Should be—and legal. Who are mannerly but bold; sometimes gruff but always kind; faster than a speeding bullet when it comes to churning out a ten-page trial brief overnight, complete of course with quotes from cites and references to facts; and able to leap continents at single bounds without complaint, sometimes two or three of them in a single week.

"Well," he said, "I don't know what you've proven when you've spent six years proving those things about yourself, except that you're exactly the animal that any taxonomist would've said you were after a moment's inspection, but whatever it is, I've proven it. I am the very model of a modern junior partner, and when I've been one for a while, I'll be a senior partner, and then I will be the model of a modern senior partner. But some day I will still die, even though I've done those things, and I will not die happy.

"The dying part I'm not looking forward to, but I understand it's mandatory. The happiness is optional—you get to take that or waive it for yourself. I'm not signing the waiver, no, if that's what you're getting at. What I've got with you, what we've got together, is far more important to me than what I've got and what I will have with Birnam, Barkey and Morris.

"No one that I've talked to about doing this—including you, although of course for selfish reasons of your own, you might have a bias—has come up with more than one substantial argument against it. That argument is the money I'll give up if I leave Wall Street. Not good enough. It comes down to 'yer money or yer life.' I want the life.

"The second most popular argument is the one from Manhattan culture. It might be substantial if we were the types out at every Broadway opening, at every Met performance, at every single new exhibit at the Whitney or MOMA. But it's not, because we're not. The lions in front of the library are less social than we are—they were lying down there last night where they're lying down today, and the chances are that's where they'll be if you go by tonight; at least we move around some. But our movements mostly are between our dwelling place and work. Sure, we got to concerts, and sure, we got to plays, and yes it is a lot of fun to stroll Fifth Avenue.

"Well, I went through my desk diaries for the last two years. You know how many times we did such things of wonder and adult delight? Seven. We averaged three-point-five cultural weekend events a year. And there's no point in searching records further back, because we both know what they'd show: we scarcely went out at all; we were working day and night. Culture-vultures we are not—more like sparrows I'd say.

"The only other argument's the mirror of the money. It comes under various labels, such as 'being on the cutting edge,' 'prestige,' and 'fast-lane legal practice.' Other names for power. True enough, no question: that practice opens doors. But doors to what? To Washington? To Treasury? The SEC, or maybe the Federal Reserve Board? Does it matter that I don't want to run the country, or the state? Or the city or a borough, or the Port Authority? Don't want 'em.

"I guess thirty's early for the mid-life crisis," he said. "I guess I'm prematurely critical. But that's okay—I'll take it." He paused. "You aren't having misgivings, now, are you?"

"No," she said, hesitantly. "I was just *stunned* when you told me you were ready to pack it in at Birnam and move up here with me, now, lock, stock, and barrel. I lost my train of thought completely, forgot all I'd planned to say. It was the virgin professor's first-day nightmare: she goes into her first real lecture, and she draws a total blank. I don't know a single person that that's ever happened to, but neither do I know a single one who hasn't been absolutely terrified it would. It's only funny afterward. Well, with me, with you, that night, it happened. I froze and drew a total blank.

"You see what I mean?" she said. "Ever since we came up here I've been getting more and more afraid that even though you certainly seemed enthusiastic about the idea, getting more so every day, actually you were doing something for my sake to be good to me—as you always are, so it's your fault I thought that. And I kept thinking: 'My God, what if he does it and comes up here, and after a year he just hates it and he can't stand it anymore? He'll have lost something most men would kill to get, and once he does it, once he quits, they'll never take him back. All the rest of his life he'll be stuck here in the woods, when he could have stayed right where he was. It didn't need to happen.'

"I don't want you doing things for my sake, Joe," she said. "That's all I'm saying. I want you doing things for me, as I want to do things for you, but I'll never do anything solely for your sake that will make me sad and bitter just so you'll be happy, and I never want you to do anything like that for me, so that you can't be happy." She paused. "Sure, I've talked a lot about Gampy's death. It's, I don't know, baffled me? Puzzled me? I don't know. It's just always been at the back of my mind. My mother, my aunt, my grandmother: all these nice, refined, cultured ladies, well-to-do, cultivated, all that, and right smack in the middle of their history—which is mine, after all—is this unsolved murder, like some Gothic novel. Well, if he was killed, *why* was he killed? Revenge? Jealousy, what? Or if it was suicide, why did *he* do it? Embezzlement? Insanity? I don't know." She sighed. "But that's not enough reason for you to junk a bright future, just because of that stuff."

"Yes it is," he said. "Especially if the bargain is a better life for me. I'm not faking this excitement. Now I'm finally doing what I was meant to do."

"Yes you are, you son of a bitch," she said. "And I'm still technically up in the air."

11

Ned Polland had become chief managing partner of Birnam, Barkey and Morris two weeks before his forty-second birthday, in January of 1979, making him the youngest man, by a margin of slightly less than three years, ever to hold that position. In his first decade of service, he had performed so passionlessly, evenly, efficiently, and calmly in the allocation of responsibilities, obligations, burdens, perquisites, and firm resources that only the few senior partners remaining active after it remembered that his sudden promotion had been forced by the stunning collapse and hospitalization of his predecessor due to chronic alcoholic toxemia that had become acute over the Christmas holidays.

Ned Polland was aggressively familial. The credenza behind his big, neat desk was crowded with photographs of his wife and seven children, and now and then, himself. They were pictured playing tennis, softball, boating, picnicking at the family home just up the Hudson, skiing at Tremblant and rafting on the Colorado. "And that's the way he thinks of the firm," Joe told Jill. "It's his second family, and when somebody junior to him in it flouts his wishes, it can't be just a career decision he's made—it's a violation of the commandment to honor your parents."

"Ned," Corey said, settling himself into the maroon leather wing chair facing the desk and crossing his legs at the knee. "I had a brief conversation with Ed, 'fore I left, told him I was thinking I might leave."

Polland nodded once. "Ed told me," he said. He arched his eyebrows. He frowned and looked down at his desk blotter. He rolled one of two freshly sharpened pencils toward the middle, and then rolled it back to the edge. He pursed his lips. "I don't mind telling you, Joe, I have to admit I was shocked."

"Shocked?" Corey said. "Surprise I could understand. But not *shock*."

Polland tilted his head to the left and then brought it back to vertical. "Well, Joe," he said, "all I can say then is that you haven't been here as long. I've been with this firm now twenty-nine years, three decades as of next June. Now that's no record for longevity, of course, compared to a Fred Barkey, say, approaching his sixtieth year. His father before him worked seventy years, and Ed Birnam's grandfather gave nearly that. You've been here now for only six years, so of course you can't have our perspective. But I can tell you, from what I know of this place, what you mentioned is shocking in this context. No one, people just don't do, haven't done, what you suggested you might decide to do, and leave."

"But people leave here all the time," Corey said. "I don't mean it's a steady parade out the door, but fourteen of us came in together as associates six years ago July, and the last time I looked, only four of us were left. Ten people must've left; there's no other explanation. And that was just my class of 'eighty-three—I haven't kept a tally, but up until the market went flat back in 'eighty-seven, about the same size groups came in each summer after us, and the same numbers left."

"Joe, *Joe*," Polland said, "that's not the same thing, and you know it." There was real anguish in his voice.

"And of course it isn't," Joe told Jill that night. "When the managing partner comes around to your cubicle after three years and tells you you're never going to make it past associate, which is the same as saying 'Beat it,' that's for the good of the firm. But when you tell Ned Polland that you're getting out, for your *own* good, that's just plain selfishness."

"He looked at me like something he stepped in on the sidewalk because some dirty rotten scofflaw hadn't pooper-scooped his Saint Bernard." They sat in the living room of their apartment in Chelsea, the air conditioners cycling in response to brown-out fluctuations in the current supply, not in accordance with changes of their thermostats, so that intermittent draughts of cooled air passed through the room and emphasized the leaden humidity of the undisturbed air mass, their chairs surrounded by cartons of the books she had stripped from the vacant shelving gaping on all sides of them.

"He pulled out my file from under his blotter and told me the firm'd spent four hundred and thirty-six thousand dollars on me before I made junior partner. I guess when partners become partners, they forget how all associates keep mental figures on the difference between what the firm pays to them and for them and what the firm collects on their billings per hour. 'And I reckon,' I said, 'that the firm made a profit of three hundred and eighty thousand dollars on that investment, which is a darned good return, Ned—eighty-eight percent, averaged over three years, is an annual return of almost thirty percent. Very few stocks or bonds pay that rate.'

"He closed my file like the door to a dirty toilet, took the glasses from his nose, and began to rub it. 'Yes,' he said. 'Well, I see your mind's made up and there's no point in pursuing this further.'

"And there wasn't," Joe said to Jill. "I went to lunch really resentful. When I got back there was a note on my desk to see Ed."

Heard you and Ned had a little chat this morning, Joe," Birnam said when he had swallowed a mouthful of potato chips. He habitually ate lunch at his desk, explaining: "It's because I'm cheap, and anyway, I like greasy food that my wife and my doctor won't let me eat. So I don't, where they can see me." He bent and drew the leather-bound wastebasket around from the right side of the desk, swept the sandwich wrapper and the potato-chip bag off the desk into it, steered it back into position, sat back in his chair and stared with amusement at Corey standing in front of his desk. "Well, sit down, sit down," he said, "the damned thing isn't booby-trapped, you know. At least it isn't yet. If Ned gets in here after-hours, it may be tomorrow."

Corey sat down. "Ned wants you hailed in on charges of desertion," Birnam said. "He was a little agitated, so I'm not entirely sure whether he means the military version, of your troops while under fire, or the surrogate's division, of your loved ones under wedlock. Either way, though, there isn't any doubt: he wants it to go hard with you. I think he'll settle for less than confinement at hard labor, but forfeiture of all pay and allowances is definitely in his plans. Gettin' sand in your shoes, lad, are ye?"

Corey shrugged. "So it appears, Ed," he said. "You know my views on all my friends here. Till today I thought Ned was one of them. I was steaming when I left his office, but I calmed down some over lunch. Now I'm beginning to feel somewhat silly. What's all the uproar about? I didn't come back here from my vacation with any plans for disruption at all. My wife got an offer she couldn't refuse, and the god-father would never renew it. I want to go with her and try something new. Maybe I'm having the change of life early, but really, it's not a big deal. I haven't gone nuts. I'm not mad at a soul. I've had a good time here. I've learned. And now I think the time has come to go and learn something brand new. Simple."

Birnam frowned. "Well," he said, "I wish it were. I mean, I know it is for you. And I envy you that fact. But it isn't simple for Ned Polland, and it won't be for some of the others. I hope you'll understand when it gets hard."

"Hard on me or hard on them?" Corey said. "Even though I still don't see why it needs to be hard on anyone."

"Hard on them at first," Birnam said, "and then because

they, several of them at least, will resent the hardship on themselves, and hold you responsible for creating it, after that they will make it hard on you." He sighed. "Well, it can't be helped, I guess." He leaned forward and rested his elbows and forearms on the desk.

"This thing that you wanted to look into when you went up there," he said. "It's some kind of murder case, right?"

"More'n that," Corey said. "It's a murder case in the family. My wife's family, that is."

"And it fascinates you," Birnam said.

" 'Strongly interests me' might be a better phrase," Corey said. "It's new and different, you know?"

Birnam smiled. "Would be from my point of view, at least," he said. "Never had one of those in my life. Don't think the whole firm ever has. Or wanted one, far as that goes, but *chacun à son gout*'s what I say.

"But *anyway*," he said, "moving right along here, even though I can't see a way in the world that this case of yours or any other puzzle you might manage to come up with in the tangled woods for the next twenty years or so could possibly involve a client we've had here, you still come under the Roger Rule, you know. Have to itemize and summarize every matter that you've worked on since you first walked in our door. Dreary business, but we can't have one of our clients suing us for violation of the attorney-client privilege on the grounds someone who used to be here is now using what he learned here to make life exciting somewhere else."

"I knew about the rule," Corey said. "I didn't realize it was known as the Roger Rule."

"Only to blood relatives of mine," Birnam said. "Inside-family joke. Roger's my brother, nine years older. By the time I showed up, Roger'd had most of the advantages and all of the detriments of being the only son and the eldest child to boot. My father was a great respecter of women, and he doted on his daughters, but his considered view was that men quite properly controlled and managed the affairs of the world, and therefore should be brought up from the cradle preparing to accept their responsibilities and to discharge them magisterially. If not majestically.

"I don't think Dad was by any means displeased when I came along, I don't mean that. He did his very best to bring me up exactly the same way he'd raised Roger. But I grew up as the spare son, you know? The bullpen pitcher. Hope you never need him, but got him if you do.

"Roger was thirty-three when I joined the firm," Birnam said. "If he had fallen from the sky he would've been acclaimed a shooting star, and deserved it, too. Roger is a brilliant man, much smarter than I am, six-two, prematurely greying at the temples even then, married to a gorgeous woman, devoted to each other and their three perfect children, among them Dad's first grandson, named Roger the Fourth, of course. In every possible respect my brother was the spitting image of the heartthrob actor that Central Casting sends over to your studio when you call up and tell them that you've got a script that calls for a man to play a U.S. senator embarking on a hopeless presidential campaign that everyone who sees him on the silver screen will know from the first instant he's a dead-sure bet to win. His specialty was bond law, and there wasn't a major city, state, or federal official between here and Waikiki who didn't recognize his name and genuflect by reflex when he heard it.

"I was in the yacht club one day, my second or third year with the firm, bag-toting for my father at some luncheon conference with a couple of his high-powered banking clients, ánd one of them started exclaiming over some routine act of genius Roger'd just pulled off: 'That son of yours, Roger,' he said, 'I don't mind telling you, I don't care how old he is, when that young man gets up to speak, every man jack in the room knows without a question that he's listening to a future Treasury secretary, SEC chairman, or head, Federal Reserve.' Dad never batted an eye. He nodded, once, and said: 'Thank you. Very proud of him, of course. As I am of Ed.' And segued smooth as silk drawers right into the conference topic.

"Have you ever felt chills and fever simultaneously? Can't say I ever have. But that day I had two feelings at once that made me blush and tremble. The blush was for the compliment. Dad never, but never, said he was pleased with something you'd done, let alone proud of you. Not where you could hear him. And he'd just said that about me. But I also knew that the only reason he'd said it was because I was there, and like a flash I knew at last *why* I was there, too: Dad'd long since reached the same conclusion about Roger that his friend'd stated, except that most likely Dad in his private projections probably hadn't seen any reason why Roger's gifts shouldn't take him somewhat further than a mere cabinet post—why not be the man who *picks* the people for the cabinet? The one who lives in the big white house, and has the Marine band in for teatime. And so now I *was* being warmed up, the relief pitcher, ready to take over when my brother headed down the Jersey Turnpike to his date with destiny.

"Then a funny thing happened," Birnam said. "Jack Kennedy came along, and Bobby right after him, right on his heels, and Roger's steady progress toward a patrician, Republican Valhalla of his own got shunted off onto a siding. By Roger himself. He became inflamed by the desire to do good, so much so that he refused to put off the day when he began to do it. He decided for some antic reason that he had to put aside his personal ambitions, by which I mean the muscular habits of greed bred into him as surely as his intellect and physique had been, and proceed at once to Washington to work for cab-fare wages and integrate the South. The public schools, the state universities, the lunchrooms and bus stops. Here he'd been nurtured in an atmosphere of relentless hostility to Big Government that pokes its nose into everybody's business and must be thwarted every time if the Republic's to be saved, and what was he doing? Heading off to join the enemy and make common cause with a bunch of colored riffraff and rabble-rousers hell-bent for election to enlist the government in a total revolution to destroy a way of life. Dad'd always been generous to the United Negro College Fund and the Urban League, but this was going too far. And Roger would not budge.

"Things were strained in the family manse when Roger and Gail brought the kids home for holidays, but that was nothing compared to the tension around here. A Birnam jumping ship? Unthinkable. But it meant that something had to be done fast to make sure Roger didn't crank up his new power at Justice against a client of the firm. And thus the Roger Rule.

"Now, the reason I'm telling you this," Birnam said, "is because after a while, Bobby decided he needed Roger more in the racketeering section, the organized crime thing there. Chasing the mafia. Roger, of course, ever the good soldier, agreed to it in a jiffy. Started off with the Hoffa pursuit, working with people who'd chased Dave Beck, too, in order to get his feet wet. Well, Dad still didn't exactly approve of what Roger was doing, but the circles that he moved in weren't exactly hotbeds of warm sentiment for Teamsters, so he could at least shrug it off—it wasn't quite as bad as seeing Roger on TV, insulting southern governors and excoriating cops. And Roger liked that assignment even more; stayed with it until he retired.

"Now, not that Roger's ever said much about what he happened to be doing, but from the little he's let out, I doubt there's been a murder case in this Republic that somebody or other didn't try at one time or another to blame on the mob."

"Until he said that," Corey said to Jill that night, "got that expression on his face, I thought the whole conversation was just Ed's studied tactic for calming me down, stroking me some, giving me hints for placating Ned, so that maybe if I tried, I could finish my string out in peace. That he was just trying to give me some perspective on things, so there wouldn't be any more rancor than there absolutely had to be until I cleaned out my desk and departed. Well, I'd been mistaken."

Birnam exhaled loudly, puffing his cheeks and vibrating his lips like a horse blowing after a race. "Sometimes," he said, "they've been right. After the Teamsters, Roger moved on to the Meyer Lansky squad, the mafia's general comptroller. And when he dug into the Lansky snakepit, what Lansky'd done with the money he placed for the Honored Society, he began to approach some of our biggest clients. Their capital accounts were involved."

"Ahh," Corey said.

"At first we had no inkling of the extent of the thing," Birnam said. "We were a bit nonplussed, of course, when one of our clients called here in hysterics because their Chicago regional headquarters'd been hit with a subpoena *duces tecum* demanding all their financial records for the previous three years, because we'd never had the slightest reason to suspect it of being a mob front. We figured it was just a coincidence that the subpoena was signed by Roger Birnam."

He snorted. "Yeah," he said, "just an odd coincidence. Well, you try telling that to a client whose company's been represented for over sixty years by Birnam, Barkey and Morris. You just try to convince the chief executive officer and the president of the board of directors and the chairman of the executive board that Roger Birnam didn't fall back on one single thing he'd learned as a lawyer in this firm when he drafted that subpoena that zeroed in, bingo, on questionable dealings by a company that'd been a client of ours while he was here. It's not an easy sell.

"In fact, it can't be done. For over a year, close to sixteen months, not a bloody week went by but that we weren't called to battle stations because Roger and his marauders, broadcasting subpoenas across the country like Johnny Appleseed planting trees across the fruited plain, had hit another client of ours. Dad and I almost lost our minds. We weren't rigged for that kind of duty. Criminal proceedings never were and never will be the kind of law we do. We had to call in criminal defense firms from here to San Francisco, to deal with those damned subpoenas. We had bar association problems by the barrow load. The only thing that saved us from insanity was Meyer Lansky's thoughtfulness—he died before they could get him to trial, and Roger moved on to some other hood, far removed from everyday commerce.

"Well," Birnam said, "that's not going to happen again. Ever. And that's why the Roger Rule.

"But," he said, "in your case, that history might by some stretch of the imagination be helpful. If what you find out in the course of your investigation of your wife's family death begins to smell like mob, it'd help you a lot to have access to the kind of knowledge Roger has. He's retired, but his memory's still in very good shape. So, if you like, I'll arrange for you to meet him before you leave here. And with that connection, well, you can check out such things in a flash."

"That's very nice of you, Ed," Corey said. "I appreciate it."

Birnam shrugged. "I don't want you to infer from Ned's reaction that your decision to leave makes you persona non grata at this firm. It doesn't. You're a distinguished alumnus. If we gave out cards like the unions do, yours would read: 'honorable withdrawal.' And it could be that someday we might find we need somebody up in your forest, Robin Hood, someone whom we know and trust, to handle a matter for us there. We have people like that in the Hamptons, in Europe and England and so forth, and they share our action while they help us. It makes for a lovely arrangement."

"Corresponding counsel, in other words," Corey said.

"That," Birnam said, "or 'of counsel' or something—as long as connections are made. We've got a fair number of pins in the map of the territory up around Lenox. Some of our bigger clients like music. They're a little too old for scrapes with police, and their major work's done in this office. But they all have property up in those hills, and they also have heirs presumptive and unruly kinfolk who require counsel from time to time. It's already been decided that among other locations, we really ought to have a liaison there, to comfort the afflicted and keep them out of our hair while they're on vacation, and we're trying to be. We don't have such a person in mind. We already know you and like you. I'll bring it up at the next planning session, if that's all right with you."

"More than all right," Corey said. "I'd appreciate it."

"Good enough," Birnam said. "Now, after Brother Roger retired from doing his Eliot Ness thing, he went to work for an outfit called ISIS, Intelligence Systems and Internal Security Company, headquartered down in Virginia. What they do is consult with global conglomerates about how to keep their businesses clean. So the mob, or the drug smugglers, if there's a difference, don't sneak into their boardrooms and get them in trouble with whoever's got Roger's old job now. We, our clients, use them a lot. Full circle, huh? Life's funny.

"Anyway, Roger's still bored. If this thing that you're working on looks to him as though it might be something along his line, I'm sure he'd like to help you out, in any way he can. Roger left this operation because civilian life was quiet. Now he's back in it again, and he's found that it's still quiet. We've got a meeting in two weeks with the family trustees here, over at the Morgan Bank. When he comes up I'll broach it to him, see how he reacts. But I think maybe I know. You two are a lot alike."

12

At 4:10 p.m. the last stragglers among the membership of the luncheon club had left the restaurant of the Windows on the World on the 107th floor of the north tower of the World Trade Center, and Corey, polishing the lines of his excuse for tardiness as he came out of the elevator, was relieved to find no one but a young male bartender in the lounge area. He took a seat at a table overlooking the southeastern tip of Manhattan where the East River, its surface flat and greyish-blue metallic, seemed motionless and molten under the dull haze of the late heat of the day, and waited for the air-conditioning to relieve the pounding in his head.

He had not been prepared for Roger Birnam's call. In the two weeks since he had returned from Shropshire, he had not had time or energy to reflect on much of anything but the relentless tedium of recapitulating every task that he had undertaken at Birnam, Barkey and Morris since he had emerged like a stunned animal from the two-day bar examination into his first day's work seventy-four months before. He had spent fourteen consecutive days at it, leaving the apartment in the mornings as the *New York Times* delivery van moved at crawl speed up the street, the papers in their blue plastic sleeves lofting out and up from an unseen hand into the still air already relinquishing the coolness of the dark to the ascending heat and then tumbling down more or less in the vicinity of subscribers' doorways. He had mechanically made his way around elderly women furtively curbing small dogs in the sunrise in pitiable evasion of the ordinance requiring them to collect and dispose of the feces, mindlessly noting the cool urine smell that floated out of the alleys, enduring without complaint the jostling he got boarding the buses with the large black women and quick-stepping Hispanic men going home from night shifts on cleaning crews, hoping only to retain his wallet.

The Pakistani counterman at the Dunkin' Donuts persisted in what Corey surmised were his daily efforts to promote the sale of lemon Danish with Corey's purchase of two large coffees with cream, undeterred by Corey's daily refusal. "At least I assume that's what he's got on his mind, and I think he's a Pakistani," Corey said to Dale Restic, the associate assigned to monitor and countersign his inventory of the files. "His command of English is about midway between the jabber of the average cabbie and the patter of the guys who run the corner store and've learned most of the words they need, but not the order they go in. I prefer the jabber myself. If you can't understand any of it, then you don't get yourself all confused trying to make sense of some of it. It's easier on a man's nerves."

He felt sorry for Dale. "She's a very diffident watchdog," he told Jill. "She doesn't know quite what to do, what to make of this assignment. I suppose when I was two years out of law school, I would've been timid myself, stuck with a detail like this one. She's as bright as hell—she was third in her class at Chicago, and a star undergrad at Northwestern—or she wouldn't be where she is, but she's also human, like I was. Like I guess that I used to be. Here she's been banging around from pillar to post the first two years of her probation and orientation, so as soon as she's gotten her bearings in one thing and learned what this new partner wants, she's been Ping-Ponged into a new section, and all she's been able to do during all of it's been the same thing I did: pray for the strength to endure the ordeal, and just hope she strikes pay dirt in some field, so they won't tie the can to her tail. One more year to go, and now what happens to her? She gets yanked off the treadmill to watch me, and then when I get through and leave, back she'll go to the rockpile again, to serve out the rest of her term.

"It's tough on her," he said. "In the past three years I guess I'd forgotten the mystical awe that you have in your first three for the senior associates over you. The ones who have made it, survived the gauntlet—they look like partners to you. Every day you have to restrain yourself from going up to them and asking if it'd be all right if you just touched them once, the hem of their garment or something. Because that might impart their secret to you: how to become one of the big three or four who sail through on to security. It must be very confusing for her, to be plopped down to watch, day after day, while someone who captured the grail she's so hungrily after goes methodically about the ritual purgation of washing his hands of the prize, renouncing what she desperately wants. She must think I'm nuts."

"Maybe you are," Jill said. "Maybe we both are. Maybe we should not only've faithfully renewed our subscriptions to *New York* and the *New Yorker*, but actually read the damned things. Maybe it doesn't count if you just move them from the mailbox to the hall table to the coffee table to the floor beside the flush, but never read them. Maybe it's like being admitted to the select company that lolls on the Isle of the Blessed, and then when the naiads come 'round with ambrosia, saying: 'No thanks, but could I have a Coke?' Maybe we didn't enjoy it, you know, because we just never *enjoyed*? Maybe this move's a great big mistake."

He pointedly surveyed the chaos of the apartment. Large cardboard boxes sealed with shiny, fibrous, ivory tape—Jill, not knowing what to call it, had asked the clerk in the hardware store for "ten rolls of that wide tape that bonds to the box so no power on earth can remove it," and he'd instantly known what she meant—were stacked two and three high in three rows of seven columns each between the fireplace and the hall door, leaving a passageway wide enough for one person to pass between the living room and the kitchen beyond. "I don't think so," he said.

She smiled. "You're not having second thoughts, then," she said.

"Well," he said, "I wouldn't go that far, go so far as to say that. But the kind that I'm having, when I get the odd minute to do some actual reflection, they aren't about: 'Am I doing the right thing, walking out of the Garden of Eden?' They're about: 'How did I ever get into this sorry mess?' "

She touched his arm. "Come on, Joe," she said. "I know you're protective, and I know you don't want me to have any doubts, or think you're just going along, but what you're giving up here is no throwaway line, no disposable pie tin or something. It's a very good job, with a very bright future, and anyone would feel a twinge."

"Well, I guess I'm not anyone, then," he said. "The only second thoughts I have are the kind an outsider would have as first thoughts, given my new view of my job. Good Lord, woman, when you just look at what I have to go through to rid myself of it, to get out of this enviable job, without even considering any of the ratcheting that I had to go through to get it, the only possible conclusion you can come to is that anyone who voluntarily subjects himself to such servitude must suffer from a congenital and pathological condition of submissiveness. Chronic meekness, aggravated by periods of compulsive timidity, characterized by obsessive and fawning obsequiousness. 'Patient incoherent at times; complains of delay in receipt of earth he expects to inherit.'

"Think about it," he said. "All right, so I like Ed Birnam. He's always been square with me. He was my sponsor, if any one partner was, the man who got me the job. He's been my mentor since I started. He's seen to it I made a good wage, and he shepherded me to the fast track. Okay, he's a very nice man.

"But now consider what Ed got for doing it. He likes me as much as I like him, enjoys my presence at work. I've always

121

been square in my dealings with Ed, and I've repaid his sponsorship loyally. I justified his claims about me. I asked his advice when I needed advice, and I followed it, each jot and tittle. I earned every dollar of that good wage, a good many of them several times over. And Ed's motive for taking me to second level was a composite of all of those things.

"I call that an even swap," he said. "A good bargain for both parties to it. So where on earth do you find a provision that compels me now to do this? I never heard of it, not since Day One, this abject procedure I have to endure for formal release from my vows. I never took any vows. What makes me submit to this crap? Why didn't I tell Ed to cram it?"

"Because," she said slowly, "you're smart enough to know that if you leave on friendly terms, he might do something nice for you later."

"Might," he said, "right. And also might not, I might add."

"True," she said, "but if you *don't* leave on friendly terms— as friendly as possible, at least—you *know* for certain he'll do something *to* you, something that you won't like."

"Yeah," he said. "But it's like accepting an invitation to swim in the nice blue warm water of Captain Nemo's secret cove and grotto, and then finding yourself in the grasp of that monstrous octopus that banged up the *Nautilus* for him."

Roger Birnam made a stately entrance into the bar at the Windows at 4:50 P.M.. He had abundant silver hair and deeply tanned craggy features that framed sniper's grey eyes, and wore his dark grey, light wool suit with louche elegance. He selected Corey on his first scan of the room and approached the table with a lounging stride that Corey had seen practiced elsewhere only by middle-aged gentlemen wearing tweeds and grey flannels, escorting younger women on cool Sunday mornings along the left embankment of the Seine. He inclined his head and said: "Joseph Corey, am I right?"

"I stood up at once, of course," Corey said to Jill that night. "He'd kept me waiting fifty minutes, far as he knew, at least, and all that I could think of was showing due respect to him. I tell you, I'm getting servile. My mother'd be astonished to see it. My father would be, well, disgusted."

"Did he give you a reason?" she said.

"No," he said. "At least, not in so many words. He languidly uttered a mild imprecation at 'bankers who take the whole afternoon to deliver reports you could read in about thirty minutes,' and I supposed, for my craven part, I could take that for an apology. Or not take it, if I liked—all one to him. Monarchs by eternal decree are on time, whenever they choose to arrive."

Birnam viewed Corey's San Pellegrino water and lime and instructed the waiter to bring him a Bombay Gibson, "two onions."

"I decided I'd either better assert myself pretty soon," Corey told Jill, "or else drop to my knees in front of his feet and lick all the sidewalk grime off them. I ordered an Absolut gimlet."

Birnam displayed a small smile that had been in his family for generations. "Ed tells me," he said, "that you're jumping ship. May I ask what provoked your decision? It's a fairly unusual one."

" 'An old murder case,' I said, 'a twenty-year-old murder case.' And then I told him in summary," Corey said to Jill. "What you told me. What Oldham said, and Amelia. And what Burt Magoun said, and what Baldo said. I rambled some, but not long. It was all right. The bar was filling up with men and women who arrived alone and joined other men and women who'd waited at the entrance, or taken tables but not ordered, and I felt like I was adding the oboe part to a concerto for discretionary instruments and bass disinformation. He didn't actually comment, unless you count the nod that told me when he'd now heard enough from me to make it quite impossible for me to judge, ever, how much Ed had told him first."

"The facts as you describe them," Birnam said, "assuming that there are no others that would flatly contradict them, suggest quite strongly to me that Warren Oldham's right. I know Warren. I've known him, oh, it must be thirty years and more. He was a young trooper when I first came across him. An ancillary matter in his jurisdiction that we thought might be related to the Maggadino operation we'd unearthed in Buffalo. It was, but its connection was too tenuous to justify diversion of our meager staff to add it to our case. And in the context, well, it wasn't big enough. At most it would've been a makeweight for our main case, a big sports-action network; the layoff men in Warren's woods weren't close enough to the center to make them tempting targets. Even if we'd made them talk, they wouldn't've known enough about the kingpins we were after to make it worth our while.

"So," he said, hesitating while he turned his glass and made the white pearl onions swim, "we triaged what he had and we went with what we had, on the understanding that if he could get resources from his regional D.A., a couple of sharp lawyers and two or three more cops, say, we'd turn over what we had to make his case complete." He frowned, picked up the glass and swallowed a third of his drink. "He couldn't, of course. Get the added manpower. He was very sour about it, bitter, in fact, and I gathered from what he said, there wasn't much question in his mind but that someone was in the bag."

He gazed at Corey. "This was not an uncommon discovery in those days," he said. "The nature of my chief assignment, and the broad scope of Mister Lansky's activities, more or less compelled me to inspect all prosecutions, all investigations, all across the country, in order to ascertain whether any one of them had unwittingly come up with something that would improve my case on him. So I was something of a free lance, by necessity, and as such I saw a lot of most remarkable situ-

124

ations which seemed to me to warrant the across-the-board conclusion that Mister Lansky never aided any local boss until he had been satisfied that police and prosecution forces had been neutralized, and posed no threat to him. The situation Warren outlined matched that template perfectly. His dark view was the correct one; it was justified.

"The incident that you describe dovetails perfectly with the classic pattern in such cases. An actually unsophisticated but materially successful man mistakes the wealth and power he's acquired in his own community, that he understands, and knows, for experience sufficient to enable him to deal with men who have no principles, on fair and equal terms. Time and time again I've seen it: a good and rich man come a-cropper to the point of facing jail time if he won't talk, or assassination if he does, because he labored under the impression that his deeds in legal commerce, tough, hard-nosed lawful business, qualified him to contend with gangsters on their terms. It's as though you trained a stray cat to use a litter box, and decided that qualified you to train tigers. Pleasing to the ego, but unrealistic, and therefore extremely dangerous. Disaster almost always comes next."

"So," Jill said, "what he said is that my grandfather was killed because he got mixed up with the mob. Well, maybe he's right, maybe not. I didn't know him, but my mother did, and she'll doubt it. Jim Mandeville may've been a big show-off, and he may've flaunted his money. But from what she's said, he wasn't a fool, and I doubt he acted like one."

"Roger Birnam," he said, "did not say he was. Although of course he didn't know him either. What he said was that he could understand those men, men like your grandfather was, because he'd seen so many of them."

"It's not because a prominent man gets too big for his britches that he falls victim to them," Birnam said. "They're able to play smart, shrewd men for suckers because they don't look like what they are. Most people, most businessmen, when they think of gangsters, see caricatures. Men in black suits, wearing white-on-white shirts and looking a lot like George Raft. Wearing big hats—Borsalinos, most likely—violin cases with machine guns in them; bosomy blondes on their arms. Your first-generation gunsels, in other words, maybe at the most your second-generation gunsels.

"Well, those guys've gone to their Godfather in the sky. The trollers that reel in straight-arrow businessmen now're at least third-, usually fourth-generation, hoodlums, and they're chameleons. Throw one of these guys on a plaid blanket and inside of thirty seconds you wouldn't be able to see him, unless you could still spot his eyes. The only difference between what they're offering and what your regular banker or broker is peddling, is absolute confidentiality, no reporting, no disclosure, no tiresome nothing like that, that leads to reports in *Banker and Tradesman*, or notes in your Dun and Bradstreet file, alerting your creditors and your competition that you've come up with something new and hot. Oh, there's a price for the service, of course, but just the one they tell you in the beginning, all in exchange for a small extra charge: one or two points over market. That's maybe not exorbitant, if discretion's of the utmost importance. Well worth the money, in fact.

"But that's not all of it. The bargain stands only until something happens that makes it more profitable for them to eject you from the deal than it is to keep you in it. 'Ejection' being a term to describe whatever it takes to make you disappear and leave them in control of the plunder, more profit than they expected, when you made the original deal. If you're a sucker for women, or maybe for boys, and you can't take a scandal, well, that's it. If you like to gamble, but aren't too good at it, that will be what they do. One way or another they'll grind you down, until you give them what they want. *But*, if you're a tough nut, an upstanding fellow, no shameful vices to work with, solvent enough to keep your end of the deal up, as honest with them as you've always been in dealing with the straight-arrows, well then, this calls for cordite, which they have lots of, and for your abrupt departure from this world. Nothing personal; just necessary.

"Now," Birnam said, "I don't like those fellas. With me it's not personal either. I don't think they contribute much to the operation and commerce of an orderly society, going out of their way to cripple and ruin, and sometimes even kill, perfectly respectable citizens who weren't even trying to steal anything."

"It's a quirk of yours," Corey said.

Birnam presented the left half of a grin. "Yeah," he said, "you could say that, I guess. A personal eccentricity. I'm retired now, in theory, but that little twitch isn't. I still get annoyed when I run up against something funny that makes me think someone got screwed."

"I think I've got a mild case of the same disease," Corey said. "Early symptoms, maybe. There's not a thing wrong with the work I've been doing for Ed and the rest of the firm, but the hallmark of it is that it's all formal. Just follow the rules, and cross all the t's, make sure the i's have been dotted, and some government drone, no reflection on you, says: 'This looks all right,' and he time-stamps it in, and it is."

"No offense taken," Birnam said, "I know the feeling myself. It's basically why I left the firm. The work paid me well, but it was stultifying. I understood why all those rules are in place, and I know people need lawyers to handle them. But they didn't need this one; they didn't need me. Any damned lawyer would do. So I cleared out, like you're doing: much consternation. Hand-wringing and gnashing of teeth.

"Now look," he said. "I'm out of the loop now. I'm retired. I'm sick of the road and cheap motels, and too old for cases I can't prove. But I still have some access that you'll never have, and it's access I think you may need. These guys you've signed on with: the D.A. and this Baldo, whoever he is, I never heard of those two, and I don't know who you are, either. And I'm not about to start ransacking files to get data for guys I don't know. So what I need to know is if you're willing to agree to let me run you. Through our computers. All three of you, to see if you're all right. One wrong number, you're all out the door. I need DOBs for that, as well as places, dates, and places of birth. S.S. numbers, too, if you can. I can do it without them, but they make it easier. Think you can manage that much? Will that be all right with you people?"

Corey shrugged. "It's fine by me," he said. "Burt Magoun was a fed and since then a D.A.; I can't see why Burt would object. And Baldo's retired from Defense Intelligence, so he must've been through this before."

Birnam sniffed. "No reflection on him," he said, "but when somebody tells me he had Q-level in that place, Fort Fumble, I mean, I run him through twice if he's clean the first time. They give Q to car parkers in that joint."

"Well," Corey said, "all I can say is I'll ask him. I'll see him this weekend. I'll call you on Tuesday, if that's all right. And I really appreciate this."

Birnam delivered the whole grin. "Odd you should mention it," he said. "So do I. This looks like an old one that slipped through the cracks. Be kind of fun to do a wake-up call on some complacent bad guys I somehow missed when I was active." Then the grin disappeared. "You're sure about this now, I hope," he said. "I hope you know what you're doing. It's a frustrating business, and those people are tough. They've been at it a long time, have lots of resources, no scruples, the patience of Satan. I had manpower, the very best, unlimited money, grand juries. I could *make* people talk, I could put them in jail. I could be just as patient as they were, and I was, and they still managed to avoid my clutches—not all, but a good many of them. And I was working fairly fresh ground, sometimes right on their heels, not trying to exhume a twenty-year-old case that got fouled up when it occurred.

You'd better know what you're getting into here. You'd best be prepared for what's coming, and to leave behind what you're leaving."

"Well," Corey said, "if I'm not now, I may never be. Tomorrow's my last day of this life."

The next night, when Corey returned to the apartment after 8:45, there was a U-Haul truck double-parked in front of the building, an aluminum ramp leading up to the rear doorway. Rock music that he did not recognize blared from the dim interior of the cargo box, and someone who he could not see said: "Well, it's never gonna happen till the Martians come and capture Steinbrenner and tie him up with a big rope, and take him to Saturn, that's all." He climbed the steps into the hallway.

In the living room, four large young men and a slender woman, all in cutoff jeans and tee-shirts silk-screened with such advice as "Live by Day, Love by Night, Kill by Profession," and "Do It in the Road," perched and roosted in boneless positions on the furniture and floor, drinking Bud Light from cans and laughing derisively at something said just before he came through the open door. There were two stained pizza cartons on the floor, piled with soiled paper napkins. The wall of cardboard cartons was gone, and all the bookshelves were empty. For an instant he thought in wild embarrassment that he had wandered into the wrong building, perhaps even chosen the wrong street, in his automatic state of mental numbness after the long, last day, ritual drinks and dry-eyed farewells.

"Mister Corey?" the woman said. When he tried to speak, he found his lips dry, and licked them quickly as he nodded. "Professor Corey's in the bedroom," she said. "She said she didn't have time to finish before we got here. She said for us to have a beer while she puts all the clothes in boxes." He nodded again. One of the young men, the pigtail of his long, curly blond hair secured at the nape of his neck by an elastic band, said: "We're the looters, Mister Corey. From the school, the summer session?"

Corey found his voice. "Ahh," he said. "Ah, well, I didn't . . . I thought you were coming tomorrow. Tomorrow night, I mean."

"We were," the woman answered. Jill emerged from the bedroom. "But the guy from U-Haul called Professor Corey, and—"

"—said the truck we were supposed to get tomorrow broke down in New Hampshire on its way here today. The transmission or something. And it won't be fixed in time. So it was either take the one he did have left here tonight, and get it back here Sunday night because it's reserved again on Monday, or else wait another week." She approached and kissed him. "Hi honey," she said, "hard day at the office? The finance company called up and said that if we don't pay up by tomorrow morning, they're coming for our worldly goods, so I thought we'd better skip tonight."

She turned and said to the students: "Okay, gang, the clothes're packed. The bed is stripped. The bureaus are both empty. Suitcases go in the Escort." They were suddenly on their feet and heading for the bedroom.

"Don't I even get to change?" he said. "I could use a shower, too."

"Yup," she said. "Your jeans, polo shirt, Docksiders, and clean socks, also fresh tee-shirt and shorts, 're all piled neatly on the floor, in the bathroom, sugar. Also one clean towel, and a hanger for your suit. And a garment bag. Wash the city off yourself, and by the time you're fresh and dainty this place will be 'To Let.' "

"I wouldn't mind one of those beers, either," he said.

She made a face at him. "Pushin' your luck pretty hard, aren't you, chum," she said. "I'll see what I can do."

"Oh, I've got faith in you," he said, going toward the bathroom. "Apparently there's no end to the things that you can do."

"Well," she said, "I'm practical, but you've always known that. I figure if what you want's a whole new life, you'd better grab it when the chance comes, before you change your mind."

"Or you lose your nerve," he said.

13

The breeze off the lake on Labor Day night seemed chilly after the warmth and exertion of the day; Michelle's suggestion of coffee and apple tart in front of the living room fireplace elicited the silent acquiescence of fatigue. "Well, look at it this way," she said as she placed a small bowl of whipped cream on the campaign table, next to the tart, "at least now you're finished. For the time being. And by the time you get your own place, and you're ready to move into that, you'll have found some muscular kids around Amherst to drag out what's in storage and what you've got here, and put it down there where you want it. And then you'll be all set for life."

"I thought seriously about having a small fire," Jill said, "while I was packing back in New York. Joe was at the office, might as well've moved in and slept there, for all the time he was home and all the good he was to me while we were back. So I was all by myself, and I thought when I finished the first day with the books, and you couldn't see that I'd made any progress at all, I thought how helpful a nice oven fire would be, if I let it get out of hand. All the stuff was insured, and what couldn't be replaced I could've sneaked out, before I torched all the junk."

"Wouldn't've worked," Corey said. "Hassan would've been there with the hook and ladder and a thousand yards of hose before the pilot light came on. All those smoke detectors he had, all that endless jazz with batteries?"

"Our landlord," Jill said to Baldo. "Hassan owned the building we lived in."

"And if anyone was going to burn Hassan's building down for insurance purposes," Corey said, "Hassan was going to do it himself. At least that was his justification for popping in at very odd hours."

"At first we didn't think anything of it," Jill said. "But then we began to think about it. Late Saturday night? Snowy Sunday mornings? Holiday weekends? Has this guy got a fetish for changing batteries or something? Or is it more likely he's weird? We decided he was weird."

Baldo laughed. "Probably thought you were watching dirty movies," he said. "Keep at it long enough, and he was sure to catch you at it."

"Or maybe making them," Joe said. "Getting out the camcorder and producing our own porn. Hassan was definitely strange." He paused. "I suppose the ratio of strange people to normal people's no higher in New York than it is anywhere else, but when you've got so many people packed into one limited space like that, you're bound to have more oddballs per acre, and it's hard to avoid running into them all the time."

"Oh, you'll find your share of them up around here too," Michelle said comfortably. "I have no idea what varieties Mount Holyoke imports, its teachers and students . . ."

"I'll give you a reading tomorrow night," Jill said. "I have to be there, in my office, by nine tomorrow morning. Which means that I'm out of here, seven-thirty at the latest. In case there are some problems with preregistration scheduling not turning out as planned. As of course there always are."

". . . but if they're anything like the bozos and nutbags and airheads that Hartford and Trinity, and UConn down at Storrs had, that I saw when I was working down there," Michelle said, "you're going to have plenty of them to keep yourself entertained. And from what Baldo tells me he's got planned for you, Joe, well, I do know some of those people, a little bit at least, and there's a couple of jim-dandies in the crew waiting for you."

"Can't wait," Corey said. "What do you figure, Baldo? Couple or three days bringing me up to speed on the stuff you got in Boston? And then get started on the registries and so forth?" They were going to work in the two rooms designed as bedrooms at the rear of the second floor of the northwesterly condo unit that Baldo had loaned to the Coreys until they bought a house. Baldo promised not to come in until Joe had first appeared and given notice Jill was up and dressed in the master bedroom at the front. The phone jacks were already in, and they would face each other, across the desks Joe had bought, through the door between the two rooms. Baldo said the second-floor location would not entirely prevent a determined snoop from spying on their documents, "but he'll either have to bring a ladder or climb a damned tree to do it, and there isn't any way to stop that."

"Oh, I don't think so," Baldo said. He yawned. "The information that I picked up in the Secretary of State's office was just about what I expected: nothing much, and incomplete. About the only use it's ever going to be is as sidelights to what we start looking for tomorrow. So I think the best thing to do is dig into that right off, starting tomorrow morning."

"What time do they open?" Corey said.

"Oh," Baldo said, "the town office at nine sharp, the register same time, but there's not much point in showing up at either one of them until an hour or so later, if you need help or anything. People in those places like to ease into their day, especially when Monday's Tuesday as it is this week, and they've had three days, not two, to let their blood congeal."

"Good," Corey said. "We should leave here about nine, then? I could use some extra sack time, after what I've just been through."

"I may throw up, Michelle," Jill said. "If I do it's not the

134

roast beef, I just want you to know that. I did all the work, and now he's the one who's all pooped out."

"Oh no," Baldo said. "I figure if we're out the door by six-fifteen or so, we'll be pretty much on schedule. Schedule that I've got in mind. It's a half hour or so up the road to breakfast, and unless you get there by six forty-five or so, forget about a table—they're all taken until nine."

"What's the matter with breakfast here?" Corey said. "I've gotten so the day doesn't start officially until I've had some of your coffee. Why go out for it?"

"Oh," Baldo said, "you can have that. Have some coffee here, I mean. But for breakfast you are going to the Bright 'N' Early Grille, where the elite meet to read the papers and then decide what's going on, and how much of what is going on they like, and will support."

"And this is important," Corey said, "to what we're going to be doing."

"It won't be tomorrow," Baldo said. "At least it won't be while we're there, eating hash browns, meeting people, laughing at bad jokes and taking digs at pols and so forth. But two weeks, two months, two years from now, it will be important. A lot of people that you're going to be doing legal business with, if things work out, do most of *their* business in the Bright 'N' Early. They have offices and courtrooms; they have businesses and churches. They have banks and they have stores, keep their papers in those places and take their phone calls there. But what they write down on those papers, what they say in those phone calls, that depends on what they know and what they think of who's involved. And that kind of data they get in that noisy little restaurant around sunrise every day— two over easy, toast and sausage, with a side order or three of some people's reputations and sly plans, fricaseed and burnt to a crisp. Think of it as though you were getting measured for a suit that you were going to have to wear every time you go outdoors for the next three years, and when somebody runs his hand up the inside of your leg, don't move a muscle, don't jump, or you'll wear funny-looking pants for the rest of your life here."

The Bright 'N' Early was a one-story, white-painted, cinder-block building set between a Mobil station and a self-service car wash in a hollow on the westerly side of combined Routes 7 and 20 north of Lenox and south of Pittsfield. At 6:40 A.M. in the light drizzle of the morning after Labor Day, all but two of the parking spaces next to the building were occupied. Corey noticed that the Boston *Globe*, Boston *Herald*, and New York *Daily News* vending machines, chained to the cement post to the left of the entrance, were empty. The *New York Times* and *Wall Street Journal* machines displayed copies, and Corey stopped, fishing for change in his pocket. Baldo took him firmly by the left forearm. "No," he said, "not going in. You want to buy a New York paper coming out, or get one at the newsstand later on, fine. But you don't go into your first day in these woods carrying a paper from the place you claim you left."

Inside, a low counter jutted out from the southerly wall and offered six chromium-based stools upholstered in red plastic to prospective diners. The counter curved about fourteen feet into the room and served about twenty more places before ending at a cash register and then a passageway four feet from a large service window opening into the kitchen in the rear. There were large stainless-steel chests against the wall behind the counter, and glass-doored, stainless-steel cabinets displaying small boxes of dry cereals over them. There were two triple banks of tall coffee urns situated one third of the way from each end of the counter, and two Bastian Blessing gooseneck water and soda fountain installations sprouted between them. Two waitresses attended to counter customers; four more in what seemed to be perpetual motion plied between the two rows of two- and four-place tables in the center of the room and the four- and six-place booths that ringed the westerly, northerly, and easterly walls under the picture windows looking out on the car wash. There was a cigarette machine to the right of the entrance; Baldo stopped and leafed through the newspapers piled on top of it until he found a *Wall Street Journal* and a *Herald*. He handed the *Herald* to Corey and turned right, heading for a vacant booth at the northeasterly corner. When they were seated, Corey said: "Why is it all right for you to sit down with a *Journal*, if I can't come in with a *Times*?"

"Simple," Baldo said, "the people in here know I live here. They've known me for a long time, and trust me. I could read *Pravda* if it suited me, or *Die Zeit* or the *Morning Telegraph*. What I read's irrelevant. What you read is not, until they decide who you are. When they've gotten finished sizing you up, then you can read what you like."

"And how long will that take?" Corey said.

Baldo shrugged. "Could take several years, you get off on the wrong foot, or it could be over this week. Don't be so impatient. You're investing time. You're presenting credentials at court in this matter—think of this step as going through customs. Before you can ask for citizenship, you have to get into the country."

"Somewhere it must be written," Corey said to Jill that night, after they had shared a pot roast with the Ianuccis and returned to their borrowed unit, "that every joint like that, no matter where it is, has to have at least one waitress who's called Millie, and if there's more than three of them, also one called Dot. There's a place called Marie's on the same street in Saint Paul where my father's office is—Marie's dead, I guess, and the grill man is Bob, but the woman who owns it is Millie. I don't care what anybody says: if our first one's a daughter, we are not going to name her Dorothy or Mildred. I don't care how much money those small lunchrooms make; I'll be damned if I'll finance prep school and college for a woman who'll gravitate right to a beanery before the diploma ink's dry, a bachelor's in serving up hash."

"Did you have it?" Jill said.

"What?" he said.

"The hash, of course," she said. " 'Two poached, wheat toast on the side.' That's what my father always had in those places. Unless it was lunchtime, of course, or ten-thirty at night in some truck stop. Then it was meat loaf with gravy and mashed, or sometimes, chicken croquettes." She sighed. "Those were good places," she said. "Better than turnpike fast-feeders. Sometimes you got poisoned, but not very often—mostly you ate genuine food."

"I did have the hash," he said. "And it was fine. For someone who never eats breakfast. Of course it was cold by the time I got finished, six refills of coffee or so later."

"What took you so long?" she said.

"Baldo wasn't kidding," he said. "When it comes to being the crossroads of America, this corner of it, anyway, that place could give Times Square or Heartburn Airport down in Atlanta a very brisk run for the title."

"Hartsfield," she said absently. "I've only been through there once, but at least I can get the name right."

"You must've not eaten there, when you went through," he said. "If you had've you'd know *they* got the name wrong. Survivors like me get it right.

"We had just time enough to put in our order," he said. "Millie gave us coffee when we first sat down. Heard my life story and went to the kitchen, and the next thing I know: company. I don't know where he came from, except it had to've been from the counter or one of the other tables, because I was sitting facing the door, and I didn't see him come in. Besides, he knew too much before I said a word. I figure that Millie dispatched him. Exactly according to Baldo's clockwork plan, and this was without a rehearsal."

The man was in his early forties, slightly under average

height, slightly over normal weight. He wore a blue blazer and grey slacks with a white shirt and a blue-and-white-striped tie. There was a Kiwanis pin on his lapel. He wore bifocals with tortoiseshell frames, and he kept his monk's fringe of brown hair trimmed close. His face was smooth and ruddy and plump, and when he smiled, he showed one gold canine tooth. "Baldo," he said, his face beaming the smile of a man who loved getting up early, "we thought you'd dropped off the edge of the earth. Where the hell've you been?"

"Dick," Baldo said, returning the smile, "I assumed you guys read the papers. Burt had to retire me to make room for the lady, Annie Oakley or whatever her name is. Siddown. Have some coffee."

Dick slid into the bench next to Baldo. "Retired, sure, we knew that. All thought that it stunk. But then you just disappeared, seemed like. One day we saw you, the next day you were gone, and damned if you didn't stay gone. The old joint's not the same without you."

"Well," Baldo said, "you know how it is, Dick. What reason'd I have to come in? You take a man's business away from him, just yank the rug right out from under him, he feels like a fifth wheel in a place like this, with people who've got news and so forth.

"But that's all changing now, I'm happy to tell you. I'm back in the saddle again. Meet Joe Corey, my new friend Joe Corey. We're going to be working together. Joe, this's Dick Putney, good friend. County Commissioner, what, sixteen years or so? Nowadays deputy register, probate. Good man to know around the courthouse—Joe's a lawyer, Dick, up from New York. Going to open a practice up here. Well, down in Shropshire, most likely."

"That so," Putney said. "Give Bob Gates a run for his money? That what you've got in mind?"

Corey forced a laugh. "I wouldn't put it quite so definitely as Baldo does," he said. "I know I'm out of New York for keeps. My wife's a professor and she's got a new job, teaching history over at Mount Holyoke. So this's the part of the country where she wants to be, and when the chance came along for her, well, I was pretty fed up with New York. Put it this way: between Jill and the city, I know which I like better, which one I'd rather be around. But what I do, where I settle down, for the long run, I mean: I don't know. For now it's all pretty much up in the air. I'm feeling my way along here. All I know is I'm out of New York."

"It can be pretty dirty, I guess," Putney said. "Okay to visit, but I wouldn't want to live there, myself. Wife's always after me, take a trip down, see a play or something like that. I've taken her three or four times. It was all right. Had a decent time, but my God if they don't gouge your eyes out. Man can't take a piss for himself in a restaurant men's room, some coon doesn't want fifty cents for letting him wash his hands after. We stayed at the City Squire, nice enough place, on one of those weekend arrangements? Well, some bargain I say, for two hundred bucks—cost me forty to park my car, and dinner, not one of those real fancy places, but the check was out of this world. You're doing the right thing to relocate here. There's plenty of business for lawyers. Bob Gates may not like it, he gets the word, but he's got no deed to the town. And there's plenty of other towns around here, if he gets snotty about it—no Gateses to deal with in them."

"Actually," Baldo said, "what brings Joe up here's the Mandeville case. You old enough to recall that?"

Putney did a theatrical double-take. "Why you old walrus," he said, beaming again and slapping Baldo lightly on his left shoulder, "you think I'm a ree-tard or something? Jim Mandeville and my uncle Guy were thicker'n thieves at a fair. To this day you can't sit down for a drink or a dinner with Guy Cooper without being mighty careful what subjects you bring up. Because if you pick a wrong one, such as hunting or fishing, old Guy'll get to snifflin' and remembering old Jim. The two of them were like twin brothers, that respect. If Guy hadn't had his business, and if Jim'd been retired, I swear they would've gone out in the woods six days a week, and griped about no hunting Sundays, which they did anyway—I heard them do it, myself."

"Well then," Baldo said, "you're probably familiar with the theories people had—that Mandeville was murdered, that he didn't kill himself?"

"Of course, of course I am," Putney said. "Everybody heard them, and for a damned good reason, too. That was complete foolishness, saying he did that. Blew his brains out, his own shotgun, almost Christmas Eve, too. Guy said it was the most ridiculous damned thing he ever heard tell in his life."

"Okay," Baldo said, "what Joe here's going to do, and I'm going to help him with it for the next few weeks at least, is see if maybe we can't make some sense out of that case. And maybe even, if we're lucky, prove it was a murder and who might've had it done."

Putney showed the smile again, but his eyes were cool above the dividing line in his bifocals. "Ah," he said, "so you're the grandson. You'd be the Mandeville grandson. Have you seen that property? Looked at it, I mean? That big house he lived in down there, and all that land and those buildings he got from the priests? That property'd be worth a lot of money today, someone got his hands on it with some kind of legal action, where he could prove the people that own it now got it by committing a crime."

"Well, actually," Corey said, "I have seen the property. But I'm not a grandson. Jim Mandeville's grandsons, well, I'm not one of them. My wife is one of his granddaughters, and as far's I know at least, the only one of all of them that seems to've thought about it much."

"Uh-huh," Putney said. "But still and all, if someone did that, proved that like I said, well, your wife might have to split it, four ways, six ways, even seven, but it'd still be a nice piece of change. Very nice piece of change."

"I wouldn't know," Corey said. "I've never seen the will,

or anything like that. I more or less assume he left the whole thing to his widow, but she's been dead now for a while, and her will was filed and governed under New York law. I haven't seen that paper, either. My wife's mother had a sister. Jill had one sister, and her aunt had four kids of her own. So without knowing, I'd assume that if the property reverted, it would go to Jill's mother and her aunt, equally. Jill and the other five grandchildren wouldn't get a thing."

"For now," Putney said. Corey shrugged. "Well," Putney said, "anyway, this interests me." He turned to Baldo. "You got any plans," he said, "to give our young visitor a tour of the model operation we run at the registry?"

Baldo nodded. "Sooner or later," he said. "It's certainly one of the items we've got on our agenda."

Putney nodded. "Right," he said. "Well, if I get half a chance today, I'll pull down old Jim's will, and have some copies made of the accounts and all that stuff. Have it waiting for you around noon, you're in the neighborhood."

"Appreciate it," Baldo said.

"Let me ask you something, though," Putney said. "What does Magoun think of all this? Or does he know about it?"

"Well," Corey said, "naturally I—"

"Well, my God, Dick," Baldo said, "wouldn't you expect a man like Joe here, maybe young, but an experienced attorney, junior partner in a major Wall Street law firm, wouldn't you expect a man with his background to let the D.A. for the county know what he was doing?"

"I would, yes," Putney said. "I just wasn't sure he did. I'm liable to run into Burt, you know, normal course of business. And anyway, this is, well, a matter of some interest. Just wasn't sure, since you've told me, how much I should feel free to tell Burt."

"Anything you like, Dick," Baldo said. "This's all perfectly open and aboveboard here, what Joe's got on his mind. No secrets involved here at all." Baldo waited until Putney was out of earshot before he said: "Meaning, of course, that he'll tell everybody he meets today until he gets the same news coming back at him, which'll be right after lunch if it isn't before that."

"We had maybe eight or nine minutes after Putney got up and left," Corey told Jill that night, "with all the casual indolence of a man who'd just discovered that his pants had caught fire, during which I actually got to eat some of my cool hash and my clotting eggs, before Ed Pratt wandered over, just by way of no harm, and sat himself down for chat. I took the chance to ask Baldo why he interrupted me."

"Simple," Baldo said, digging into his potatoes and bacon. "you're a lawyer, not an actor. If I'd primed you, what to do, you'd've done it all right—you would've overdone it. Because even though you're not actors, you like to think you are, and when you're putting on a show, it's obvious as hell. Dick Putney's got a mouth on him like those power mowers they advertise on TV all the time: it came with a lifetime guarantee it'll start on the first pull. His father was County Commissioner; that man had real power. Dick inherited his seat and his taste for politics, along with all his money but almost none of his power. But if Dick knows that, he's not letting on. He thinks he's a regular broker. Like wishing would make it come true. It won't, but that's all right with Dick. He's basically a lazy man, satisfied with what he makes for not doing too much work, because it lets him spend his time pretending to play politics, and kidding himself that he's got an in with the big players. Governors, state treasurers, and so forth. Gossip's his stock-in-trade, but not just to repeat it—he likes to think he's real shrewd, can predict things that never got mentioned. What people really have in mind when they tell him something—is usually to plant a rumor that they think might do them some good, by the time Dick gets through spreading it for them, but Dick's never figured that out. He's the insider's insider, that kind of thing—that's how Dick sees himself. A man like that is an all-day sucker, but suckers are useful sometimes.

"What I wanted him to think is that Magoun may not like this much, the idea of you coming up here, poking around into things, digging up old smelly scandals. So by cutting you off, I gave him the notion that he's onto something juicy, something that you would've tipped him off to, if I hadn't stopped you."

"What's the point?" Corey said. "I don't see the point of it."

"The point is that Dick smelling intrigue will take care of advertising, save us lots of legwork that could take a lot of time. Everywhere we go from here on out, we will be expected. We'll still have to go through all the introductions and the tail-sniffings and so forth, that the old dogs gather 'round to do when new dogs come around. But all the people that we see now will be just a little bit distracted. Not only sizing you up, but seeing whether they agree with Dick's firm conviction something funny's going on. It's not much of an edge, but it's still an edge, sort of a dime on the sidewalk—it isn't worth much, but it doesn't take long to bend down and pick it up, and it'll still buy you a phone call."

"We didn't get out of that place until after nine," Corey said to Jill that night. "I met Eddie Pratt, the chief court officer. I met Ralph Llewellyn, chief court clerk. I met Evelyn Murtagh, big real estate agent—Baldo let it slip that we'd most likely be in the market for a nice house, 'fore the snow begins to fly, and she seemed to find that cheering news indeed; made me take her card, and promised to call me up as soon as she's gone through her files. Forbes McKinnon, the sheriff, dropped by. Basil Granger, the Fire District supervisor, stopped for a coffee with us, and Connie Lewis, the State Police major, said his stomach was demanding oatmeal: 'Always does after holiday weekends, all the crazies out on the pike.'

"My breakfast was three bucks. Baldo's was two-fifty. Coffee's sixty cents, all you can drink. The check came to twelve bucks plus two bucks for Dot, or Millie, whoever she was. Not much in money, but my God, in work? I felt like a primary

144

candidate must feel, working the Iowa caucuses; my bladder was full to the bursting. I told Baldo I had to hit the head before we left, and he said he thought that was a good idea. That we'd made a good start, nothing more, and the day was ahead of us yet. 'Take your time,' he said. 'We'll want to give them an hour to get on their phones about us. Then we'll go up to town and start pounding the pavement, maybe see one or two more people first.'

"The 'one or two people' that we saw," Corey said to Jill, "were automobile dealers. Baldo explained to them that you and I're interested in a new car or two, and by the time he got through nudging them this way and noodging them that, I got the impression if we'd just come by, and be kind enough to remove two sets of wheels right off their showroom floors, they'd be happy to pay us a good fee. 'Always trade with the locals,' Baldo told me. 'It's amazing how fond that makes them of newcomers. How favorably they are impressed.' "

"But actually," she said, "did you actually get anything done out there today, in all that? Or was it like my day? All hoopla and flesh-pressing, handshaking and smiling and that stuff—but really just conventioneering?"

"Well," he said, "I got pages of notes and copies of documents it'll take us tomorrow to catalog. But did I get anything? If Baldo's right, I did. 'When Sherlock Holmes went out into the country to work on an important case, everyone knew who Mister Holmes was—he was the famous detective, and to snitch to him was an honor. You'll never be Holmes, even Holmes wasn't Holmes, but if you're just a little bit known, people'll be curious about you. And by the time they get through being nosy about you, they'll feel beholden to us.' "

14

By the end of the first week, Corey had mastered the pattern of Baldo's investigatory procedure. "Baldo does it by rote, of course, all the years that he's been at it," he told Jill. "For him it's like finding a comfortable pair of old pants at the back of the closet, that he'd given up for lost, putting them on and relaxing. But for me it's something entirely new. The past six years I've been structuring factual situations to conform to what the SEC Act and the regs say directors and the shareholders have to do to satisfy legal standards—taking known facts and making sure laws are obeyed.

"What I'm doing now is exactly the opposite: starting with an event that we're sure was a crime, and working back to the facts that must have accounted for its commission. It's much more complex, working backward and blind, and it's not just the twenty-year time lag. The time lag exists—no one figured it out then—because the people involved in committing the crime were concealing the means that they used, in order to hide if not all the facts of them, at least those that were most important. And they did a fairly good job of it, too. There's a hell of a lot of inference involved, of deduction instead of induction. I used to say: 'Well, what should we do now?' Now I say: 'Why'd he do that?' While keeping in mind, as Baldo keeps saying, that maybe his only reason—whoever 'he' turns out to've been—for doing a thing was to hide something else more important, and also, of course, sinister."

"It sounds to me like you're working my side of the street," Jill said, "practicing history without a license."

"I am," he said. "That's precisely what we're doing. This time line we're doing: at first it was two-tracked, because we hadn't yet reached the point at which James Mandeville Senior perfected his title to Overlook Hills. There seemed to've been a cloud on it. And until we resolved that we couldn't proceed to where Jacob Stritch inherited the parcel adjoining, that he later deeded over by his will to the Claretians, and then go on to where your grandfather acquired it, and our two starting time lines converged."

"Why was this so important?" she said.

"Well, we didn't know it was," he said. "But as Baldo keeps drilling into my head, we also didn't know for sure it wasn't. 'When you don't know whether something's important, then you know it's important to find out. Don't assume anything. That's how cases get lost. It's not unimportant until you know it is, and even then you don't forget it.'

"In this case what we didn't know was important. Maybe not really significant, but it helps us to know what we didn't, in case it takes on significance as we get closer to the present day. All of this land, Overlook Hills and Claretian Shores, was sold off by one Arthur Hammersmith right after the Civil War. It was all he had left of a grant to his family made by King George the Third just before the king's grants became worthless as a result of the ruckus that began at Concord and Lexington shortly thereafter.

"The purchaser was Herman Stritch. He paid cash for the parcel, cash he'd made as a wholesale supplier, a merchant of blankets and uniforms to the Union Army, from wool that he bought in Vermont. A war profiteer, in other words, operating out of New York, but taking good notes while the war continued, for his own guidance when it was over. And he learned a lot, about many things. Among them were railroads, and routes they might take, and what his fellow moguls were buying. He probably cheated them every chance he got, just the same as they tried to cheat him, but he still respected their judgment. When they bought land up here, Herman did, too. He got all this for twelve hundred dollars.

"By the time Herman died in eighteen eighty-two, and left the land to his son, Emil, it seemed pretty obvious that he'd guessed wrong. This was not going to be a new hotbed of industry, or anything else, for that matter. The textile market was all taken care of, up in North Adams at this end of the state, in Holyoke on the Connecticut River. Machinery manufacturing gravitated that way as well; the natural routes from those cities to the major distribution ports were much better. The land was still pretty, there was agriculture, but it wasn't a stunning investment. When your great-grandfather scraped enough cash together to look for a homestead for himself, Emil was quite willing to sell him twelve acres—that still left him with over four hundred. Later on, best we can tell now, they added two acres to Overlook Hills, to square off the metes and the bounds on the southerly side; if more money changed hands then, we can't tell.

"Emil's luck changed a little before he succumbed to vile habits, high living and gin, and handed the four hundred acres on to his son Jacob. This would've been about four years after the purchase of Overlook Hills. Jacob doesn't seem to've shared his father's taste for Lillian Russell–type blowsy blondes, or Delmonico dinners with the swells. The library's collection of microfiched papers is spotty until you get to eighteen ninety-three, because there was a fire that destroyed the morgue at the paper in eighteen ninety, and it didn't occur to anyone then to replicate the collection that'd been lost. But there's a 'ninety-four photo of Jacob when he announced he was building his house, and the paper did a big story on it—biggest thing ever hit Shropshire till then; could be it still is, to this day. He had a lean and hungry look, clean-shaven under his top hat except for his muttonchop whiskers, looks to've had all the genial good humor of a professional hangman. The story was very emphatic about what an upstanding citizen he was. And he had enough money so he could declare he followed the Roman religion. Most likely everyone who had the good sense to respect big money understood clearly that the pope of the millionaires wasn't the kind of lowlife that the pope of the immigrants was, and Jake had enough millions so it didn't matter if some couldn't make the distinction. Jacob was just my age then.

"Upstanding or not, though, Jake took his lumps in the Crash. To the point at which he thought that it might be prudent to unload his mansion when he died, and most likely save the other holdings he had from estate-tax confiscation. Reserving a life-estate to himself, he deeded the parcel, by then with the main house and a barn and some buildings since torn down, to the Claretian Fathers as a charitable bequest. That wiped out his tax liabilities. He made out the will in 'thirty-one, and he didn't die until 'thirty-nine. He was seventy-four lean years old. He spent the last seven of them a papal Knight Hospitaler, more commonly known as a Knight of Malta, to the displeasure of Masonic knights of that name who say it's as much theirs as it's Rome's. Charity has its rewards in this life, too, if it's showy-enough charity.

"Anyway, that got us up to 'thirty-nine, when the good fathers got this blessed plot, just before lunch yesterday. So that meant we could merge the two lines on our chart in nineteen sixty, twenty-one years later, when your grandfather bought out the priests. I was a little discouraged, if you want the truth. 'Cripes,' I said, 'will you look at this? We're finally up to what looks like a milestone, and where are we actually? Seven years before Mandeville gets his head blown off, and it's taken us most of a week.'

"Baldo didn't know whether to hit me or laugh at me. 'If you had any brains, New York lawyer,' he said, 'you'd be turning cartwheels we've come this far. Plug what we've picked up into what we knew from the beginning, and you'll see we've made some real progress. Until we did this, all we had to go on was that your wife's grandfather bought up this parcel *when he couldn't afford it*. Now, we did have an inkling before this, from things Amelia told us, and from what Katherine McCormack told you, although they didn't know they were telling us, that Jim Mandeville Junior had a mild playboy streak. He was a romantic, you know? Nothing really disgraceful, nothing outrageous, but still on the impulsive side. The neglect of bank business when big fish were biting, or when he could hunt upland game. The dogs in the office, the big Christmas parties, the whole squire role he liked to play so much.

" 'So that explains why he took the flier that put him into the hole; he risked half a million, most if not all of his liquid assets, on what was high-risk speculation, which smart bankers just never do, and then he doubled the ante by hocking a future no one then could have predicted. He was going double-or-nothing. Even dumb bankers don't do that.

" 'Well, we know Mandeville Junior was not dumb. So, did he know something that made this flier low-risk, that the land was bound to climb sharply over the price that he paid? So that it was smarter for him to borrow the other half million he needed, instead of forming a syndicate to cut down his risks, but which would've required him, if everything worked right, to share the big profits with others? Not very likely. The loan was for only ten years. Property values can go up pretty steeply, but to double in ten years, for sure? Cautious banker'd never bet his whole wad on that. So he must've had some other reason, that made him an *in*cautious banker. And that was the appeal of owning the whole tract, that his father could only buy part of. He was bigger'n his daddy'd been. He bought this big parcel because he *wanted* it—no other reason at all. That was Jim Mandeville's motive.

" 'So now,' Baldo said, 'now we can start digging into where he got the money, who the people were that loaned it, with the confidence we've got from knowing that we're not being nuts at all when we suspect they were bad guys. So bad that he must've known it. And didn't care. He was obsessed to get this parcel. Enough, in all likelihood, to ignore the better judgment that told him he was crazy to deal with reptiles if that's what it would take to get it. See how knowing the victim's motive helps us? This narrows things down for us more than a little, and at least should improve our morale. Now when you call up your aristocrat crime buster, and ask him to run some names for us, you'll know at least he is earning his snootiness, and that should make you feel good. He probably does have their files, or'll know where to get them right off.' "

"What'd he mean by that?" Jill said.

"Roger Birnam," he said. "Baldo didn't feature telling me his date and place of birth, and his Social Security number, so Roger could run a check on him. 'Rich amateurs,' he said. 'Dick Tracy in spats, Nick Charles on a damned polo pony. Think the only investigators who get anything right're the dabblers from their better *clahsses*. Think high-powered evil's beyond comprehension, except by high-powered good, the higher orders chastising the lower.' Not that we're ready to call Roger in yet. We've still got our tracking to do.

"The deed that we got from the register says that Gil Rogers represented your grandfather. No surprise there. But there is a small surprise in the fact that Rogers was also one of the lawyers for the Claretian Fathers. He was cocounsel with one Henry M. O'Hara, Esquire, of Myerson, Cohen, O'Hara and Boyd, Twelve East Forty-first Street, New York. As best we can make out, O'Hara and his firm represented the Congregation of the Missionary Sons of the Immaculate Heart of Mary—which is the formal name of the outfit—in all their dealings in this country. It's a comparatively young order, founded by Saint Anthony Claret in Spain in eighteen fortynine, not especially prominent or acquisitive, and our guess is that Henry inherited their business from his father, Henry F. O'Hara, Esquire.

"Henry F. was Jake Stritch's lawyer for the legal work that transferred the land to the good fathers when Jake died in 'thirty-nine, and we think Henry F.'s good offices in that respect probably account for *his* designation as a Knight Hospitaler with Jake back in 'thirty-two."

"In other words," Jill said, "Henry F. talked Jake into leaving the property to the Claretians, and got his own sword for the service."

"Right," he said. "But probably not much of anything else, in the way of money, I mean. Prestige is the coinage of payment to law firms that represent monks, big charities, and major museums. The intended effect, the one they talk about, that is, is goodwill earned from big, rich clients who have charitable or artsy-craftsy enthusiasms. *Pro bono publico.* I did a fair amount of that wheel-spinning at Birnam, Barkey. Flip and Dip for example, the two electronics geniuses? There they are, a couple of nerds in boat shoes who made four hundred million dollars apiece doing magic tricks with silicone chips you can't even see with the naked eye, and what's their main passion in life? Sailboats. Racing sailboats. Which they want to design and build from scratch at extravagant costs, that they want to deduct from their taxes. So I do one of our money-losing 'incorporations of convenience' for them, Wilmington, Delaware, shell corporation named 'Silent Wanderer Yachts,' and they go happily out to play, messing around with boats, and beating the Treasury out of what was then fifty cents of every dollar they threw in the water.'Course they later made a good piece of change out of that little frolic, too, being the type of guys that can't help making money no matter how crazy they look, but the point is that nobody, including them, expected them to when we started their company for them. We were just out to preserve their goodwill, and keep their regular business." He paused. "And then of course there's the other motive, the one the firms don't talk about: doing good works free makes it unlikely they'll get caught, or punished too severely, when, as, and if they get tempted some day and steal something.

"A prosperous New York lawyer like Henry M. O'Hara,

apparently having inherited his father's monks for clients, but not his father's pressing interest in a papal decoration, often does not regard monks' business as a priority concern. It's more like a nuisance that gums up his life, something to get out of the way. There's no point in running up billable hours if all you get paid's a cockade, and your more secular partners concur. Henry M. in all likelihood reviewed the files and considered the monks' bank accounts. Most likely he hired a local appraiser and found out that your grandfather's offer was fair—indeed, it was near-generous. So what Henry M. did was call up brother Rogers and propose a convenient procedure. Gil, who was getting paid actual money by Granddad, would draw up the deed, which meant: have his girl copy the Stritch deed and will, and insert all the new signature spaces. Gil would then send the new deed to Henry M. Henry M. would study it—which meant that Henry would have an associate drone read it against the old Stritch deed, and then if it parsed, Henry would initial it, page by page, very meticulously, and sign it as the monks' general counsel. But Rogers would sign on as cocounsel, too, when he got the deed back from Henry, and then when the papers were passed up on Bank Street in Pittsfield, some distance from Henry, Gil would represent both parties, your granddad and the monks, too. Thus saving our Henry a time-wasting trip, for clients who didn't pay much."

"Was that legal?" she said.

"Oh, absolutely," he said, "perfectly legal and ethical. There was no conflict of interest involved, none apparent and none hidden, either. A willing seller and a willing buyer, a price certified fair by a disinterested third party, licensed as an appraiser? Hell, if it weren't for the laws on transfers of land, your grandfather and Father Dominic Cleary, the Claretian's financial man, could've done it by handshake and X marks on birchbark. The lawyers weren't involved to protect the parties; they were there to make sure that society's interest in traceable titles was covered. And to turn a neat, though small, profit for themselves. The deal itself was clean, quick, and honest. It was what was hidden behind it, on Jim Mandeville's side, that made it poisonous later—where Jim'd gotten the money.

"Half of the money behind the bank check he endorsed over to the congregation. And that's what we go after next. But for that we need Burt Magoun and subpoenas, to meet bank-privacy acts and that stuff."

15

Burt Magoun drove down to Shropshire late the following Tuesday afternoon so that Ianucci and Corey could bring him up to date on their progress in the case. He explained on the phone that he preferred Ianucci's home as a meeting place because "your gossips've got the press to the point of staking out the courthouse, and ferreting the list of grand jury witnesses, but so far they haven't started following me when I leave here. And that's another thing we probably ought to talk about, while we're at it: how we're going to handle the reception they'll give us when we get together Thursday."

They conferred in the northeasterly room on the second floor of the first condo unit, dragging a chair in from Baldo's office and situating it to the left of Corey's desk, so that Magoun and Ianucci flanking Corey would also have a clear view of the wall chart of the time line and the two large sketching pads displayed on the easels on each side of it.

"Let's deal with the really significant issues first here," Magoun said, smiling crookedly. "Not this minor matter of a murder gone unsolved, but the truly cosmic matter of the state of the media's digestion and disposition."

"Let me guess," Baldo said. "They're unhappy. They think you're holding out on them."

"And, of course, they're right," Magoun said. "I haven't found it necessary to explain that I'm holding out on *them* because you're holding out on *me* and I've been letting you get away with it, because that would make me look worse—being called 'stupid' is worse than being cursed as 'uncooperative.'

"What's gotten them—'them' being good old Beth Warren—into her current state of high agitation is what you guys've done so far. As we expected, Dick Putney and his morning-coffee posse did their usual efficient job with the jungle telegraph, so she's got an idea what it is. She tends to be rather closely focused on whatever she is doing—she's a damned solipsist, in fact—but when somebody else's doing something that gets talked about all over town, she notices. To her way of thinking, it would be perfectly fine if you hadn't made any progress. But since the scuttlebutt says you must've, because you're still at it, and you need some grand jury time, well, that's honey for the bear.

"Now Baldo," he said, "you may not think this is much, after what Dame Budget did to you, but what's happened here is that the same problem that forced me to terminate you has also obliged me to cut down on grand jury sessions, and use what I've got like they're bullets. Twenty-three jurors, at twenty-five a day, plus their mileage to and fro, well, you add it up: it costs the county just about eight hundred bucks a day to assemble those good men and women to ponder evil doings and, where it is appropriate, order me to round up those who should be punished and see to it that they are.

"In bygone days it used to be a leisurely affair. One week out of every month, sometimes six days, or seven, we'd have the clerk call up the folks impaneled for six months, and we'd present the cut-and-dried stuff and perhaps make a little progress on a complex investigation. If we got a big case, one that made the headlines, well, we'd have a one-hour session, get the bum indicted and then jugged in lieu of bail. And my God, my federal days, we always had one working. Sitting every day. Quite often we had two of them, sometimes even three. One to deal with day-to-day stuff, one for mafia, and one if some bunch of crooks sneaked into the banking business, or started buying politicians or buying bureaucrats at group rates instead of individually. Ah, life was easier then—more spacious, if you know what I mean.

"Now I have the jury in one day each week, each month. And every hour of those days, every *quarter* hour, is budgeted in advance. Investigative function? Hah. This is the fourth jury we've had since the cash drawer jammed shut last year and put us on starvation rations, and nothing goes in front of those good people until it's been neatly trimmed and freeze-dried and then pressure-packed in cubes. Now, the rest of the assistants take a tolerant view of things. Officially they don't know any more than the public does, but just like her, they know damned well what's really going on. It's exciting, for a change. Not just some bing-bang exercise, that can only have one outcome that we all already know, but a real investigation that could lead to a fat case. This's what we're s'posed to do.

"Beth doesn't think so, unless something comes out of it that makes a big headline. What Beth thinks is what the paper thinks, and what the paper thinks is what the voters think, and I'm up for reelection in two years. So therefore, as I know you'll understand, when I choose to preempt the ninety minutes I've reserved for you this Thursday, it'd be real good if something came out of it. We're gonna have ignition and lift-off, and as soon as she gets outside the courthouse and down to the paper where she reveals her soul to Berkshire County, we'll have first-stage separation as well and orbit is guaranteed. Beth hasn't printed anything yet, but only because she can't go on unsupported claims. So that's why she started camping out at the courthouse, and therefore why we've now got three or four more of her ilk also perched out front every day with her now; they may not like her any better'n I do, but they do respect her nose.

"Anyway," Magoun said, "what all of this means for you guys is that you'd better be prepared to get hounded as soon as you surface on Thursday. And to keep your big mouths shut when you do. So here's the script: on Wednesday, I'll hold a press briefing. I'll remind the knights and ladies of the keyboard that grand jury proceedings are secret. They'll remind me that the records of subpoenas issued are public documents that the clerk has to let them see, and publish if they like. This will reestablish our mutual determinations to hold tenaciously each foot of bloody ground the law says belongs to us. I will then inform them that the grand jury will convene the next day, and that in the morning, while my assistants are presenting evidence in their usual routine, I will be appearing before Judge Malcolm Weatherbee in the first criminal session, where I will present a motion in the matter of *Commonwealth of Massachusetts versus John Doe*, a proceeding to commence before the grand jury that afternoon. In that motion I will ask the court to grant admission to the bar of Massachusetts, *pro haec vice*, to Joseph Corey, an attorney admitted to practice before the bar of the State of New York and in good standing thereof, for a period of more than five years next preceding the date of my motion, for the purpose of assisting in the presentation of evidence, and in presenting evidence, to the grand jury, in the captioned matter. I will give as reason why the motion should be granted Mister Corey's detailed and specialized knowledge of the case and his consequent unique ability to assist the grand jury, and myself, in the orderly presentation and elucidation of complex matters which I have probable cause to believe, and accordingly so state, would reasonably warrant the inference that a crime or crimes have been and are being committed in this jurisdiction, and that his assistance would materially aid the grand jury in its deliberations.

"All of which, you will agree, is a much more elegant way of reiterating the substance of the discussion I had with Malcolm in chambers this morning, when I told him I wanted you, Joe, admitted for the purposes of this case because if we're ever going to find out what skulduggeries went on here, it's only going to be by taking shameless advantage of any otherwise-rational volunteer who shows up, and hustling him aboard as a Special Assistant D.A. to chase the mischief down for us, before he has a chance to change his mind. Malcolm thought that sounded eminently reasonable—Ralph Llewellyn, his clerk, was in there of course, too, far be it from Ralph to miss out on something; he said he's met you and you look all right, so you passed muster with him—so the whole thing is in the bag.

"After Malcolm pops it in officially, I'll move to have you sworn, so that you can be present during any and all testimony offered, and other evidence presented in the secret sessions of the jury. And you will be. Some further bowings and scrapings, and then out to face the lions of the media, whom I will inform of my simultaneous reemployment of Baldad Ianucci as a special investigator attached to my office, for the purpose of assisting in this investigation as head scrutator and guru, at a salary not to exceed one dollar per annum. Then, again citing the secrecy rules, I will lapse into uncommunicative silence while I am bombarded with questions that I will refuse to answer, a good time will be had by all, and tomorrow night's news along with the morning papers will be stuffed with unsubstantiated speculation that we're hot on the trail of the people who had Jim Mandeville killed back when Lyndon was our president and the Berlin Wall was forever.

"So," Magoun said, "are we? In full cry after the prey? Because after all this dust gets tramped up and settles back down to earth, I think we'd better be, gentlemen, or I'll have some explaining to do."

Corey and Ianucci exchanged glances. Corey nodded. "I'd say 'tepid on the trail,' I guess."

Ianucci shrugged, then nodded. "Closer to the trail'n we were two months ago," he said. "No question about that. But probably a good month or six weeks or so until we can say we're getting hot. If we get lucky, first. But that's why we need the grand jury here. To see if the evidence bears out what we think it'll show.

"Take a look at the charts," he said. "Mandeville borrowed the money from Principalities Financial. That was a Delaware consortium represented in this state by Samuel Lewis of

Springfield. Mister Lewis was a lawyer in nineteen sixty, with offices at Forty State Street. The offices are still there and Mister Lewis's name's still on the door and on the stationery, but it's also on a headstone in a cemetery in West Springfield and he's under it, so we'll never know whether he would say that the attorney-client privilege forbids him to tell anyone who his actual clients were.

"The paper on the keeper of the records for the Congregation of the Sons of the Immaculate Heart of Mary's kind of a shot we took in the dark where Mister Lewis's demise leaves us. The guy we're hoping for is Father Dominic Cleary—he was the Claretian money honcho when the whole land deal went through, but—"

"Forget Father Cleary," Magoun said. "I had a call from the good fathers in Chicago just this very morning. Father Cleary's with his Savior, has been since 'eighty-two. The official keeper of the records since then has been the Reverend Luis Delatorre, rector of the Eastern Province of the United States, assisted by the Reverend Anselm Dawes. I took the liberty of telling Father Dawes that either he or Father Delatorre could satisfy the terms of the subpoena by just copying the documents and expressing them to us, assuming the good fathers planned no Illinois proceedings to resist our jurisdiction. Well, he had some reason why that could not be done. Said they'd prefer not to entrust them to anybody else. So then I said that either one of them could do it, appear in person with the documents you asked for, and he immediately told me that if it was all right with me, they would both like to come. Why this is I didn't ask him—although I certainly have a right to, being's how travel expenses for witnesses come out of my budget, but I didn't. Maybe one's afraid to fly and the other holds his hand—or then again, they may be bookends, I dunno, you've got to take the pair."

Baldo gazed at him with disapproval. "You know, Burt," he said, "I think you've slipped into bad habits since I stopped supervising you. Looks to me as though the first thing Joe and I'll have to do here is get you shaped up again.

"The papers they bring with them aren't going to tell us much more than the papers that we've got, in all likelihood. Having them bring in the papers is just our pretext to get some warm body, any body, in before that jury, so that after he assures us that these records are all made and kept in the usual and ordinary course of daily business, we can butter him all up and see if there's a shred of information in his fertile brain that we could certainly use and he doesn't know he has. Now you know that, Burt, or used to, so when we put a paper on some unsuspecting soul and he wanders in to chat, you don't send the nice man home—you let him come in and sit down with us; let him testify, while we hang on his every word and a steno takes them down. He'll be a better person for it, and we'll have a better case, after we shrive him."

Magoun stared at Ianucci. "Maybe," he said, "just maybe, I should reconsider my evaluation of this contribution to my farflung operation."

"The results will be predictable," Ianucci said. "You've come up with nothing since I left your little vineyard that a borderline detective couldn't've reasoned his way to, out of the morning papers. But enough of this badinage—on to business here. Joe, you talk some now."

"You look down that time line," Corey said, "and when you come to June of nineteen sixty you start seeing blanks. We don't know where the loan cash came from, how it got to Shropshire before it got to Jim Mandeville. We have no more names, no places, and no dates. We hope the priests have got something, written down or memory, hearsay, anything, that will maybe give us at least a hint of that. But frankly that's a long shot; we think it's worth a try, but we don't think it's likely to come through.

"Anyway, after we try the priests out, then we come to Foothills National. Now we've looked into this, first through

Katherine McCormack, and then through her successor. And both of them confirm that Foothills then was just the same as all banks I've worked with since I started practicing law. By the late fifties, before this whole thing happened, every bank that had more than a dozen customers had converted or begun to convert all its paper records to microfilm records. All checks in and all checks out, and all other documents. Compact to store, and durable if not left out in the sun, which they very seldom were. The result in my old line of work was that when I absolutely had to prove the details of a transaction that happened twenty years or so ago, I could do it—where the old, bulky papers would've been destroyed after seven years or so, the microfiched files were complete. Dusty, but complete. So we know Foothills has the records—all we've got to do is ask.

"Now, the paper that we put on the bank, calling for whatever they've got for 'sixty through 'seventy, is pretty comprehensive. It may take two men two days and a dump truck to deliver, but we know they've got the stuff. To authenticate it to the jury? Fifteen minutes, max. An hour to label the various crates. And then two weeks, or three weeks, or maybe ten years, to itemize and chart what's on those spools of film. Then, if we get what we hope we're going to get, at least, then we'll need the jury back, for further fun and games. Most likely a whole day. To go after some more stuff."

Magoun frowned. "Yeah," he said. "I figured that, of course, this being all preliminary. But then I looked at those subpoenas in detail. The bank one there, I understand the first two paragraphs: all documents relating to transactions between Mandeville and anybody else between one/one/sixty and twelve/three/one/sixty-seven; and the same thing for all business through Claretian accounts. No headlines in that item; anyone who knows we're on the Mandeville homicide would expect we'd want his records, and no one who knew about his interest in that land would be surprised that we'd want the priests' checks, too. Naturally we would.

"But the third one, where you ask for all copies of bank

records for the Shropshire Inn between one/one/fifty-seven and twelve/three-one/seventy—now that's gonna start a bit of a stir. And so is the fourth one, where you ask for all Jack Davis's accounts, and Winifred with him. Not to mention the fifth one: all bank records for our late estimable brother, Gilbert Rogers, Esquire, for the same period of time. I realize the bank's not about to raise a stink, but if they did and said: 'Well, this is over-broad, too burdensome, a hardship,' and all that other stuff, I think you might be a little pressed to stop a judge from quashing it and getting mad at you. And let's not leave out the buzz that's going to start when the names on those accounts hit the front pages, friends: we don't actually come right out and say that Jack's a prime suspect, or that we think that Gilbert might've had a hand in it, but nobody who hears the story will have too much trouble figuring that's exactly what we think—why else would we ask for all their paperwork?"

"In other words," Ianucci said, "even to your nasty prosecutor's eyes, this looks like no more than a fishing expedition."

"That's about it, yeah," Magoun said. "I appreciate what you guys're doing here, and I'll back you all the way, but keep in mind that I'm the guy who's going to have to go into a courtroom if somebody takes the heat and says you've been unreasonable. If I have to, fine, I will, but when I do I want to win, not get my head handed to me out in front of God and all the damned reporters for letting my two volunteers go berserk and start their own private witch-hunt, out of my control. I agreed with your suggestion that you and Joe might as well plant the seeds of the gossip yourselves, so we'd get the weeds we wanted, but the crop that's going to spring up when these billets-doux go public could be poisonous. You're going to alert Davis, for one thing, and all his shady pals, and if you're right about them, give them time to destroy files or maybe even light out for the border."

"Okay," Ianucci said. "Let's take those things in order. It *is* a fishing expedition. As Joe's already told you: there's no way we can fill in those blank spaces on the time line until we get the names of the people who were involved. We think Jack Davis knows those names, because we think his is one of them. Burt, there's a lunker in the deep pool where Jack Davis swims. I haven't seen him, can't describe him, but I know he's there, and when we get our hook in him we'll have the bait we need, to get the sharks who sent him here. I hope. Jack showed up from nowhere, like he dropped down from the sky, conveniently one step ahead of Dawson Nichols's certain downfall either from gin or foreclosure. He had the financing, and management he knew. Jim Mandeville's most fervent prayers, answered by one man. Most convenient, I think. Where did he come from? New York? Not quite good enough. There's lots of people there. Why him and not somebody else? And if an inn was his heart's desire, why this inn here, of all inns, and not some other one?

"We want to know the answers to those perplexing questions," Ianucci said. "But before we ask them, we should have a good idea of what the truthful ones might be, so that if Jack doesn't give them, well, he gets a nasty choice: come coco with us, or else pack his grip and go to jail, either for perjury, if he lies, or contempt, if he clams up and we decide to get him immunized and he still won't talk.

"The truth, or the leads to it, is preserved in those records, which before Jack finds out we want them, will be in the bank's safekeeping, and after he finds out, well, they will be in ours. I grant you Jack and his sidekicks can sanitize their files, but I doubt very much that that would take them long, if it takes any time at all—dirty dealers like they are don't write many memoranda when they're up to wickedness.

"So, first we get the records, and then we go over them, and after we have done that, then we have Jack in to chat. And see which route he chooses—liking none of them."

Magoun nodded. "Neat, Baldo," he said, "very neat. I do admire a careful man. In the Lord's sight he is good. I just hope his luck holds out, because his luck is mine."

16

Luis Delatorre was a trim man with excellent posture, total physical composure, a fine head of curly silver hair, the facial features of a sculptor's idealized Caesar, and what seemed to be a fixed, wan, imperial smile of forgiveness as well. Anselm Dawes took Corey aside in the corridor outside the grand jury room after he was sure that Delatorre had seated himself as comfortably as possible on the oak bench in the anteroom, and asked if he might talk to him, "in full privacy." Corey showed him into the small, bare office next to the anteroom, and closed the door behind them.

"Father Delatorre," Dawes said, seated on an armless chair made of grey metal, with a thin grey cushion, "does not speak English quite as well as he believes he does."

"Would he like," Corey said, "would he prefer to testify with the help of an interpreter?" That night he told Jill he had already made up his mind to dispense with Father Delatorre's testimony entirely, "if Dawes gave me the wrong answer. God only knows what interpreters cost, but whatever it is, Burt ain't got it."

"I could've come in," Jill said. "I don't claim I could guide the Sunday tourists through the Alhambra, but rusty or not, it's still there."

"No, you couldn't, my dear," he said. "This here is the courts, not real life. To translate for the record you have to be certified for accuracy, truthfulness, and sweet breath. To get certified you have to be pals with one of the certified people, or someone a certified person's afraid of, such as a judge or a clerk. You can't get experience without experience. You know how these union shops work."

"My goodness, no," Dawes said, recoiling, "that would upset him most greatly. Father Delatorre is Hidalgo. His family is very old. Of the nobility. Very close to El Caudillo, during the regency. You have perhaps heard of his cousin, Francisco Delatorre."

"No," Corey said, "I can't say I have."

Dawes raised both eyebrows. "Well, of course the passion for the art is limited in this country. But when Father Luis was in the Panama, of course, much of his ready acceptance and his honor by the peasants whom he dealt with originated, he told me, in his blood connection to the famous matador. It was felt by many at that time that Francisco was in truth superior to both Dominguin and Ordoñez. But of course I do not know.

"But this is of no matter. Father Luis has been a proud man all his life. Not in the sense of the cardinal sin, but as he conducts himself. The dignity, I mean. To require or even to accept assistance in any aspect of his life would be repugnant to him. He prides himself on his mastery of languages. For many years after he was first ordained, when he served in the mission to the Panama at Darien, as he calls it, he spoke his Spanish, of course, and was most comfortable. Then for a time he was assigned the Eastern Province, after its creation in nineteen fifty-four, for about seven years. But he was in the office of the rector solely then. This was before he went to the mission in the Philippines, and I am told that he became most fluent in the Tagalog—but of course I do not know. His English, as it was required during his studies here and then in the mission fields, is quite adequate for life's necessities, certainly, since he has returned here, but not for abstruse conversations. So that is why I assist him, and travel with him when it becomes necessary that he conduct matters outside of the congregation. For the matters of purely intellectual concept, if I have made myself clear." He paused. "But Father Delatorre does not acknowledge this fact."

"Well," Corey said, "the questions that we have for him are certainly not abstract. The only things that we'll be asking pertain to whether he has knowledge of transactions that occurred here back in nineteen sixty, and his recollections, his memory, of people who were involved."

Dawes looked worried. "Yes," he said, "I understand that, and it is possible he does. That he does have such recollections as you will be asking for. But what I am suggesting is that he may not realize this, you see? And become confused about the meaning of a word. It would be best, therefore, I think, if you would question both of us at the same time. At once. If that could be done. From someone that he knows, with whom he is familiar, from such a person who is circumspect about the matter as he knows I will be, Father Delatorre will permit aid to be offered. He is most anxious always to collaborate in every way with secular authorities. So long as it is done, my help is, so that it does not appear to be that. If you understand."

"Well, I think I do," Corey said. "It doesn't seem to be that complicated a matter. But I'm afraid, you see, that that won't be possible. Unless Father Delatorre informs the District Attorney that he will be unable to testify before the grand jury without the aid of a translator, he must appear alone before it. I'm afraid that is the law."

"Alone?" Dawes said. "No one else in the room?"

"Well," Corey said, "the stenographer, of course, and I will be present, too. And the chief investigator, Mister Ianucci. But except for us and the witness who is called, only members of the jury may be in the room. And everyone who's in it, with the exception of the witness, is sworn to secrecy of everything they hear and see."

"Twelve persons of a jury?" Dawes said. "This stenographer, and you, and the policeman as well? Fifteen persons keep a secret?" He smiled. "Your sanctions must indeed be very strict, if this can be done. The Church, as you may know,

167

permits but one to hear a secret, and punishes that one severely if he discloses it. And even so, from time to time a trusted person strays and a secret is divulged."

Corey grinned. "Well," he said, "I'm new to this myself, so I can't say how well it works. But actually there're twenty-three members of a grand jury—the petit juries that hear trials, they're the ones made up of twelve. But I guess it must work, pretty well at least. It's been around for several centuries, since it was first put in, in England. The idea, as I get it, was to stop King John or one of those guys from railroading people that he didn't like into jail or to the gallows on trumped-up offenses. So they made it a law that no one could be accused of having committed a crime unless at least twelve ordinary people out of twenty-three who probably knew him, and maybe knew the king, too, heard what there was against him and said: 'Right, looks to us as though it was done, and this rascal might've done it. So bring him in and let's see if the king can prove his case.' But if most of them said: 'Nope, we don't see a crime here, just the king getting riled up,' or: 'Yup, there was a crime, all right, but we can't make ourselves believe that this guy probably did it,' well then, the king was out of luck, and that was the end of it.

"Which accounts for the secrecy rule; wouldn't make much sense to protect the innocent, if you let the king or his sheriff slander him all over the place before you said: 'He didn't do it.' As I say, it may look kind of clumsy, and I understand it seldom happens these days that a grand jury refuses to indict a guy the prosecutor thinks should be indicted, but it still seems to work—I doubt it would've lasted so long if it hadn't."

"Remarkable," Dawes said. He put his hands on his knees and then stood up. "Well," he said, "I shall with your permission do my best to acquaint Father Luis with the protocols involved here, and then we will await your pleasure to make our appearances."

Corey told Jill that night that Father Delatorre "was no more nervous than a drowsy alligator when he came in that jury room. Aristocrats do not have nerves; they have people to have nerves for them. Father Dawes was doing that. Father Luis was relaxed. Baffled, maybe, but relaxed.

"I was grateful to him, in a way. Burt'd come in with us, first, introduced Baldo and me to this bunch of perfectly nice people, all white, most looked to me like they'd retired from decent jobs and had the kind of time that lets you take an interest in what's going on out in the big world, and up to then I did just fine. But then Burt started winding up his little speech, summarizing Baldo's long, distinguished record, doing his level best to make my short and undistinguished one sound reasonably impressive, and he still hadn't gotten into the facts of the case.

"I think what Burt'd overlooked, making me look good, was that never having done this before, I literally did not know what I was doing. And therefore, last night at the very latest, better yet three days ago, I hadn't known I should sit down and write out the presentation I was now called on to give. I'm beginning to understand why Ed Birnam always became such a distracted son of a bitch when he had a hearing coming up. Big one, small one, in-between one, the first time to the last time that I saw the man transformed from a generous, patient, kindly guy into the best two-legged imitation I've seen of a real Tasmanian devil, I never ceased to wonder what in God's name set him off.

"Now I know. He knew from experience, or maybe just from observation of his father or a friend, the kind of paralytic fear you get when you see you're going to have to stand up and give a reasoned argument *that you have not prepared*. When I worked with Ed in preparation for some hearing on a matter that I'd handled in the office, I thought that he got crazy because he had pride of craftsmanship, and didn't want his client seeing him flounder around. I was wrong. Today I found out that his reason had zilch to do with clients; what made him crazy was the fear of how he'd look to himself, if he did a lousy job. All the times I worked with him preparing detailed notes, cross-referenced to files and pleadings, studded with citations and direct quotes from cases, I never once saw him rely on them, when the big day came. He always spoke *ex tempore*. And brilliantly, I might say. Those bales of notes and loose-leaf binders that I'd thrown my back out lugging up and down and back and forth, sat there on the table undisturbed, and unneeded. And that was why he didn't need them—because he had them, and he knew it. He was confident.

"Well, today I wasn't. So I winged it, best I could. It seemed like I was up there talking to those nice strangers about what happened to your grandfather for at least three hours. I desperately needed to go to the bathroom, and that was only natural because there wasn't any moisture in my mouth or throat or nose, and even though my palms and armpits were pouring out the sweat like lawn sprinklers at full throttle, there still had to be a spillover, and that'd gone down to my bladder." He laughed. "I looked at my watch when I sat down. I'd been on my feet nineteen full minutes."

She nodded. "So I can assume then," she said, "that we've heard the last crack out of you about what a cushy job it is, lecturing nine hours a week to a roomful of smart people who've got more time than you have to look up the facts you haven't studied since back when you were their age? And that we'll have no more of the easy supercilious condescension about how insecure a teacher must be if she can't find her research notes half an hour before she starts a seminar?"

"I think that would be a fair assumption," he said.

Father Luis Delatorre required what seemed to be a considerable amount of time to arrange himself to his own satisfaction in the oaken chair provided for witnesses in front of the dais where the foreman, deputy forewoman, and secretary of the grand jury nominally presided over the hearings. Corey and Ianucci sat to the deputy's right, the windows behind them, and in front a large oak table with their notes and documents. Delatorre at last folded his hands loosely in his lap, having carefully straightened the creases in his black trousers before crossing his left leg over his right at the knee. He showed his smile punctiliously around the room, dismissing unsaid, as quite unnecessary, the apologies he was certain the grand jurors would wish to volunteer for taking up his time, tacitly assuring them that he humbly served God by patiently serving them.

"State your name for the record, please," Corey said. "I was still flustered," he told Jill that night. Baldo'd trained me down finer'n a Kentucky Derby favorite: first have the foreman swear the guy, then ask him to state his name. So naturally I ask him first to give his name, and then Baldo gives me a dig and I asked that he be sworn."

Delatorre looked perplexed. The foreman, a semiretired Unitarian-Universalist minister, bald and lanky, who dressed in business suits but wore a black dickey and collar and preferred to be addressed as Phil—he pronounced his last name, spelled with two vowels and six hard consonants, as "Sheffley"—rose and raised his right hand. "Solemnly swear, affirm," he inquired brightly, "tell the truth, whole truth, nothin' but the truth, 'n'all matters which may be 'quired 'bout 'fore this grand jury, s'elp-you God?"

Delatorre remained seated and immobile, except for his facial muscles. He frowned and studied Sheffley as a grave five-year-old boy ponders his first boiled lobster, willing to concede that someone had placed it on his plate for some good reason but quite unable to conceive of what that reason might be.

Baldo dug an elbow into Corey's ribs. "Tell the reverend he has to be sworn," he hissed.

Corey nodded. "Ahh, Father Delatorre," he said, "the foreman, the Reverend Mister Sheffley, the procedures require that before you testify you must first be sworn to tell the truth."

Delatorre directed his clear brown-eyed gaze to Corey. "Really," he said.

"I'm afraid so," Corey said, "so if you'd stand and raise your right hand and be sworn now?"

Delatorre shook his head twice, glancing around the room at the jurors in the evident expectation that they shared his inability to fathom what was going on, but finding no sympathy in their faces, returned his gaze to Corey's. "Ah, Father Delatorre," Corey said, "if you would, ah, just *stand* now, and raise your right hand and so forth?"

"This was not a speedy business," Corey told Jill that night. "I'd already resigned myself to the fact that the only sensible thing to do with Father Delatorre was get him sworn, ask him a few harmless questions for appearances' sake, and get him the hell out of there so that Father Anselm could trot in, drop the papers and begone with him in tow. But first I had to get the guy sworn. I'd long since given up sweating sweat—now I was sweating lead bullets. But we got it done, at last. And then after that Father of course had to recompose himself for the taking of his formal portrait, exactly as he'd been before— it wouldn't've surprised me in the slightest if he'd complained about the lighting, in a polite and civilized way, of course: 'Perhaps a backlight, do you think? To put highlights into the hair?'—but it did seem as though we were at last under way, and this was not going to take long. After all, how much could this clerical boulevardier know? And on the off chance that he did know something, how in the world could I ever hope to get it pried out of him? 'Three minutes for you, pal,' was what I'd decided. 'Both of us can breathe easier, you just state your name here and be nice.' " He sighed. "Wrong again."

"Mister Corey," Ianucci said, after Delatorre had stated his name and address for the record, and said he was responding to the subpoena served upon the keeper of the Claretian records in Chicago, "would you mind if I, in the interest of brevity, put one or two of my questions first?"

"Not at all," Corey said.

"Father Delatorre," Ianucci said. "We haven't met. My name is Baldad Ianucci. I'm a special investigator for the District Attorney here. Working with Attorney Corey, beside me, on the early stages of this investigation."

"An unusual name," Delatorre said. "Your father, I take it, knew to cherish his friendships, be thankful to God for their solaces."

Ianucci smiled. "As I grew older, Father," he said, "I came to the understanding that my father indeed valued, most highly, the manifold blessings of friendships, but his main consolation, the years that I knew him, was in study of the Holy Scriptures. A contemplative man in his own nature, I think, apart from the world though thrust into it, but happiest in sole communion with God."

"Yes, yes," Delatorre said, beaming. "So often we see, do we not, Señor Baldad, the pain of the men, and the women, of course, souls whose great thirst for God can never be slaked because of commitments on earth."

Ianucci shook his head and showed sadness on his face. "You put it so well, Father," he said. "I've many times wondered, as I've grown older, if a vocation discovered too late does not ask of its bearers just as great sacrifices as the calls that come early exact. The joys of this world my dad had in plenty, but those that he craved were of the next."

Delatorre nodded twice with serene sadness. "Very common, sir," he said, "very common indeed. We soldiers of Christ encounter it often in our ministrations to lay men and women whose devotion consumes their own lives. It touches us deeply and serves to remind us how doubly blessed God made us."

"And I'd imagine, Father Delatorre," Ianucci said, "that during your years of service assisting the late Father Cleary, you encountered many such people. In the world, surely, but not of the world, and humbly devoted to God's will. Such as, for example, the late Jacob Stritch, who donated his beautiful estate in these hills to the benefit of your congregation."

"Ah, Jacob Stritch," Delatorre said, his smile radiating goodwill, "I must confess I did not have the pleasure of ever encountering him. But Father Dominic Cleary, my wonderful mentor and predecessor in my post now, he spoke with fulsome and unbounding affection of his Jacob. 'A generous, godly generous man.' "

"The estate being valuable, you mean?" Ianucci said.

"Of course, of course," Delatorre said, "but greater in the spiritual sense. For the nearly forty years that the congregation occupied it, the Shores was a place of comfort, light, and hope, a refuge from the world of ardor for those returning from the field, a warm bastion of sanctuary for awakening postulants, and a harbor of surcease from care for those who sometimes had professed no vows, or not their final vows, but had undergone the breakdown of the spirit in their quest. What I think is called today the intervention of the crisis, I believe."

"Yes," Ianucci said. "But to your knowledge, there came a time at last when it seemed best that the congregation seek an offer to purchase the Shores, correct? Father Cleary told you this?"

Delatorre nodded. "Yes, Father Dominic, he did tell me of this. As it transpired I was with him when the reaching of decision was accomplished. This was nineteen fifty-nine, after much prayer for divine guidance that we did not act too rashly or too foolishly in this. But in the years since Mister Stritch had given the Shores to us, our work in Chicago had expansioned greatly through the National Shrine to Saint Jude, and then in nineteen thirty-two, a long time then, the Police League for patronage of all engaged in the keeping of God's peace in this world as we know it. So it was thought appropriate, and then with the further center we set up in Kankakee, that with almost ten thousand members in that flock alone, it was best that we concentrate our efforts in this part of America in the heartland, as they say. And so after the meditation and much planning, it was determined that Father Dominic would notify our secular attorney to begin the undertaking to convert Mister Stritch's very generous gift into the means to be employed for the further furtherance of those undertakings. As I say."

"In other words, to sell it," Ianucci said.

"That is right, yes," Delatorre said. "To make it better possible that Mister Stritch's gift to the congregation for the repose of his soul would be applied as he would wish to the congregation's needs, as God had worked an alteration of those needs."

"And do you know who this secular attorney was, that Father Dominic contacted?" Ianucci said.

"I do of course," Delatorre said, smiling. "This would have been Attorney Henry M. O'Hara, Esquire, of Manhattan, New York City, the son of Attorney Henry F. O'Hara, Esquire, a most devout, devoted man, very loyal to the Church, to Holy Mother Church, and especially to our order, for many, many years. As was his son whom I met, and the father as well, too, although he was by then retired so I did not see him, to meet. It was not an active part, but a very devout, devoted man, a true son of the Church."

"And Father Dominic requested him, this would be Henry M. O'Hara, to find a buyer for the Shores?" Ianucci said.

"Yes," Delatorre said. "That is what he did."

"And do you know what steps Attorney O'Hara took, if any, to find such a buyer?"

"Yes, I do," Delatorre said. "I know those steps because there was an illness at this time in Father Dominic's family, a very serious affliction of portacted—long duration, that his mother who had become quite elderly became also very ill with. And he was called to her side to be with her when she went, and it was a duty that called him to Troy, New York, where he remained for many weeks. So it became my authority to do as Father Dominic had expected that he would participate himself, with Attorney O'Hara, and this is what I did. As Father Dominic preferred."

"And what was it exactly that you did?" Ianucci said. "Did you talk to Attorney O'Hara by phone? Confer with him in New York? Approve papers for the congregation? Confer with other parties as they came into the deal?"

Delatorre looked puzzled again. He paused. He canted his head to the right. "Yes," he said.

"Perhaps I'm not making myself clear," Ianucci said. "While you were substituting for Father Dominic as the congregation's financial officer, did Attorney O'Hara mention any other names to you?"

Delatorre resolved his expression into a smile again. "Oh," he said, "of course, of course. Other persons' names. Yes. I recall a Gilbert Rogers. Attorney Gilbert Rogers, Esquire, of the same town as the Shores, in which the Shores are located. Attorney Rogers was involved. Attorney O'Hara spoke of him with great admiration, kindly, and said that he would surely represent us in the town and in the matter quite as well, with all the skill and honesty we could expect of him. Of Attorney O'Hara, that is what I mean to say. Or he meant to say."

"So you trusted Attorney Rogers, on Attorney O'Hara's say-so," Ianucci said.

"Yes, yes, I did," Delatorre said eagerly.

"And did you ever have occasion to meet Attorney Rogers, or talk to Attorney Rogers on the telephone?" Iannucci said.

"Yes, yes, I did," Delatorre said. "I did this several times."

"Which?" Ianucci said.

"Well, both of those things," Delatorre said. "As you said, I talked to him, I spoke with him by telephone. Many, several times, that I recall now, at least that. And then I met him also, when he brought the papers down, that I had to sign. And I was there to sign them."

"You were where to sign them?" Iannucci said.

"In Attorney O'Hara's office," Delatorre said. "In Manhattan. In New York. I went there in nineteen sixty. I recall it being hot, very very hot. I believe the train I took there was the Empire Limited, or the Empire Builder, perhaps, and I went there in the summer because I had to sign the papers, Father Dominic's dear mother's illness having kept him away so long. And although of course he was there, Father Dominic was there, he thought it best and I was pleased to do as he requested, that since he had not been present during so much of the matter, that I should be there with him and advise him if he wished. And Attorney Rogers was there when we went into the room, Father Dominic and I, and I remember seeing him, a very handsome man. I think about your age, sir, Mister Ianucci, fifty-three or -four, perhaps, but much taller in his stature and quite most distinguished-looking."

"And what happened then?" Ianucci said.

"Father Dominic introduced me first to Attorney O'Hara, with whom I had spoken so many times by telephone but I had not met, and then Attorney O'Hara introduced us both to Attorney Rogers who was also a most impressive man. And they said, both attorneys said, that we should read the papers, which the buyer had all signed, and that were we satisfied, or if we had some question first, we should ask it of them, and then that if we felt that this was all done in good order and according to the understandings we had found in our discussions, conversations we had had, then we too should sign the papers and the money would be given."

"This would have been a million dollars," Ianucci said.

"As I think I recall, it was. It was a million dollars. I know it was a large amount, much greater than the sums that I had worked with in the past as Father Dominic's assistant, and I had not seen before a check for such a sum, and I think it was one million dollars, yes."

"And you signed the papers," Ianucci said.

"We read the papers," Delatorre said, "Father Dominic and then I, and we did this carefully, and it all seemed to us to be as we had discussed what would be done. It was to our comprehension. And there may have been some little questions, very little ones, *pequeño*, that were trivial, as you know, as those questions they answered, Attorney O'Hara and Attorney Rogers answered them for us, and to our reconciliation.

"And then Attorney O'Hara said to Attorney Rogers: 'And you have the check with you of course, Gil? So that we may see that it is also all drawn properly and quite correct, according to agreement?' And Attorney Rogers took out of his pocket an ordinary white envelope with his name and address on it, but without an address of a person typed on it, and opened up the envelope and showed the check to us, and handed it to Attorney O'Hara, and he inspected it, and then he handed it to Father Dominic and me, and we too inspected it to make it sure it was the right amount, and certified and so forth, and that it was made out as we had agreed, to Gilbert Rogers, Esquire, as attorney for the buyer, Mister James Mandeville Junior, and then on the back a place for Attorney Rogers to endorse, beneath a typing which said that it should be paid to Henry M. O'Hara, Esquire, as attorney for the congregation. And it was. It was as we had agreed. For a million dollars. That was the amount. And then as they directed us, Father Dominic signed the papers and I witnessed him do that, and Attorney Rogers signed the check on the back as it was called for, and handed it to Attorney O'Hara back again after so doing. And that was what we did. And it was completely done."

"Do you recall, Father," Ianucci said, "do you recall whether there was any conversation while all of this was going on?"

"Well, there was conversation, certainly," he said. "It was all, well, for the attorneys it was business in the usual, as they were accustomed, but for Father Dominic and me, it was the big event, a kind of thing in size of magnitude we were not used to or accustomed. So we both were quite excited, and most happy, gratified too, as well, yes. For the congregation, and the money of Jacob Stritch, whose generous gift those years ago had multiplied in talents as the bible tells the prudent to make sure they invest wisely." He chuckled. "I would not say to you today that everything, that everything we said then was, well, quite sensible, but certainly we talked, yes, and laughed—we also laughed."

"And did Attorney O'Hara and Attorney Rogers," Ianucci said—"try to focus in on this now, Father, and I know it's long ago, but did you hear either of them say anything to the other when that check came out?"

Delatorre nodded. "Yes," he said. "I did that, yes. I remember it quite clearly, and if Father Dominic were here, he would recall it too, I'm sure. Because it was not something that, you understand, I hope, that we had expected. We had both come to Manhattan, to Attorney O'Hara's office, in the understanding that the matter was concluded and resolved and everything, just now the paperwork, as the two of them called it. And then Attorney O'Hara, when Mister Rogers showed the check, he said: 'Well now, at long last, Gil, I see it, right before my very eyes. Until now, I wasn't sure this would ever come to pass. But damn, I do believe it now. After all that stuff we went through, back and forth, this way and that, your man with his chilly feet—"I guess I will," "No, maybe not," "Gee, I don't know—I've got to think"—there were an awful lot of times there when I thought this wouldn't happen.' " He hesitated. "What all this meant we did not know."

"And did Attorney Rogers make any response to this, to what Attorney O'Hara'd just said?" Ianucci said.

"Yes, yes he did," Delatorre said. "Both Father Dominic and I, of course, we were completely silent. Because we did not know what this was, what was being said, or what it meant to us, or to the congregation, the whole matter we had worked so hard to do. And it bothered us. So we were interested. And most concerned, as well. That there had been a doubt, it now appeared, we had not known about. And Attorney Rogers laughed and he slapped Attorney O'Hara's back in a comradely fashion, and he said: 'Henry, Henry, I told you. I told you not to worry. These small-town tycoons play it cautious. That's the way they are, because that's the way they live, and when they do business, well, that's the way they do that, too. Very deliberate, very slow, very careful, think things over a long time. Especially when it's something or it's someone they don't know, something that they have't done, or something that they have done, but not with a new guy that they don't see every day. Their underwear shrinks under them, right while they talk to you. And they have to adjourn, you know, and go home and change, and all the whole time they're changing, well, they're thinking, worrying.

" 'Jim Mandeville's the kind of guy, you meet him in a bar somewhere, like the clubhouse down at Gulfstream or a drink at Twenty-one, and he'll come on like J. Paul Getty, small-town but big-time guy. But when it comes to putting zeroes on a paper that'll be his IOU, and he hasn't always known the guy whose name's there as payee, he gets jittery and nervous. Takes him time to take the plunge.

" 'Marco Piantidosi to you is just a guy you've always known. Principalities to you is just a thing that Marco does, just a minor sideline operation by a client that you met and got to know from his really major interests. So to you a guy like Mandeville should be giving thanks to God that you know a man like that, like Marco who can carry him, who will bail him out on this. But to Jim, well, he's not sure. And that's really all it was, Henry, just a matter, soothing Jim. Just getting Jim calmed down and all. I told you: "Don't worry about it, Henry. Let me handle it." You did, and I did it. Now it's all over with.' "

"Did Attorney O'Hara respond in any way to this?" Ian-ucci said.

Delatorre shook his head. "No, no," he said. "Attorney O'Hara seemed to think, and then he looked at Father Dominic and me, and then he coughed and said that much water had gone over many dams since he first encountered Attorney Rogers, and this was just the latest overflow, and we should finish it. Complete what we had come to do. So we did, and Attorney O'Hara had us come with him to a bank, Attorney Rogers, too, and he endorsed the check and we saw him make it a deposit in his firm's account, and then he wrote another check, to Father Dominic as the rector of the province, and had this certified, and gave it to Father Dominic for us to take back with us. For one million dollars."

"Neither Attorney O'Hara nor Attorney Rogers deducted any part of that million for a fee?" Ianucci said.

"No, that is correct," Delatorre said. "They did not. It was my understanding, from Father Dominic, that Attorney O'Hara's habit was to bill the congregation at the end of June each year, for the services he had done during the previous twelve months. But his bill was always the same, for a thousand dollars, as it is today, and he always sends a check in the same amount, as soon as we have paid him, to some special project we have started in that year. I think Attorney O'Hara does this work for us as an offering to God, and that he seeks no profits from it in this world."

"Tell me, Father Delatorre," Ianucci said, "in the course of your dealings with Attorney O'Hara since that day, when the congregation got the million for Claretian Shores, have you ever had any subsequent dealings, through him or anyone else, directly or indirectly, with this Marco Piantidosi?"

Delatorre shook his head. "That is the only time I have ever heard that name," he said. "I proposed to Father Dominic before I left for Manila, which was shortly afterward, that we ought to ask Attorney O'Hara for that gentleman's address, in order that we might entreat him for assistance since he seemed to be a man of great personal resources. I was making a small joke, but I was also serious. But Father Dominic did not find this humorous, and merely made a sound, what one would call a grunt, and then shortly afterward I was commissioned to the mission in the Philippines, and I did not return to the province office for several years since then. I did not speak with Father Dominic again before he died about this Marco person. I have not heard the man's name since."

"Upon your return," Ianucci said, "and upon reviewing the books when you succeeded Father Dominic in his office, did you find any record indicating that he or any other member of the congregation had had any dealings whatsoever with this Piantidosi?"

Delatorre shook his head again. "No, no," he said. "I must confess I was not intending to find his name recorded, but I do not think I saw it in any form of a notation that would suggest that Father Dominic or anybody else had ever had a contact with him. Not one that I remember."

Ianucci sat back and nodded. "You've been very helpful and forthright, Father Delatorre," he said. "I thank you, and I'm sure the members of the jury join me in that sentiment. Mister Corey, I'm sorry to have taken so much time. Have you any questions of the witness?"

"I had one," he said to Jill that night. "Well, actually I had several, but most of them were to the effect of how the hell I'd managed to practice law for six years, taking depositions, preparing testimony, doing all those things for Ed and the other litigation partners, without getting so much as a faint glimmer of how a man who really knows what he's doing mines the gold out of a solid object that looks like nothing more to me than a big, black, solid ordinary rock. But that could wait, I thought. So all I asked him was whether he had signed or not signed papers on that day in New York."

Delatorre showed the frown again. "Signed papers?" he said. "Yes, I was in New York, Attorney O'Hara's office, the day of signing papers. As I told Mister Ianucci when he asked me that."

"I'm sorry," Corey said. "I didn't make myself clear. I'm just trying to clarify something in my own mind here. I thought at one point you said that you signed some of the papers, and then at another point, somewhat later on, or perhaps it was before, you said Father Dominic signed them. And implied you did not."

Delatorre's smile reappeared. "Ah," he said, "I think I see. No, I did not take my pen from its pocket and put my name on them. Father Dominic did all of that, for the congregation, I mean. I meant to say that I was there, because he had missed

182

so many days when I had been his substitute, so that was why he desired me to attend the signings with him. In case there was some question. But to place the signature upon the papers—Father Dominic did that. I was only there."

"But there's no question in your mind," Corey said, "of the exchange you heard between the two attorneys, Rogers and O'Hara? That you didn't understand?"

Delatorre shook his head emphatically. "No," he said, "no question, none. That was as how I have accounted it. It troubled me that day because it was something that I did not understand. That there had been some reservation, or some difficulty, in the sale of the Shores to Mister Mandeville. And I had thought I understood the entire incident, and had made it my duty to do that in case Father Dominic required assistance from me. So I was somewhat, just for a short time, somewhat troubled then, and for that reason it remains clear in my mind. Because even to this very hour, I do not understand."

"And then we excused him," Corey told Jill that night. "The jurors had no questions, of course, not knowing what was going on, and all I'd done was maybe shortstop a small problem later on of that small inconsistency in his testimony. Because of course we'd seen copies of the documents that we were going to get, and got—it took about eight minutes—from Father Dawes, and nowhere on those papers is the Delatorre name."

"Nice going, kid," Ianucci said, as the grand jurors took advantage of a ten-minute break to smoke, visit the toilets, or merely stand and stretch. "I got so wound up in what I was doing I missed that little contradiction. Just the nasty little land mine that blows up under you, six months down the line."

"Yeah, right," Corey said. "I don't know what you would've done without me."

17

When the subpoena directing Jack Davis to produce his personal and business records became public record, he seemed not to have had any inkling that his financial dealings might interest the District Attorney. Beth Warren of the Pittsfield *Courier* visited the Shropshire Inn for his reaction comment. She called him to the registration desk by tapping the small bell on it, and he emerged from the kitchen, wiping his hands on a dish towel, appearing harassed and recovering slowly after having been momentarily stunned. She had to repeat she knew that the grand jury had demanded to receive the next day copies of virtually all of his records—his own, his wife's, and those of the Shropshire Inn, and asked again whether he had any comment. He dropped the towel on the floor and said: "You must be shittin' me. How did you go and find this out?"

When she told him subpoenas became matters of public record as soon as return of service was made to the Clerk of Court, he said: "Well, I don't know what to make of this. It just beats the hell out of me." When she asked him whether he knew of any possible link between his dealings and the 1967 homicide of James Mandeville, he said: "Homicide? No homicide—that was a suicide, lady. Jim killed himself, poor screwed-up bastard. Everyone knows that. Not why he did it, no one knew that, but that he did. Killed himself. That was no homicide. Now you will please get out of here."

When she asked if that implied he had not heard or read about reports that Burt Magoun had reopened the case as a murder investigation, he did not respond. When she repeated the question, he bent down, his face for a moment out of her sight, and picked up the towel. When he straightened up he was expressionless. He rested the heels of his hands on the edge of the desk and said: "Miss, I've asked you politely to get off my property. Now I'm *telling* you to leave. I've talked to my lawyer and I don't want you around when I talk to him again. Or any other time, either. And since this's the only phone on this floor, and I don't feel like going upstairs to call him or want you here while I talk to him, I have to order you to leave."

To later inquiries, including one last predeadline follow-up call from Warren, he responded uniformly with: "Neither Winifred or I will have any comment on this matter. If you have any questions, call our attorney, Mister Robert Gates. His number is in the phone book." Gates answered the calls by reading from a sheet of paper typed by his secretary:

"Jack and Winifred Davis are aware of no facts or suspicions about their conduct which would warrant a criminal investigation in this county or anywhere else. As owners and managers of the Shropshire Inn for nearly a quarter of a century, they have established themselves as honest and respectable business people with strong ties to and a considerable personal stake in their community. As their attorney, I have advised them to make no comment at this time on any slander, rumor or innuendo prompted by this or any other outrageous and irresponsible action by the District Attorney, or anyone acting in questionable authority on his behalf, and we put him and all such persons on notice that we are considering legal action for any and all damages caused by this gross and unsubstantiated speculation."

"My, my," Michelle said that evening from her kitchen, where she was preparing a salad while Jill tended to a roasting chicken, "sounds like our two wayward boys have struck a tender nerve."

"Can they sue?" Jill said.

"Oh, probably," Michelle said. "No one ever actually has in any of the cases Baldo's ever had, but the first time he nabbed a big one, after I knew him, the other lawyer blustered all over the place with the same kind of threats, and I asked Baldo if he could. And Baldo said: 'Yeah, sure, it can be done. Malicious prosecution. But to prove that and get some money, he'll have to show we didn't have a reason in the world to go after his guy, and that after we went after him we couldn't come up with anything. Which'll be pretty hard to do this time, same's it always is, because no one who knows his business, and how much of it he's got, ever needs to go out scavenging for more by making cases up. We've got him by the short hairs.' So since Baldo's been at this a pretty long time, and Joe's working with him on it, I don't think you really need to worry yet about your life's savings or your silverware."

"Joe was absolutely in awe of what Baldo did in that grand jury today," Jill said. "He said he was magnificent, questioning the priest."

Michelle laughed. "Baldo's a piece of work," she said, "so long as Baldo thinks he has a real piece of work to do. After we got involved down in Hartford—it turned out it wasn't sabotage, or anything like that; just one squad of incompetent installers out of about four that worked at an assembly plant out on the West Coast, where the planes were put together—I began to watch him, you know? And also naturally I got a lot of feedback from the plant floor, once people knew we were a thing. Between the people who thought I must know something about the guy that'd explain him, to them, and the people who thought they knew something that'd explain him to me, so I'd stop going around with him, before I let him ruin my life, I didn't have a minute's peace.

"So I decided then and there there must be about six Baldos, at least. The three I knew—first the one that's just all business, the one that first came in the office; then the bear we met when he got mad; and then the nice older fellow that took me out to dinner and smooth-talked me right into bed—plus one that seems like an innocent little boy, one that doesn't really understand what it is you do, so you have to explain it to him maybe fifty times, until it dawns on you that he understands it fine, and did long before he talked to you, but wants to know for sure if you do, and he takes some convincing. And, lemme see, then there's the father confessor, knows you've done wrong even if you don't, and wants you to confess for your own good, just for your own peace of mind; and the sixth one would be the insidious one, which he says is the one that makes money."

She laughed. "I should explain that to you," she said. "When Baldo says he thinks he's going to make a little money today, he's not talking about anything that you can spend on something silly, or will pay taxes on. 'Making money' is his term for making progress on a case. The other stuff he does okay on—we're comfortable enough, have everything we want—but the money-making that he's good at, really good at, I mean, is the other kind. He really does have an uncanny ability . . ."

Baldo, followed by Corey, entered the kitchen as she spoke. "Now don't be telling family secrets, sweetie," Baldo said, patting her buttocks. "Let's just all have a nice drink and celebrate a good day's work. Because the only other reward that we're going to get from it's exactly the same one that you always get from one: the right and obligation to put in lots more days of work, and hope to God that one or two of them will turn out good."

"Lawyer Gates is annoyed at you two," Michelle said, as he poured wine. "He as much as said that you and Burt're being very mean to that nice man and his wife who clip the tourists at the inn."

"Imagine that," Baldo said, pouring glasses of chardonnay. "The effrontery of the man."

"Can he do anything?" Jill said. "He said 'legal action.' "

"Smokescreen," Baldo said. "He could do that, but he won't. What he's really doing, or I would be if I were in his place, is burning up the phone lines, as his client's doing, too. Assuming that he knows just as well's his client does what it was his client did, and who he did it for. As he certainly does, of course, and has for many years, ever since he signed on with old Gilbert and old Gilbert clued him in."

"Well," Jill said, "that can't be too good, can it? If they've been alerted now? All these years when no one's said as much as boo about the case, they all must've thought they had nothing to worry about. And now all of a sudden you two come around and start making all this noise—won't this sort of give them time, to cover up their tracks?"

"In the first place," Baldo said, "it's way too late for that. If this was the morning after your grandfather was found murdered, then there might be something still lying around that they hadn't erased yet, because they hadn't had the time. But this is over twenty long years later, so everything they thought then that they should make disappear has been long since disappeared.

"That means the only things that might be still around are either the things they didn't think of disappearing then, so they're still worth looking for, or the things they couldn't erase then because they weren't in their control. And that's where they still are: out of their control. The fossils sure don't tell us as much about the early dinosaurs as we could learn, if we could come up with six or eight of them alive, but those fossils still tell us a hell of a lot, and they're much easier to catch, nowhere near as dangerous. Besides, we're not out to make a working model here, of a dinosaur: all we have to do is prove the dinosaur existed.

"And in the third place," he said, following Corey into the dining area, "much to what I think was Joe's mild consternation here, the first thing that we did when we started in on this little Boy Scout project was make sure all the creatures who've been happy in these woods for all these many years, since they killed a man to steal then, got the news informally that two new bears've come to town and they have revenge in mind. So Bob Gates and Jack Davis and the shady higher-ups've had two or three weeks before this to wonder what was up. And you can bet they've chatted once or twice in the meantime, the big villains somewhere else being soothing, confident, the petty villains around here sweating maybe just a little, trying hard to reckon what we knew, or might find out.

"So all we did today was drop the other shoe. Now Jack and Bob and Winifred, and the folks they work for, now they all know that we know more than Al Feldt did, and Burt cares more about the case than the guy who ran it, back when it happened, more'n he even dreamed. Now they can do some serious sweating, especially our Jack and our Bob. Nobody ever spotted Jack's part in this whole thing before. Well, we have, and he knows it. What we've spotted, he does not know. Neither do we, of course, but Jack doesn't know that. And by now Jack's forgotten quite a bit of what he did himself, what the actual details were. And Bob, not having learned about it until three, four years afterward, is even more at sea. Did Jack make some dumb mistake, in 'sixty-eight or -nine? Did Bob, before he knew the score, mention some little detail that gave it all away? Did Gil maybe overlook some telling item back then, one that Bob skipped over, too, when he succeeded Gil? Tossin'-turnin' nighttimes now: 'Did we give it away, ten or fifteen years ago, but nobody noticed then?' "

He laughed. "That'd be the best thing," he said, "if the buggers panicked. If they sat upright in bed in the middle of the night and said: 'My God, I wrote that check.' Or: 'I signed that goddamned paper. If they find that we'll be sunk. I've got to get it back.' And then did something stupid so we caught them in the act."

He sighed. "Well, that won't likely happen. We've got pros on our hands here. Guys who've been at it a long time. If we ever catch these guys, it'll be the hard way, by our own legwork and sweat. But never fear, Joe, we will catch 'em. We will catch 'em good. And when we catch 'em, the live ones will be looking at the outside from the inside, a long time to come."

He swirled the pale gold wine in the glass. "I do declare," he said, "I just love making trouble for real deserving people. Beats loafing every time. By the time your snooty buddy Roger calls us back with Marco's file, we'll be halfway to setting up Brother Davis's big chance to tell his own side of the story to all of those nice people in that big room in the courthouse there, few miles up the road."

Corey settled easily and comfortably into the routine of autumn days and evenings on the lake. Around six-thirty in the morning the light coming through the eastern windows of the bedrooms-become-offices on the second floor grew strong enough to lift the darkness of the western-facing bedroom that he shared with Jill, and leaving her curled up in sleep, he disposed of the first hygienic details of the morning in the bathroom before putting on his robe and padding downstairs to the kitchen to get the coffee started. For the first half of September, enough stragglers had lingered in the condominium compound to warrant the paperboy's prolongation of his summer route—one couple, Corey did not know whether they lived in the development or on a farm nearby, elegantly rode shining roans along the lakeshore each morning for about two weeks, one or the other of the riders occasionally pausing to allow the mount to drink while the sun rose above the trees behind them and began to rinse the lavender out of the hills across the lake, but those visitations ended after the third weekend. Then came what Baldo said was the lull before the foliage season would bring some weekend traffic for about a month; the paperboy had stopped appearing, and Corey had become accustomed to irritably depending on the *Today* show for inadequate informational distraction while the coffee brewed. The birds that had tormented him as a late-sleeping city dweller in the warmer months seemed to have lost their voices, or perhaps departed, too, and the random cry of an eccentric loon that sometimes plied the lake was the only sound he heard that he had not caused himself.

Jill, finding him one morning absently cradling his mug of coffee in both hands while he sat on the couch and ignored the TV set, theorized that he was rapidly proceeding on his way to seed. He took it as a joke, grabbing her wrist and caressing her hand as she sat on the arm of the couch and said: "No, I'm becoming meditative, darling. I've sent away to a *bhagwan*, he takes MasterCard and Visa, for my personal mantra, and by Christmas I should be in Nirvana state. If not, I get a full refund, plus a complimentary set of famous Ginsu knives, just for accepting the trial offer."

"I'm serious," she said. "You're slipping into something here, and I'm doing it myself, that's as pernicious in its own sweet way as the life we left behind. You're treading water, Joe. Not making progress here. And so am I, right in step, too, one day at a time, and isn't life just bliss."

"I am not 'treading water,' as you so gently put it," he said. "You've seen those three-foot boxes full of bank records upstairs there. There're twelve of them. One for the good fathers, which we've been through. Four for Jack Davis and his wife and the inn, two an' a half of which we've cataloged, item by every item. And seven that we haven't even touched yet, for Jim Mandeville himself.

"Now I grant you, and I wish it wasn't so, but I grant you that ninety-nine and forty-four one-hundredths of what's in them isn't worth a damn to us. What Jack paid his wholesale suppliers for kitchen staples, and how much it cost him to get the squirrels evicted—four times so far, we know about, persistent little rodents—from the attic of the place; that does not advance us much. Or what it cost him to get all the drains derooted and freed up. Doesn't help much either. But Baldo says, and I believe, oh, I do solemnly believe, that the other fifty-six one-hundredths of the stuff is exactly what we're looking for, and therefore we have to find it. Which means we have to look for it, because we don't know which one-hundredths those fifty-six are until we look through all of them. Dull and very time-consuming, dear, but necessary. And that does not take into account the stuff that we don't find there, that we would expect to find, and how come it wasn't there. About which we will want to talk to Jack again. That will take time, too."

"That isn't what I mean, Joe," she said, pulling away and rising. She headed for the kitchen, talking as she poured her coffee and began to drink it, black. "I know if you're going to do this, you have to do it right, and I think it's wonderful that you enjoy it so damned much. But what I mean is that I think both of us are really almost wallowing in this, taking this to an extreme that's really just as bad for us and bad for our well-being as the rat race that we left.

"Look at me." She returned to the living room. "Tuesday and Thursday I give my classes. Monday mornings, research at home. Wednesday mornings, research at school. Wednesday P.M.s, for two hours or so, office hours at school. Fridays, all day, writing at home. Weekends? Oh, hell, I sleep late, one day at least, maybe catch an old movie or read a new book, or actually shop for food. And then in a great show of boundless energy, cook Sunday dinner for all four of us, the one meal a week that Michelle doesn't cook. And where do I do that? In her kitchen. She cleans up. Because she knows where things go.

"We've been here now coming up on a month. We're still driving the rented car. Sure, we make do—one's all I need, and when you go out, you're with Baldo. But what've we done about buying our own cars? Mister Hertz gets a good rate, you know—he'll let us keep that thing as long as we like, and he'll go to Paris. We won't. And, while we're at it, how many times has that Murtagh woman called here? Have we looked at one dream house she's mentioned? Or even one miserable house? Have we studied one town around here? Have we acted as though we're mature adults now, hardy professional types?

"We've done no such damned thing. I'll tell you what we've done: we've reverted, that's what. We're in the same sluggardly, slovenly mode that my seniors lapse into each spring. 'Hey, go with the flow. We're graduating. Let's have a few beers, a good time. And then after that, let's hit the beach, and when it gets cold, we'll go home. Mom and Dad'll be glad to see us.' We're using Baldo and using Michelle as our surrogate Mom and Dad. And they're using us, in their happy way, as Junior and Sis, but housebroken. I tell you, Joe, if we're not careful, we'll become a prime-time sitcom. You can be Desi and I'll be Lucy, and they can be Ethel and Fred. Or Baldo can be Ralph and she can be Alice, and you and I'll be Ed and Trixie.

"It's time we got cranked up, husband of mine. It's time to pull socks up, to wash. It's time to stop mushrooming our way through life. We're too old, and I'm getting unhappy. I want to be free, upstanding and adult, and worry too much, just like grown-ups." She paused. "Besides, I think I'm knocked-up."

18

Ten days later Corey in the middle of the morning heard Baldo grunt, and grunt again, at his desk in the adjoining room. Corey had just started on the first of the three-foot boxes holding Mandeville's bank records. Baldo said: "Say, Joe, this inventory, that we've got on Davis? Is there something missing here we ought to think about?"

Corey stood up and stretched. He took his time crossing into Baldo's room. He leaned against the door frame. "Got to say, Baldo," he said, "there very well might be. But what it is would be harder to say. I thought we fine-tooth-combed him pretty well."

Baldo was frowning over his half-glasses. "Yeah," he said, "we did. But I've lived in this state awhile now. And there's something missing in his stuff. How far're you on Mandeville? You finished 'sixty yet?"

"Finished it?" Corey said, "God, no, I just opened the box. I'm up to the middle of March, nineteen sixty. No dazzlers yet that I've found."

"Yeah," Baldo said. "While you're going through it, keep an eye peeled for all canceled checks he wrote for car insurance, repairs, excise taxes, stuff like that."

Corey allowed his expression to go blank. "Don't recall any so far," he said. He straightened himself. "Lemme get my list here." He took the list from his desk and returned to the doorway. He leafed through the two sheets. "Well, I don't know," he said, "guess this could be one. The sixteenth of January, two hundred and nine bucks, made out to the Town of Shropshire. There's a notation on the back of it: 'Excise tax on personal car.' "

"Yeah," Baldo said. "Well, maybe he had a Jeep or something, or that was Mimi's car. But I'll bet you it wasn't the Caddy. As you go through the rest of his stuff, watch for any items like that. Anything that looks like car expense. I bet what you find is that those items just stop. Sometime in late May or June, and then there won't be any more."

"I don't follow," Corey said. "Why won't there be any more?"

"Because there aren't any at all in Jack Davis's records," Baldo said, "and that fact just caught my attention. If you pulled all my records, any month, any year, and you went through them, check by check, you'd find lots of that kind of stuff. Renewals of car registration. Those excises to the town. Repairs. Routine service. Very impressive insurance bills, bigger checks every year. But I will bet that you're not going to find any canceled checks that Mandeville signed after spring, nineteen sixty, to cover those little items."

Baldo nodded and hummed. "And when you don't," he said, "that's going to be very interesting. Same as it is with Jack Davis, who doesn't have any either. And neither does his dear wife, Winifred. Or the fine Shropshire Inn that they run." He put his papers down on his desk. "But Jack did have a car. And so did the late Mister Mandeville. Since I have a car, and I have canceled checks, a good many checks every year, none of which I really liked writing, that makes it seem strange to me that this gentleman, Jack, driving a car in the same state where I drive, didn't write any checks for it. Why do you think he didn't write checks, and complain just as loudly as I do?"

"I don't know," Corey said. "You've got me there. Why didn't he have bills like yours?"

"Because, I think, he didn't own the car. The cars that he's driven over the years haven't belonged to Jack Davis. Somebody else's owned those cars for him. And I'll bet that same someone bought a Cadillac for Mandeville, and that's what hooked him for the deal. Remember what that Spanish padre told us? How Rogers and O'Hara let it slip in front of him that Mandeville'd been suspicious, and it took quite a lot to convince him? He didn't trust their good friend, Marco, and it took some time to persuade him? Well, what was it Marco did to convince him? Did Marco give him a car? Was that Cadillac he drove corporate property, a little deal-sweetener that Marco gave to him, and knocked off his company taxes?"

"Jeez, I don't know," Corey said. "Jim Mandeville wasn't hurting for money. He was a well-fixed guy. He could've bought his own Cadillacs, three or four at a time."

"Could've," Baldo said, "but if he'd had a choice, between buying and getting, he would've taken the gift. Rich guys love little sweet deals like that. Makes them feel like they're in the know. Little people buy their own cars, and take a whipping on them. But rich people's companies buy rich people's cars, and the taxpayers foot all the bills. That's how rich people get rich, Joe, and that's how they stay rich, too. And feel superior to boot."

"Could be, I suppose," Corey said. "I never knew him. I don't know what would've tempted him."

"And Jack Davis's car," Baldo said. "Not a Cadillac, no, Jack was not in that league, but still good enough transportation. How come our Jack paid a mortgage each month, but didn't have any car payments? The original loan was for one-forty-three; Jack put thirty-two grand down. Straight thirty-year commercial mortgage, written at eight and a half. His monthly payment was eleven hundred—ten-ninety-nine, sixty-seven—plus his real estate tax bill, about seven hundred a month now. Jack's been religious making those payments. Just as steady as anyone could be. He's only been overdue four times since he bought the inn, and those four times were all in Aprils—Uncle Sam must've been mean to Jack those years, so he had to scrape for the mortgage.

"You look at his capital outlays for that place: a new stove, a walk-in refridge. A roofing job, two painting contracts, storm windows, and fourteen room air conditioners. A new boiler, new furnace, eight new bathrooms: all of those things he financed through the bank with installment loans for the useful life of the given improvement, whatever that happened to be. And Jack's made those payments religiously, too. He's the banker's dream of a borrower. So if he wanted a new car, or really needed one, he could've gotten a loan. And if he'd gone through General Motors Finance, or maybe some small credit union, he would've made out checks for those payments just the same, and those checks would be in with our copies. But there isn't one single one.

"Now you tell me something: How did Jack do it? Did he own his car free and clear when he came here, and he hasn't needed one since? Twenty-six winters of salt on the roads, and Jack's car's still in fine shape? I've seen Jack often, out and about, and never noticed his car. But if he'd been driving a 'fifty-eight Chevy, I think that would've impressed me. Jack gets a new car about as often as any man, every four or five years. Where does he get it? How does he pay for it? Does the Commonwealth give him the plates? Did he and Jim Mandeville have the same arrangement, so the state gave them number plates free?

"I was with you two nights ago, when you and Jill took Homer's deal. He treated you all right, I'd say, but I don't recall hearing Homer tell you that because you bought two cars, the state would waive both the sales taxes. If Homer said there's a special provision that exempts guys like you who pay cash for a green Jeep, and cash as well, a red ragtop, from needing insurance or plates, he must've whispered it. I missed it. The way I recall it, you sat there writing checks, and Homer sat licking his chops. Two customers, two cars, all in an hour— that's more profit than he's made in weeks, even with rebates deducted. Aren't you as nice a guy as Jack Davis is? So how come you had to pay?"

"Good question," Corey said.

"Yeah," Baldo said, "I think it is. I think it's a very good question. In fact, I think that it's such a good question, I'm going to put it to Oldham. Warren's a former card-carrying state trooper, right? When Warren calls up the registry and asks them to cross-check a driver's license with the principal-operator files on leased cars, they don't get all huffy with him. I think I'll have Warren do that for Jack Davis, and also with Jim Mandeville. We know they both drove—now, where did they get, and who actually owned, the cars that they did it in?

"And that," he said, "brings me to the second thing this morning, which is that we've got to go back to that nice lady at the bank and get us some more records. I find myself becoming very curious indeed about Jack Davis's predecessor as proprietor of that quaint old inn."

"Dawson Nichols?" Corey said. "The guy Amelia said was the guy who had it right, but got it right too early?"

"The very fella," Baldo said. "The young tycoon who became a rum-soaked tosspot when his great scheme collapsed under him. Have you ever seen *The Music Man*, the Broadway show?"

"The movie of it," Corey said. "On television, I mean. Old movies on the boob tube weekends are Jill's secret vice, so I humor her in that one the same as she does me in mine, which is watching basketball. The one with Robert Preston, guy that cons all the bumpkins out of their life's savings by promising a band? And knows nothing about bands, but they get one anyway?"

"That's the one," Baldo said. "You see any resemblance between what Preston started out to do to the folks in River City and what that Nichols guy did here? Oh, Harold Hill's bait was a boys' band, and Nichols's was the inn. But the principle's about the same—just worked out differently.

"The only stuff we really know about this Nichols guy is what Amelia told you. Which isn't all that much. The guy comes out of nowhere—'down south' is pretty vague—and all we really *know* about his background's what she said. In other words, we don't know much, because she didn't know—all she knew was what she'd heard. God knows who she heard it from—if it was Al, not from Nichols, then it was double hearsay. Hotel school and Sheraton; loads of natural charm—well, the only detail on that list that we can count on is we know he did have the charm. Enough to buffalo this town at least, and that was all he needed.

"The reason that he interests me, why I want to know more about him, is that looking at it from this chair, twenty-five years later, close to thirty in his case, is that when you come right down to it, Dawson and the stupid medic, Doctor Lowden, there, look like they have something in common. And not only with each other—also with Jack Davis, too. The three of them show up here, one by one, starting back in the fifties, all coming in from somewhere else. Not that Dawson and the doc were in cahoots or anything, or that Jack and the doctor had an understanding, either, but all three of that group came here from somewhere else for the same basic reason: to make a lot of money off unsuspecting people who didn't know the worth of what they had in them thar hills.

"Well, the locals caught on to Doc Lowden. They knew malpractice when they saw it. But even though the inn went bust, and Nichols had to leave, they really didn't catch up with him. As far as we know, they still don't know where he came from, where he went, or what is most important: that he looks to me as though he must've made a decent profit from running that inn into the ground."

"He couldn't've," Corey said. "The whole reason Mandeville was so glad to see Jack Davis was because Nichols'd been missing payments."

"Right," Baldo said. "But what we don't know, because Amelia didn't seem to—or did, but didn't think it was important—and we haven't bothered asking anybody else yet, is *why* he was missing those payments, or how many of them he missed, either. Hitting the sauce doesn't make you miss payments, unless you get so drunk you start missing work, too, and you get fired from your job. Well, no one could fire Dawson Nichols from his job—he was the owner, the boss.

"Now Davis's canceled checks from his purchase, when I put them beside the deeds for it, show me a funny transaction. If I compute from the tax stamps on Nichols's deed what his purchase price probably was, I come out with one hundred and ten thousand dollars. This is not cheap for a shutdown and run-down country inn in the middle fifties. But assuming the building was structurally sound, it was not an inflated price either. And the building seems to've been basically sound— none of Jack Davis's checks are for main beams or big stuff like that.

"Amelia believes Nichols had a big mortgage, not having much cash to put down. She guessed ninety to ninety-five percent, which would've been one-oh-four-point-five, if the hundred and ten's all he paid for it. But my figures say that's too low. Twenty-five thousand too low. My figures and Jack Davis's. Jacks're the ones that count here.

"I don't think Jim Mandeville fronted him that much. I think the deal included improvements, which everyone knew the place needed. So Nichols would sink twenty-five in the inn, besides the down payment, and that would enhance the collateral. What Mandeville did was advance on one-ten, on Nichols's word the inn would be worth one-thirty-five, so his payments would be on the one-ten. If everything works out, everyone makes out. Nichols's payments are nine-forty-five a month, manageable, and the inn would become rentable.

"The trouble was, everything didn't work out. So nobody made out as planned. Our friend Nichols did not keep his word. The repairs and improvements that he underwrote either didn't get done, or he cheaped them, so they had to be done over again. But Davis still paid one-seventy-five, a sizable profit, forty big ones, for our friend the faithless Nichols. My question's why Davis did that."

"You've lost me," Corey said.

"No," Baldo said, "*they* lost both of us. Just what they meant to do. Then or now, many years later. And long before that they lost Mandeville. The secret of this deal's the Las Vegas gambit. They get you to bet on the come. The reason they do that's to make you use your dough. And then *lose* your dough when the deal craps out. These guys never use their own. That's why these guys never lose.

"Back in the fifties the mob's second team came out here from Providence, all right? They bought the old Rabouin farm in Hancock and called it a racetrack. Berkshire Downs. And set about purchasing all kinds of officials, and all of it worked like a charm, because everyone thought he'd get rich. The rosy dreams were all over the papers, what a tourist attraction this would be. A gambling hell and a paradise, too, the land going a hundred a square inch.

"Well, everyone didn't get rich. The people who came here didn't know squat about running racetracks or anything else except the rackets, and they made a big mess of things. They didn't get too badly hurt, never do, but lots of the locals got creamed.

"I think that was what was going on here, too. I think Dawson Nichols was the first outrider, or one of the first ones, at least. I think he was sent here, or maybe recruited, by some other mafia family. Or maybe he started off as a bright-eyed volunteer, ran out of his money and had to go to them—dumb move. But anyway, one way or the other it happened: they bought him fair and square and they owned him. And then when he screwed up, well, they pulled him out. Or maybe they just reeled him in. And sent Jack Davis in to replace him."

"So why does he make a profit?" Corey said. "If they own the guy and they own Davis too, why give him forty-K profit?"

"A very good question," Baldo said. "That's why we need more bank records. All I've said is that it looks to me as though he made it—but who says they let him keep it? Especially if one of them'd loaned him the twenty-five K some years before, and he owed that and vigorish too? And so also we need from

201

your high-class friend Roger the background on Dawson and Jack."

"Okay," Corey said, "I'll get on that right now."

"Not so fast here," Baldo said. "I made a mistake when we had that priest in. When we had both of them in. Neither one of them was here when this property got sold. This was a going concern. Generally, people in going concerns develop a certain attachment. The guys in Chicago may look at the ledgers and say: 'Well, we'll liquidate this one. We need more money out here for new stuff, and what's on that lake's worth a million.' And that's the decision that sticks. But the people who live in the impacted area, as the federal government says, are nowhere as dispassionate when their beds're involved. They get cranky about the whole thing. It doesn't matter what vows they've taken; they're human and they hold their grudges. And if they're around, their memories are good. Resentment's a powerful goad. I should've asked both of our good fathers there who was running this joint when they sold it, the house mother or whatever they called him. And where he is now, or if he is dead now, who was the next in command. All the way down to the janitor, if that's all that's left that's alive.

"You know who knows more, what goes on here now, than any person who lives here? Remember the Deacon in the Yankees hat? The guy who cuts grass? He rakes leaves, too, and he shovels snow. He knows who's around, what units're occupied, and how many people're in them. He knows that because he collects rubbish, and three people create more'n two people do. He knows that you're living here now with your wife, and he knows who both of you are. He knows where you came from, and what you did there, and what your wife's doing here. And how does he know this? From the trash pickup. You bring your mail here, and most of it's trash, and some of it comes from New York. Forwarded. And Jill has to throw out a lot of junk mail, as you do, because teachers get that stuff too. If the Deacon missed the papers, or the evening news, he didn't miss much else. He already knew quite a lot

202

about you, and what he's overlooked, he'll find out. Just like your old landlord that came visiting—Deacon sees all, and remembers. They all do, all the Deacons.

"So tomorrow, while you're chatting up Amelia about our friend, Dawson Nichols, I think I'll look up my pal Deacon, and ask him a few probing questions. See if by chance *he* might've been here then—he's certainly old enough to've been. And if he was, what he saw around here. It can't do us any harm."

19

"Oh land, yes," Amelia Feldt said the next morning, "Dawson Nichols seemed to have all the equipment, and do everything, that everyone else in this town did. He was a Rotarian, as I think I told you, and he met a good number of the men that way, and then it turned out he was a Mason, too, so that was another thing. Not a particularly regular churchgoer, I seem to remember him saying once he'd been raised as a Presbyterian, but he wasn't a bit particular. If there was some reason why it seemed as though he ought to attend a service at First Parish—that would be the Congregational—Dawson would be there, and the same thing with First Baptist and Saint Francis, or Saint Mark's, the Episcopal. Dawson the first few years he was here was on good terms with everybody. Everybody liked him."

"How about hobbies?" Corey said.

"Well, the same sort of thing," she said. "Al was never a golfer or anything like that—said his job didn't leave him time enough for hobbies. About the only real hobby Al had was reading books about the Civil War. I swear he bought every one that came out, but I must say he did read them all. That was always one of his big plans for when he retired. Summer being the big season up around here, traffic and that sort of thing, Al never did really feel comfortable taking a real vacation then, but what he always said we were going to do was take our first summer, when he retired, and tour the battlefields. Didn't see much point in that in the winter." She smiled.

"That's another thing you men do. You make all these plans for the day you retire, and then you work yourselves to death before it comes time to do them.

"But Al was sort of unusual for the men his age that he knew. Jim Mandeville, of course, hunted and fished, played some golf, too—all of those things."

"And Dawson?" Corey said.

"Why yes," she said. "He went with him. You see most of the other men Jim knew didn't quite have the same freedom. To take off whenever they liked. Had to attend to their businesses. So anyone who knew Jim and could do what he did, well, Jim was glad to know him. Oh now and then they'd make up a party, deer season or something like that. Gil Rogers would close up his office for the day. Bruce Tappett'd tell his clerk he wouldn't be in until late afternoon, and if anyone wanted a prescription, well, if it was an emergency, he'd have to make arrangements to get it somewhere else. And when Dawson was here, he'd put up a sign, if he had any guests, that the muffins and so forth were in the baskets, coffee all made in the urns, and a whole bunch of them, six, seven or eight, would go out looking for deer."

"So Dawson could shoot," Corey said.

"Dawson was special to Jim,' she said slowly. "Jim sort of adopted Dawson. When Dawson first came here, when he came up from down south, he went down to the station one day to see Al and see what the gun laws were here. And he told Al that before he went down to the south he'd had a permit, New York State, I guess, to carry a concealed weapon on him. A revolver, I guess, don't know what it was. But anyway, what he wanted to know was, what the gun laws were here. This would've been 'fifty-one, 'fifty-two, around there. He was quite young, twenty-five, twenty-six, very handsome, quite good-looking. Very anxious to please. And Jim didn't have a son, the way his father and grandfather did, to train and bring up in his image. You know?

"Well, anyway, I don't know whether the Bartley-Fox

law'd been passed then, the gun law we have up here now—you're supposed to go to jail for a year just for having a gun with no permit—but whatever it was, he and Al came to their terms, and Al was very impressed. As Jim'd been.

"See, Al was always a stickler on handguns. Very concerned about handguns. The long guns—the rifles and shotguns, you know—they didn't worry him much. He felt the only reason anyone wanted one of those was to use it for hunting. Well, the only way you could do that was if you had a hunting license, and the only way they'd issue you one was if you'd either taken a course in gun safety—the sportsmen's club ran those every year—or you'd had a license for several years running. Al felt you must know what you were doing, and it was perfectly legal.

"But the pistols and revolvers bothered him. Al thought the only people who ought to carry those were either policemen—law enforcement officers—and bank guards, people like that; people who had a good reason why they needed to have one. And even that kind of people got no license from Al unless they could prove that they knew how to use one. Well, Dawson's reason was that he kept a certain amount of cash on hand at the inn, had to meet to make change and pay tradesmen, and of course he was open all night. Al thought that was good enough. So he took Dawson down to the range, where the policemen all practiced, and saw how he handled a gun. And he told me he'd been very impressed. 'No Wyatt Earp,' he said, I recall this, 'but a very competent marksman. He handles a gun very well.' And so Al gave him the permit."

"How about social life?" Corey said. "Did Dawson have any you knew about? Aside from the manly pursuits."

She frowned. "You're awfully interested in Dawson, aren't you," she said. "Do you think he had something to do with Jim's death?"

"I don't know," Corey said. "Did Al think he did?"

She looked puzzled. "If he did," she said, "I can't recall that he ever said anything about it to me. I don't know why he would've, really. Dawson'd been long gone from Shropshire when Jim died, was killed. *Years* since he'd been around here, since anyone'd even mentioned his name. He was just someone who'd come and stayed for a while, been quite popular for a few years, and then he had the business problems, and the drinking problem and so forth, and when he couldn't hold out any longer, he left. Very charming, of course, and people felt bad about it for a while, not that many of them were really surprised at what'd happened. But he'd seemed so promising, young and bright, and he had had the right idea about fixing up the inn. Which did mean a lot to the town. So they were disappointed, not only for him but for the town, for themselves. But, well, I guess most of them just felt he'd had a streak of bad luck and didn't know how to handle it, what to do about it, and it was too bad, but that was it." She paused.

"Dawson, well, it seemed like he made an awful lot of friends in this town, in a very short time—people in small towns, I guess, tend to want to look you over some before they, you know, really warm up to you. But not with Dawson. People liked him, it seemed like, from the first day he was here, and the more he was here, the more people he met, the more friends it seemed like he had. I don't know of a single soul who knew Dawson at all and didn't like him. It was just that, well, after he left, it seemed like they forgot about him just as fast as they'd made friends with him. They'd liked him, his company, the stories he told and all that, but when he was gone, well, he was gone. Nobody missed him at all. When Jack came in and took over, well, he was an older, steadier Dawson, and people took to him the same way. Not as quickly, perhaps, but they took to him." She hesitated. "Jim always said the inn was the centerpiece of the town. As it went, the town went. That's why he made the loans on it. For the town. Jim Mandeville loved this town. And he was right. Dawson just wasn't the right man to handle it. When he left, he was gone."

"So maybe he didn't really have any friends," Corey said. "Here, I mean. Maybe he just had acquaintances."

She nodded. "I'd say that's just about right," she said.

"Does that answer my question about social life?" he said.

She sighed. "Most likely," she said. "Oh, there were the rumors, I may've told you, that more'n one calculating woman or her mother took a close look at him and decided he'd make a good prospect for a husband. But so far as I know, he never went for any one of them, never took any of the young ladies out to dinner, on dates, things like that." She laughed. "The only one he ever seemed to take a shine to, that I saw at least, was Mimi Mandeville."

"Really," Corey said. "Now that could be interesting."

"Oh, heavens," she said, "I didn't mean *that*. That there was something going on between them. Far's I know the only times they ever saw each other were at parties at Jim and Mimi's house, dinner parties, the Christmas open house, things like that. Or when Jim and Mimi'd drop into the inn for a late supper after they'd been off someplace for the day. I doubt the two of them, Dawson and Mimi, were ever just by themselves.

"It was simply that, well, it was natural that he'd take to her. Mimi was what I think they call one of those 'strikingly attractive' women. Very good posture. Nice figure. Very good bones—her face, I mean. And very sure of herself, too—she *carried* herself so well. Money does that for you. For a woman as well as a man. And she was always, well, she always kept herself well. The women in Shropshire who consider themselves 'stylish' go up to Pittsfield to get their hair done. The rest of us poor little mice in those days went over to Bess Henderson's house when we needed a perm or a cut." She snickered. "Every six or eight months or so. But winter and summer, all year 'round, Mimi went to New York like a regular churchgoer, every month, faithful as clockwork, to have her hair seen to down there. Leave here on Tuesdays, Jim'd take her to the train, come back Saturday afternoons. All done up like a queen and carrying boxes—she got all her dressses there, too. Her hats and her shoes and her furs." Amelia giggled. "Most likely her underwear, too, although I never did ask her that."

"Really?" he said. "Every month? To get her hair done and go shopping? Where'd she stay in New York?"

"You know, Joe," Amelia said, smiling, "you've become much more inquisitive since the last time we talked, since you've spent all this time with that Mister Ianucci fellow who called me up out of the blue. You've really become quite nosy."

"Well," he said, "I know a lot more now about what I'm talking about, so naturally I know a heck of a lot more as well what I *don't* know about, and I'm hoping you can help me fill in some of those things that I don't."

Amelia's smile became a grin. "Yes, yes indeed," she said. "If I were a few years younger I might begin to wonder if this nice young man who's talking to me might be thinking about something that his wife wouldn't like to hear about." She uttered a mock sigh. "But I'm not, darn it. I remember how, every time there was some gossip going around about some woman people knew making a silly goose of herself over some man, usually after he was supposed to have gotten what he was after and then just forgotten about her—the people spreading it around always saying what a stinker he'd been, and of course loving every word of it—Al would always say it was her fault, not the man's. 'Any female over the age of consent who either takes her clothes off or lets a man take them off for her, knows exactly what's going to happen next. And wanted it to happen all along. Especially if she's already got herself a husband. She gets no sympathy from me, any more'n he does.' Maybe Al was right. Even about me."

Corey smiled. "Well, do you by any chance know what hotel Mimi used on those monthly trips to New York?"

Amelia cleared her throat. "And persistent, too," she said. "Yes, as it happens, I do. Well, not what hotel—where she always stayed. She had a friend, Harriet, there, and she always stayed with her. Mimi was very conscientious, about everything, and knowing Jim's habits of traipsing off into the woods whenever he felt like it, she wanted someone to be able to reach her in a hurry if there was some emergency at the house while she was away and no one could find Jim. So she gave Al the number of this Harriet in New York, and the address as well. I've forgotten the address and the number, before you ask, and Harriet's last name as well, too. Old age, you know. But I remember that it was 'Harriet,' her first name, and that Mimi told Al they'd been roommates at Wellesley, and stayed best friends all their lives. It was a very fashionable address, though, in the city. I always had the impression, from the way Mimi talked about her, that Harriet'd come from lots of money, always had it. Now, how much that was, or how much Mimi's family had, how much she'd had before she married Jim, well, I couldn't say exactly. They were not hard-up, though; I can say that for a fact. But from what Mimi said, compared to Harriet's, it wasn't much. But that's really all I know."

"Warren Oldham," Corey said. He cleared his throat. "Look, Amelia, I know you loved your husband."

"I thought the world of Al," she said. "Just the world of him."

"So I don't want to offend you here now, and I don't mean to if I do, but I have to ask you, or tell you, this: Warren Oldham told me he never should've allowed your husband to do all the questioning of Mimi."

"Did Warren say why, why he thought that?" she said.

"Well, I guess what it came down to was that he thought Al and Jim, and you and Mimi, the four of you'd just been too close to each other, that Al'd taken Jim's death so hard he couldn't be sure, Warren couldn't be sure, that Al, well, had enough distance from the case to take all that on himself."

She nodded. "That's about what I said to Al myself," she said. "I could see, I could tell much better than Warren, I think, how hard Al'd taken it, how it just *tore* at him. And *I* knew—well, I didn't *know*, but I was sure afraid—that, that that had to get in the way of how Al was looking at it. That he shouldn't take it all on himself to solve, or as much of it as he did anyway. But when I mentioned it"—she shook her head—"and I only said it once, when I said something like that to Al, he was, well, he wouldn't hear of it. It was *his* friend, in *his* town, and *his* responsibility, and he was the one to handle it." She paused. "I never brought it up again."

"When Mimi came back and sold the house, and left," he said, "I know Gil Rogers was her lawyer for the sale and all, but do you know who the real estate broker was who found the buyer for it?"

"I assume it was Gil," she said. "It was all done so fast. She had the memorial, the service, I mean, for Jim, and then she left, and the next thing we knew, the house'd changed hands. From what Al said, I gather the buyer was the same person, the company that took over Claretian Shores later on, two or three years later, I guess. But of course we didn't know that then. I'm not sure—Al wasn't sure—she got a fair price for that place. I'm not sure that mattered to her, what the price was. All she wanted to do was get rid of it and get out."

"And go to New York," Corey said.

"I believe so, yes," Amelia said. "I'm not exactly sure where in New York, the city or somewhere outside it, but I think she went to New York."

He began to gather up his note pad and files. "Well," he said, "I appreciate this. You've been very patient with me, and the coffee's good, too."

She frowned, smiling at the same time. "Is it my turn now?" she said.

"Sure," he said, laughing, "fire away."

"Pardon an old woman's curiosity, but have you two got some idea now of who it was, really, who killed Jim? I suppose it's silly of me, but I more or less feel like a caretaker here, trying to do my best to settle something that my husband didn't finish, couldn't finish, before he died. That murder ate at him. I watched it happen. Al died before his time, and part of the reason was Jim Mandeville's death."

Corey pondered. "Some idea of the type of person who wanted him killed: yes, and a pretty good one, too. Some idea of how he went about it; not pretty good, but good. A very firm idea of what the motive was. But some idea who killed him, who actually pulled the trigger? No more than suspicions so far."

"Who else're you two talking to, may I ask?" she said. "To narrow down those suspicions, I mean."

He laughed. "Well mostly," he said, "to each other. We sit in our offices and go over papers, and yell back and forth at each other. As a result of that, we decided I should come over and reinterview you, and Baldo should talk to the real caretaker. The gardener at the Shores there."

She chuckled. "The Deacon," she said.

"You know him?" he said.

"I didn't, no," she said. "I saw him two or three times, on the street, but we were never formally introduced. I only knew him by sight, and from Al's description—I never spoke to him. But Al knew him—Al knew him well. I've forgotten his name—you can probably get it—but he came here, oh, must be thirty years now, straight to this town from Chicago. To tend grounds for the Claretian Fathers."

"Then how did Al know him?" Corey said.

"Well," she said, "Deacon'd been in prison, somewhere in Illinois. And—I'm not sure of the details on this, but the gist of it I know's right—apparently the only way he could get out on parole was if he had someone to vouch for him. Otherwise he'd've had to finish his term, and he still had a while to go on it. But some policeman out there got some one of the fathers to say they'd be responsible for him, and get him to leave Illinois. They'd get him a job somewhere else. And this was the place that they picked.

"Oh, Al was wild," she said. "When that kind of thing

212

happens, parole supervision gets transferred to the place where the prisoner's headed. But then that was Springfield, at least I think it was, and that's a distance away. The probation people seldom got up here, so they farmed out the job to the police. And Al, being chief, was the one that they called, every week, every two weeks, and so forth, to see if the man was behaving himself. So that meant more work for Al. He had to check on the man at least once a week, make sure he was working and so forth. Not drinking and staying where he was supposed to be, and then talking to him once a month. And then making reports to the people in Springfield—oh, how Al hated that job. From the day Deacon came to the day that Al died, he went on about that kind of thing. 'We don't have enough bad eggs of our own—they send us their rotten ones, too.' "

"Do you know what the Deacon'd done?" Corey said. "I mean out there in Illinois, that is."

"Oh, not exactly," she said. "I know what they called it back then. He was a sex offender. Al never discussed the specific offenses of any of those 'lousy cases.' Obviously it must've been something serious—rapes, or something like that; maybe molesting children. To me he just looked like a creep, the kind of shifty-looking creep who'd run around at night in backyards, stealing women's underwear off their clotheslines." Corey laughed. "Well," she said, "of course it wasn't anything as petty as that, as minor. It must've been something serious. But that's how he looked. Like a weasel, you know? A wet muskrat, or something like that."

"Did he ever get out of line after he came here?" Corey said.

"Not that I know about," she said. She reflected. "I think he was probably too old. Either that or too tired."

"The other interviews," Corey said, "the reports on the plain white paper. I assume ABF's your husband. Who's this PFB on some others?"

She looked thoughtful. "That would've been Paul Barry," she said. "He was the sergeant here under Al, and, everyone knew, the next chief. Al thought a lot of him. Tried several times to get a lieutenancy for him, give him a little more money, but the selectmen insisted on the exam, the Civil Service exam. I guess they were afraid that one of the others, nowhere near as qualified as Paul was, nowhere near as good a policeman, would sue them if they let Al promote Paul without taking a test for it first.

"Well, Paul just wouldn't do it. Paul *couldn't* do it. He'd barely passed the sergeant's. He often said it'd been just his good luck, he happened to be the only one who took it that time, when the opening came up. Paul was as smart as a whip, and he worked like a dog. 'A cop's cop' was what Al called him. 'The most valuable man on the force.' Hours meant nothing to him. If he'd ever been able to do it, go to law school, pass the bar, he would've been a fine lawyer. But he couldn't, and it was the same reason he couldn't take the exam for lieutenant—there was one thing Paul couldn't do, and that was sit down for a test. He froze, was the way he put it. 'I sit there and stare at the paper,' he said, 'and my mind goes totally blank. Oh, Bob Gates could take it, no trouble at all. He'd pass with flying colors. And then be a lousy lieutenant. But not me. I can't do it. This world isn't fair. It isn't a fair world at all.' "

"I talked to Bob Gates," Corey said. "After I read the reports. He was certainly all right to me. Barry didn't like him?"

"You're a lawyer," Amelia said pityingly. "Of course Bob would be nice to you. Especially since you're a *New York* lawyer—you might come in handy someday. That's a little trick he learned from Gil Rogers. Gil was as smooth as a new baby's bottom. And he had lots of connections outside this county, especially down in New York. Which he had for one reason: they made money for him. Oh, Gil was as cute as they make 'em. And Bob was Gil's protégé. He does business just the way Gil did. Bob Gates uses people, any way he can.

"He's always been that way. Paul didn't like him; Al didn't like him; and the other men didn't trust him. I'm sure part of it was envy on their part. Bob made no secret of his plans. The only reason he was working as a cop at all was to finance his way through school. That didn't sit too well with the other patrolmen. They were working as cops to be cops. But it wasn't just jealousy on their part, either. They had their reasons for feeling that way.

"Bob didn't come from a well-to-do family—his father was a house painter. But there was no question that Bob was ambitious. Bob planned to make money, lots of it, fast. Just as fast as he possibly could. And Bob, well, he sucked-up to money.

"The other man said that that made them nervous, because they thought Bob might bend the rules. If he thought it could do him some good, later on, he might look the other way some weekend night when some rich person did something he shouldn't. Building up favors for when he finished school, banking on gratitude somewhere down the line that would help him make big money, fast. Gil Rogers, for example. Gil was the biggest lawyer in town then. As of course Bob Gates is now. Oh, Gil was certainly capable enough, as I'm sure Bob Gates is now. Gil did most of the bank's work, which he wouldn't't've if Jim hadn't thought he was up to it. He also represented the Barlow Company—they do almost all the grocery-supply business around here, except for the chain stores—and two or three car dealerships. And he did some union work, too.

" 'Well,' the other men said, on the force: 'Just suppose this: Gil Rogers gets himself a good skinful up at the Mountainview Club, when he's out romancing some honey'—which Gil was known to do quite a lot, both things; he ran around on Cecile—'and then he decides to drive home at a good clip. And he sideswipes some car that's parked on the street, with Bob Gates sitting right there. Now what do you think Bob Gates will do? Will he arrest Gil, bring him in? Lock Gil Rogers up in the tank overnight, and charge him with what he was doing? Will Bob arrest Gil for drunk driving, endangerment, and make sure he loses his license? Or will Bob just put plastered Gil in the cruiser and drive him home to bed, and write up the whole thing as an accident?'

"Well," Amelia said, "Al didn't know the answer to that and he admitted it to me. 'Furthermore,' he said, 'good thing they didn't think of this, but how do I know that hasn't already happened? That or something just like it, with Gil or some other rich fella? And the answer to that one's the same as the first one: I don't, and that's all I can say. But until I find out Bob's done something like that, I can't toss the guy out on his butt.'

"And Bob could be mean. He used to ride Bill Slinger a lot. Well, Bill wasn't much good as a cop, even though he wanted to be one, and had been one for some twenty years. He had a big family, six, seven kids, and he couldn't get by on police pay. So what he would do when he finished his night shift was drive over to Lee to Carl's Liquor Store, and open it up for the day. He was the day manager, and he didn't get off until two. Then he'd go home and sleep maybe five hours until he came in for the night shift. And that meant he could support his family.

"Well, Al knew Bill had a hard time on that routine. A younger man would've had trouble, and Bill Slinger was in his forties. Al knew that Bill fell asleep at the desk. He worried that some night something would happen, and Bill wouldn't wake up for the call. 'But he says that it won't, that he's a light sleeper. A cat stamping its feet wakes him up. Well, I'm not sure of that, but I hope it's true, and until he lets me down, he's safe.' Al always had a good deal of respect for a man who worked hard in order to take care of his family.

"Anyway," she said, "no, Paul didn't like Bob. And the rest of the men liked him less. But Al couldn't fire him. 'And anyway,' he said, 'do I want to set that precedent? That you can't be a cop if you've got an ambition to study and better yourself? That doesn't sound good to me.' But Al didn't trust Bob himself, and since he knew Paul was right when he said that Bob would certainly take the test if Al gave it, and do well on it too, if he did, Al couldn't give it and Paul stayed a sergeant. So Paul had a personal reason, too, for not thinking too much of Bob.

"So," she said, "the only way Paul could get promoted was if Al gave up the job, because the selectmen appoint the chief, no exam, and they can appoint anyone. And everyone knew that when Al did retire, Paul would be the new chief. But he died. In 'seventy-two. Forty-six years old. Left a family, three kids, mortgage, all that. Just keeping in shape on a nice summer night, playing basketball down at the playground—a lot of the younger men did that; the firemen used to play too— and he dropped dead right on the court. Al said he was dead before he hit the ground. Doctor Williams, Fred Williams, said he'd had a stroke, not the slightest sign of it coming on, nothing. Just a young man cut down in his prime."

She shook her head. "That was another thing that didn't help Al. Didn't lengthen Al's life, I mean. He wasn't as bothered as he'd been about Jim—Paul's was, after all, natural causes; nobody *done* it to him—but Al said many times, long before Paul dropped dead: 'Paul Barry is my right-hand man. Or maybe I'm his, I don't know.' " She sighed.

"Paul wore a suit to work, suit or sports coat, and a shirt and tie, same's Al. It wasn't Paul's idea to stop wearing the uniform. He said the others would ride him, a sergeant dressed up like the chief. But Al said: 'No, you do it. You're deputy chief, because that's what I need, even though I can't make it official'—see, that isn't in the staff tables; there's no deputy in the bylaws. 'And you're chief of detectives, because you're the only one. So dress for the jobs that you actually do. It'll make both our jobs easier.' "

"They made a good team. Paul ran the day shift until lunchtime, so Al could get paperwork done. Then Al ran the shift until suppertime came, and Paul was out keeping tabs on the town. After Jim's death, even while Warren Oldham was still down here almost every day, Paul spent most of his time talking to people who might know something that would help.

217

He'd go back four or fives times, checking out the tiniest things, time and time again, until he was sure he had it right. Except for Mimi. Al thought it would be better if he did her interviews, since he knew her well, and how much it'd hurt her, and he wanted to make it as easy as possible for her to tell her whole story. So he took those . . . I know he dreaded every single one of them, the time he had to go and talk to her. How many interviews are there?"

"Four or five, I think," Corey said. "The first one's pretty detailed. The other ones're brief. Just a stray fact here and there."

"I'm sure," Amelia said. "Al said before he talked to her the first time that he was determined to be as thorough as possible, even though it was going to be hard for her. 'I don't want to have to keep going back there and back there, six or eight times to get it. I'm not going to be like the kind veterinarian who only cut an inch or so at a time off the Doberman's tail because he didn't want to hurt the dog.' "

"She didn't seem to know much that would really've helped," Corey said.

"That was what Al said," she said. "Jim snored, and she liked to read herself to sleep with the radio on, and the light kept him awake, so they had separate rooms. He had a phone in his room. She didn't have one in hers because she was such a sound sleeper she wouldn't've been able to hear it anyway. So if he got a call, which she assumed he must've, she wouldn't've known who it was. If it'd been the hunting season, or fishing season, no one in the house would've been surprised at all if Jim'd gotten up and left before dawn, and he'd gotten very good at being quiet doing that, not disturbing anyone, so they didn't hear him leave anyway.

"Then there were what Al always called 'the other questions.' " She smiled. "Like I told you," she said, "I never read what's in that file, but I think I know it by heart. As far as Mimi knew, Jim had no financial problems, of his own or at the bank. He didn't have a girlfriend, that she knew about at least, and as far as she knew, he never did. He didn't gamble, unless you call when they went to Saratoga two or three times a season 'gambling,' or the times they went to the races in Florida in the winter. He certainly liked to take a drink, but in the thirty-odd years they'd been married, she'd only seen him drunk half a dozen times, and the first one was at the rehearsal dinner the night before the wedding. He seemed to be in good health. He'd had a checkup in September and the doctor'd done some tests, and Jim was out of town when the tests came back and the doctor called with the results and said Jim was in tip-top shape, fit as a fiddle, 'the physique of a man fifteen years younger.' He wasn't despondent. She said she'd never seen Jim depressed in his life. 'He loved life. He loved his family; he loved the outdoors; he loved his work at the bank. I never in my whole life saw a man with more energy. More eagerness to start the day. Some mornings, when I was absolutely bushed, I could've throttled him for that.' They hadn't quarreled. They *never* quarreled."

Amelia shrugged. "She told Al she couldn't think of a reason in the world why Jim Mandeville would want to kill himself. And if she *had* been able to, which she wasn't, why on earth he'd choose to do it right at Christmas, with his daughters coming back with their families and two of the grandchildren that he'd never seen—his favorite season of the year. It baffled her.

"It baffled Al, too," she said. "It baffled everybody. And as Al said: 'Sometimes when you just can't make yourself believe that something could've happened, it really *didn't* happen. Jim's dead all right, no question about that. But that man did not kill himself. And that's why Mimi couldn't believe he did, and you can't, and Paul can't, and I can't. Jim Mandeville was murdered.' "

20

Four days later Corey, Jill, and Baldo saw that Evelyn Murtagh had chosen as her costume for their first inspection of a house she thought had "promise" a double-breasted iridescent brown silk suit that matched her henna hair exactly when it caught the slanting afternoon sunlight, and emphasized her rangy build. She stood square-shouldered next to her copper-colored Buick Regal on the knoll in front of the eight-room Victorian-style farmhouse in Norwich, as Jill murmured while they got out of the new Jeep, "like an impatient Brunhilde waiting her turn to perform." It was clear from her expression that she had not expected Baldo to accompany her customers, and did not like it, either.

"Well, Baldo," she said, her voice resonating in the cool air, "Homer Forbes told me you were like a mother hen with these two nice people when they came in to see him, and now they come to see me, and you show up here, too. Do you and Mickey tuck them in and read them bedtime stories too?"

Baldo wore oil-stained heavy-duty khaki pants and a blue windbreaker splotched with white paint; he carried a six-cell flashlight in his left hand and used his right to toss a golf ball to her. She caught it with a stylish major league first-baseman's sweeping motion and flipped it back to him. "Only engineering matters, Evvie, dear," he said, grinning, catching the return throw and putting the ball in his pocket. "Biological concerns aren't part of my expertise. But having a pretty good idea of what's in your trick bag, I thought maybe my advice might come in handy, so I asked to tag along."

"Yes," she said grimly. "Well. Should I assume you know the house, too, or should I go ahead and show it as though I do and you don't?"

He shrugged. "Suit yourself, Evvie," he said. "I've never seen the place, inside or out. All I know is engineering, things like that, and that's all I came to see."

"Yes," she said. "Well, as you can see, this is a truly breathtaking location." She gestured with her right hand to encompass the stands of maples that framed the property on the northwest and southwest sides. "It's three and a quarter acres, very good natural drainage, and the owners before the present ones let the meadows stay just as they are, so in the spring and during the first part of the summer, you can expect a show of wildflowers almost as beautiful as the leaves here will be in a couple of weeks. Your kitchen and the family room are on the back, so they get all the benefit of the morning sun, and they both open on a lovely redwood deck with a new awning that the owners put in just two years ago."

"And in the winter," Baldo said, "you can look forward to getting all the benefit of the nor'easters and those brutal Montreal Express winds that'll suck all your heat right through those old clapboard walls like a riptide made of air. While also giving you some really memorable drifts in what I'd say looks to me like a seventy-five-dollar plowing bill for that long and lovely winding drive."

Murtagh stared at him. "As we go inside now, notice the lovely front veranda. The floor was new two years ago, and it's a shame you didn't see it when you first came up last summer, because the owners have left rockers for it and a glider swing. The railings, as you notice, are all lathe-turned spindles and pillars . . ."

". . . which are the devil's work to paint," Baldo said quietly to Corey, "and sheer hell to scrape."

". . . and the roof, of course, shades the front bay window

221

from the hotter sun," she said. "Notice the detail of the front door. This is all handwork, and the frosted etching of the main pane with the stained-glass windows framing it so beautifully." Murtagh's key operated the lock smoothly but the door creaked as it opened, resisting the pressure she put on it. "Now, the lovely entryway," she said. "Matched boards here, as there are throughout the house, and you can tell from the appearance that they've had the best of care."

Baldo opened his windbreaker and took a carpenter's six-inch aluminum level from an inside pocket. He knelt on his right knee and rested the level on the doorsill. The air bubble in the bright green fluid of the center glass came to rest two thirds off the plumb line to the left. He frowned. He stood up and applied the level vertically first to the left and then to the right uprights of the door frame. The bubble in the glass at the top of the level came to rest dead center on the right, but off center on the left. "Sill's out of line," he muttered. "Frame's out of line. Sills've settled here."

Baldo crouched in the entryway and studied the floor. He took the golf ball from his pocket and placed it carefully on the floorboard nearest the baseboard of the interior wall to his right. It remained where he put it for a moment, then began to roll in a slowly curving arc toward the left baseboard, making what seemed to be a considerable noise before coming to rest about nine feet away on a heating-register grate.

That was only the beginning. Baldo predicted that the heating system, forced hot air by an oil-fired furnace, would have to be torn out and replaced. He said the material that looked like sawdust on the attic floorboards was evidence of carpenter ants. "And the place needs insulation," he said. "It may be 'winterized' now, if your idea of winter's late October, mid-April, but anyone who tried to live here in January, February, might not agree with you." He said all of the thirty-one openings would have to be fitted with combination storm windows and doors, and stated his opinion that the fixtures, tile, and cabinetry work done in the bathroom upstairs and the half bath on the first floor were of mediocre quality that would not last. He doubted that the Coreys would find it convenient to raise a family without adding at least one full bath, and predicted the washer and clothes dryer would fail within six months of family use. He said they would almost certainly find that they required as well a garbage disposal unit and a dishwasher. "And when you'd added all that stuff, you could very likely find that your septic system and your leaching fields aren't up to handling the extra discharge, and you'd have to get a backhoe in here and install a whole new plant."

Murtagh said progressively less as Baldo pointed out more flaws, and when he inspected the frayed insulation and chipped china insulators of the wiring in the attic, pronouncing it "dangerous right now, has been for a long time—should've been torn out years ago. Plug a toaster in downstairs, whole place could go up. Too dangerous to move in until it's all been ripped out and replaced," she shook her head and sighed.

She said, "Well, I can't help it. I just show the things I have."

Baldo nodded. "Jill," he said, "Joe, you two asked my advice. My advice is: you don't want this place. It isn't worth anywhere near what they're asking, a hundred and sixty-five thousand. If you wanted this place for what they used it for, a primitive, roughing-it, summerhouse, and you had the time and the patience to live somewhere else—take me and Michelle up on our offer to stay with us for the next six months, or as long as you want, far as that goes—while all the heavy work's going on here, with all the delays and frustrations that always go along with those projects, then I would say: 'Sure, lowball an offer. Say: "Eighty-two, take it or leave it." ' But you're telling me you want your own house now. So you need a house you can move into now, and at no price is this that kind of house."

"Sorry," Jill said to Murtagh. "Does this mean we won't be hearing from you again? I'd like to, you know, if that matters."

Murtagh smiled. "If I come up with another place," she said, "will you show up with him in tow again?"

"Depend on it," Corey said. "I would've caught the furnace and storm windows, and the plumbing stuff sort of stands out. But the structural stuff, and that worn-out wiring, that would've gotten by me. What Baldo said's right: there's too much work here for us to take on. We need something a little more polished."

Murtagh nodded. "Well," she said, "nothing like learning the rules of the game—better by the third inning than never. You guys making any progress on your other project I hear so much about lately?"

"Hard to say," Corey said. "We know more than we did, but the more we find out, the more it seems that just means there's more to track down."

She nodded. "It must be pretty tough, unraveling Jim Mandeville's dealings. He always seemed like the nicest man in the world, but doing a deal with him in it could be hell."

"You had some business with him, did you, Ev?" Baldo said.

"Oh, more'n a little," she said. "I was working out of the Hough Agency then. Bill Hough always told people he'd handle anything—commercial, industrial, pure residential, mixed-use or straight agricultural. And he did a good bit of business. But the truth was that Bill only liked the first two—commercial, industrial stuff. Only way you could get him to sell a house for you, or show you a better one, maybe, was if you were one of his commercial accounts, and the bigger your account the better. If you listed with Bill, say a hundred thousand square feet of warehouse or manufacturing space, or he sold you a lease on a freight terminal, something along that line, then Bill would work hard to get you a new house, and a good price on your old one, same time. But without that connection, he wouldn't do you much good. His mind just was not residential. He knew people had to live somewhere, of course—he had to live somewhere himself—but unless you were building, or buying or selling, a place with at least a dozen apartments, he had trouble getting worked up.

"Well," she said, "that was fine for Bill, and the other guys, too, but back then that kind of stuff was all male. Men bought what Bill sold, and men sold what Bill listed, and so all of us broads got shut out. And naturally since the men handled all that business, their sales records were bound to be better than ours—a fact which Bill, nice a guy as he was, could not seem to get through his fat head. There he was, the guy who'd set it all up so his female reps don't get any listings, and when our records show lousy sales volume, he says: 'What's the matter with you dames, anyway? Don't you know how to sell property?' So it got pretty frustrating there, and not many women stayed long.

"Anyway," she said, "through some kind of a fluke, I actually sold a house one day. And it was a pretty good sale, I do say so myself, two hundred and twenty-five thousand, back thirty-four years ago, this was, and well, serious money in those days. The buyer was a woman, which naturally helped me, some rich dame who taught art at Williams but wanted to live down this way—'Keep the students out of my hair.' She wanted a place with room for a studio, she painted when she wasn't teaching, which she only did one term a year. And also enough room for a small gallery—she ran one-man shows in the summer.

"Well, that just impressed all the hell out of Hough, and before he recovered, I said: 'I assume that I'll handle the closing and all—the client's used to me now.' Because that was another trick that Bill had—when we did get a sale, one of us women, Bill or one of his boys always horned in, as though we'd screw up on the closing. Like I say, we didn't stay long.

"But this time I kept it all to myself, and pretty soon I regretted that. The seller was an absentee owner, lived down in New York State, on the Hudson. He'd inherited the place from an uncle, along with, I gather, all of his uncle's bad habits. The uncle was a big-time horseplayer and gambler, apparently good at it, too. The nephew was a high roller himself, but his luck wasn't so good. So when he got the house, he had to unload it, to cover a few minor setbacks, and I guess he resented the fact. And not only the fact but also everyone who got involved in changing the place into money—he was just plain uncooperative. I could understand why he didn't like answering letters—I doubt he even opened the ones I sent. But he wouldn't return phone calls, if you left a message, and you always had to do that, of course, because this guy was just never in. I suppose he was getting hounded by creditors, and took no chances by taking calls. But anyway, there weren't any real problems with the sale except the ones that he created, and my purchaser was getting mad.

"Jim Mandeville was getting pretty grouchy himself—he'd been responsible for Bill getting the listing, through the guy's lawyer down in New York; I guess Jim knew this mouthpiece socially, but how, I really don't know. And now Jim'd committed the money, eighty, ninety grand, to the mortgage for my buyer, so he couldn't loan it to another customer, who'd start paying interest right off, so it was just lying there, idle and useless, and Jim was all over my case. So was Gil Rogers, that son of a bitch."

"Gil Rogers?" Baldo said, an instant before Corey started to say it.

"Oh," she said, "Gil had his nose in everything those days. If there was a dollar in it, Gil was poking around in it, seeing if there might be some way he could grab some of it himself. I mean, *really*: here was the richest lawyer in town, doing everything he could to knock a broker out of a lousy commission, and he did it every time. You know who brokered the sale of Jim's house? Overlook Hills? No broker. The people who bought that place for a rest home from Mimi bought it through Gil. He took the legal fee, and he took the brokering fee, double-dipping if I ever saw it. That greedy snake. I hope he's in hell."

"Do you know who bought it?" Corey said. "Who he sold it to, I mean?"

She shrugged. "Some corporation," she said. "Some outfit down in New York. I never did bother to look it up, because obviously he hadn't gone to one of my clients behind my back—I didn't *have* any for a place like that at the time—so there was nothing I could complain about. But I know, I just know, that part of his pitch was that he could get the zoning changed so they could turn it into a rest home. And I couldn't have guaranteed that, either."

She took a deep breath. "But *any*way," she said. "I went to Bill—and I hated to do that; another weak, helpless woman, running to Daddy, can't handle her problems herself—but I really didn't have any choice. And I said to him: 'Bill, for God's sake, is there someone this guy will talk to if he calls? I mean where did we get him, anyway?' And Bill was quite nice, actually; he said yes, he thought Dawson might help. 'Dawson and this guy're friends,' Bill told me. 'Dawson referred him to us.' "

"This would've been Dawson Nichols," Corey said.

"Yeah," she said, "the innkeeper there. So Bill said: 'Go see Dawson. Tell him your problem. See if maybe he can help you out.' So I marched myself down to the inn, found Dawson in the bar, naturally—this was maybe a year or a year and a half before he sold out to Jack, and by then that was the first place that anyone looked for him, and you seldom needed to look for him anywhere else after that—and put it to him. That I had the guy's house sold if he'd just sell the damned thing and stop driving everyone nuts. And about all the grief I was getting from Mandeville, and how my buyer was edgy. And

Dawson, well, he told me to relax, and he called up the guy at a Manhattan number, one I never heard before, and got through to him just like that. And, this was in the winter, the late winter, March, the two of them talked for what seemed like an hour, and Dawson's making notes like a madman—I thought he forgot I was there, or even why he made the call."

"Do you remember what they talked about?" Baldo said.

"The general subjects, yeah," she said. "Basketball, college basketball, I recall. Pro basketball. Horse racing. I think there was a heavyweight fight, too. Or maybe a middleweight fight."

"It was gambling stuff, in other words?" Baldo said. "They were swapping gambling tips?"

"Sure sounded like it to me," she said. "Anyway, after maybe half an hour or so of this—Dawson's got the phone between his shoulder and his ear, making notes with his right hand and pouring drinks for us with his left, and I'm getting gradually bombed—I finally poked him and said: 'Can I talk to him? Tell him it's his real estate agent.' And Dawson holds up his finger and signals 'a second,' and writes down about fifty more things, and then he says: 'Now look, Rafe, I've got a friend here, and you're not treating her right. She's sold your house for you, the one that's up here, and you're giving her a hard time over it. Now in a minute I want you to talk to her, tell her you'll be a good boy from now on, and all of those usual lies. But when she hangs up, I want you to call my lawyer, the one that I use up here. His name is Rogers, Gilbert Rogers, and he's all right—I vouch for him. And you tell Gil to handle everything for you, because we both know you won't really reform. Give him your power of attorney on this, and get this damned show on the road before someone starts breaking your legs.' "

"And that's what happened," she said. "As much as I hated the bugger, I have to admit that Gil did it. A couple days later he went down to see the seller, probably met him in the cellar of some abandoned building, and came back with a power of attorney, and after that the whole deal went through like a nice breeze. Old Dawson may have had his faults and all, but he sure helped me out that time."

"As you've helped us out, this time," Corey said. "Give us a call when you get something good."

21

As Jill brought the Jeep down the long drive from the knoll, Baldo in the backseat said if she and Joe did not mind, he would like to take a different route back to Shropshire. "If you take a right down at the highway," he said, "in a couple miles or so you'll come to Route Seven-one, which will take you onto Twenty-three, and after that a left. That'll bring us into East Lee and we can stop at Carl's. I'm running out of chardonnay, and I could use some reds as well."

"Do you treat Carl as roughly as you did Evelyn?" Jill said.

"When Evvie offers you two a discount on a house," Baldo said, "I'll start treating her the way I treat this guy. He gives me a discount. Bill gives one, that is. Twenty percent off the case price. Bill Slinger's Carl these days. Bill Slinger, the retired cop."

"The one that Gates abused," Corey said.

"Same fella," Baldo said. "Bill's life's improved a little bit since those days, I'm glad to say. The reason he retired was that, oh, sometime around 'sixty-four, -five, Carl decided he'd worked about as long's he needed to, and Carl didn't have a family so he offered Bill a deal. He didn't quite give Bill the store, but that's what it amounted to. As long as Carl was on the ground, and not under it, Bill had to pay him a fairly big percentage of what his profits'd always been. But every dollar that he paid Carl went toward the purchase price, the understanding being that when Carl went to his meeting with the Lord, Bill would have a good leg up on buying it from his estate. It amounted to Bill paying Carl a retirement annuity, in exchange for another piece every year of the equity in the business. Good deal for all concerned, and no grubby little tax problems to make sharp lawyers rich.

"Then Carl finally died, and that's when Bill found out the old bastard hadn't told him the whole truth. The store wasn't in his estate at all. The only provision for the whole business was one paragraph in the will: It said that on whatever date it was, Carl, 'being of sound mind and dispositive intention,' had 'entered upon an oral contract, the nature of which was aleatory, whereby William Slinger, of Shropshire, in the county aforesaid, did agree to pay over to me twenty-four percent per annum of the gross profits of Carl's Liquors, Inc., for as long as I should live, for my subsistence, care, and maintenance, should such become necessary, and in exchange for said undertaking on his part, and for good and valuable consideration of one dollar, receipt of which is hereby acknowledged, I did agree and undertake to convey to him, the said William Slinger, all right, title, and interest, including but not limited to ownership of the said corporation, value of physical premises, Class A license for the sale of beverage alcohol not to be consumed on premises, inventory of goods, and goodwill, to him and his heirs to have and to hold in fee simple forever, by appropriate provision of this, my last will and testament, as I hereby do.'

"Which of course Carl hadn't agreed to do at all," Baldo said, "but Carl was smart. If Bill did the right thing by him, he'd let the provision stand. And if Bill didn't, he'd change it, throw the store into the residual bequest clause where he gave everything else he might be owning when he died to the Swedenborgian Church. Which Carl, so far as anybody around here ever knew, had never been inside one of in his life. So Bill'd get all tied up in all kinds of probate nuisance, which wouldn't do Carl any good but would punish Bill for shortchanging him while he was alive, because there's nothing that'll fight like a church when it smells a unexpected bequest.

"So," Baldo said, as Jill turned onto Route 71, "you wanted to know if I treat Carl, who's now dead and therefore is Bill, the same unkindly way that I treated our friend Evelyn. My answer is that I treated Evelyn the same way that Carl treated Bill, and I treat Bill just like he treats me. With some respect. And I treated Evelyn, at your invitation, the same way she was treating you. When she showed you that derelict, she was seeing whether you're a pair of pouter pigeons. When she saw me get out of the car, she knew you weren't. That's why she was pissed off, and showed it. She'd scheduled that tour to see whether you'd buy a pig in a poke, but she knew before she gave it that you wouldn't, because you'd dragged me along. And that's why she didn't raise much fuss when I pointed out exactly what was wrong with the house—because she knew it, too.

"For hardbitten New Yorkers," he said, "you guys seem to be awful damned trusting. You don't know the first principle, which is that people live up to your expectations. If you let them know you expect them to hammer you, well, they won't disappoint you—they'll do it. So the first thing they go about finding out, when you start to do business with them, is whether you think that they're going to gyp you, and expect it, as I just said. Now Evvie knows you won't stand for it. She'll show you another house, take my word, and the next one'll be pretty decent. You take my advice, you won't buy it. When she gets contrite and tells you that she has to show what she's got on her list, she's leaving out that the dogs and the cats are the first things she wants to get off it. I'd make her show me four or five more, if I were in your position, and I'd also call another broker, and look at a couple with him. She'll know about it by that afternoon. That'll be good for her, too."

Carl's Liquors, Inc. occupied two thirds of a small convenience shopping center located on a steep ledge between the right shoulder of Route 20 westbound and a broad stream about sixty feet down. The other two businesses were a 7-Eleven store and a branch post office. The young man behind the cash register addressed "Mister Ianucci" by name and said "Mister Slinger" had gone to the bank and would return within half an hour. Baldo introduced the Coreys and said he had come to stock up on wine. The cashier invited them to browse.

Slinger came in less than ten minutes later. He was a wiry man in his mid-sixties, his face and neck permanently browned by exposure to the sun, and he regarded Ianucci with pleasure. "Baldo," he said, "in good health, I hear. Raising your share of hell still."

"I admit to that, Bill," Ianucci said. He introduced Corey as "my sidekick on this," and introduced Jill as Joe's wife, "but unlike her husband, not a damned lawyer—professor. Deserves your respect."

Slinger shook hands and expressed his pleasure. "I should warn you," he said, "this guy always takes all the credit for anything that turns out right, that he's been involved in at all. You nail the guys that had Mandeville killed, the scuttlebutt out of the Bright 'N' Early'll be that our friend Baldo did it. All by himself, in fact."

"The scuttlebutt'll be about right," Corey said. "I'm playing the same part in this whole exercise as the showerhead plays in the shower: the hot water gets made someplace else in the house, and then gets delivered to me—all I do's turn it into a spray."

Baldo selected four cases of white wine and three of red, one Chilean cabernet and two California merlots. Jill picked out the makings of a rudimentary bar stock, to which Corey added a cognac. Slinger at her insistence and over Baldo's protests tallied the orders separately, deducting twenty percent from each total. Baldo stopped protesting. "As long as you do the right thing by them, Bill," he said. "As long as you do the right thing."

Slinger rested his hands on the counter and straightened his arms. He stared first at Baldo and then at Corey. "I'm assuming," he said, "that's what you've got in mind. Doing the right thing, I mean. Are you gonna nail our friend Gates in this lash-up, after all of these years? I know the bastard was tangled up in it. Maybe not from the start, but he joined up."

Baldo allowed his shoulders to slump. "I dunno, Bill," he said. "It's too soon. You wouldn't know anything that maybe might help us, about that guy Dawson Nichols?"

Slinger rolled his upper lip over his lower. "I knew Dawson all right," he said. "Not a bad guy. Had some problems he couldn't get solved by himself, little weak, but not a bad kind of guy."

"Tell us about him," Corey said.

Slinger relinquished his support on the counter and stood up. He told the cashier to load up their purchases and take them out to the car. The young man fetched a two-wheeled cart and began stacking the cases. Slinger waited until he went out.

"I used to see him in the old place. He'd come in when I was on. Carl taught me the rule, and I follow it now, that the manager gives all the discounts. If there's a good reason why you should have one—as there is in your case; you buy enough good stuff from me so I can stock it, all year 'round, and pick up the carriage trade, summers, without losing my shirt on inventory—well, damned right, you're going to have one. But only the owner makes the decision, and a manager okays the price when you come in to stock up and the owner's not in the store. Otherwise all the clerks' friends drink cheap, and your whole place goes to hell down their throats.

"Dawson was one of the people Carl duked. He said Dawson's business was worth it. He said Dawson's business, supplying the inn, made the courtesy a real smart move. Jim Mandeville got a rate from him, too. Not that he bought near as much—his Christmas party was about the only big ticket a year, when he showed off for the whole town. But Carl said his trade was worth it. I think that was one case where Carl stretched a point—I think he liked having Mandeville's trade 'cause he thought it gave him prestige. Prestige doesn't sound like dinner to me, but Carl thought different. His privilege. 'Nother possibility, of course, is Carl thought Mandeville could be a good friend to have in case somebody got it in his head, start another store in Shropshire. You never knew, with Carl, what that man had up his sleeve."

"Mandeville came in then, to place his own orders?" Baldo said innocently.

"Oh yeah," Slinger said. The clerk returned with the cart; Slinger directed him to go to the cellar and finish sorting fresh deliveries. When the clerk had disappeared on his hands and knees on the conveyor belt leading to the basement, Slinger said: "He just started. Nice kid. No need messing his mind up with a lot of stuff he won't understand.

"Jim Mandeville was very particular about what he bought. He'd call up and order three, four days ahead of time, so we'd be sure to have it on hand. And then he'd come by in his Land Rover, I think he had, to pick it up. All the best brands. All the top labels." He shook his head. "I know he was rich, but I thought he was a show-off. Yeah, he was generous, but he made damned sure you knew he was being generous to you. Made sure everyone else did, too.

"The weekend before he got his head blown off, he was in here an hour or so. We were busy, of course, Christmas coming, everybody in to get a bottle for someone they didn't like but were afraid of, like the mailman, because he could do something to them and he would, too, if they didn't. But old Jim took his time, struttin' around, shootin' his mouth off, throwing his weight around, making a big stir for himself. Bought about four, five hundred dollars' worth, nice piece of change, but did himself at least a thousand dollars' worth of showboating, I thought."

"Recall anything specific he might've said?" Corey said. "Who was coming, that sort of thing?"

"I was pretty busy," Slinger said. "We all were, of course, it being Christmas and all. Not quite's busy's New Year's Eves are, Labor Days, Fourth of Julys, but busy enough for most people. Only thing I recall was that Jack Davis came in, apparently needed a few things, and I had the two of them at the register, same time, and Jim said to Jack was he coming. Up to his party he meant. And Jack said he wasn't sure if he could—wanted to, but he did have guests to think of. And Jim said Jack should come if he possibly could, because he'd see an old friend if he did. And Jack got the funniest look on his face and said: 'Whaddaya mean? Who will I see?' And Jim wouldn't tell him. He liked teasing people. Gave him a feeling of power. All he'd say was he'd talked to an old mutual friend that they hadn't seen for some years. And if things worked right, this guy would be there, Jim said: 'Passing through on his way somewhere else.' But then of course something happened before that, before the day of the party. So there wasn't any party that year."

"And you have no idea who that mutual friend might've been," Baldo said.

"Well," Slinger said, "I've got one idea, but that's all it is—I think it was probably Dawson. Dunno who else those two had in common. He came in here the night after that—this's the old place I'm talking about now—wanting a bottle of booze. Dawson seemed kind of surprised to see me. I never was in on that day of the week, but it so happened Carl was sick. It was my day off from the cop shop, so I was just filling in. And I hadn't seen Dawson for a long time. I must say he looked pretty good. Bought a quart of vodka, I guess it was, and I asked him what he was doing. Said he was on his way up to Halifax there, up in the Maritimes. Claimed he had relatives there, he hadn't seen in some time. He was based in New York again, still didn't like it, and when the holidays came around he decided to take some time off. Which is a funny time to take a vacation, if you're in the hotel business, but I don't know if he still was. 'Rented a car for myself,' he said, 'going back to see the old folks.' And I asked him if he'd seen anyone here, any of the people he knew when he was running the inn, and he said he'd like to, but he had to hit the road the next morning, early. But whether he'd seen Jim, or talked to him? I dunno. He didn't mention it. I didn't ask. I didn't see Dawson again."

"And didn't talk to him, either," Baldo said.

"Oh," Slinger said, "sure, I talked to him, on the phone. I wasn't avoiding the guy. I wouldn't say we'd ever gotten to be that good-ah friends, back when he still owned the inn. But Dawson cold sober was not a bad guy. He knew lots of stories. And he liked to talk, and I like to talk, and that time of day, when Dawson came in, it was always quiet in the store. From what I could gather, he had some ambition, but that was about all he had. He said to me once, I remember this, that something'd gone wrong and he'd missed it.

" 'I did everything right, Bill,' he said to me that time, sort of stuck in my mind, and I don't mean he was moaning and groaning. He was very matter-of-fact, the way a drinker can be when he's sober but knows very well he's gonna get himself smashed again, as soon as the rush dies down. 'I knew growing up what I had to do. Go to school and work hard, get a job. Then work hard some more, and be nice to the boss, and marry a nice wife and so forth. And I did all that, except the nice wife. I didn't have time for the ladies. I was working too hard, and playing too hard, too, and I wasn't going outdoors.

" 'I took stock of myself. I was twenty-six years old. I was running in place on a treadmill. The stuff that I knew I was selling cheap to a big corporation that bought me. And my owners kept all the profits I made. Well, to get a break from that what I did was gamble, win two days, lose big the next. I had to get out of that system. And that was why I came up here. Run my own place, no casinos here, a few years and I'll own myself. And I will treat myself right.

" 'Except that I left about three things out. The first one was that if you took the smart money's advice about Sugar Ray, but went against it alternate fights, you could make enough money to go buy an old inn, and stop working for guys that clipped you. But what you could not do was go back to that bank when you needed more for the inn. Because then you would pick the wrong horse, the wrong team, the wrong boxer, or maybe just the wrong side of the spread. And that is just what I've done.

" 'The second thing is that when you dump an old weakness, you shouldn't take on a new one. And that's what I did when I got up here. No bosses watching me now. The first two or three years I was working my tail off, but things were going all right. So I thought I'd relax, a few drinks. Then things weren't going so all right, so it took me more drinks to relax. And then back to the old weakness, right? Which didn't go any righter the second time around'n it had the first time around. Needed more drinks to relax. But you probably guessed that—I see you too much for you not to've. I don't come in here for the papers, and you know I don't get enough customers in my saloon to account for the booze that goes through it—that booze is going through me.

" 'The third thing is that when your old habit comes back, and your new one's making things worse, nothing you do, either one of them, makes things any better for you.' "

"I know the kid was concerned," Slinger said. "The last year or so he was running the place, he told me he was getting counseling. That wasn't a usual kind of thing then—'You killed your whole family, your neighbors and two cops? Well, we're going to deal harshly with you, my boy. You get six months' suspended—but only if you get therapy. You've got something wrong with you, son.' "

"Did he tell you who was counseling him?" Corey said.

"Oh yeah," Slinger said, "the head priest. The one at the monk house. Apparently he was a former lush himself. Sort of specialized in that kind of problem."

"Recall his name?" Baldo said.

"Are you kidding?" Slinger said. "I've got all I can do to remember yours, and I see you every six weeks. It's been twenty years since I've so much as *heard* his. I've got kids I've seen the past two or three years, and my wife has to remind me of *their* names."

"Did Nichols say whether this priest was doing him any good?" Corey said.

"Oh yeah, at first," Slinger said. "But that's what they all say, at first. I didn't see him for our regular chats for maybe a couple of months. He still phoned in his orders for the inn, of course, but they were quite a bit smaller. Then, like I say, a couple of months, I started seeing him again. I didn't say anything to him of course. Man's got a problem with how much he drinks, I figure his problem, not mine. But when he can't wait for the delivery truck, well, I can figure out that he's got one." He paused.

"I can't say I was really surprised when he bailed out fairly soon after that. He said to me, Dawson said this: 'It's only a matter of time now, you know, before I'm on the market again. I'll have to put myself there. Sell what I've got to the highest bidder, the inn and what I'm worth myself. And think: well, I'm thirty. What I tried didn't work. Five years in another place, maybe it will. Maybe I'm due for some good luck.' Then he laughed and said: 'And also, maybe I'm not.'"

"Let me ask you this, Bill," Corey said, "did you by any chance ever see this priest? Ever meet him, the course of your business?"

"My cop business, yeah," Slinger said. "Met him one night doing that. He came into the station for some guy. Some guy that'd banged up a car. I forget who brought him in. Anyway, this would've been late 'fifty-nine, early 'sixty, somewhere in there. Not too long before the priests left. He seemed like a very nice guy, least to me. Don't know as I would've been so polite, some alky got me out of bed at that hour, come down and get him from the lockup. But it took the prisoner a little time to get his bearings and so forth, and the priest and I got to talking, nothing in particular. And I'd hear some rumors, everyone had, that they all might be pulling out.

"He made no secret of it. Said it was true. And he looked like he really regretted it. 'We've done some good work here,' he said, 'at least I think so. I'd like to continue that work.' I had some idea what he meant by that, naturally, but I didn't let on what I knew. 'But those in high places think that we'd do better to concentrate our efforts and resources elsewhere.' Then he told me how much he admired Mandeville. I didn't, so I kept my mouth shut. You want the truth, when he said it, I didn't get it. I didn't know that he wanted the property, Jim Mandeville wanted it, I mean. And of course that explained why the padre thought so much of him, right? And figured all of us poor natives did? 'Never can tell,' this's what he was thinking, 'this cop might soft-soap the guy for us.' But if he did, it was wasted on me."

"Why didn't you like Jim Mandeville?" Corey said.

"I had no reason to," Slinger said. "I had as much reason to like Jim Mandeville as I had to like Eisenhower. I'd met Mandeville, sure, and I'd seen him up close, and that was more'n I could say for Ike. But he never did a damned thing to me or for me, anymore'n old Ike ever did. So when it came to Mandeville, well, I was neutral. And I stayed that way till he died.

"Then the priest said again how much he'd hate leaving Shropshire. I didn't have much to say on that. And he started in on what nice people we all were, and how much he liked Gilbert Rogers. That stuck in my mind more'n the priest's name did, I guess, that he called Gil Rogers 'Gilbert.' Most of us called him 'that SOB Rogers.' But I was still just the cop on the desk in those days, and I was used to not saying anything. 'Lawyer Rogers is representing us now,' and I thought: 'Well my God, I hope you're praying real hard, and if I was you what I would do is keep a sharp eye on the collection plate.' 'The good man who ran the inn up the street, he sold it a few years ago, recommended him to us soon after he came to Shropshire. Well, we had no need then, of his services, but now this comes along and we do. And what do we find out from our New York lawyer? Lawyer Rogers is his lawyer here, too.' I was doing all right up to that point, I thought, keeping my mouth shut and all, and so that's what I kept right on doing, and pretty soon the priest's drunk stumbled out of his cell, and off the two of them went."

"This was some time after Nichols left," Corey said.

"Yeah," Slinger said. "After Nichols left. Before the priests cut out."

"Do you know where he went when he left?" Baldo said. "Nichols, I mean, when he left?"

Slinger shrugged. "He told me Chicago," he said. "But I don't know if that was the truth. He didn't say what he'd be doing. He called me a couple times, years after that, to me sounded like he was in good shape. Once from Lake Tahoe, asked me to come out and visit him there. He was working at some big hotel. 'Security,' that's what he said. 'I'm chief of security here.' He said: 'Look, it won't cost you a dime. I'll comp you the whole deal, the rooms and the meals. Kids can swim, water ski, you see shows? I'll give you and the wife five hundred apiece, chips, you win and you keep what you get.' Right. Just like he'd kept what he'd won when he won. 'Come out and have a good time.' I said: 'How do we get there? Mighty long walk. You run an airline or something? Give us all free seats on a plane?' He said no, he couldn't comp that.

"And then the last time, maybe four years ago, by then I'd moved the store here, sold the old house, so both the phone numbers'd been changed. He had to chase me down some. That time he told me he was in San Juan, and I asked him was he on vacation. He said no, he wasn't. He's semiretired. 'But I'm okay. I'm doing real good.' And I haven't heard from him since."

The next morning Baldo was pouring fresh coffee into the thermos jug when Corey entered his kitchen. They sat down at the table and made it potable in silence, sipping at it as long as the caffeine took to poke their minds to the edge of functioning consciousness. Ianucci spoke first. "Jill isn't up yet, I take it?"

Corey shook his head. "No," he said, "she's got more sense'n we have. And I don't look forward to when she does get up. She's not only going to have the same hangover—she's going to have guilt things, too. Her doctor told her to watch out for the booze. He didn't exempt wines from Chile, or say that Kahlua's all right."

"Ahh," Ianucci said. "She does it every day, then it's a problem. She does it once, it won't be. One toot won't hurt the kid."

"It was still stupid," Corey said. "That's what she'll think. No need of taking that chance. And she'll be right. I can't argue with her. This is not going to be a good day. I'm glad we're going to Pittsfield."

Ianucci sighed. "Well," he said, "it won't help to tell her this, but what she did last night, when we got back here, wasn't as stupid's what we did."

"What?" Corey said. "What the hell did we do?"

"You called Birnam from this phone," Ianucci said. "I thought nothing about it. It didn't cross my mind until after you did it, that we should stop using this phone, except when we want to know what time's a movie, or maybe to get tomorrow's weather."

"You think the phone's bugged?" Corey said.

"I know that the phone is not bugged," Ianucci said. "I know because I took my gadget to the junction box down in the basement this morning, and the power draw's just what it should be. But what I also know is that I must be slipping, because I should've done that before this. I should've been doing that every day, and some other things, too, that go with it. We've left lots of tracks, and Birnam's left some more. By now those birds know we're on to them. We should have perimeter security here. We don't, and that's dangerous."

"We haven't got anything here," Corey said. "Nothing but transcripts and copies."

"That's not nothing, that's something," Ianucci said. "And furthermore, the kind of questions we've been asking make it seem like it's more than it is. We've got some leads now, not as good as we'd like, but we're sure to get better ones. The people we're after must be getting nervous. They'll overestimate us now, and start thinking about what to do. We've got to start being more careful what we do, and where, and how we go about it."

22

The following Monday afternoon Roger Birnam's response to Corey's telephone call about the status of the background reports he and Ianucci had drafted failed to satisfy Baldo. "I make it over three weeks since you expressed the Piantidosi sheets down to him," Baldo said. "O'Hara's was in the same batch, and Davis was a week before that. Roger's had one week tomorrow to get Nichols's current whereabouts to us, and nothing is what he's come up with. By now Nichols's had time enough to relocate to Ougadougou if he wanted. Principalities might as well've been the lost colony of Atlantis, for all the success our mandarin's had so far, profiling it to us. It took Warren Oldham three days to get back to us with who owned Davis's car, and tell us it was the same company that also owned Mandeville's Cadillac. So we dutifully ask our friend Roger to check out Bon Ami Motorcars, Inc., of Jamaica, Long Island, New York, and what he comes back with is that it's an outfit that's been supplying car fleets at corporate rates to hundreds of satisfied customers now since right after the Korean War." He snorted. "One thing about Roger: with him on your side, you don't need a Yellow Pages, and you can skip the Chamber of Commerce."

"I don't know what to tell you," Corey said. "I worked for the guy's brother. I liked him and trusted him. His brother plugged me into Roger. Roger said he'd give us a hand. There must be some reason why it's taking so long, but I don't know what it is."

"Neither do I," Baldo said, "but I do know it's got to be one of the two or three things I think of right off, and I don't like any of them.

"First possibility: the guy's too busy. Can't find the time to get on it, but won't tell us that because he's embarrassed. I don't buy it. He's retired, 'cept for ISIS, and the only other thing he's got on his mind is checking his brokerage accounts and remembering to put his false teeth in before he goes out for the day. What we asked him to do is make some phone calls, not to scavenge the files personally. He's got plenty of time. He just hasn't done it. Therefore he must be stalling.

"Second possibility: he's stalling because he can't get what we want, but he's ashamed to admit it. We'd know he's been frozen out of the net since he retired and turned in his badge. That dog won't hunt either. Nobody lasts as long as he did in the jobs that he had if he isn't trustworthy. And no one who's trustworthy ever retires, in the sense that people clam up on him. Once you've been in, really in's what I mean, you've got a lifetime appointment. There'll always be someone who knows your name and'll field a tough question for you.

"Third possibility: he's stalling because he's not really with us. He never intended to help. He's a decoy for some other person we don't know, or maybe do know but don't yet suspect. I think we ought to start suspecting, should've some time ago. The guy I would start with is this phony's brother, the guy that you used to work for."

"Ed Birnam?" Corey said. "Ed Birnam's an honorable man. Worked under Ed for six years of my life. If he'd been underhanded, I'd know it. The idea of Ed being mixed up in this, well, it just won't compute. The guy has got ethics most men never heard of. He wouldn't touch something like this."

"That's probably *why* he's involved in this," Baldo said. "He's involved on ethical grounds. Remember what he told you when you were leaving—he's been through this maze before. It happened when his brother quit. If he didn't know before what happened then, he certainly knew afterward. The minute he heard what you had in mind, the bells and the whistles went off.

"I'm not saying your old boss is some kind of gangster, carries a gun with a silencer on it when he goes out to make a house call. I'm saying he's been around long enough now so he knows he might have a client who's one, but looks like he's something else. And if he's as scrupulous as you think he is, that means only one thing to him: find out what could threaten that client's best interest, and keep tabs on it after you do. And what better way to monitor something than set up a listening post? Do the same thing with your brother that Marco did with Jack Davis at the inn: get him in and have him keep you posted. And if that's what he had in mind when he plugged you in to Roger, it's worked like a Swiss watchmaker's dream.

"Whenever we've picked up a promising lead, the first thing we've done is call Roger. And where do the leads end? So far, at Roger. The only one who knows more since we picked up the phone is our pal and good buddy, old Roger. Until we told him, he didn't know and we did. Now he knows at least what we knew when we called, and we're still right where we were.

"Therefore," Baldo said, "from now on we don't call Roger again. We lose nothing 'cause that's what he's good for. And maybe we gain at least some privacy, not to mention some stuff we can use that might give us a leg up on this."

"I don't know," Corey said.

"Neither do I," Baldo said. "But I do know that anything Roger gives me now is not something that's going to help me. How do I know if it's on the level? That it's not some red herring to fool me? The answer is: I don't. I have to think that whatever he gives me, if he ever does give me something, is disinformation, meant to mislead me, and in the end make me give up."

"What do we do instead?" Corey said. "We can't tap those computers from here."

"We call my friend Harry in Florida," Baldo said. "Harry's

still in the net and he'll help. And we set up a meeting in Springfield with Oldham. We'll double the hunt that way, telling both of them what we're doing. And we'll work down there because Warren's got what we don't: machinery, and security, too. By the end of this week we'll be where we should be. Where we should've been, two weeks ago."

Michelle Ianucci claimed sympathy when she picked them up at 8:25 on Thursday night at the corner of Fort and Main streets in Springfield. "I've had a long day myself," she said. "I've been up as long as you have. Hairdresser, shopping, lunch with the girls—I'm leaving out the damned gynecologist. It's very fatiguing, I tell you. If I had any sense I would've caught Jill's cold, miserable as she said she was. I could've stayed home and sniffled, shared cold medicine with her, kept her company, made you two guys drive yourselves down." She slid over to the passenger side of the Buick. "Things still going along good?"

Corey yawned in the back seat. "Uh-huh," he said. "I'd said we made real good progress today. Burt sent out subpoenas this morning, called the grand jury in for next Wednesday, and told them they might have to sit Thursday, too."

"Maybe Friday as well," Baldo said, putting the transmission in gear, "if we get what we hope to the first day. I don't like to be too optimistic about things, but if what comes in's what we think will come in, we could go to indictments on Friday."

Shropshire was quiet just before 10:15. One cruiser heading north on Main Street passed them in front of the CVS Drugstore that had replaced Tappett's Drugs. There were two cars parked in front of the inn. "We could pop in on Jack for a friendly drink," Corey said.

"Doubt he'd be glad to see us," Baldo said. "He's probably been fairly busy today, another piece of bad news, right on the heels of the last one." He turned right onto Berkshire Street.

"Another one?" Michelle said. "What've you two done to him besides the subpoena? What else did you do to the poor guy that's never done you any harm?"

"Hit Bob Gates with one, too," Baldo said. "Gates is his lawyer. But that paper knocks him out of that job. He can't represent Jack; he's a witness himself. He'd be a fool if he tried."

"Who else'd you go after?" she said. "Anyone that I might know?"

"Probably not," Baldo said. "A priest that's retired from a seminary in Compton, California. A gentleman by the name of Marco Piantidosi, who says that he's retired now and lives on Key Biscayne, and most likely won't show up—this's not the first time that someone's invited him to fly up where it's cold and talk about his long career, and he's got a couple of tame doctors and a whole squadron of lawyers who always show up to tell judges elsewhere he's way too frail to travel."

"Can he get away with that?" she said.

"Oh, for now," Baldo said. "It'll get a little harder for him when we type his name in on the indictments we expect—no one's ever favored him with that kind of a greeting, though a couple of federal strike forces've come very close to it. Judges generally look a little harder at excuses from defendants in murder cases than they do when a mere witness says he's too sick to testify." The venetian blinds had been lowered in the front windows of the police station; one cruiser idled vacant with its lights on in the drive. "Now there's your tipoff, Joe," Baldo said, "you're in a small town now. You left the keys in your prowl car where you used to live, while you went in to take a leak, damned thing'd be long gone before you got your zipper back up.

"And then," Baldo said, "let's see. Well, we've got Dawson. Dawson Nichols, I mean. Dawson's definitely coming, wouldn't miss it for the world. Says he was out of the country when his old friend Jim went down, and when the news caught up with him, well, he was all upset."

"Did he say where he was?" Michelle said.

"Joe's the one talked to him," Baldo said. "All I did was listen until I got afraid I might bust out laughing at him."

"He was 'traveling in Europe,' " Corey said. "I asked him if he could narrow it down some, and he had me hold on while he went to look for his passport, and then he got back on the line after fifteen or twenty minutes . . ."

". . . which you know he spent talking to his lawyer on another line," Baldo said.

". . . he was all apologies. Seems it hadn't crossed his mind he's got a different passport now. And he has no idea at all where the old one went. I told him that was all right, just to do the best he could, and we'd go over it again when he got back here."

The big lantern suspended over the front doors of the house at Overlook Hills was bright against the dark hills and sky. "There you go, Joe," Baldo said. "They've got the light on for you at the old homestead, 'case you'd like to drop in and see for yourself what a fine old place Jill and all her family got swiped from them."

"Or if I'd like to check myself in," Corey said. "I could plead premature senility, couldn't I? If we're nuts enough to think we can catch them now, shouldn't we be put away? Plainly incompetent?"

"That's what Dawson seemed to think," Baldo said. "I got the definite impression he was choking back a laugh. A man of his accomplishments, summoned for this foolishness."

"What accomplishments?" Michelle said. "Everything I've heard from you two, Nichols was a wreck. A gambler who became a lush, and God knows where he went from there."

"No no," Corey said. "You've got it all wrong, Michelle. Dawson's a success now. Very big success. He's in charge of personnel relations, labor management, for Escape Resorts Worldwide. Executive vice-president—that's what his title is. I said: 'What exactly is it, Mister Nichols, that you do in your job?' He said he's 'basically a roving troubleshooter.' "

"That's when I began to laugh, and signed off on the call," Baldo said. "That's the neatest euphemism I have ever heard for what Dawson Nichols does. But give the devil what he's due—he must be good at it. If he's been at it all these years, and no one's caught him yet . . ."

"Assuming as we do, of course, that Jill's grandfather was his first," Corey said.

". . . he must have the drill down pretty good. He doesn't make mistakes," Baldo said.

The trees that rimmed the empty parking area at Claretian Shores had begun to shed their leaves. The pavement was littered with small piles of them collected along the berms where the wind had eddied them. Baldo parked the Buick. The three of them walked slowly between the condominiums, darkened except for the automatically switched lights next to the front doors. The leaves crumbled softly under their feet, and small waves on the lake raised by a light breeze washed quietly onto the shore. The lights from the rear windows of the units in Baldo's triplex were the only interior illumination visible in the compound.

"Ahh, home," Michelle said, taking Baldo's upper right arm and squeezing it with both hands. "I've become an old stick-in-the-mud. Too old for that big-city life anymore, the wild social whirl of old Hartford."

"That's odd," Corey said. "There's a light on in the second floor."

"We didn't go up there this morning," Baldo said. "I didn't, at least—did you?"

"Nope," Corey said. "I can't think of a reason why Jill'd go in there. It's the office I use, but there's nothing of hers there, nothing that I'd think she'd want."

"The phone, maybe?" Michelle said. "She used the phone, and then just forgot to turn the light off, when she went back to lie down?"

Corey shook his head. "Don't think so," he said. He picked up his pace. "We got a long cord for it last Saturday. I brought it into the bedroom for her this morning, put it right next to her side of the bed, so she could call up the college and cancel her classes today. She felt so lousy, I doubt she would've put it back, or wanted to make any calls where she would've needed my desk."

Baldo extended his right hand and grabbed Corey's left hand. "Wait a second," he said. "Let's not rush into things all unprepared. Now you just stand here for a minute with Michelle, make no noise, and I'll be back here in a jiffy with a couple things."

"He doesn't leave a gun in that thing, does he?" Corey said.

"No, no," Michelle whispered. "He keeps his guns in the house. What he's got in the car is a couple of clubs. Air Force potato mashers. They're made of aluminum and filled with lead. He calls them his 'persuaders.'"

Baldo returned with the two clubs, each about a foot long and dull silver in the dimness. He handed one to Corey. It was cold. The grip was sized to fit the average hand, and the business end tapered out from it to a thickness of three inches. "Apply it anywhere," he said in a low voice. "Joints are good—ankles, wrists, knees, and of course the jaw. Wonderful sedative effects. In a pinch, the skull."

"If somebody's in there," Michelle said, "they'll hear the back door open."

"No they won't," Baldo said, "the back door's already open. See that thin wedge of light spilling out? Whoever went in left it ajar. The question's whether he's still in there. That's what we find out now."

The door showed no sign of having been forced open. The door to the cellar stairs was locked from the outside. They found no one in the kitchen or bedroom of Baldo's residence. On the couch in the living room of the double unit, they found Jill lumped up under an afghan, the fringe of it up to her chin, Baldo's TV showing commercials for tires and Ford Thunderbirds. On the campaign table in front of the couch was a tumbler half full of what looked to be water, next to an open bottle of Advil and a capped bottle of green Nyquil cold medicine. "Well, at least she found my medicine," Michelle said absently, so that Baldo glared at her. There were wadded-up Kleenexes scattered around on the top of the table and floor, and when Corey carefully uncovered the rest of her face, she snored once. He looked up grinning, about to say she was all right, but Baldo shook his head and pointed toward the other unit to the north.

The downstairs there was unoccupied. The stairwell was lighted and so were the two bedrooms they had converted to workspace. Baldo led Corey quietly up the stairs. All the second-floor rooms were vacant, but the offices had been ransacked, the papers and charts spilled off the desktops and easels, the desk drawers pulled open and dumped.

"A very impressive job," Baldo said.

"What the hell were they looking for?" Corey said. "It obviously wasn't here."

"Our nerves," Baldo said. "Someone's sneaked off their reservation. This is a work of frustration. Whoever did it didn't know what he wanted, or maybe didn't want anything, really. What you're looking at here is furious vandalism. Somebody making a point. The point is he doesn't like what we've been doing. He didn't come here to stop us from doing it—he knows it's too late for that. He came here to show us he's really pissed off. He came in, wrecked the place, and then left. I'm surprised he didn't crap on the rug or something, spray-paint bad words on the walls."

"Well, at least he didn't go after Jill," Corey said. "Thank God she decided to sack out in your end till we got home, and that nighttime stuff zonks her out."

"He didn't come here to terrorize her," Baldo said. "I doubt he knew she was here. He probably figured she'd gone with us, or maybe knew this was a teaching day and figured she'd gone down to South Hadley—Deacon would've known her schedule. Called both lines, got no answer, since she'd gone to our end of the place and wouldn't've picked up our phone, so he thought the coast was clear. 'Nobody home,' he said to himself, came right over and had a fine rampage."

"Well, what do we do now?" Corey said. "Call Burt and have someone who knows what he's doing come in and finger-print things? Get Deacon up and grill him?"

"No point in it," Baldo said. "No point at all. Deacon'd be on the burglar's side. He'd stonewall you and he'd make it stick. When I talked to him he actually had the nerve to tell me he did work for the priests, but he didn't remember any of their names, and he came here because he needed a job. He's a lying SOB and we don't need him. No. And as for the prints, well, ex-cops don't leave any prints when they go nuts, no more'n they use battering rams to open locked outside doors. Rubber gloves and a good set of picks. I should get better locks for this place."

23

Jill Corey said the weekend's mutterings over what Baldo called "the order of the proof" between her husband and Michelle's gave her a bigger headache and a more unruly stomach than the Chilean cabernet, Kahlua, and the virus had. Michelle said Jill should get out of the house with her and let them work it out. Following her directions, Jill on Saturday afternoon drove eleven miles east into Sussex, Massachusetts, where Michelle's favorite restaurant, The Blissful Dove, overlooked the town common. They had fresh crabcakes with a half-bottle of sauvignon blanc and Jill did not notice the white cape with the ell and For Sale sign on the other side of the green until after the waiter had presented her credit card slip for signature. "That might be worth looking at," she said. "Can you see if it's Multiple Listing?"

Michelle had a better angle through the bright leaves of the maples fringing the common. She said, "It says 'By Owner.' Some thrifty Yankee trying the market out, to see if they can beat the agent's commission and keep the whole price for themselves."

"Any reason not to encourage them?" Jill said. Michelle said she could not think of one. After the elderly woman had shown them its nine rooms, two of them small, second-floor earring bedrooms with ceilings that sloped down to the eaves, Jill said that the place had some possibilities and asked if the woman would consider an offer of $110,000.

"No," she said pleasantly, "no, I will not. My niece is a

real estate agent in Mystic, down on the Connecticut shore. And she told me what a reasonable price was, after she did some research. She said one-twenty-two-five's a fair price all around, for me and whoever buys it. So that's what my price is, and I'm sticking to it, at least until Armistice Day."

"What happens Armistice Day?" Michelle said.

"That's when I'll have just about three weeks left before I go back to Florida," the woman said. "I've got an apartment south of Jacksonville that I share with my late husband's sister. Irene's always been very good to people, and now she needs some of it back. She's getting too feeble to live by herself, and I could use company myself. It's a cosy place that I have here, had it for forty-three years. I know I'll miss it after I'm gone, but I do have to face up to facts. The rosebushes are lovely and so are the lilacs, and I'll miss my tulips in May, but I've reached the age where this is a burden, not only to Irene, but me. If I haven't sold it by Armistice Day, as Averill always called it, not 'Veterans' Day,' I'll find an agent and have it listed, and start thinking about what I can't bear to part with, and call up a mover and pack. The agent will hike the price up to one-thirty, if my niece is any judge, and then you or someone very much like you will fall in love with it, just like I did when Ave and I first laid eyes on it back in 'forty-seven, and you'll bargain her down to one-twenty-seven and think you got a bargain for yourself. As you will have, and I'll end up with two thousand less than if I could've sold it myself. Well, if that happens, so be it, but until it does, you've heard my price: one-twenty-two-five, that's it."

"What do you think, Michelle?" Jill said.

Michelle shrugged. "Sounds to me like she means it," she said. "I didn't see anything major wrong with it, and after my years with Baldo, I would've. I'd tear Joe away tomorrow morning and bring him back here to see it, and tell him if he won't come then his next chance will be when he finds out which bedroom you're going to sleep in."

"Or I could just write out a deposit check now," Jill said.

"Another possibility," Michelle said. "I didn't think of that one myself, but it's a definite option. That way he'd probably come here for sure, you get his attention like that."

"Will five thousand be a sufficient amount?" Jill said to the woman, taking her checkbook out of her bag.

"Oh, I should think so," the woman said. "Just let me get the agreement forms my niece left with me, and we'll get them filled out here right now."

On Tuesday afternoon the discovery that Rev. Donald D'Avolio depended on a wheelchair and immediately required transportation from Bradley Field at Windsor Locks, Connecticut, to the Hilton Inn Berkshire in Pittsfield, and would need it again to return to the airport when he had given his evidence, resolved all lingering doubts about the order in which Corey and Ianucci would have the witnesses testify on Wednesday. After Corey and Ianucci had delivered him to the hotel in Baldo's Buick—"Of course they both had to go pick him up," Michelle said to Jill. "Otherwise they would've lost a good three or four hours of bickering time, and my God, they couldn't have that"—they agreed that the sooner the gentleman said his piece and was delivered from the Commonwealth, the better it would be for all remaining in it.

"I worked with a guy like that once at Defense," Baldo said over dinner that night, spearing a meatball vengefully with his fork and using it to mop marinara sauce into a pool on his plate. "I didn't work with him long, and I didn't work with him well. Nobody did. Nobody could. He was the damnedest difficult article I'd ever seen in my life. He was deaf—this was before deaf people were 'hearing-impaired'—and he knew exactly whose fault that was: everyone he met who could hear. That son of a bitch had a supercharged hearing aid that could've picked up whispers in the Kremlin, but he said it amplified background noise too much, so he wouldn't leave the thing on. The result was that everyone heard what he said, when he had something on his mind, but he didn't hear what any of us said, because his machine was turned off. If he asked you something, and your answer was short, he got what you had to say. But if his simple question needed an explanation, and you tried to give it, you were dead. The son of a gun just tuned you out. And forget about ever having a discussion with him, or God forbid, setting him straight, when he got wound up on some damned-fool idea and started expounding on it. When something went wrong, as things always do, it was never remotely his fault. It was because no one'd listened to him, or hadn't advised him properly."

"Passive-aggressive," Jill said. "I took a few courses in psychology, before I came to my senses. The types that have it use their defects like judo holds."

"And that's exactly what this living saint does," Baldo said. "We engineer him out of the terminal—you know, I bet the bastard *can* walk—and I would say by the time we got him to the car, we were fully convinced he held no grudge. How many times would you say he told us, Joe? That he hadn't minded not being met, or having to call up Burt's office. And then having to wait till we showed up. 'It really wasn't that long of a time, I suppose. It's just that the moments seem to pass so slowly, when a person can't get around.' "

"I'd say about fifteen or twenty," Corey said. "Could've been more'n that, though. And he understood perfectly well that the delay was all his own fault, and he should've known that we didn't know he's not able-bodied these days. It was all his fault for not telling us when we called that he's lost the use of his legs. But he just assumes that the people in charge of the home where he lives tell the people who call that he can't get around very well. Not that, of course, he doesn't forgive them, poor stupid people that they are. They do the best they can, with limited powers, to make up for society's habit of discarding anyone who is disabled."

"He is good at sighing, though," Baldo said. "We really should give him that. I'd say we heard sixty or seventy sighs between Bradley and the hotel. Deep, heartfelt sighs, followed up with apologies for being so much of a burden. Jesus is in for it when this guy dies—he's going to get up there and forgive God to distraction for all the bad things that God did to him down here, that he's forgiven us all here for, too. Too bad Adolf Hitler didn't meet this guy: D'Avolio would've forgiven him. He would've forgiven him until he had der Führer screaming for cyanide mercy."

"Does he know anything that will help you?" Jill said.

Corey nodded. "Possibly," he said. "He might. He might even tell it to us, too, if we make it very clear in advance that we're humbly grateful for his humility in telling it in total disregard of any thought a proud man might have had of the toll we've inflicted on him by this ordeal."

"I leave that entirely to you, Joe," Ianucci said, using a soup spoon and his fork to coil strands of linguini into a sizable mouthful. "I await your performance with great interest."

"You do," Corey said. "Here you're looking at a man who didn't see the house he bought until a day after he found out he'd bought it; a man without a steady job whose sole source of income is a wife who does have one, but's pregnant; a man whose only link with anything resembling adult professional responsibility is a twenty-plus-year-old unsolved murder case which if he doesn't solve it will do pretty well as his professional obituary in a state where no one knows a bloody thing about him except: 'Isn't he that damned fool who barged in here thinking he could find out who killed Jim Mandeville back in 'sixty-seven? I should hire *him* as my lawyer?' And who won't remember anything about me ever afterward except that I was that damned fool who couldn't do it either, and you rely on me? To do with this popish Mahatma Ghandi what Gunther Gebel Williams used to do with nice peaceful wild animals? Forget about turning me in at the Home for the Uncertain, where Gampy used to have his parties—you're the one who belongs there."

D'Avolio was pink-scrubbed and pleasant as the grand jury's first witness. Foreman Sheffley stood and said: "Now 'peat after me, please," and administered the oath. D'Avolio gave his name and address and beamed at the jury.

"You knew Dawson Nichols, Father D'Avolio," Corey said, "during your tenure as administrator of the residence of the Congregation of the Sons of the Immaculate Heart of Mary in Shropshire, Massachusetts?"

"I did," D'Avolio said. "I knew him as a troubled soul, as so many of us are, in need of consolation of the spirit and the mind. I endeavored, best I could, to provide what aid I might. You understand, of course, that I must invoke the priest-penitent privilege to shield the matters we discussed."

"I understand," Corey said, "that you are bound by your vows to invoke that privilege as to communications made to you as a priest, by a penitent."

D'Avolio frowned. "Yes," he said.

"And I further understand," Corey said, "as I hope you do as well, that observations which you made, observations of conduct or behavior that any person, layman, might make, and communications between you and other persons that occurred within the hearing of third persons, are not comprehended by that privilege."

"I believe we are agreed," D'Avolio said.

"I hope so, Father," Corey said, "because if we are not, you and I will soon appear before Judge Malcolm Weatherbee, whom I will ask to sort out any differences we may have."

D'Avolio did not say anything.

"For the record, Father," Corey said, "Dawson Nichols was not a member of your congregation. Or a Catholic either, was he?"

"I had no congregation, as such," D'Avolio said. "I was entrusted with the management of the souls entrusted to my care at, and the physical premises of, the community established by the congregation in Shropshire between August, nineteen fifty-six, and the time when it was sold, in the summer of nineteen sixty."

"And Mister Nichols was not one of those souls," Corey said.

"He was not," D'Avolio said. "He was a member of the community at large of which our community was a part, and consistent with my mission I considered it my duty to afford whatever aid I could to anyone who approached me and indicated that he felt a need for it. I never inquired what denomination, if any, Mister Nichols belonged to. I don't think Our Savior does, when a sheep that's been lost comes to Him."

"And this community at large included persons who had trouble with alcohol," Corey said.

D'Avolio frowned. He thought. He said: "It did. I had had experience as a counselor to the League of Saint Jude ministering to the members of the police department in Chicago, before I came to Shropshire, and in that capacity I felt I gained a certain empathy for persons so afflicted."

"And Mister Nichols was one such person whom you counseled here," Corey said.

D'Avolio sighed. "Now I fear, Mister Corey," he said, "that your question if I answered it would cause me to infringe upon the privilege that I mentioned. Which is not mine to waive, but the penitent's."

"Very well, Father," Corey said, "without conceding your point on that by any means, I'll move on. At some time before the summer of nineteen sixty, you were informed by your superiors in Chicago that the congregation had decided to sell the property in Shropshire, were you not?"

"I was," D'Avolio said.

"And in keeping with that decision, you were instructed to inquire discreetly in the area for prospective buyers," Corey said.

"I was," D'Avolio said.

"Did you tell that to a man named Jack Davis," Corey said, "whom you had met through Mister Nichols?"

"Mister Corey," D'Avolio said, "the communications between me and Mister Nichols—"

"Father D'Avolio," Corey said, "now we really must exert ourselves to understand each other here. I didn't ask you whether Mister Nichols told you he'd done something. I didn't ask you, and I'm not asking you, if he told you that he coveted his neighbor's wife, his ox, or anything else. I am asking you whether Dawson Nichols introduced you to Jack Davis a few years before the property went up for sale. That question implies no sin on his part or yours. It pertains strictly to a business matter.

"We are not in this room, Father, in order to render to Caesar what properly belongs to God. We are in here to render to Caesar what you know and I know is Caesar's. Did you tell Davis that or did you not?"

"I told him," D'Avolio said.

"And then or later, Father D'Avolio," Corey said, "did Mister Davis at some time inform you that he believed James Mandeville Junior would be a prospective buyer?"

"Yes," D'Avolio said.

"And did you communicate that possibility to your superiors?" Corey said. "Specifically, to one Father Dominic Cleary, who was then in charge of financial matters for the entire eastern province?"

"Yes," D'Avolio said.

"And at some time thereafter did you become aware that Father Cleary had communicated what you'd told him to Henry O'Hara of New York?"

"Yes," D'Avolio said. "His firm handled all of our American legal work, what little legal work we had."

"And as a result of that," Corey said, "you had some discussions with Mister O'Hara, and on the basis of them you did something."

"Mister O'Hara informed me that Gilbert Rogers of Shropshire might call me," D'Avolio said, "in his capacity as the buyer's lawyer. And then, later on, as ours, too. I may have mentioned this to Mister Davis. That I don't really recall, but I may have. This was a long time ago."

"At any rate," Corey said, "the transaction went through and all parties involved were delighted."

"I wasn't," D'Avolio said firmly. "I was very attached to the Shores. I understood, naturally, what had to be done, but I didn't like it a bit. And it took a long time. Much longer than anyone thought. So I got my hopes up somewhat. Mister Mandeville was the only real serious buyer, but there was some trouble with money. I couldn't imagine what that might be. I knew he had lots of it. And as far as his bona fides were concerned, well, I knew the man pretty well, and I knew he loved the land we owned. Ever since I'd been there he'd been hunting our fields, with my blessing and all my good wishes. Mister Nichols and another friend, Cooper, often hunted with him on our land. I guess they must've been pretty good hunters, too." He smiled.

"Mister Mandeville and his friends shared their bag with us," he said. "We had many a bird from their guns, and many a bottle of wine with them, too, from Mister Mandeville's cellar. Well, the others did. He was a superlative neighbor. It was hard for me to leave the Shores, but easier to leave them to him."

"Have you any idea how those were worked out?" Corey said. "The financial problems, I mean?"

"Only a vague one," D'Avolio said. "I saw Mister Davis one night and he told me that our mutual friend, meaning Dawson, had told him—I assumed that Dawson had called him—that he heard the deal had gone through, and that some other man that they knew, or that one of the lawyers knew well, had come through with the money up front. But that's really all I can tell you."

"That's more than enough, Father," Corey said. "You've been very helpful this morning. But just to recap, so I'm sure we've got it right, let me run through this again. Tell me if I mix anything up.

"You came to Shropshire to run the community during the middle fifties, and while you were here you became acquainted with Dawson Nichols, the innkeeper."

"That's correct," D'Avolio said.

"Mister Nichols was a friend of Mister Mandeville's," Corey said, "and introduced you also to Davis."

"That's correct," D'Avolio said.

"In the course of time the community property went up for sale, and Mister Mandeville bought it. With financial assistance from someone you don't know, but whom Nichols and Davis, and for that matter, Rogers and Mister O'Hara as well, all knew."

"That's correct," D'Avolio said.

"So to summarize here," Corey said, "if I may, this is the chain of connection among them, at least as it's known to you: Nichols was here when you arrived. He was running the inn, not too well, and he went hunting with Mandeville. Nichols introduced you to Jack Davis, who bought him out later on. Rogers was Nichols's lawyer, and became Davis's, too. Nichols and Davis both knew O'Hara, and the three of them all knew the man you don't know who financed the Mandeville purchase. In other words, Nichols is the link here. He knew everyone who was involved."

"I hadn't thought about it before," D'Avolio said, "but yes, I think that would be right."

Corey nodded. "Thank you very much, Father," he said. "I think that's all I have. Mister Ianucci, have you any questions?"

"Not a one," Ianucci said.

The jury had no questions, either. "Very well," Corey said, "we'll excuse you now. We know you have travel plans made. The District Attorney has made arrangements to drive you from here to the airport, and we thank you again for your trouble."

24

P ersonally," Baldo said that night, munching cheddar and Wheat Thins with his wine, "I thought the kid was magnificent."

"I wasn't bad," Corey said.

"The priest," Baldo said, as the aroma of roast pork drifted through the living room, "the kid put the priest in his box right away, and said: 'Now stay in there, you got that?' And he did."

"Not really," Corey said. "I didn't really do that."

"Then we had Warren Oldham," Baldo said. "If you told him this, Warren'd get mad, but it's true and he knows it and he knows I know it: Warren's embarrassed to be a success. To be wearing the good suits and neat haircuts. Warren still thinks that a Mass. State Policeman's God's noblest creature on earth. So when he swaggers in now to pontificate, Warren's a little defiant. He doesn't want you to say anything to him that might indicate he's sold out, or maybe he's over the hill.

"Now a man of my years and vast experience senses such problems right off, and knows what to do to avoid them. But when a mere stripling like this lad here shows such sterling grasp of intangibles, well, I can tell you, this old dog was impressed." He seized another cracker. "You can go ahead and have the kid, Jill," he said, "I changed my mind about you two today. Now I think that Joe is the one that married beneath his station."

"Take the roast out now, Jill," Michelle said. "Heave it

ight at his head. Pan drippings, hot grease and all. It's my
house—you have my permission."

"Well, I'm serious," Baldo said. "The kid was good. He had
Warren in, and then Warren out, before half an hour was up.
Warren was all business, once he was satisfied learned counsel
was all business himself. Yes indeed, he had the documents,
signed, sealed, and certified. Car registrations to start with.

"One nineteen sixty-six Cadillac Coupe de Ville, color maroon, registered to owner Bon Ami Motorcars, Inc., Jamaica,
Long Island, New York. Principal operator, James Mandeville
junior, Overlook Hills, Shropshire, Mass. One nineteen fifty-
one Oldsmobile Super Eighty-eight Holiday coupe, green on
green, registered to owner Bon Ami Motorcars, Jamaica, Long
Island, New York. Principal driver: Dawson Nichols, Shropshire Inn, Shropshire, Massachusetts. One nineteen fifty-seven
Chrysler Town and Country, color black, registered to owner
Bon Ami Motorcars, Jamaica. Long Island, New York. Principal driver: John Elmer Davis. Shropshire Inn.

"Then we moved on to the corporate records, all also
signed, sealed, and certified. Bon Ami Motorcars, it seems,
was what we call a shell company, wholly owned by a Delaware front. The Delaware front was Principalities Ventures.
The people behind that are harder to find, it being a privately
held trust, but since grand juries can act on hearsay, Joe was
able to ask our good friend Warren whether he'd seen any
other materials on which he could base an opinion of who was
behind the smokescreen.

"Warren was up to it," Baldo said. " 'Marco Piantidosi,'
he said. Whom we've asked up for tomorrow. And had Warren seen some more documents that might enable him to say
whether that same gentleman had other connections with land
deals in the town of Shropshire? Indeed he had, and he did.
He said based on his review of other documents, which he was
not at liberty to disclose, he has probable cause to believe that
Dawson Nichols purchased the inn with a down-payment
check from Principalities. And that when Jack Davis bailed

Dawson out, he did it with funds from Principalities. And further that when your grandfather purchased the land with his own check in the amount of one million dollars, drawn on the Foothills National Bank, one half of that sum represented monies that he deposited in his account the previous day in a check drawn upon Manufacturers Hanover Trust of New York, account of Principalities Ventures, signed by Marco Piantidosi aforesaid. And further that said sum in Warren's expert opinion was the consideration for a loan of five hundred thousand dollars secured by a note and a mortgage of real estate of even date given by James Mandeville Junior, said realty being the land and improvements at Shropshire commonly known as Claretian Shores.

"This set the stage for the bank lady's second visit with us," Baldo said. "She produced copies of canceled checks and deposit slips conclusively showing that Warren's opinions were right. By now it was time to excuse the grand jurors for luncheon and whatever other errands they might have in mind, after which they were promised they would return to a real, rip-snorting good time."

"They actually seemed to be enjoying it themselves," Corey said.

"Oh, they'd gotten into the spirit of things, all right," Baldo said. "I've seen it happen before. Days and weeks go by, on grand jury service, when knitting begins to look like excitement, because they're not really doing that much. Sure, they hear about all of the gore and the scandals, but all of it's cut and dried. There's no conflict between lawyers, no arrogant judge, nothing to grab their attention. But when they get something that grabs their attention, when they can see something unfolding, something that they're figuring out, it has a galvanic effect.

"I have to say," Baldo said, "that we gave them their money's worth this afternoon. It was a corking good show. Our first featured guest was Robert Gates, Esquire, who made it clear he was offended. First words out of his mouth after he gave his name were that he didn't know why we'd asked him. Joe said if he'd just be patient with us, it might become apparent to him.

"Then he led Gates back through the reports, what he'd seen at the bank on the day of the crime, how long he talked to Jack at the inn, what they said, and the weather, of course. This of course gives the grand jury a nice capsule rundown on how your grandfather got scragged, but Gates wasn't noticing that. He became very curt, in fact. 'Yes,' 'No,' and 'I guess so,' or 'If that's what the report says—it's been so long I can't be sure now.' Until we came to the phone call Jack got while the Danish were still in the oven. Then Attorney Gates got somewhat cross.

" 'I'm sure the report's clear on that,' he said. 'I remained in the kitchen while Jack took the call. He answered it at the front desk. I couldn't hear that clearly what he might have said. All I know's what I stated: he came back to the kitchen and told me it was a wrong number—that's all.'

" 'Mister Gates,' Joe says, 'at some later date did you come into possession of facts which made it clear to you that that call was not a wrong number?' "

" 'I don't understand,' Gates says.

" 'I think you do understand,' Joe tells him. 'I think you know very well. I think you know now who placed that call, where he was, and why he was calling. I think you learned those things from files that you saw in the office of Gilbert Rogers, when you went into law practice with him. And that what was not in those files when you saw them, you learned directly from him. And furthermore, I submit, you were initially troubled by those facts. And later, confronted Jack Davis with them, and he confirmed all you suspected, along with telling you more of the circumstances. In other words, Mister Gates, you unearthed a conspiracy several years after it started, joined it at that time for personal gain, and remain part of it to this day.'

" 'You must be out of your mind,' is what Gates says.

" 'No, I'm not,' Joe says, 'we've got this thing figured out, sir. Now it's you who should do some thinking. As I see your options at this stage of things, you really have only three choices.' "

"Joe," Jill said, "have I missed something, or did you know that? All of what Baldo just said."

"Know it? Sure," Corey said. "Could we prove it? Not tonight we couldn't. But bluffing's allowed in grand jury hearings. It's considered all in good fun."

" 'The first one is to tell us that you're an attorney,' " Baldo said, grinning, " 'and anything you learned from Rogers or his files, about his clients and thus yours, is privileged information. If you do that, you will run up against the big exception to that rule: an attorney may not cite the privilege to withhold the fact that he joined in commission of a criminal act.' "

" 'I've committed no crime,' Gates tells him.

" 'That's a matter for these jurors to decide,' Joe says. 'If you've read the statute books recently, you know that a conspiracy to commit murder comprehends all agreements and acts later done to prevent its detection. No lawyer would hesitate for the merest instant to get up in front of a judge and tell him that such a conspiracy continues until all of its parties are dead, and that furthermore, those joining it late become accessories after the fact, punishable as principals. Is that right?'

"Gates didn't say anything. 'Your second option,' Joe says to him, 'is to lie to the people in this room. There isn't a thing we can do to prevent that, but there's something they can do to punish it. They can indict you for perjury, sir, and as their attorney, if you do lie to us, I will so recommend.'

"Gates still didn't say anything. 'Your third option is to take the Fifth. You know what its exercise will mean. When you go to trial, the judge will tell those jurors they can't hold it against you. But by then an acquittal won't help you much, and you know it as well as I do, and furthermore, I doubt that you'll get one.

" 'Now we understand, sir, that all of this probably comes as a nasty surprise to you. If I were in your shoes, as I would not want to be, I'd want some time to sort matters out. So what I'm going to do is excuse you for now, for the rest of this afternoon. But you're still under subpoena, and we want you back here at ten o'clock tomorrow morning. If you believe you should seek your own lawyer, we will understand that. In your place, that's what I would do. But do be aware that you're due back here at ten in the morning tomorrow, to answer the rest of the questions we have for you, or state a reason why you won't.'

"Gates was breathing like a goldfish," Baldo said, dropping his lower jaw three times. "There wasn't any blood left in his face. 'By the way, Mister Gates,' Joe said, 'while you've been in here, State Police officers have served a subpoena on one Maurice Coble, otherwise known as "Deacon," to appear before this jury forthwith. We intend to ask him whether you have had a conversation with him recently in which you ascertained from him where Mister Ianucci and I were conducting this investigation; whether he told you that we had employed the two bedrooms at the rear of the second floor of the northerly unit of Mister Ianucci's condominium at Claretian Shores; and whether he informed you that the home was unoccupied last Thursday. For your information, Mister Coble has made a statement to Mister Ianucci to that effect. Mister Ianucci has recited that statement in an affidavit presented to Judge Malcolm Weatherbee this morning, on the basis of which he signed warrants to search your law office and your home. State Police officers have executed those warrants during your appearance here this afternoon. They are authorized to seize any and all devices, instruments, tools or appliances, which have been or may be employed as burglarious implements, including but not limited to skeleton keys, lock picks, and rubber gloves. You're excused until tomorrow at ten.' "

"We brought the Deacon in right after Bobby," Baldo said. "He didn't take too long. First time I ever saw Deacon respectful. He said yup, Bobby called him on Thursday, vacuumed his small brain for what we were doing and where we were doing it, who was around the place that day. And then for the closer, Jack Davis.

"I didn't quite feel sorry for John Elmer Davis," Baldo said. "If I liked him, even a little bit, I would've felt sorry for him. But I don't, and he'd earned it, so I just sat back and enjoyed it.

"Joe went through the car registrations first, and Jack came coco with us. He said Piantidosi was his employer, when he worked in New York, and he confirmed Dawson worked for him, too, and Marco was the guy who bought the inn both times, using those two as his straws. Said he didn't know whether Marco'd loaned your grandfather the Claretian Shores money, but then he looked around the room, and he could see no one believed him. So he changed that a little: he said he thought so, but he didn't know it for sure.

"Then we came to the phone call," Baldo said. "The call that he got from Dawson Nichols to make sure that Gates'd completed his bank check and he was where Davis could see him.

" 'Mister Davis,' says Joe here, 'now directing your attention to the early-morning hours of December twenty-second, nineteen sixty-seven, I ask whether you at the Shropshire Inn received a telephone call from Dawson Nichols, whose voice you recognized, between four-fifty and five-thirty A.M.?'

"He waffled," Baldo said. "He stammered. He did everything but throw up. He finally said that he didn't recall that, it was a long time ago. 'And further, whether the purpose of that call was to enable Mister Nichols to find out whether the only patrolling policeman in the entire town was then in your place of business?'

"He didn't want to answer that one, either," Baldo said. "He settled for saying, as best he remembered, he hadn't seen or talked to Nichols for some time before or after that date.

That as far as he knew, Nichols'd gone west and found a new job for himself.

"Joe read him the perjury statute. 'Now,' he says, 'I advise you, Mister Davis, that the question I've put to you asks for information regarding a fact material to this jury's work. And that therefore, if you lie in response, while you are under oath here, and we can prove it, as we can, you may be charged with that crime. Now we know, as you do, that Nichols was here then, in this area, I mean. And we have strong reason to believe also that he was here by arrangement, which arrangement you were well aware of. And that when you told him what he called to find out, that Officer Gates was with you, he made another phone call. Which phone call prompted James Mandeville Junior to go to the bank that December morning, where he was murdered in cold blood.' "

"What did he say?" Jill said.

"He licked his lips first," Baldo said, "and then he said: 'You'll never prove that.' And Joe said: 'Thank you, you are excused.' "

"Is that it?" Michelle said. "What happens next? You haven't got a case yet."

"What happens next is tomorrow," Baldo said. "Orphan Annie was right—it's only a day away."

271

25

Dawson Nichols wore a camel-hair blazer, a maroon bow tie, a white shirt with a gold collar pin, pleated grey flannel trousers with one-inch cuffs, and highly polished brown cordovan shoes. His grey hair had been recently styled, and his face, neck, and hands were deeply tanned. His mustache was perfectly trimmed. His teeth were even and white; he showed them when he entered the grand jury room and went to the table that Corey shared with Ianucci to shake hands. Corey suggested that he stand in front of the chair provided for witnesses, be sworn, and be seated. Nichols did so with aplomb, arranging the skirt of his jacket and crossing his legs. "Yes?" he said.

"Yes," Corey said. "Mister Nichols, I advise you that this grand jury is conducting an investigation of the homicide of James Mandeville Junior, of Overlook Hills, Shropshire, Massachusetts, on December twenty-second, nineteen sixty-seven, and that you are a target of this investigation. I further advise you that under the Constitution and Bill of Rights of the United States, you have a right to remain silent, and that your exercise of said right may not be used against you in any way in any court of law. You have a right to an attorney. If you cannot afford an attorney, the court will appoint one to represent you at no charge. If you decide to answer any of our questions, you may stop at any time. If you give any answers, being aware that you have these rights, those answers can and will be used against you at a trial in a court of law. Do you understand these rights, sir?"

Nichols smiled. "Well," he said, "yes, I understand them. But what possibly causes you to think I'd need to be reminded of them here is quite beyond my ken."

"I take that to mean you choose to answer questions at this time?" Corey said.

"I can't see why I wouldn't," Nichols said. "Fire away."

"Where were you, Mister Nichols," Corey said, "on the afternoon of December twenty-first, nineteen sixty-seven?"

Nichols smiled again. "As I told, I believe, you, Mister Corey," he said, "that was quite a long time ago. All I can tell you for certain is that I was traveling in Europe. And Africa as well. And in Asia Minor. Where exactly I was on a given date during that period I really can't be sure now."

"Where did you spend Christmas day in nineteen sixty-seven?" Corey said.

Nichols's expression went blank. "I'm not really sure," he said. "I know I went to Europe, to London, right after Thanksgiving. I'd been working very hard, built up a lot of vacation time, and having no real family, really, I decided I might as well make use of it. All at once. So I notified all my people that I'd be gone for a month or six weeks, made my plans and so forth, and, well, I just *went*. It was a very nice trip. I may have been in Egypt on Christmas. And I went to Israel, too. The Holy Land. It's difficult for me to remember, after all these years have gone by."

"But at any rate," Corey said, "while you can't specify now where exactly you were, either on Christmas Day or on the twenty-first preceding it in nineteen sixty-seven, you are able to state, unequivocally and without any doubt whatsover, that you were not physically present on the continent of North America on either of those days. Or the twenty-second, either."

"Yes," Nichols said. "I am able to say that, and I do."

273

"This grand jury, Mister Nichols," Corey said, "has information which would indicate that during your period of ownership of the inn at Shropshire, you suffered from a drinking problem. A problem with alcohol. Is that correct?"

Nichols exhaled loudly. "Goodness," he said. "Has it become a crime in this state to like the sauce more'n you should? There'll be a lot of people in deep trouble if it has, I think. You won't be able to build new jails fast enough. Yes, I had some trouble with alcohol. My business, the inn, wasn't bringing in quite the returns that I'd hoped and depended on, really, when I bought it and reopened it, and so I was under a good deal of stress. I drank too much. What can I tell you? It's under control now, I'm happy to say. Has been for the past thirty years or more."

"You've had no further business problems in that time?" Corey said.

Nichols laughed. "Well, Mister Corey," he said, "I can't go so far as to say that. It's a rare bird in business these days who doesn't always have some kind of problems, every year. But I've been able to keep the ones I've encountered since under control, and myself, too."

"And when did that period start?" Corey said.

"I don't follow," Nichols said.

"To the best of your recollection," Corey said, "when did you regain control of yourself, and solve your problems with alcohol?"

Nichols laughed again. "Well," he said, "you're young, Mister Corey, and I not only can forgive you for that, but envy you quite a bit, too. When you're my age, you'll find that specific dates become rather hard to come up with. I really couldn't tell you just when it was. It was after I sold the inn, and signed on with Escape Resorts. I just wasn't cut out for the independent's role. I was born to be a salaried employee. Once I found that out, well, things went more smoothly. I came to grips with them better."

"When you went to Europe in 'sixty-seven, Mister Nichols," Corey said, "do you recall if you were drinking then?"

"Sure," Nichols said. "I recall that I wasn't. I'd been on the wagon for years. Ever since I got out of Shropshire. Not that the town had anything to do with it—it was my business problems. But once they were gone, well, I licked it. Still, no easy thing when you travel in France. They do make fine wines over there. Nothing like Belon oysters and a crisp Graves in some Paris café as the snow falls. But I persevered. I stuck to my guns. Perrier and the wholesome life."

Corey read him the perjury statute. "I understand what it means, Mister Corey," Nichols said, "but why you read it to me, I do not."

"I'll tell you why," Corey said. "You were the out-of-town talent. When you leave this room, you will see William Slinger. Mister Slinger is a former Shropshire police officer who knew you when you ran the inn. And he will testify that you came into the liquor store he managed and now owns, the day before James Mandeville Junior was murdered. He will testify that you bought a bottle of vodka, and told him you were on your way to spend Christmas with distant relatives you had up in Nova Scotia. That means that so far you've lied twice to us today. Once when you said you were out of the country, when James Mandeville was killed, and once when you said you were off the hooch in nineteen sixty-seven.

"You now have two choices," Corey said. "You can leave this room, and take your chances that Jack Davis won't tip you in. You called him up at the inn the grim morning to make sure the cop was detained. That cop is now an attorney, Robert Gates, Esquire, and he's got a few problems, too. People with problems tend to think first of themselves. What they'll do to you, I don't know.

"Your other choice is to purge yourself now of the perjury charges that you're flat-up against at this moment, not as serious as the murder charge, certainly, but no laughing matter, either. You're looking at prison time. If I were you, I'd leave the room. Our final witness this afternoon is a telephone company person. He has the toll records for Jack Davis's phone up to and including this morning, and one of them, sir, is to you. At the Sheraton-Hartford Hotel. It lasted about twenty minutes. Since Judge Weatherbee authorized the State Police to tap Mister Davis's phone yesterday, we know what you said to each other. I suggest to you, sir, that reasonable persons could infer from what the two of you said that he knows and you know who killed Jim Mandeville. I don't think we need to look far."

Nichols said nothing. "So it's possible, sir," Corey said, "that when you leave here you will see a man you know. Marco Piantidosi. And it's equally possible that you will not, if he's hanging you out to dry, after all these years you've worked for him. So really what you need to decide is how far you're willing to carry this. And whether you think that we've found out where you got the twelve-gauge shotgun shell that you used to kill Jim Mandeville."

"You're excused."

Ianucci rose from his seat and followed Nichols from the room. When he closed the door behind them, Sheffley said: "Mister Corey, if you don't mind my saying so, aren't you playing a dangerous game?"

"There's no question about it," Corey said. "But the danger isn't to me. When this little band of brothers cobbled up their plan to kill Jim Mandeville in 'sixty-seven, it was purely a matter of business. Marco Piantidosi wanted a profit he hadn't seen coming, and the people who worked for him wanted Marco to be happy. When he was happy, he made them happy. That was the way they saw life.

"Now they've all gotten older. They see life differently— they see it in terms of survival and comfort, taking each day a bit easier. The question that we're putting into their minds here is whether their past happiness as his pawns is worth spending their futures in jail. We only need one of them, Mister Foreman. Only one of them has to crack. I doubt it'll be the man who just left, but I want him worrying, too. My guess would be either Gates or Davis. But even if neither one of them folds, we've got them both where we want them. And that's two more than anyone had when this dirty business took place."

Ianucci opened the door to the grand jury room. "Mister Corey?" he said. "Couple people here'd like to talk to you."

Corey excused himself. He went into the anteroom and found Edward Birnam and Ned Polland sitting relaxed on one bench. Birnam stood up and offered his hand. "Joe," he said, "good to see you." Corey took it and shook it. "Ned and I came up in response to your subpoena directed to Marco Piantidosi, whom you no doubt remember as one of our clients. Marco bought Silent Wanderer bedding compound from people you worked for, and then Marco became our client. You remember that."

"No, I don't," Corey said, "but that's all right. What you've got in mind's to immobilize us by claiming I did work for him. Well, I didn't. I probably did do some work on some file for some company in which he had an interest—after all, I was there for six years. But the badminton game you and Roger ran so long's over now, Ed—it won't work. While the three of us stand here grinning at each other, Bob Gates is making a statement. He's in Mister Magoun's office upstairs. And when he's finished he's coming up here, to say it all over again.

"Mister Davis will follow him into the room. He's had some second thoughts, too. He will corroborate what Mister Gates says. I know this—we've got 'em on tape.

"The game's over, Ed. We're in garbage time now. The deliberate fouls aren't going to help you. Gates and Davis sink Nichols, and when he gets life, he'll start thinking about making deals. I'll be here, as will Baldo, and we listen good. Get frequent-traveler cards."

Birnam smiled. "I assume you've thought about what problems this creates for any liaison between our firm and any office you may establish up here."

"About as much as I've given to the average annual rainfall in Tibet, Ed," Corey said. "Now I think I have it: jam yesterday, jam tomorrow, but never jam today."

You move in when?" Baldo said.

"Next Tuesday," Corey said. "I'm about to become a country squire. If the kid's a girl, I'll name her 'Scout,' and change my first name to 'Atticus.' "

"You did a good job here, you know," Baldo said. "I wouldn't depreciate that. Dawson Nichols is gone, on what we've got, and that means Marco should worry."

"Oh," Corey said, "we all should. In a hundred years it won't matter."

"Sure it will," Baldo said. "Did Baldad the Suhite live in vain? Did he sit down on the ground seven nights for no reason at all?"

"I really couldn't tell you," Corey said.

"Well, I can tell you," Baldo said. "You did good."

"I'm glad it's over," Corey said.

"Yeah," Baldo said, "but we'll see."

"I may get a dog," Corey said. "I really like dogs."

<u>TRUST</u>

George V. Higgins

Trust means knowing someone owes you a favour and will pay it when you call it in. It also means that you know exactly what a favour's worth – which means not really trusting anyone at all.

Earl Beale, psychopathic ex-basketball player trying to make his fortune as a used-car salesman after being jailed for corruption, knows all about trust . . .

VICTORIES

George V. Higgins

Henry Biggs, ex-baseball star, is still something of a celebrity in rural Vermont. He also has ambiguous political ambitions which Ed Cobb, Speaker of the House, encourages him to fulfil.

But just in case Henry needs a little more than encouragement to run for Congress (and, given the opposition, he will) Ed has a nice little line in blackmail hidden up his sleeve. So Henry goes for it. At best it will be a welcome escape from his disastrous family life and at worst . . . who knows?

Henry doesn't, that's for sure . . .

☐	Kennedy for the Defense	George V. Higgins	£4.50
☐	Penance for Jerry Kennedy	George V. Higgins	£4.50
☐	Imposters	George V. Higgins	£4.99
☐	Outlaws	George V. Higgins	£4.99
☐	Trust	George V. Higgins	£4.50
☐	Victories	George V. Higgins	£4.99
☐	Wonderful Years, Wonderful Years	George V. Higgins	£4.50

Warner Books now offers an exciting range of quality titles
by both established and new authors. All of the books in this
series are available from:

Little, Brown and Company (UK) Limited,
P.O. Box 11,
Falmouth,
Cornwall TR10 9EN.

Alternatively you may fax your order to the above address.
Fax No. 0326 376423.

Payments can be made as follows: cheque, postal order
(payable to Little, Brown and Company) or by credit cards,
Visa/Access. Do not send cash or currency. UK customers
and B.F.P.O. please allow £1.00 for postage and packing for
the first book, plus 50p for the second book, plus 30p for
each additional book up to a maximum charge of £3.00
(7 books plus).

Overseas customers including Ireland, please allow £2.00 for
the first book plus £1.00 for the second book, plus 50p for
each additional book.

NAME (Block Letters) ....

....

ADDRESS ....

....

....

☐ I enclose my remittance for _____

☐ I wish to pay by Access/Visa Card

Number ☐☐☐☐☐☐☐☐☐☐☐☐☐☐☐☐

Card Expiry Date ☐☐☐☐